PRAISE FOR K.J. SUTTON'S RESTLESS
SLUMBER

"A fantastic urban fantasy series that I highly recommend. Massive thumbs up from me!" —Beckie Bookworm

"During my whole read, I was either laughing, crying, or sitting on the edge of my seat... I'm so glad this series will be multiple books long! I'm already craving more." —Bibliophilic Ferret

"There are no rules in this dark fantasy, but don't worry, you won't even miss them!" —Jenacide by Bibliophile

"If you are looking for a new paranormal series, this is the one for you." —The Book Curmudgeon

"I absolutely loved this book!" —Pages of Chapters

"An excellent sequel to an exciting new series. Fortuna Sworn is a great addition to an echelon of kick-ass women of fantasy." —Life in Words and Lyrics

"A unique and compelling fantasy series that will grab you right from the start and hold your attention." —Mindy Lou's Book Review

"I am totally invested in these characters." —Life in the Book Lane Reviews

"A whirlwind of action, emotion, and turmoil that never lets up!" —Tome Tender Book Blog

RESTLESS SLUMBER

K. J. SUTTON

ONCE UPON A TIME
book 2

ISBN 978-1-0879218-5-3 (hardback)

ISBN 978-1-7334616-7-2 (paperback)

ISBN 978-1-733-46168-9 (e-book)

This is a work of fiction. Names, characters, places, and incidents either are the products of the author's imagination or are used fictitiously. Any resemblance to actual persons, living or dead, businesses, companies, events, or locales is entirely coincidental.

Front cover image by Gwenn Danae

Typography by Jesse Green

Published in the United States of America

Please be aware this novel contains contains scenes or themes of slavery, profanity, a car accident, violence, domestic abuse, suicide, sex, death, murder, demons, and rape.

Angels are bright still, though the brightest fell.

—William Shakespeare

PREFACE

A boxelder bug writhed on its back.

I stood in front of the window and watched it die. The bug was a frantic, mindless thing. Its wings were two blurs as it struggled against the inevitable. While I observed the creature's final moments, waiting for dusk, it emitted a high sound that no one else cared to hear but me. Then, all at once, it went silent. Its legs, which had been wriggling, no longer moved.

Night was finally drawing near. Multiple people had come and gone since I got back, attempting to talk to me about getting some sleep or stepping in the shower. I probably looked like an extra from a horror movie. It didn't matter, though. Nothing mattered but that darkening horizon.

A clock on the wall counted into the stillness. *Tick. Tick. Tick.* It was almost time.

Thinking this, I turned around to face the body on the kitchen table.

CHAPTER ONE

*S*ome call him Laurie.

Like a flock of birds, my mind burst into a dozen different directions, a chaos of feathers and flapping wings. King? The faerie who I'd trusted, befriended, and depended upon... was sovereign of the Seelie Court?

The werewolf at my side probably felt the turmoil roiling inside me; he shifted restlessly and made a sound deep in his throat. Something halfway between a whine and a growl. I looked at him, not really seeing him. My memory was flying backward, halting at every interaction with the faerie I'd known as Laurie. His comments and behavior were just as bewildering, despite this new knowledge.

What's with these goddamn kings taking such an interest in me? I couldn't begin to guess at Laurie's motives. Had he been here to keep tabs on Collith? Did he hope to use me against him?

A second later, I realized that Viessa might be able to answer some of these questions. Just as I gripped the bars tighter, opening my mouth to ask, Lyari chose that moment to reappear.

She didn't announce her presence, though; Viessa's blue-white gaze shifted past me. It was so subtle that, normally, I would've missed it. But I'd already sensed Lyari coming somehow. I wasn't ready to explore the implications of this. Instead, I turned my head to acknowledge her. She was a tall, stiff figure in my peripheral vision. "Sorry to interrupt," the Guardian said, sounding anything but apologetic. "I figured you'd want to know that someone just tried to kill your brother."

At this, I jerked toward her. "What? Is he okay?" *Don't tell me he's hurt. Don't tell me he's dying.*

In facing Lyari, I'd consequently put my back to Viessa. A split second later, I realized the foolishness of this, and stepped away from the cell. Lyari smirked. The werewolf didn't like that —his lip curled. Her gaze flicked to him and she touched the hilt of her sword. "My brother, Guardian," I said coldly, resting my hand on the wolf again. Strangely, I found it as comforting as he seemed to. "Is Damon alive?"

Lines deepened around Lyari's mouth. I couldn't tell if they were made of distaste or regret. Then I decided I didn't give a rat's ass. "He was cut, but the healer is with him now, thanks to His Majesty," she answered.

Relief shot through my veins, more overwhelming than any drug. I nearly sagged. It was never far from my mind, though, that I had to keep up a facade of power around these creatures. So I just allowed myself a curt nod and moved toward the stairs. The wolf instantly followed, keeping his large body between me and Lyari. Ironic, considering she was my personal guard. "Good. Please take me to him."

"I look forward to our next meeting," Viessa called to my retreating back. Her voice sounded stronger than it had when I'd first arrived. I wasn't sure what that meant—I already regretted offering her a boon, however intriguing her information had been—but her words were a reminder of my original purpose in coming down to this dank, foul place.

"Wait." I rushed back to the cell. Viessa had begun retreating into the darkness. I could only see her ragged skirt as she turned. My mind was struggling to gather itself, think ahead, see every angle as a faerie would. It took all the discipline I had; every instinct and urge was with Damon. "One last question. Is there a place, here in Court, where I won't be overheard? No cameras, no guards."

After I'd finished, only silence came from the gloom of her cell. I bit my tongue to avoid saying anything that would get me in trouble later. One boon was enough, and pissing off an assassin was the last thing I needed to do right now. Maybe that meant I was growing.

The three of us stood there, in the belly of the Unseelie Court, unmoving and unspeaking. That didn't mean nothing was happening, though. I felt power in the air, more substantial than smoke or fog. We were testing each other. Tasting each other. I didn't know what these females had been through, but I knew what I had survived, and I was more powerful. Without a doubt. There wasn't anything more motivating than protecting someone you loved. The blood of multiple innocents and guilty monsters already covered my hands. A little more hardly felt like an obstacle now.

Maybe Viessa saw the truth of this in my eyes. After nearly a minute of silence, she said at last, "Tell your entourage you'd like to pay a visit to Nym."

Thank you. I swallowed the automatic reply, nodded again, and backed away. She watched me go, her expression fathomless, unnaturally still. I couldn't help but feel as though I'd just made a deal with the devil. After another thick, stilted moment, I forced myself to turn. Viessa didn't call out again, but as I rushed up the narrow stairs, she began to hum. It was an amused, happy sound. It followed us even after we'd reached the upper passageway.

One question haunted me now, filling my ears like a spirit's whisper, floating after us no matter how much I quickened the pace.

What have I done?

CHAPTER TWO

*D*amon was sleeping by the time I arrived at his rooms. *No, Jassin's rooms.* I hurried to my brother's side, knelt, and examined him from head to toe. He rested in the middle of that gigantic bed, so silent and pale. When I took his hand, it rested limply in mine. Behind me, the werewolf padded to a corner of the room and sat. It was unnerving how something so big could move without a sound.

The court's healer, Zara, stood on the other side of the bed. I arched my neck to see her face. Firelight flickered over her flawless skin. She wore colors so bright that they felt like a shout in the stillness. Her hijab rivaled a sunflower, and she wore a button-up shirt with blue and yellow stripes. "It was a shallow wound," Zara said by way of greeting. Her gaze flicked to the enormous werewolf. I waited for a reaction. Surprise, wariness, disdain. But the faerie revealed nothing. She focused on me again to add, "Tomorrow morning it will be nothing more than a scab."

Though Zara's expression was distant as always, I recognized that she was being kind. After the way I'd treated her, she was trying to offer me comfort. Was it genuine? Or just another faerie trick?

I realized that I was glaring at her, but she hadn't noticed it yet, thankfully. I refocused on Damon, still frowning. My time at Court had proven that some faeries were more than beings of cruel instincts and basest desires. And yet my prejudice had been well-earned; it was not so easily forgotten.

"Do we know anything about who did it?" was all I said in response.

Zara shook her head. "His Majesty had assigned a Guardian to this room."

Hearing this sent a pang of gratitude and guilt through me. I hadn't thought to leave someone for Damon's protection. "Oh."

"She saw a cloaked figure slip inside," Zara continued. "When your brother started shouting for help, she entered. The would-be killer fought his way out and ran."

"He was probably hired," a familiar voice said from the doorway. Zara and I both turned toward Collith Sylvyre, King of the Unseelie Court. Tall, bright, and beautiful, he was every inch of him a faerie, a race that I was supposed to despise. He had a voice made of chocolate and eyes full of sin. His body invited anyone to touch, with its hard planes and sharp ridges, but there was a price. Oh, was there a price.

He was also my mate.

I wanted to blame that magic between us for how Collith's appearance made my stomach flutter, but it would be a lie. We hadn't laid eyes on each other since my coronation; he'd been mysteriously absent. He hadn't even slept in the bed we currently shared. I took in the sight of him, feeling as though I were seeing Collith for the first time all over again. He was dressed as a human today, wearing tight-fitting jeans and a button-up shirt. His brown hair was artfully gelled and the pale, smooth angles of his face looked ethereal in the fire's glow. In this moment, his hazel eyes looked brown.

"Has someone checked the cameras?" I asked, striving to seem unaffected by his presence. Too much time had passed since his comment, but thankfully, no one acknowledged this.

"Nuvian is watching them as we speak," Collith answered. His expression was neutral and the bond between us curiously still. Almost as though he was trying to hide from me. "Thank you, Zara."

The healer took it for the dismissal it was. She inclined her head in a fluid, graceful movement, and started toward the door.

"Zara," I blurted. She paused at the threshold and raised her eyebrows in a silent question. I hesitated, the battle within me raging on. *Faerie. Cruel. Untrustworthy.* "I... appreciate what you've done for my brother."

"You're welcome," she said simply. Strangely enough, I liked that she didn't tack on any titles or formalities. She didn't mean it as an insult; she was simply acting as though we were equals. For someone that had gone from prisoner to queen in a matter of days, it was refreshing. Zara's face softened, somehow, probably responding to something she saw in mine. Before either of us could get uncomfortable, she nodded and left.

Leaving me alone with Collith.

Even now, after spending several nights together, my pulse quickened at the realization. But I'd be damned if I let it show and betray everything life had taught me about faeries. Pretending to be absorbed in Damon—although at least half of my mind was painfully aware of every shift and breath Collith made—I brushed Damon's bangs out of his eyes. His facial muscles twitched. I wondered what Damon Sworn dreamed about. "Arcaena was probably the one who put out the hit," I said without turning. I should've killed that bitch when I had the chance. "What are we going to do about it?"

Collith went to the fire. There was a dull sound, then the room brightened and faded. He must've shifted a log with the poker. "I've already made inquiries into that, as well," my mate replied. "She is still recovering from performing the Rites of Thogon. She hasn't uttered a word since then."

"What about her creepy twin?" I demanded, finally twisting to look at Collith. "Did you 'make inquiries' about him?"

"Have you eaten today?" he asked abruptly, approaching the bed on soundless feet. He said nothing about the werewolf, though there was no way he hadn't seen him. "The food in our room was untouched."

Our room. Something fluttered in my chest. Why should those two words affect me?

"Not yet," I answered. I didn't miss that he'd changed the subject, but right now, I was more resigned than annoyed. I was starting to understand this evasive faerie, despite so many unknowns haunting the space between us. His refusal to say anything spoke volumes—I'd asked a question he didn't want to answer, which meant I was probably right about the twin. If the king wouldn't do something about Arcaena's brother, then I would. There was probably a solution in one of the dusty volumes still awaiting me.

Collith was moving toward the rope now. He pulled on the fraying strands. I realized that he was going to order something. "You don't need to—"

"Please stop talking, Fortuna."

I was so startled at his interruption that the rest died in my throat. Collith raised his brows in a silent challenge, as though he *wanted* me to argue. I was about to comply, quite happily, when there was a timid knock. Breaking our stare, Collith went to the door and poked his head out. He murmured to whatever servant stood in the passageway.

After that, he spent the next few seconds dragging chairs across the room. One of them Collith placed next to me. I slipped onto the faded cushion and observed without comment, thinking that it was annoyingly likable that he did things himself, rather than relying on the slaves all around us.

Despite the noise and movement, Damon didn't stir. I longed for and dreaded the moment he did—I knew that hatred would burn in his eyes, just as it had during our last conversation.

Once he was finished with his rearranging, Collith situated himself in the chair opposite me. He leaned forward, resting his elbows on his knees, and looked at Damon. His gaze lingered as though he'd never truly seen my brother before. The fire crackled into the stillness. For a few minutes, we just sat like that, neither of us speaking. I held Damon's frail hand and came to the realization that I couldn't just write a handful of letters and leave him like this, injured and alone and grieving. Which meant that I couldn't stay here. Would I be breaking my promises to Collith by returning to Granby?

"When Jassin brought him to Court two years ago, I noticed him immediately. Such is the nature of a Nightmare," the king said suddenly.

I focused on him, unable to hide the surprise I knew was drifting down our bond. Though Collith's gaze didn't move from Damon's face, it was obvious he was speaking to me. I didn't dare respond, for fear he would see my interest and stop talking.

Thankfully, Collith seemed to be lost in a memory. "But it was more than that," he added. "I felt a pull toward him. An... investment, for lack of a better word. I'd seen slaves being mistreated my entire life, yet there was something about Damon Sworn that I couldn't shrug off."

"Why didn't you do something about it, then?" I couldn't help asking. The question should've been biting, sharp as the teeth of the werewolf lying just a few feet away. It came out softly, though.

Now Collith met my gaze. "I did."

I waited for him to elaborate, but apparently we'd hit one of those walls. It was becoming a pattern—Collith would begin to reveal himself to me, inch closer with a secret or a thought from the mind beneath that crown, and then he'd abruptly construct a barrier of brick and mortar. Effectively keeping us apart and rendering him untouchable.

Instead of my usual burst of frustration, I just studied Collith's distant expression and wondered what had happened to make him this way. His jagged scar looked deeper in the firelight, and I remembered what he'd told me about it. *I wasn't born with this scar; someone bestowed it upon me.* "Trust goes both ways, you know," I told him. "You claim you want to know me, and yet I'm not allowed to know anything about you."

At my words, another surge of sensation traveled down the bond, this time from Collith. The feelings were too swift, too numerous for me to catch each individual one and define it, but what I felt strongest was... pain. Collith's mask had fallen away, revealing the weary king I'd met once before.

I opened my mouth to speak again—without any idea of what was about to come out—when he ran a hand through his hair and nodded. "You're right. I'm sorry. I know it's not fair."

He'd surprised me again. "So let's start with something small," I suggested, hoping I didn't sound as eager as I felt. "What did you do to help Damon?"

A muscle flexed in Collith's jaw. "It's... difficult for me to make significant decisions without knowing something of the outcome," he said haltingly. "I am not a decisive king, which I realize is probably the worst quality a ruler can have. When my conscience wouldn't rest because of Damon Sworn, though, I sought... counsel. In hopes of discovering what effect taking him from Jassin would have."

Here he fell silent.

It was always my first instinct to keep pushing, keep fighting for what I wanted, but I didn't know Collith's limits. Not yet. For once, I decided to let something rest. I looked down at Damon's slender fingers and absently noted that his nails needed to be clipped. The room was too quiet; I could hear the whisperings of bad thoughts and dark memories drawing nearer.

"So…" I ventured desperately. "We haven't exactly talked since my, uh, coronation."

Since I dueled with Jassin and left him dead in a pool of his own blood, a small voice corrected. Images from the ceremony assaulted me. Had it really only been yesterday? I tried not to wince at the flashes of my mother's unblinking gaze, the blood-stained sheets around my father's body, Damon hunching over his dead lover on the floor.

Collith frowned. Firelight flickered over the smooth planes of his cheeks. God, he was beautiful. "No, we haven't," he replied. "I suspect you haven't prepared yourself."

I blinked, all thoughts of beauty rushing from my mind. "Prepared myself? For what?"

"I told you the crown came at a cost."

For a moment, I had no idea what Collith was talking about. After a few seconds, though, it came back to me. Those murmured words in the softness of a shared bed and crowding shadows. *In the same way you and I are bound, so you would be bound to them,* he'd said.

All at once, I realized why he was being so careful about letting any emotions down the bond. Collith was worried. "How do you propose I should prepare for hundreds of faeries setting up camp in my head?" I asked tightly, a reaction to the knot of apprehension forming inside me. Maybe I'd let myself forget about something so monumental because I had started to hope it wouldn't happen.

"By staying near me as much as you can," Collith answered without hesitation. "When it happens, I can use our bond to ease the transition."

His words made my stomach quake. More time with Collith meant more temptation. More resistance. More chances for him to corrupt me. I would never forget that terrible moment in the throne room, that handful of seconds I'd thought about killing my own brother.

When I didn't say anything, Collith went on, his voice even tighter than before. "Magic is unpredictable, Fortuna. The spell is already working differently on you; it should've materialized at the coronation. There have only been fae queens."

"You're right, I'm not a faerie. I'm a Nightmare. So maybe the magic is just scared," I said snidely.

Thankfully, Collith didn't acknowledge this childish response. He tilted his head and appraised me. Shadows flickered across his features. "May we set the issue aside for a moment? I've been meaning to offer you a proposition."

Oh, shit. His last proposition had resulted in an irreversible bond between us. What else could he possibly want from me? I eyed Collith warily, fighting against the instinct to bolt from the room. "What is it?" I asked, curious in spite of myself. I glanced at Damon, wondering briefly if he was hearing any of this.

Collith's next words, though, made my gaze snap back to his. "What if we tried to be friends?"

"Friends?" I echoed.

"It's a companion, of sorts. A confidante, if you will."

At this, I rolled my eyes. "I know what a friend is, you ass."

The insult slid off him like oil on water. "Excellent. So what do you say?"

There came another knock, saving me from an immediate response. Because, truthfully, I had no idea what to say. My friendship with Laurie, if that's indeed what we were, had happened like a cold coming on. Gradually, unexpected, and without giving me much say in the matter. To be *friends* with the Unseelie King... it went against the natural order of everything in my head. Friendship meant giving him a certain degree of trust. Of deliberately spending time together. Of laughter. Was that even possible with a creature that had manipulated me into being his mate?

Collith returned to the door in just a few long-legged strides. He took a tray from the awaiting slave—it was the young girl I'd given shoes to, which now adorned her small feet—and thanked her. He shut the door with his foot, the movement oddly graceful. As Collith crossed the room again, he didn't move toward the chairs or the desk. Instead, he placed the tray right on the bed, within my reach. He then dragged his chair to rest beside mine and busied himself buttering a bread roll. The familiar scent of him drifted through the air, a combination of cologne, earth, and male.

Desire filled my center, unexpected and wildly inconvenient. It wasn't like we were in a place, emotionally or physically, where I could do anything to satisfy the urge.

"Now that I'm queen, am I able to make changes?" I asked abruptly.

Collith took his time responding. He continued his painstaking preparations, setting plates and bowls in front of me. Fruit, a boiled egg, bread. Eventually, he started on his own bounty. As I watched him, I realized I'd never seen the Unseelie King eat before. He did it like he did everything else—thoughtfully and deliberately. "What did you have in mind?" he replied at last, speaking only after he'd swallowed.

I glanced at the food and could only think of the poor creatures who'd prepared it. My stomach still growled, though; I couldn't remember the last time I'd eaten. "I want to make it illegal to have slaves at Court," I said, reluctantly picking up the bread roll. "I also want to abolish the black market."

A faint smile curved Collith's lips. He set his fork down and focused on me. Having this faerie's full attention was always unnerving; I couldn't decide if I was more aroused or nervous. I began tearing the roll into pieces and popping them into my mouth. "Before I met you, I thought Nightmares were creatures of pain and darkness," Collith said softly. One of the pieces lodged in my throat. "Why, then, are you constantly seeking freedom and light?"

I swallowed the bread. Collith watched each movement

intently, and I refused to let the frank admiration in his gaze affect me. "Why are you avoiding this? Why have you let it go on so long?" I demanded once I could speak again.

This got to him. Barely perceptible, a muscle ticked in his jaw. "Fine. Tell me something," he said. His voice was cold; it was obvious I was talking to the king. "In the time of Prohibition, did humans stop drinking? If I shut down the market, it will only be rebuilt somewhere else, and they'll make it harder to find. Why do you think I was at the market on the day we met? I spend what I can spare of my small salary buying those captives and setting them free."

The revelation he had a salary made me frown in surprise. But that wasn't relevant right now. "What if the Union had shared your mindset? Oh, why bother freeing them, since people will just own slaves anyway?" I challenged, resisting the impulse to stand. "It's *wrong*, Collith. Simple as that."

His eyes were dark and pained. Any hint of appreciation was long gone. His hand, where it still gripped the handle of a fork, was white. "Don't you think I know that? Do you think so little of me? I'm trying to free them without shedding any blood, Fortuna, and that takes time. A comment here, a deal there, a planted thought—"

"And in the meantime, there is suffering. Not just the ones down here, being beaten, raped, and forced into servitude. There are also the ones aboveground, left without answers or closure. Not even a body. These slaves are sons and daughters, parents, friends, and... siblings." My voice cracked. Worried Collith would offer comfort, which might make me break completely, I hurried on. "You said you brought me here because you wanted more power. You said you wanted to survive the backlash when you took away their toys. Well, here I am. Let's take them away."

In a fluid movement, Collith abandoned his supper and moved to the fire. He said nothing, but I was a Nightmare who'd touched his skin—I felt the fear rolling off him. I stared at the tense line of his shoulders in astonishment. In the admittedly brief time I'd known this faerie, he'd never revealed anything more than longing or sorrow. Maybe Collith had brought me here for reasons even he wasn't aware of. I was the fire to his ice. The shout to his whisper. The run to his walk.

Thinking this and watching him, I once again decided to let it go. For now.

"Where do you go when you disappear?" I asked next. Absently, I stroked the back of Damon's hand. Throughout our entire conversation, he hadn't stirred. More than anything, I wished I could use my abilities to ensure his dreams were beautiful. "When we first got to the Unseelie Court, you vanished. Every time I wake up, you're gone. After my coronation, there was no sign of you."

It was obvious, even through his clothing, that the lines of Collith's body were tense. He stared down into the flames and spoke as though there were a hand around his throat. "Usually I'm... visiting someone."

He's trying to open himself to me, I realized. It was so difficult that he couldn't even meet my gaze. "Who?" I prompted.

But apparently Collith had reached his limit for truths. Once again, he turned to me. At some point, he'd dragged a hand through his hair, because it was wilder than before. His eyes burned hotter than the fire at his side. "What did Jassin say while you were in the warded circle?"

The words had hardly left his mouth when the memory came skipping back, tearing into me with the ravenous ferocity of a redcap. I could feel Jassin's breath upon my cheek again. See his emerald eyes burning into mine. His voice slithered all around me. *Did you like my gift? I would've used your brother, but they wanted him alive for the third trial, so I made do.*

If I could go back in time and kill the bastard again, I'd do it. "He was the one who arranged for Shameek's death," I told

Collith flatly, focusing on my brother again, a physical reminder of why I'd put a blameless human in harm's way. "Apparently he wanted to rattle me with that knowledge right before our battle."

Collith absorbed this silently. After another moment, he left the fire and settled back into the chair beside me. Once again, he clasped his hands between his knees. As the quiet swelled, one of his fingers began to twitch. Were he sitting on his throne, I knew he'd be tapping it against the armrest, that silver ring flashing. I waited, somehow sensing—or maybe I was just starting to know this mate of mine—that he was about to reveal something.

For once, Collith didn't disappoint. "I should tell you that I saw some of what you faced," he said, his gaze meeting mine again. In the dimness, his irises looked more brown than hazel. "Your emotions were so overwhelming that I'm not sure I could've blocked it out, even if I'd wanted to."

It was my turn to process. The idea of Collith seeing one of my most private memories was akin to him reading my journal. If I'd ever bothered to keep one. For a few seconds, I fought an irrational rise of anger. "I guess fair is fair," I sighed eventually, the indignation leaving me in a rush. "I've seen plenty in your head."

Collith tilted his head and appraised me. There was no sign of the Unseelie King when he murmured, "I'm sorry that happened to you, Fortuna."

Usually, when people said something along those lines, it was automatic. When Collith said it, though, sincerity drifted down the bond. Studying him right back, I felt my lips curve into a sad smile. "This might be a weird thing to say, but I think my dad would've liked you."

Strangely enough, Collith didn't smile back. My words seemed to have a sobering effect on him. He was silent for a breath, then he spoke softly. "I would love to know more about him."

It had been so long since anyone had asked about my parents. Granted, I didn't exactly make it easy for them—Bea and Gretchen used to try, once in a while—but after reliving the worst memories of them, I welcomed a chance to bring back better ones.

Now, I pictured the man that had taught me so much. The man who had left this world far too soon. His too-big ears and dear, crooked smile. I'd never thought to accuse Mom and Dad of playing favorites, and of course I loved my mother, but Dad had been my best friend. "He was everything I'm not," I said. I looked at Damon, seeing Dad in every line of his face. "Soft-spoken, patient, and kind."

"But you are kind."

I snorted and refocused on the male sitting next to me. "I know faeries can lie now, Collith."

He didn't try to argue, but yet another small smile hovered around his mouth. "I like when you say my name," he commented.

Warmth spread through my chest. I didn't trust myself to respond, so I picked up a hard-boiled egg and started removing its delicate shell. Still smiling, Collith followed suit. Neither of us spoke for a time. The only sounds in the room were the fire and the sporadic clinking of silverware. At one point, Collith wordlessly poured a glass of wine and handed it to me. Either it was later in the day than I thought or faeries didn't adhere to the human practice of avoiding alcohol until a certain time of day. Either way, it was much needed, and I didn't even think to be cautious or remember my mother's caution about faerie drinks. The flavor was dry, too dry for my preference, but I sipped on it between bites.

The only words we did exchange were light and brief. I

glanced at Collith, paused, and pointed the fork I held. "You've got some egg on the corner of your mouth. Right there."

To which he shocked me by winking and saying, "But it got you looking at my mouth, right?"

My lips twitched in response. Collith returned his gaze to the food and left the egg exactly where it was.

After that, we finished our meals in a comfortable silence. My plates were clean before Collith's. At a loss of what to do with my hands, I started stacking my dishes and putting them on the tray. Collith immediately stood to help, ignoring my protests. The coolness radiating from his skin teased my own. I didn't edge away as I might have done just two days earlier.

Maybe Collith realized this, as well—halfway through our task, he startled me by reaching over and taking my hand. His fingers folded in the spaces between mine. I darted a glance at his face, expecting to find desire in his expression, but there was nothing. He was touching me without wanting more.

Guilt tugged at my mind with the insistence of a child pulling on its mother's shirt. "I made a vow to be honest with you," I whispered, raising my gaze from our entwined fingers. Collith waited patiently. I studied the lines of his lovely face. They weren't obvious, didn't detract from his allure, but undeniably there on either side of his mouth and between his eyebrows. It was physical evidence of the burdens he carried, when most of his brethren still had the flawless skin of living without thought to consequences. In a rush I said, "I'm leaving the Unseelie Court. Just for a while. Long enough to take Damon home and get him settled."

The faerie king didn't react. "Okay," he said.

I didn't know what I'd been expecting, but it wasn't this simple response. I searched Collith's gaze, wondering what the catch was. "Okay?"

He shrugged. "You're not a prisoner here, Fortuna. You're a

queen. I come and go as I please; why shouldn't you? Shall I show you the way?"

"I think I've got that covered, actually," I said, still trying to hide my incredulity. "No offense, but whenever you go somewhere, it's not exactly subtle. If there's a target on Damon's back, I want to leave without anyone knowing."

Collith raised his eyebrows, clearly intrigued. If I was truly being honest, I probably should reveal that I'd befriended the Seelie King. Something held me back, though. Maybe I was afraid he'd dodge the question and upset this strange peace between us. "It's a long story," I hedged. "But... may I still use your name if I do end up needing you?"

He began stroking the back of my hand with his thumb. An involuntary shiver went through me. Strange that such a simple touch should affect me so strongly. "It's as I said. I like when you say my name," he murmured.

All at once, fear rushed through my veins. I pulled my hand free none-too-subtly. Collith's expression returned to its usual neutrality, and if my withdrawal bothered him, it didn't show. He settled back in his chair. "When will you go?" he asked, as though nothing strange had just occurred between us.

"As soon as Damon wakes," I said without hesitation. "He probably won't come easily; I'll tell Lyari and Omar to carry him out if necessary."

"And the wolf? Is he going with you?"

I'd actually forgotten that we shared the room with an enormous wolf—at Collith's words, I twisted around to look at him. However long he'd been trapped in that form, the beast still understood bits and pieces, because he lifted its head and fixed yellow eyes on us. A growl rumbled through the room. I turned back to Collith and raised my eyebrows. "I don't think he'll allow me to leave him behind."

"I think I might be jealous," the faerie remarked.

At that moment, Damon shifted, and once again I was saved from responding. I perched on the edge of my seat, watching my brother's face closely. His eyes fluttered. They would probably open any minute now. Shit. He needed to sleep just a little longer.

I lowered my voice to avoid waking him. "There's something I need to do," I told Collith. "Will you… will you stay with Damon, please?"

The significance of my request was not lost on him; it meant I trusted him with the person most precious to me. "It would be my honor," Collith answered.

His voice was soft, more caress than words, and it felt like he'd trailed a feather along my skin. "I'll be back soon," I managed as I stood. The werewolf immediately stood, too.

After another brief nod of acknowledgment, Collith turned to Damon. He leaned his elbows on the mattress, creating slight indents. The fire had gotten weaker during our conversation, so now the light it cast was darker. Dreamier. Damon looked like a handsome, sleeping doll, and the faerie beside him was ethereal. As though God had sent one of his own down to watch over my brother. Collith's skin was lit from within, alive and flickering with embers.

With that strange image imprinted on my mind, I left to find the King of the Seelie Court.

CHAPTER THREE

One of the torches wavered and spat as I reentered the passageway. *Yeah, well, the feeling's mutual.* The werewolf, whose name I still didn't know, stayed so close that his warm snout brushed my elbow. I couldn't hold back a flinch, ever aware that he could kill me in an instant if he so chose. The contact left a damp spot on my skin and a flash of his fear. In that instant, I saw a woman's face. She was not beautiful—her scowl was too fierce and her frame too wiry—but there was something about her that demanded attention.

There was no time to speculate on it. I pulled the door shut as firmly as I could, a futile effort to keep Damon safe while I was gone. The werewolf watched every movement with his bright, flaxen gaze.

Lyari and Omar were right where I'd left them. As I moved to stand in front of them, I experienced a sense of déjà vu, and it was beginning to feel like this day would never end. Had it really only been a couple hours ago that I'd spoken to Viessa in the dungeons?

Omar, a round-faced fae who radiated timidity and an eagerness to please, immediately bowed. He didn't come back up. I stared at the back of his head, nonplussed, and it took me a few seconds to realize he was awaiting a command. "Oh. I, uh, need you to keep guarding the door," I told him, sounding more like a bumbling human than a queen. "Please don't let anyone besides Zara go into that room."

"Yes, Your Majesty," he said without hesitation, finally straightening. I had no doubt that he would sooner die than allow someone past him.

With Damon now adequately looked after, I turned to Lyari. She stood with her back to the wall, staring straight ahead, holding the hilt of her sword with a grip that looked painful.

"Please take me to Nym," I said, hoping no weariness leaked into my voice. Something told me this female's already less-than-stellar opinion of me would worsen at any sign of weakness.

If she was surprised by the request, Lyari didn't show it. Her body practically thrummed with tension, but she moved in front of me to lead the way. As we plunged back into the maze, I didn't let myself look back, despite how the bond ached as we moved further away. For an instant, my brow crinkled with bewilderment. Then it hit me—whatever part of myself that was tethered to Collith didn't like how much distance there was between us. This was a new development, and it was one I found particularly disturbing.

The silence was too absolute, too ready to fill my head with unwelcome thoughts. At first, I tried to put all my focus on the sound of our shoes against the stones. When that didn't work, my gaze went to the tense line of Lyari's shoulders. There was no sense of fear emanating from her, which meant it could only be loathing. "Why do you hate me?" I blurted.

"Do you really care?" the Guardian asked without turning around.

It was exactly the distraction I'd been looking for, and I truly thought about the answer before saying anything. Maybe there was a part of me that admired Lyari. Understood her. We lived in a world dominated by men. They earned more, they ruled more, they spoke more. Any female who fought back—literally, in Lyari's case, as I suspected her weapon and armor weren't just for show—was worth my time.

"I guess I do," I said finally. "I'm not hoping we'll become besties and braid each other's hair, but I'd hoped to gain an ally when you made your vow of fealty."

"You didn't give me much choice in the matter."

"Neither did you, once," I retorted, glaring at the back of her head now. "Or have you forgotten how we met?"

The memory was easy to relive; Lyari's careless, supernatural strength as she backhanded me. I could still taste the bitter tang of blood in my mouth and see the ground rising to meet me. Few times in my life had I felt so powerless, so degraded. Fresh hatred surged through my heart, and just like that, I felt no remorse for separating this female from her comrades. If she considered guarding me a punishment, so much the better.

Before the petulant Guardian could respond, something moved up ahead. Thinking of the wendigo I'd fought in these tunnels, I jerked to a halt. The werewolf shifted so that he was mostly in front of me, and there was a ringing sound as Lyari unsheathed her sword. It glittered, looking every inch the weapon of a faerie. "Show yourself," she commanded, not a trace of trepidation in her voice.

A dirty face peered around the corner, and each of us in the passageway relaxed. It was just the girl I'd given a pair of shoes. Her blue eyes found me in the shadows. "Be careful, Your Majesty," she whispered, sounding more like something ancient than a child. "That way lies madness."

I mustered a smile, though I was more on edge now. "Thank you for the warning. I'll be careful."

The girl ducked out of sight, doubtless going to serve the faeries we both despised.

"You're something of a hero to them," Lyari said, starting to walk again. "After your performance at the coronation and that stunt with the shoes, I suppose they believe you'll save them."

"And I will," I said without thinking. There I went again, making promises that were too big, too complicated, too impossible.

Lyari snorted, which felt distinctly inappropriate for a guard addressing her queen. However much these creatures feared me, they didn't respect me. Really, though, did I care?

We finished our journey in silence. Eventually we came to a dead end—the first I'd seen in this place that felt endless—and Lyari inclined her head toward a narrow, wooden door that was hidden in shadow. A single torch adorned the wall, but no one had tended to its flame in a while, because it was floundering like my courage. "Here we are," the faerie said.

Before the last word had completely left her mouth, something on the other side of the door crashed. The werewolf's ears flattened against his head. "We won't be here long," I told him, hoping he didn't sense my trepidation. A nervous werewolf and an anxious Nightmare seemed like a volatile combination. "You could always wait out here if you—"

Another one of his growls vibrated through the dirt tunnel. Guess I had my answer.

Lyari waited for my command. I was tempted to have her accompany me, protect me from whatever waited in that room, but this was another conversation that I didn't want an audience for. "Well, I'll probably scream if something goes wrong, so keep your ears open," I said. Her eyes narrowed but she didn't argue. I wasn't certain if that was good or bad. I took a breath. Then, to avoid giving myself a chance to hesitate, and thus change my mind, I pushed the door open.

Like the royal kitchens, the sight that greeted me was a

series of rooms with high ceilings. Every space, however, was filled with clocks instead of fires and slaves. Broken clocks, ticking clocks, grandfather clocks, pocket-sized clocks. The werewolf entered in front of me, radiating tension. I followed him, taking it all in, and realized why Viessa had thought of this when I'd ask about a place where I wouldn't be overheard—anyone trying to listen in wouldn't have much luck.

In the farthest room, sitting at a workbench, was a faerie. He didn't react as the door hinges whined. Thinking there was a good chance he hadn't heard, I pushed the door shut as hard as I could, slamming it against the rickety frame.

"Hello?" I ventured. Still, the faerie didn't react. I started walking toward him, sidestepping obstacles along the way. The floor was littered with various trinkets, tools, and books. But mostly books. Some open, some closed, all of them curling with age. My instincts were warning me to stay out of his reach, so I halted several yards away. I raised my voice to be heard over all the ticking. "You must be Nym. My name is Fortuna. I'm here because I was told it's difficult to eavesdrop in this room. Now I can see why."

Finally, the faerie glanced at me over his shoulder. He didn't do a double-take like most creatures meeting me for the first time. Instead, he promptly returned to his work. I decided to risk it and get closer. The werewolf didn't like this; he pressed against my thigh, the fur along his spine standing on end.

Now I stopped a couple feet away. The space in front of the faerie was within view. I didn't know much about clocks, but he appeared to be repairing one. Its insides were spilled across the surface of the workbench, gleaming silver and gold against the dark wood. There was a tiny tool in the faerie's hand. His movements were frantic and desperate as he twisted it. "By ignorance? Is that their happy state? The proof of their obedience and their faith?" he muttered. It was obvious he didn't expect a response. Did he even know I was here?

I studied the faerie's profile. He had a handsome face, but its allure was lessened somewhat by his wild hair. It hung just past his shoulders, ratty and tangled. He wore a white button-up, but it was so thin, the outline of his gaunt body was visible underneath. "Is it all right if I stay with you for a little while, Nym? I need to summon someone," I added.

Nym glanced at me again. His watery eyes widened and the tool he held clattered to the table. "Watch out for the cow!"

His panic was so real that I actually spun around, expecting a huge animal to ram into me. "Uh, what cow?"

When I turned back to him, the faerie was frowning, as though I'd done something terribly rude. "Did someone mention a cow?" he questioned, sounding for all the world like another courtier in the throne room. Before I could answer, Nym turned on the stool. He stared blankly at the table for a moment, then retrieved the tool he'd been holding.

What was it the girl had said? *That way lies madness.* Another mystery solved. Though I had no way of knowing if this faerie was dangerous or not, compassion stirred in my chest. "No, it was my mistake," I murmured. "I'm sorry for confusing you."

Without warning, Nym uttered a curse and threw the clock at the wall in front of him. It shattered instantly, and I discovered what had caused the noise when we'd been in the passage. Once the pieces lay broken and scattered, Nym pulled at his hair, looking like a child that had misplaced his favorite toy. Acting against my usual instinct to avoid physical contact, I dared to put my hand on his shoulder. His fears whispered through me instantly. There were many, but I didn't have a chance to properly analyze them.

In a movement that belied his fragile appearance, Nym seized my wrist. His grip was painful. Something glinted against his chest—a silver chain—but the rest of the necklace was hidden beneath his shirt. "I remember you," he whispered urgently, his near-black eyes like a bottomless hole. His breath smelled like alcohol. "You're the one who lets him out!"

I didn't let myself flinch. Instead, I met the faerie's frantic gaze. "We've never met before, Nym," I said calmly.

Slowly, he released me. His brows were drawn together, his eyes glistening with confusion now. Somehow, though he was probably decades older than me, Nym emanated the innocence of a child. "We haven't?"

"No. I'm just here to summon Laurelis."

A second went by. Two. Three. I waited longer than I would've with anyone else, giving the faerie a chance to release me on his own. I really, really didn't want to use my abilities on him... but it looked like there would be no other alternative.

Just as I was about to reach for the monsters that kept him awake at night, Nym's focus shifted to a point over my shoulder. Something in the air shifted. A familiar scent filled the air. "So good of you to join us, Your Majesty," I said without turning, keeping my focus on the faerie who could break my wrist with a flick of his own.

A sigh came from behind. "Be a good boy and let the pretty lady go, Nym."

Lines of confusion deepened across Nym's forehead, but slowly, finger by finger, he obeyed. The moment I was free, I spun and found myself face-to-face with the King of the Seelie Court.

When I'd imagined our confrontation, I'd pictured him with a smirk or a teasing smile. Instead, Laurie looked irritated. Irritated and kingly. He wore a black outfit that clung to every subtly-defined muscle. The tunic was stiff and, when he moved just right, faintly glittered. The collar was high and somehow highlighted Laurie's startling coloring. A sword hung from his narrow hips. His boots gleamed in the firelight.

"How did you find out?" he asked, seemingly oblivious to

how I stared. A beat later he shook his head. "No, don't answer that. Viessa, of course. Collith should've killed her years ago."

"You said you weren't my enemy," I accused. And there it was, the truth of why I'd turned down Collith's much simpler offer of taking me to the surface. I didn't give my friendship, my trust, to anyone these days. When I learned of who Laurie was, and came to the inevitable conclusion that he'd gained my trust for his own purposes, I had felt... betrayed.

Wearing an expression of harried resignation, Laurie leaned his hip against one of the tables. Now that I knew the truth of who he was, I didn't know how I'd missed it. How I'd ever believed he was a slave, despite his act when we first met. Laurie radiated arrogance and power. It wasn't in his frame, which was more slender than muscled, like Oliver was. It wasn't in his clothing, either, however well-made the tunic appeared to be. The truth was in the tilt of his chin, the glint in his metallic eyes, the caress in his voice. He also had cheekbones that were to die for.

"I'm sorry," Laurie said with raised brows. "Have I harmed you? Hindered you?"

His words made me pause. Because, no, I didn't have any veritable proof that he was against me. In fact, he'd helped numerous times. I frowned and raised my gaze to his. "Then *why*?"

There was no flicker of remorse in the gaze that stared back. "I'm not at your beck and call, little queen," Laurie snapped. "I've already given you too much of my time. Others have begun to notice my absence."

The response reeked of typical fae evasion. Well, I would just put some pieces together, then. What was it Viessa had said? *He has a history with Collith.* Apparently it was more complex than rival monarchs; he was going out of his way to protect my mate. He left his own Court often, just to keep tabs on what was happening here. Yet I hadn't seen Laurie and Collith interact. Not once.

If I had any enemies—enemies that weren't currently dead or bedridden, that was—I wouldn't work so hard to avoid them. No, the creatures I avoided were the ones that mattered in more powerful ways.

"You love him," I whispered.

In an instant, I knew I'd guessed right. Laurie smiled, but it was nothing like the smiles I'd seen until this point. There was also something in his eyes that captured my attention; this faerie was not all games and fun. There was a soul behind the flesh and bones. "Faeries only do things for three reasons, little Nightmare," he answered. "Boredom, greed, or lust."

"Liar."

Laurie's generous mouth tightened. He swung away and strolled past some of the clocks, seemingly absorbed in their faces and woodwork. Nym hadn't gone back to work, but he wasn't watching us, either. He stared straight ahead at... nothing. I tried to keep one eye on him and one on Laurie. It was unclear which one I should be more worried about.

"My spies brought word that Collith had taken a mate," Laurie said suddenly, making me forget Nym. He touched the top of the clock and rubbed his fingers together, almost in an absent-minded way, though I suspected nothing he did was without purpose. "I was curious, I suppose. Then I began to like you against my better judgment."

"The horror," I drawled.

Amusement cracked his cold facade. "You know, they say that sarcasm is the lowest form of wit."

"Well, I try to cater to my audience," I volleyed back. At this, Laurie grinned, and there at last was a glimpse of the faerie I'd befriended.

My own smile quickly dimmed, though. It was impossible to ignore the seconds ticking by. Every one had the potential to be when Damon's would-be assassin decided to try again. "Someone is trying to kill my brother," I told the Seelie King without preamble. "I need you to use your abilities to get the two of us through the door undetected."

He didn't look surprised. In fact, his expression was carefully neutral, as though I had just made the first move in a game of chess. "It's as I told you the day we met; I am loyal to Collith. Why should I aid in his queen's escape?"

So the Seelie King wasn't as omnipotent as he'd wanted to seem. He clearly didn't know that Collith had given me his blessing to go. "If you're so dedicated to Collith, why are you avoiding him?" I challenged, keeping this fact to myself. This entire endeavor would fall apart if Laurie didn't believe he was acting against Collith.

There was a notable pause. He picked a piece of imaginary lint off his sleeve. The clocks around us continued to *tick, tick, tick.* Eventually the faerie king said, his tone light as a dust mote, "He may not be my biggest fan at the moment."

I wondered if there was any point to asking follow-up questions. *No time for that,* I reminded myself. Back to the matter at hand.

However I felt about faeries, I'd gotten good at understanding how they thought. The mistake I'd made with Jassin still haunted me, though; I had to be more careful in what I said down here. "You should help us because you're invested in Collith's survival," I said slowly. "I'm tied to both him and his entire Court. If you do this, I will swear a blood oath"—I'd read about them in one of Collith's books—"to send word if I sense he's in danger. I mean, even you can't be around all the time, right?"

Now Laurie did smirk. "You're not heartless, Fortuna. You'd send word anyway."

I raised my brows. "That's quite a gamble to take. These creatures tortured my brother, beat me nearly to death, and put me through trials no one should ever be forced to endure. Collith is their fucking *king*."

Laurie tilted his head. It was impossible to discern whether he was still amused or seriously considering what I'd said. His gaze bored into mine. In response, I felt myself drift to that mental place made of whiteness, ice, numbness. The place I had gone in the goblins' cabin and the Unseelie dungeon. After a second or two, I knew that the face looking back at Laurie appeared as empty as I felt.

Apparently Laurie wasn't the gambling sort—at least, not when it came to Collith—because he bent and pulled a pocketknife from his boot. In a practiced movement, he flicked it open. Nym made an odd, strangled sound as Laurie pressed the edge into his palm. Once the cut was made, he extended both the knife and his injured hand toward me. Bright blue blood dripped to the floor. "You have yourself a bargain, Fortuna Sworn," he said.

For once, I tried to think about consequences. *How much do I really know about this beautiful creature standing in front of me?* He was a faerie, which was already a mark against him. He might like me, but it was Collith he would serve and protect, despite any bargains between us. Would I regret needing to contact him someday? What if Collith betrayed me and I needed him dead?

That way lies madness, I thought. What If Road was twisty and never-ending.

The ticking clocks echoed in my ears as I made a cut of my own. There was hardly any pain. Within seconds I wrapped my fingers around Laurie's. He smiled again, this one impish and seductive, and pulled me closer. It was so startling that I pressed my other palm against his chest to keep some distance between us. He was so warm compared to Collith. Did it have something to do with their being from different courts?

"Does your mind never stop?" Laurie murmured.

I looked up at him, unable to deny a flutter in my stomach

that had nothing to do with our blood merging. Unlike when Collith and I had created the mating bond, I didn't feel anything happen. Maybe fae magic truly didn't like me. As if I would be so lucky. "I could ask you the same question," I responded. Thankfully, my voice was even.

"When would you like to depart?" Laurie asked. It effectively ended the strange spell between us.

"Now, please." I stepped away, feeling like I'd just done something wrong. I cleared my throat and sought the other faerie in the room. "Nym, thank you for letting me use your space. I hope I can trust you to stay quiet about... everything."

Still perched on the stool, Nym dipped his head. His eyes were bright and clear, as though nothing were amiss in that head of his. "Of course, Your Majesty. Your secrets are my secrets."

Smiling my thanks—Nym looked dazzled at the sight of it—I went to the door and pulled it open. It took me a moment to find Lyari, glowering in the shadows. "There you are. Excellent. I need you to guard the door to Collith's rooms and act like I'm there."

"Where are you going?" she asked. It sounded like she was talking through gritted teeth. Was it the deception she had an issue with, letting me leave unguarded, or still having to follow my orders? Oh, wait. I didn't care.

"The fewer people that know, the better," I chirped. "Thank you, Lyari."

She was silent as I shut the door in her face yet again. My heart pounded hard and fast now. I faced Laurie, uncertain how his ability worked. Did we need to be touching? But Laurie just bowed and swept his arm in a dramatic arc. "After you, my lady."

I didn't move. There was a question I had to ask, no matter the futility of it. A question that would follow me even into

Oliver's peaceful dreamscapes. "Why does Collith hate you, Laurie?" I said.

It was his turn to raise those silvery brows. I couldn't tell if it was another act or he was really surprised. "Darling, you didn't know?" the Seelie King crooned. "I'm the one who gave Collith that lovely scar."

CHAPTER FOUR

*T*wenty minutes later, freedom was up ahead, a jagged opening of light and sound.

I had a sullen brother, a silver-haired faerie king, and an emaciated werewolf in tow. Damon and I both carried bags, since he'd been adamant about bringing some of Jassin's belongings with him. While the idea of having that black-hearted faerie's things in my house wasn't exactly appealing, I'd decided to pick and choose my battles. This one wasn't worth fighting.

Just like the battle of getting any answers out of Laurie, once he'd revealed the fun fact about his scar. The Seelie King had stopped answering my questions after that, responding to everything I said with clever innuendos or barbed questions of his own.

Collith and I exchanged a brief farewell. I had been awkward and uncertain—both of which weren't like me—and his lips quirked at this, as though he knew something I didn't. Arrogant bastard. "Well, guess I'll see you soon," I said, standing there in the passageway, laden with bags and worries.

"Sooner than you think, I'd expect," my mate replied, so annoyingly lovely and collected. He didn't touch me, but he may as well have, for all the effects the fire and ice of that look had on me.

Painfully aware of his guards, Lyari, Laurie, Damon, and the werewolf observing us, I'd given him a lame wave and turned away. With every step I put between us, our mating bond quivered with reluctance and longing. *I waved at him. I can't believe I just waved at him,* I kept thinking.

None of that mattered, though, when I stepped into the open.

For some reason, I'd been expecting it to be nighttime. The sight of sunlight filtering through the treetops was a welcome surprise. Birdsong filled the air. In the brief time I'd been trapped underground, fall had arrived in its entirety; the leaves that stirred in a slight breeze were vibrant, varying shades of red, orange, and yellow.

Some distant part of me knew I needed to stay alert, stay aware of every movement around me, but I'd been on edge from the moment I'd followed Collith into the darkness. In that moment, all I was capable of was breathing deeply and silently absorbing this feeling I'd missed. A sense that the world was so much bigger than faeries, Fallen, or crowns.

Unaware that I'd stopped, Laurie, Damon, and the werewolf had started in the direction of Granby. I lingered there for another moment or two, reveling in the sensation of air moving along my skin. It felt like I'd been trapped underground for years rather than days. My nostrils flared as I inhaled clean, mountain air. *I never want to go down there again,* I realized.

But sooner or later, I'd have to. The thought made me want to run. Run fast and run hard, until I was so far from this place that there was no hope of any faerie finding me. Even Collith.

Are you sure about that? an inner voice mocked.

A voice made of silken sheets and stolen kisses reached me. "Fortuna? Do you sense something?"

I blinked and Laurie's face came into focus. He was standing within arm's reach, a frown tugging at the corners of his mouth. Until now, I'd only ever seen him in the light of torches or chandeliers. In the harsh light of day, he was still infuriatingly perfect. His long face and pale skin were so smooth, so fae, and his metallic-looking hair was even more complex as it shimmered in the brightness. His eyebrows were dark swoops over eyes that I'd believed to be a pale blue, but no, they were just as silver as his hair. There were slight lines on either side of his mouth, marks that indicated he smiled often.

As I watched, those lines deepened. Laurie had started to smirk—he knew exactly what was occupying my thoughts now.

I was about to wipe that smirk off his face when, without warning, Damon uttered a strangled sound and dropped to his knees. His precious bags fell unheeded onto the dirt. "What...?" I started, then trailed off when I comprehended Laurie had stopped hiding his presence. Nausea gripped my stomach at the sight of my brother prostrating himself before a faerie; it reminded me too much of what Jassin had done. I started to kneel beside him, at a loss for words, but Laurie beat me to it.

With a growl, he hauled Damon upright. "You should only kneel to someone if there's a sword at your neck," he snapped. "You are a Nightmare; even the bravest creatures tremble at your touch. Don't degrade yourself and your race by acting like a worm. Worms get stepped on."

"Okay, that's enough," I interjected. Damon wore a stunned expression. He hung in Laurie's hands like a ragdoll, his legs dangling slightly above the ground. The Seelie King obeyed, but not because of anything I said—the wolf had his teeth clamped down on Laurie's pale wrist. I could see, even from a few feet away, that he hadn't pierced the skin. It was a warning.

"A loyal werewolf," Laurie murmured with more speculation than I would've liked. He regarded the beast with those bright eyes of his and slowly lowered Damon to the ground. "How useful."

"Are you holding up your end of the bargain, Oh Majestic One?" I asked, hoping to take his attention away from the wolf. "Damon can clearly see you now."

Laurie flapped his hand, which the werewolf had just released. He seemed completely unruffled. "Yes, yes, of course. It just takes energy to extend the illusion to one more mind. Why hide from him anyway?"

I wasn't sure whether he meant this as an insult to Damon, but I'd had enough confrontation for one day. My brother hadn't heard, anyway; he was preoccupied with the bags on the ground, opening each one to make sure whatever he'd packed was undamaged. I took advantage of everyone's stillness to open my own bag and find my cell phone. Now that we'd left the bowels of hell, there was probably service again. I held down the power button and the screen came to life, blindingly white. It would take a few seconds to reach the home screen... and to receive the angry texts Bea probably sent me.

"Shall we set up camp here, then?" Laurie asked, practically twitching with impatience.

Now that my phone was back on, it was all I could do not to play the recording of Collith's wedding vows and demand that Laurie translate. This wasn't something I wanted Damon or the werewolf hearing, though. It was... too personal. I shoved the phone into my back pocket and hoped there would be a chance to ask Laurie later. "Tempting," I responded. "It'd be fun to watch you get eaten alive by mosquitos."

The Seelie King sniffed. "It's too cold for mosquitos. Don't you know anything?"

His playfully haughty expression coaxed a smile to my lips. When Laurie saw this, he smiled back and winked. He turned away, and in that moment, I realized the werewolf had watched our exchange. He sat there, so still, yellow eyes inscrutable as ever. A strange sense of guilt enveloped me. Frowning now, I shouldered my backpack and followed Laurie.

We walked the rest of the way in a silence broken only by crunching leaves and snapping sticks. It wasn't a long way to the house—five miles, at most—but by the time the tree line broke, revealing a familiar gravel driveway, the rusting van that once belonged to goblins, and my little ivy-covered home, the sun had started its descent. Dusk spilled across grass that someone had obviously just mowed. *Cyrus*, I thought with a pang. I owed him yet another apology.

A few yards away, Damon had paused in the yard. Though I couldn't see his expression, it was easy to guess the direction of his thoughts. It was where my own had gone the moment the house came into view—we were thinking about that night. Thinking about the last time Damon had stepped through that front door. We were strangers to the two people who'd lived here together. I wasn't the sister Damon had known, and he wasn't the brother I had adored. Could the people we were now learn to be a family again?

Before I was able to say anything, Damon finally approached the house. Something told me he wanted to go in alone, so I pulled my cell out and scrolled to Savannah's name. If we were going to stay in Granby, we'd need a cloaking spell. She also deserved to know that the boyfriend she'd loved and searched for so desperately was back. But I couldn't bring myself to start a message. *Hey girl, great news, that guy you dated a few years ago is actually alive! Fair warning, he's a little different now. Also, could you do us a small favor?*

Leaves crackled behind me. A moment later, Laurie peered over my shoulder. At some point during our journey, I'd moved to lead the way, and the faerie had paused often to touch this or play with that. It made me question more than once whether or not Fallen were capable of having ADD. "What are you doing?" he asked now, his pleasant scent drifting past, carried on a breeze.

I let out a breath. "Having a moral crisis over whether or not to ask a witch for a favor."

"I'll send a witch tomorrow," he said dismissively. "She'll place some wards and spells to protect you. It probably won't be permanent, mind you, but you'll have a few days of peace."

Was it our bargain that made him so generous, I wondered, or something more? Trying to pinpoint Laurie's motives could easily drive someone insane, and I also couldn't deny a sense of relief at not having to contact Savannah just yet. I typed Cyrus, Bea, and Gretchen's names instead. *Home safe. I'll be there tomorrow for the dinner shift.* I pressed SEND and left it at that; the news of Damon's return seemed bigger than a text.

Since I have my phone out anyway…

"Before you go, will you translate something for me?" I asked casually. "It won't take long."

Laurie didn't try to hide his curiosity. He waved an elegant hand, signaling that I should continue. My stomach fluttered. I opened the video and it immediately started playing, but no sound emerged. It took me a heart-stopping second to realize that it was on mute. I breathed a sigh of relief and turned the sound back on. Collith's voice emerged into the stillness, solemn and unmistakably sincere. Laurie's expression didn't change as he listened. Within seconds, Collith had finished and the other me began—it was so strange hearing my own voice— and I hurriedly stopped the recording.

There was a moment of tense silence. Then Laurie said, his brows raised, "What a lucky female you are. Truly, I envy you."

Whatever facade of nonchalance I'd managed melted away like a sheet of ice. "What did he say?" I asked, hoping Laurie couldn't hear my wild heartbeat.

His pale gaze met mine. "I, Collith Sylvyre, do take Fortuna Sworn to be my lawfully wedded wife, to have and to hold, from this day forward, for better, for worse, for richer, for poorer, in sickness and in health, until death do us part… unless she gains far too much weight, asks for too many favors, or reveals herself to be an unbearable harpy. In which case, these vows are forfeit, and I reserve the right to dump her miserable ass and mess around with far hotter females in my Court."

Pain radiated through my jaw from clenching it too hard. "You're an asshole," I growled. Any feelings of warmth I'd started to feel toward him froze over.

The faerie just smirked again. His form began to lighten. "Well, you know what they say. Never be nice to an asshole; all you get is shit in return."

"Hold on there, shithole," I snapped. "One more thing."

"Do I look like a wishing well? Toss a penny in and I'll just give you what you want?" Laurie asked, becoming solid again. Despite the harsh words, Laurie's tone was bemused.

"The werewolf," I said, ignoring this. "I want to help him. Do you know where I can find a pack? Maybe if I show them a picture, someone will recognize him."

Laurie's glance flicked toward the creature himself, who was creeping around the van, his nostrils flaring. Doubtless the goblins' stink hadn't faded yet. "Werewolves are unpredictable, little Nightmare. Best keep your distance. Especially from a pack," he advised.

"Most would've said the same about the Unseelie Court, and I left that place with a crown. I think I'll manage."

He shrugged. "It's your funeral, I suppose. I'll look into it."

The silver-haired king must've been eager to return to his Court, because he vanished without any of the usual parting remarks. One moment he was there, the next I was standing alone, staring at a dying lawn and some swirling leaves.

Now that I didn't have an audience, my shoulders slumped. God, I was tired. I wanted nothing more than to put on some sweatpants, curl up in my own bed, and sleep for the next twenty-four hours.

Really, what was stopping me from doing exactly that?

Encouraged at the thought, I finally started toward the house. The few steps it took sapped what little energy I had left. The werewolf hurried to follow. He loped over the threshold as though he'd lived here his entire life, his tail swinging for the first time since I'd met him. I had to keep reminding myself that I hadn't adopted some dog from the shelter—this was a Fallen creature, with his own trauma and loved ones that were probably wondering what had happened to him. I couldn't get attached. There was no point.

Once we were inside, I leaned against the door and released a long sigh. Home. We were home. It was hard to wrap my head around; there was a niggling fear at the back of my head that this was all a vivid dream, and any second now, I'd wake up and none of it had happened. Meeting Collith, finding Damon, leaving Court with him at my side. The air smelled slightly stale, but familiar, and I breathed in and out as though it were the aromatic scent of a candle.

Thinking about my brother made me notice how quiet it was; my sense of peace immediately dissipated. I pushed off the door and began a search of the house. The werewolf had stretched out on the faded living room couch. "Still don't want to change back, huh?" I asked him as I passed. He closed his golden eyes in response.

I found Damon moments later, in my shadow-filled bedroom. My heartbeat slowed and I schooled my features into a neutral expression. He stood in front of the dresser, looking down at a picture in his hands. It was the last family portrait we'd taken. Dad, Mom, Damon, and me. All smiles and crinkled eyes. Usually I kept it close, so that when I felt an overwhelming expansion of hollowness, a barren wasteland crying out inside me, I could remember that it wasn't always like now. That there was a point in time when existing wasn't so hard.

"Can I borrow this?" Damon asked without looking at me.

He's talking to you. That's a good sign. I cleared my throat before saying, "Of course."

He tucked the picture beneath his arm and brushed past me without another word. The small trickle of hope I'd allowed through dried up. Swallowing another sigh, I checked my phone. Bea still hadn't responded, which was odd. Maybe the bar was busy or she'd actually gone to bed at a decent hour for a change. Mentally shrugging, I changed into an oversized T-shirt—it felt so good to wear something other than the one outfit I'd brought to Court—and blearily made my way toward the bathroom. The sight of the toilet almost made me dissolve into tears of joy; if I never saw another bucket again, as long as I lived, it would be too soon.

A few minutes later, the taste of mint in my mouth and thoughts of Oliver in my head, I moved to go to bed. Knocking disrupted the stillness. I halted in the middle of the hallway, exasperated and wary.

I knew right away that it wasn't Collith; the bond was still taut and agitated from the distance between us. My reaction should've been relief, but I couldn't deny a sense of disappointment. Whoever it was knocked again, harder this time. Growling, I grabbed a knife doused in holy water from my nightstand —the mysterious ring I'd inherited from the dead goblins rattled across the bottom of the drawer—and went to open the door.

The werewolf was still in the living room, standing now, his eyes alert. I'd almost forgotten he was here, and the sight of him reassured me. No goblins would be taking me hostage tonight. I steeled myself and opened the door. Bea's tall form filled the space. A bug flitted around the light bulb above her. Her mouth was a white slash of fury. "I just needed to see for myself that you were—" she started.

Floorboards creaked behind me and Bea's gaze shifted. I knew the exact moment she saw Damon; her face slackened. For a moment, she didn't move or speak. Then Damon said, his voice soft and sad, "Hey, Bea. Long time, no see."

For once, Bea was speechless. In three long-legged strides, she reached Damon and jerked him into a bear hug. He offered no resistance. Seeing this, I tried not to let myself feel any jealousy or resentment. I'd done what I had to do. Damon would forgive me eventually. Hopefully.

Though part of me longed to stay and watch their reunion, I had one of my own to attend. I closed the door and left Bea and Damon to their embrace, quietly slipping down the hall and back to my room. I crawled into bed for what felt like the first time in weeks and fell face-first onto the pillow. The edges of my vision began to dim.

At long last, sleep and Oliver claimed me.

CHAPTER FIVE

I opened my eyes to see Damon tied to a wooden chair.

We were on a hill, surrounded by storm clouds and howling gusts that flattened my shirt against me. For an instant, I was frozen with shock—this was my safe place. Nothing bad ever happened here. Then Damon opened his mouth and cried, "Remember your promise!"

The sound of his voice jolted me into action. I leapt forward, so horrified that I could hardly breathe. I fumbled at the knots imprisoning him, and all the while, Damon whimpered. The sounds tore at my heart. *Why won't the knots come undone?*

Rain drops pelted me like needles. I blinked rapidly and dropped to my knees, still working at the ropes. When one of my nails bent backward, I let out a frustrated, pain-filled scream and clutched my hand against me. Damon had gone utterly still. I lifted my face, thinking to comfort him, but he stared at me with such dark, empty eyes that the words died in my throat. I frowned. "Damon, what's—"

"For the rest of our lives, I will hate you," he intoned.

Before I could form a response, his face started shifting and cracking. I recoiled so quickly that I fell on my backside, and I crawled backward, acting on instinct. Damon's skin bubbled like a pot of boiling water. Even when there were yards between us, I couldn't stop watching, no matter how much I wanted to. Within a few, tortuous seconds, I found myself looking at the face of the prisoner I'd killed. He didn't say anything, because he was dead. His eyes stayed on mine, wide and vacant. Bile surged up my throat. I turned and vomited in the grass.

Just as I started to push myself up, Oliver was there, wrapping me in his strong arms. In the blink of an eye, the storm was gone. Crickets chirped into the stillness and we now knelt alone on the hill. The moon was full and bright, casting a serene glow over Oliver's world. "I'm sorry," he whispered, cupping the back of my head. It effectively kept me from looking in the direction of that chair. "I'm so sorry. It takes a lot of concentration to keep them away. I was distracted."

There was vomit on my chin, I could feel it. Breathing hard, I wiped at it with the back of my sleeve. Then I reached up and gripped Oliver's wrists so hard that it must've hurt. I kept my gaze trained on his, afraid that if I so much as blinked, the image of the prisoner would be waiting in the darkness. "Keep what away?" I rasped. My throat burned.

His eyes were dark with guilt. "Your dreams."

"I... I didn't know you still did that."

"I haven't had to for a long time. It was mostly in the beginning, after your parents..." His jaw clenched. "Let's go inside. I've been working on a surprise for you."

I let him pull me up and lead me down the hill. Every time our feet touched the ground, a musical note crooned through the air. Diamonds glittered in the center of the flowers. We passed a tree and I noted that its bark was made of candy. The leaves were slips of paper, and there was writing on them, but we walked by too swiftly to make it out. "Think you might be overdoing it, Ollie?" I asked dryly. He shot a grin over his shoulder. He used to do this all the time—go overboard to make me smile. Make me forget. It had been a long time since he'd needed to.

When we reached the house, the shadows it cast on the ground quivered and made shapes like fingers creating silhouettes on a dim wall. A bird, a heart, a flower. I looked back at them as we crossed the threshold.

Inside, everything was the same. The entire left wall was a built-in bookshelf. There was the faded couch set in the corner, the soft bed on the other side of the room, and the softly-lit kitchen to the right of the entrance. Candles burned on the dinner table. By all appearances, Oliver had been making dinner when I arrived. Food and dishes littered the counters. The fridge door was wide open; he must've been in the middle of getting something when he sensed me on that hill.

"What's all this?" I asked, jumping up to sit on the counter. Oliver handed me a glass of wine. I smiled with pleasure and took a sip. Not too sweet, not too dry, just the way I liked it.

"I've painted canvases, I've molded clay, and I've carved wood," he told me. "Now I'm intrigued by the idea of making art out of food."

He stretched to reach the small cupboard over the fridge. In doing so, his shirt rode up a little. I tried not to look, I really did, but I couldn't stop myself from sneaking glances at his golden skin. Admiring the sinewy muscles that flexed with each movement. If he was truly was just a product of my imagination, damn, I knew how to make 'em.

"So what's on the menu?" I asked abruptly. My voice was normal, thank God.

"I'm making us a Mexican feast. Here, try this." Oliver took a chip from a colorful bowl, dipped it in something, and brought it over to me. I got a glimpse of a green dip before it was in my mouth. Flavor burst on my tongue. I chewed slowly, savoring it.

"That's amazing. What is it?"

"Salsa verde. I added my own flair to the recipe."

"Well, if that's just the salsa, I can't wait to try the rest." I smiled up at him.

It was in that instant I noticed Oliver was standing so close that I could smell his cologne, something spicy and dark. He'd already realized it; his hands gripped the counter on either side of me. My breathing quickened. I wanted him. There was no pretending otherwise. Oliver was struggling too; there was a bulge in his pants where there hadn't been just moments ago.

"Ollie, we can't—" I started. He growled, gripped my hips, and dragged me to the edge of the counter. His cock, hard and insistent even through his jeans, throbbed against my core. I moaned, fighting the instinct to touch him. In the past, I would've wrapped my legs around Oliver's waist and ridden him until we were both panting. Now, sensing my restraint, he just pressed his lips against the hollow of my throat. I swallowed— the movement only made his administrations more torturous— and repeated, "Ollie, I know I've crossed some lines already, but I can't do this anymore. I made vows."

He must've heard something in my voice, because Oliver pulled away, looking frustrated. "I always thought..." He dragged a hand through his hair, making it stand on end. The result was adorable. "Maybe it was a childish thought, but I always assumed we would be each other's firsts."

Oh, Ollie. I stared down at my hands, now clasped tightly. Why couldn't I be the sort of person who had the right words? Who always knew what to say? I let silence poison the air between us until it was killing us both. "That's not childish," I said at last. It wasn't enough, I knew that. But telling him that I'd believed the same wouldn't help either of us.

Oliver let out a breath. He leaned his hip against the kitchen island. "I'm going to ask you something. I never have, not once in all the years we've known each other, because I think I know the answer. And saying it would hurt you... which is the last thing I want, Fortuna. The last thing."

Dread gripped my stomach. *Wake up, Fortuna. Wake up.* "Then why ask it now?"

"Because I need to know for sure." He searched my gaze. "Why did you always say no?"

Shit. No. I didn't want to have this conversation. My first instinct was to lie, to say anything that wouldn't hurt him. Oliver was staring at me with those brown eyes of his, though, so earnest and *Ollie*. The seconds ticked past. I started to speak so many times, but I couldn't do it. Which is why I heard myself say, the words soft and hesitant, "I wanted my first time to be with someone real."

The following silence felt like a scream. I had no idea what to expect. Cold anger, maybe, or white-hot pain. Instead, Oliver slowly took my hand and put it on his chest. I could feel his heartbeat, strong and rapid. Compared to Collith, he was so warm. "Is this real?" he murmured.

My own heart felt like it was breaking. I tried to tug free. "Ollie..."

He let go, only to cup my face between his palms. His scent surrounded me, familiar and intoxicating all at once. "Is this real?"

Stop it, I said. Or tried to say. The words wouldn't come. Because Oliver was kissing me, and I was kissing him back, no matter what my intentions had been. I buried my hands in his thick hair, loving the familiar taste of him, aching at the feel of his hardness against my shorts. It would be so easy to slip them off and finally know what it was like to have him inside me. Filling, thrusting, coming...

The sudden, bitter flavor of salt exploded on my tongue. Oh, wonderful. I was crying. Again. The wave crashing over me—so much guilt and pain—was too much, especially after everything I'd just endured at the hands of the fae. A strange, ragged sound tore from my throat just before I wrenched free of Oliver's grip. The room was a blur as I slid off the counter and ran. He called after me, but I didn't stop.

I burst from the cabin and into open air. It smelled like my mother's perfume, a scent that was usually comforting. Now, after reliving her murder so recently, it was agony. Blinded by tears, I stumbled down the path without any idea where I was going. It just helped to *move*, to feel like I was heading somewhere.

A few minutes later, I came upon an immense, ancient-looking oak tree. Something made me stop beneath it. Though it wasn't cold and I wasn't human, I wrapped my arms around myself. I leaned my shoulder against the tree trunk and tilted my damp face up at the moon. Those paper leaves stirred in a breeze.

When I was a child, I used to come upon my mother meditating. She didn't do it like I'd imagined one was supposed to meditate, sitting on the floor with her legs crossed. No, Mom preferred a chair on the front porch, holding a warm cup of coffee between her palms. She always heard my footsteps and murmured, "Join me, honey. Close your eyes and make your brain quiet. It's nice."

"I miss you," I told her, hoping she could hear me, wherever she was. My eyes fluttered shut. For a while, everything was quiet, just as Mom taught me. It pulled me back from the abyss I had been hovering at the edge of.

He gave me more time than I expected. But eventually, Oliver did come as I'd known he would. He made sure I heard his approach, the soft footfalls that sent musical notes into the night. Then Oliver wrapped his arms around my waist, gently, an embrace meant to comfort rather than seduce. We stood like that for a while, gazing toward the stars, and at some point a drop of wetness landed on my arm. Though I didn't turn to look, I knew that he was also crying. "I'm sorry," Oliver said. "I shouldn't have done that."

A thousand responses rose in my mind and still none of them felt right. Stalling, I touched one of the paper leaves with the tip of my finger. It unfurled without any resistance. It took me a moment, but then I realized they were the fortunes usually found in the center of cookies. I smiled a little at this charming detail Oliver had conjured. Such a small thing, such a silly thing, but it had the exact effect he'd intended.

"You have no idea..." I took an uneven breath. "You have no idea how much I wish you could be free. With me. Out there. I used to daydream about it constantly."

"Used to?" he echoed. I couldn't see his face, and the coward in me was grateful for that.

"It became too painful. Like I was... picking at a scab and wouldn't let it heal."

"So what now?" Oliver asked, his hold tightening. I didn't think he was even aware of it. "I don't know if I can just be your friend, Fortuna. Where does that leave us?"

Friend. I trembled in an effort to stop myself from spinning around and grabbing hold of him. Distracting ourselves with passion and heat, like we'd been doing for so long. As I tried to find the right words for the millionth time, I realized all I had was the truth. "I don't know," I whispered.

More tears disobeyed me, escaping my eyes and sliding down my skin. I could feel Oliver looking at me, but I squinted at the horizon as if I'd never seen a sunrise before. To fill yet another silence, I reached up and freed one of the fortunes from a branch. I untangled myself from Oliver to face him. The pink light of morning made his skin seem to glow. "'You are the master of every situation,'" I read.

Something in his eyes flickered. It was there and gone so quickly that I wondered if I'd imagined it. Despite all the fortunes—women with crystal balls, cookies with a slip of paper, ancient legends that lingered on—there was no predicting what would happen. There were only the choices that led up to it.

Oblivious to how solemn I'd become, Oliver plucked a fortune of his own and unfurled it. "'There's no such thing as an ordinary cat.'"

I pursed my lips to suppress a laugh. "Uh…"

"It was hard to come up with a million of these," Oliver explained with a rueful shrug. He took my fortune, crumbled them both into a ball, and tossed the pieces above our heads. Mid-air the papers transformed into a pair of hummingbirds that darted away.

Together, we watched them vanish into the awakening sky.

CHAPTER SIX

*M*y stomach growled as I returned to reality.

For the first time since I could remember, I was glad to be awake. Not to mention that it was already after 11:00. I swung my legs to the side of the bed, stood, and hurried into the bathroom. Afterwards, wet from the shower and still avoiding thoughts of Oliver, I made a beeline for the kitchen.

A sour smell hit me the moment I opened the fridge; it hadn't been cleaned out since before the incident with the goblins. I swore quietly. Damon would be getting up soon and he needed food even more than I did; he looked one breeze away from turning to dust.

Nails clicked on the linoleum. I realized my towel was gaping open and hurried to secure it better. A second later, the werewolf filled the doorway, looking more alert and clear-eyed than I'd ever seen him. I made a mental note to hose him down at some point. His coat was the color of soil now, but that could change after a good dousing. "I have to run to the store. Would you mind staying here?" I asked, hoping he understood. "People might panic a little at the sight of a giant wolf."

He didn't respond, of course. Weirdly, though, I was optimistic. A glance out the window showed a gray sky and swaying trees and... my truck? I rushed back to my room to dress accordingly in jeans and a woolly turtleneck. Within minutes I was running out the door. The werewolf whined unhappily as I left, but he stayed in the living room.

There was a note pinned beneath one of the windshield wipers. *Welcome home,* it read in Cyrus's deliberate handwriting. *We found this for you. I replaced the left taillight. It was in otherwise excellent condition.*

They'd gone to all this trouble... for me?

Climbing into my tall truck sent a soft warmth through my chest, like I'd turned on a space heater. For a minute, all I could do was run my hands around the steering wheel and over the worn seats. It was a 1970 GMC pickup that I had saved up for and bought with my own money, back when I still lived with Dave and Maureen. I'd always liked old things, and all those afternoons cleaning kennels at a veterinarian's office hadn't been much of a sacrifice, considering how much time I got to spend with the dogs.

Smiling, I turned the key—which Cyrus had left in the ignition—and the engine turned over with a cheerful rumble.

It was good to be back.

I sang along to a song on the radio all the way to the store. There was a light drizzle as I hopped out, so I raised my jacket hood. Nightmare or not, my hair did *not* respond well to rain. Once I got inside, I was also cheered to find that the aisles were practically empty. I threw everything in the cart that I remembered Damon liking—string cheese, cereal, apples—and added some raw meat for the wolf. I promptly put it all on my credit card.

I was walking back to the truck, thinking I'd actually managed a visit to town without having to interact with anyone, when a voice called, "Fortuna!"

Groaning inwardly, I turned. The speaker was a tiny girl with big eyes and a smile so bright it was blinding. It took me a few seconds to remember her name—Ariel. The server Bea had hired before I left for the Unseelie Court. She rushed at me and I found myself in a hug. Her hair stuck to my chin; it smelled like wildflowers.

"It's so nice to see you!" she chirped. She pulled away and must've finally noticed my stiffness. Thankfully, due to all our layers, her skin hadn't made any contact with mine. "Oh, I'm sorry. I'm a hugger. I forget that it can scare people. Bea said you were out of town again! Or maybe she said you're back... anyway, are you home for good now?"

"Maybe," I hedged. It occurred to me that I hadn't come up with what I was going to tell people when they inevitably asked where I'd been. *Better keep this short*, I thought. "I'm definitely going to work a few shifts. So... I'll see you at the bar."

Ariel either took the hint or had to work herself. She gave me a little wave and smiled again. "I hope so. See you around, then!"

She flounced away in a swirl of perfume and long hair. I watched for a moment and realized that I liked her. Weird. I shrugged and moved to get into the truck. Just then, a nearby sign caught my eye. It hung above the front door, a single name glowing in green letters. ADAM'S. I stood there and stared at it, tapping my fingers against the steering wheel. Finally I shut the door, locked it again, and crossed the street.

The parking lot was empty save for one car. It was rusted and had the looks of something that had lived too long. Weeds grew through cracks in the pavement. Either business was bad or it was a slow day. Feeling hesitant now, I pushed the door open, setting off a small bell.

Warmth instantly embraced me. I lowered my hood and looked around. The smell of oil and metal permeated the air. Screamo music burrowed beneath my skin. I could see through the window to my right that the office was empty. I took in the familiar posters of the near-nude girls, the cement floor, the workbenches and scattered tools. There was a huge truck in the middle of the room, suspended in the air. I circled it quietly, and the sound of something clinking against the floor reached my ears. I paused. All I could see was a pair of boots sticking out from beneath the truck.

"Hello?" I ventured.

Thud.

"Shit!" a voice growled. Its owner rolled into sight, scowling and rubbing his forehead. Adam Horstman. He didn't have boyish good looks or ethereal beauty. Even so, he had a... raw quality about him. His skin was pale, almost translucent. He kept his hair shaved close to his skull. He'd grown a beard since I last saw him, but it didn't quite hide a streak of grime across his cheek. He had eyelashes any female, human or otherwise, would murder for.

In another lifetime, we'd gone on a few dates. Our relation-ship hadn't gone beyond that; he wasn't one for talking and I wasn't one for his preferred method of communication. Namely, sex.

He was also a vampire.

"Sorry," I said, shoving my hands in my pockets. Doubt seized me; maybe this was a ridiculous idea. "I probably should've called first."

Adam's dark eyes settled on me. Though his expression didn't change, something shifted. Whatever face he saw gazing back at him, he wasn't immune to its effects. I had been among the faeries too long—they were so accustomed to beauty—and somehow forgotten that most creatures had a reaction to me. Now I became very, very still, like a small animal in front of a predator, and waited for Adam's next move.

After another moment, he gripped the bumper above him and the muscles in his arms flexed. "You hungry?" he muttered. No small talk or questions about why I was there. I liked that.

Before I could say anything, my stomach rumbled. This seemed to be enough for Adam; he hauled himself to his feet and headed to the office, probably to order a pizza. It was pretty much all he ate. Well, that and the obvious source of nutrition all vampires needed. It was another myth that they couldn't or didn't eat human food, along with their having no reflection or possessing the ability to turn into bats. Supernatural speed, life, and strength were the only perks of vampirism. There were fewer in the world that movies and television depicted—the transition process was a lot more difficult than it was with other species, like a werewolf, who was simply bitten or born.

When Adam came back, I was studying one of the posters on his walls; some girl with inflated breasts and what barely passed as a scrap of clothing. "That bother you?" Adam asked as he pulled a cigarette out of his pocket. He put it between his lips and felt for a lighter. Why bother with healthy habits when you were immortal?

I lifted one shoulder in a shrug. "Not really."

He lit the cigarette. The tip of it glowed orange for a moment, then released a thin column of smoke. "What's going on, Sworn?" Adam asked after taking a long drag. He squinted at me through the haze.

Well, he had to ask sooner or later. I decided to come right out and say it. "I remembered you mentioning that you're trained in self-defense."

"Yeah. I am."

"Great. Will you teach me some moves?"

I waited a beat, but he didn't ask me why. Adam was a man of few words and even fewer questions; I'd always appreciated that about him. Maybe I'd been too quick to dismiss him back in the day. "Sure," he said. "When?"

"As soon as we can, as often as we can," I answered. "I only know the basics and I've managed to acquire enough enemies to make that a problem. What are your rates?"

Now Adam eyed me. He tapped on the cigarette and sent ashes to the ground. "You think I'm going to charge a female for learning how to defend herself?"

How gallant. Apparently there was a side to Adam I'd never seen. Well, while he was feeling generous, I had one more request. Adam and I had never discussed how old he was, but there was something very, very old about him. "I also want to learn the sword," I added, taking a gamble.

The vampire released yet another cloud of smoke. His expression revealed nothing. After a few seconds he just said, "That takes years."

Excitement burned through my veins. I tried to contain a smile and failed. "Then I guess we'd better get started, huh?"

ONE WEEK LATER

I was floating.

No, actually, I was drowning. Water was all around, a shimmering blue so deceptive in its beauty. It was rushing into my mouth, my ears, my lungs. I tried to scream, but this only accomplished a stream of bubbles. I waved my arms, frantic to reach the surface. Wherever I was, it was deep. There was no bottom and no top. Just a cruel death, waiting to take me into its embrace. As I flailed, hair clouded in front of my eyes, and I raised wrinkled fingers to pull it away even though there was nothing to see. Pain ripped through me as I swallowed more water. Wait... was that something moving in the shadows? Coming this way?

In the next moment, it didn't matter, because my vision was going dark. Suddenly I knew that this was it. This was the end. There was no time for regrets or memories; there was only the panic.

Then I gasped and shot upright.

For a few seconds, all I was capable of was breathing. Gulping in greedy, relieved breaths of air. Okay, I knew this place. I was Fortuna. This was home. There was no water and I wasn't drowning. My room was shrouded in darkness, save a slender slant of moonlight pouring through the window. I looked around, still panting, and tried to extract my mind from the dream's claws.

Why hadn't Oliver kept it away? Why hadn't I gone to our dreamscape?

Panic crept near again, this time because of the unanswered questions. *There's nothing you can do about it now.* Damp with sweat, I peeled the covers aside and moved my feet to the floor. Every muscle in my body protested the sudden movement—I was still sore from the training session with Adam—but the cool air felt so good. I reached for my phone, raking my hair away from my face, and the screen brightened. 5:58 a.m. Everything was quiet, which was a refreshing change. Since we'd gotten back, I'd woken up each night to the sound of Damon crying through the wall our rooms shared. At least one of us had finally gotten to slumber in peace.

I knew there would be no going back to sleep for me. Resigned, I shoved some slippers on and opened the bedroom door. I nearly tripped over the werewolf lying in the hallway. Annoyance rose up, but I shoved it right back down. The image of him being chained and yanked at was never far from my mind. "Is this for my comfort or your own?" I asked the creature.

He gazed up at me with those yellow eyes. I shuffled past him, sighing, and made a mental note to summon Laurie today. The wolf needed to shift back soon, or he'd lose whatever conscious thought he had left. Plus he was killing my vacuum.

The floorboards moaned as I made my way to the kitchen, but I didn't worry. However much his dreams troubled him,

Damon seemed to prefer them to reality—he was impossible to wake up.

When I passed the living, room, though, I realized I shouldn't have bothered. My brother was right where I'd left him hours earlier, sitting on the couch with a remote in his hand. 9News lit up the room. "Good morning," I said, just as I had every other morning since we'd come home. Keeping up with our newly-established tradition, of course, Damon said nothing in return. I pushed down yet another surge of annoyance and went to pour myself a bowl of cereal. I carried it to the doorway and leaned my hip against the wall as I ate. The wolf was now stretched out on the loveseat, just a few feet away from Damon. The sight was a little comical.

"Did you ever call Savannah?" I asked through a mouthful of Honey Nut Cheerios. A second later, the noise from the television increased—Damon had turned up the volume to drown me out. I gritted my teeth. This time, the irritation wouldn't be ignored. It filled me to the brim, then overflowed, spilling over the edges. I pushed off the wall, approached the couch loudly, and plopped down on the cushion right next to Damon. A bit of milk sloshed precariously. I swore and righted the bowl.

The old Damon would've laughed, but this one didn't react in the slightest. I sat back and just studied him, hoping I'd get some idea of how to help him. His hair was getting long again; it fell into his eyes even more than mine did. The blue glow of the television revealed beads of sweat on his temple. So he *had* slept. Not that it did him any good—Damon Sworn was a shadow, a photograph forever imprinted with grief, a shell anyone could fill. And if something didn't change, the werewolf wasn't the only one in danger of fading away.

My gaze fell upon the spaghetti I'd made for him last night, still resting on the coffee table, clearly untouched. "You have to eat, Damon," I said softly. The wolf's ears twitched. His eyes were closed, but his breathing was light and even, proof that he was awake and listening.

"Don't worry about it," Damon mumbled. They were the first words he'd spoken to me in days.

"Are you going to call Savannah?" I asked again, more forcefully this time. *Don't push him too hard,* an inner voice cautioned. A news anchor on the TV laughed. Her teeth shone an unnatural white.

Damon changed the channel and a cartoon filled the screen. "No."

"Look, I know things are... different." *Understatement of the century,* I thought grimly. Desperation urged me on. "But you two loved each other. That doesn't just go away."

"I'm not the guy she fell in love with," Damon snapped.

I didn't know what to say, because it was true. I turned my gaze to the show and watched without really absorbing anything. The quiet was full of a thousand unsaid words. Part of me wanted so badly to rage at my brother. He wasn't the only one that had been broken. He wasn't the only one that had been through hell. In all our time together this week, never once had Damon asked how I'd come to be at the Unseelie Court or how I'd coped during our two years apart. The other half of me, though, could never forget the vow I had made when we were children. I was his older sister. I was his family. And maybe if I had done a better job of that, those two years never would've happened.

"Help me understand," I said suddenly.

Frowning, Damon glanced at me. "Understand what?"

"You and... Jassin. If you need to talk about your"—I swallowed—"relationship, please know that I'm here. I'm listening."

For a few seconds, it seemed like this was the right thing to say. Damon looked at me, and within the depths of his gaze, I thought I caught a glimpse of the brother I once knew... then it was gone. Damon turned back to the TV and I almost screamed in frustration.

Deep breaths, Fortuna. A few stilted seconds ticked by and I eventually forced myself to take some bites of the cereal. It tasted like cardboard now. "You know, I fell in love with a faerie once," I told my brother without looking at him.

This got his attention. "What?"

"Back in high school." I shrugged as if the memory didn't still cut my insides to ribbons. "Her parents came to town on Court business. They were Guardians, I think. God, she was beautiful. I used to bike past their hotel just for a chance to see her."

"What happened?"

My spoon hit the bowl with a *clink*. I met Damon's gaze and tried to sound matter-of-fact. "Sorcha was a faerie—she lost interest in me and moved on, of course. That's what they do."

It wasn't what he'd wanted to hear; his expression shuttered. Damon shifted on the cushion, subtly angling his body away from me, and returned his attention to the TV. This time, I did sigh. "I'm going to shower," I said, getting up. I put the bowl next to his abandoned spaghetti and made a note to do the dishes tonight; the pile was getting pathetically high. "Bea has me working a couple breakfast shifts this week. Did you set up the new phone I got you? I'll keep my cell on me in case—"

"I'll be fine."

I hesitated. *I love you, Damon,* I wanted to say. But there were only so many times you could be rejected in the span of an hour, so I stayed silent and left him to his grief.

CHAPTER SEVEN

White puffs of air marked each exhale of breath as I opened the door to Bea's. Just before it closed behind me, I cast a wistful glance toward Adam's shop. There was no time for a training session, though. *Maybe it'll be a slow day and Gretchen will cut me.* Right. Maybe Damon would welcome me home with a smile and a tight hug, too, while I was at it.

The smell of grease and coffee assailed my senses. Gretchen must've been out in the alley, smoking her first cigarette of the day, because she wasn't in her usual spot behind the bar. Neither was Cyrus. I headed for the back, where Bea's office and the wall of lockers were. My boss was at her desk, peering down at a mess of receipts. Her gray braid gleamed. There was a pair of purple-rimmed glasses perched on the end of her nose. *Since when does she need glasses?*

I muttered a greeting—we'd all learned the hard way what would happen if we messed her up in the middle of crunching numbers—and rummaged for my apron. I looped the strings around my waist twice and, order pad in hand, shut the metal door a little too hard.

"I was going to ask how things are going, but I think I know," Bea said dryly.

"Sorry." I rubbed my forehead, where an ache was starting to build. "He's not getting better, Bea. I don't know what to do."

"It's only been a week, hon. It takes longer than that to recover from the hell he's been through."

Oh, you have no idea, I thought. The story I'd given Bea—and through her, the rest of Granby—was simple. Damon's kidnapper had grown tired of him and abandoned the cabin they'd been holed up in. My brother found his way to the nearest house and called me. It took a few days to drive there and get him.

When the sheriff showed up at the house to ask Damon for details, I'd quickly intervened and done all the talking for him. *He's still in shock, I think,* I told the old man. When I gave him Jassin's physical description, since the kidnapper was still at large, of course, Damon stiffened. Thankfully, though, he didn't speak up. And that was that. I could only hope it was all behind us.

"Okay," I said now, my shoulders slumping. "You're right. Thanks, Bea."

"How about I put him to work?" she asked as I started to turn away.

I faced her again, brows raised. "What? Really?"

Bea picked her pen back up and shrugged as if it was no big deal, but I knew running a small-town bar wasn't exactly a lucrative business. "Sure. He can bus tables and wash dishes."

The mental image was encouraging—Damon showered, dressed, and doing something besides sitting on that damn couch. It wasn't exactly medical school, which was what he'd been heading toward before his disappearance, but it was a step in the right direction. For the first time in a week, I smiled. "That's great. Really. I'll text him right now. Thanks, Bea."

"Fortuna..." Something in her voice caught my attention.

Once again, I turned back to her. Bea pursed her lips. In the harsh, florescent light, the action made her worry lines all the more prominent. Just as I started to ask her what was wrong, she asked, "Did you see the paper this morning?"

"No. Why?"

In response, she held out today's newspaper. My eye lit on the headline instantly: GRANBY MAN FOUND ALIVE AFTER MISSING FOR TWO YEARS. "Which one gave them the story?" I asked without looking up. I scanned the article, not really absorbing it. Brief snatches of sentences stood out. *Kidnapped by white male... cabin's location still unknown... can't speak...* Tight-lipped with fury, I refocused on Bea. "It was either Regina or Angela. I'm going to find out one way or another, so you might as well just tell me now."

"It was Angela," she admitted. "Who, by the way, won't be coming in today. You need to cool down before you talk to her, got it? The last thing your family needs right now is for you to end up at the sheriff's station."

I didn't trust myself to respond rationally, so I just gave my boss a curt nod and left her to the receipts.

Ariel was just arriving when I emerged from the back hall-way. Her dark hair was a riot around her head and the charming redness in her cheeks made her freckles stand out. She didn't need to be a Nightmare to draw more than one male glance as she hurried toward me. "Good morning!" she singsonged. "Is Bea in the back?"

"Good morning. She is, yeah." I mustered an answering smile. Ariel passed in a rush of floral perfume, patting my shoulder as she went. It was difficult to hold onto my anger in the face of such positivity, so I sighed and approached the order counter. Cyrus was back in his usual spot, his hair standing out in the faded kitchen like a fiery, exploding star. I still hadn't figured out how to properly thank him for finding my truck.

He had clearly been doing dishes, but I must've caught the

cook deep in thought; the bubbles in the sink were evaporating and becoming nothing. "Hey, you. I'm starving," I said. Startling, Cyrus set the water spout down and dried his long fingers on his apron. His bright, emerald eyes focused on me. This time, smiling wasn't so hard. "Do you think you can make me some of your amazing—"

"Well, look what the cat dragged in," a voice drawled from behind.

My stomach dropped. A second later, an overbearing cologne washed over me. Slowly, I turned to the person I hated most in all of Granby. I took in his greasy blond hair and the beige uniform. When I'd been in the Unseelie Court, thinking I was going to die, it had crossed my mind that at least I wouldn't see this human again.

"Ian," I said by way of greeting, my voice flat.

He winked. "That's Deputy O'Connell, to you."

Ian O'Connell had been obsessed since the day we met... and he'd been making my life hell since then, too. At first, when I was eighteen and still naive, I'd blamed myself. I thought that whatever face Ian saw drove him to say things he normally wouldn't. Words that were crude, then demanding, then cruel. Some humans, though, were dark at their core. Some of them liked to cause pain simply for amusement.

And when you were the sheriff's son, you got away with it.

"It is really 'deputy', though?" I replied sweetly, unable to resist. "I heard a rumor that you failed your exams and Daddy had to make a phone call."

Something hard and predatory entered Ian's eyes. "Which section is yours again?" he asked. "Never mind, I'll just ask Gretchen. She's such a sweetheart."

Damn it. You couldn't just leave it alone, I thought to myself, scowling at Ian's retreating back. He bent over the bar, exchanged a few words with Gretchen, then lumbered off toward my section. His badge flashed in the morning light coming in through the windows. Halfway to the other end of the room, he halted beside a girl with platinum blond hair. Whatever he said made her frown. I debated whether or not to intervene, but with my current mood, I'd probably regret it later.

For once, I decided to keep my mouth shut, and I slipped behind the bar to get the coffee pot. Hot, black liquid splattered across the counter as I snatched it up. Gretchen, who'd been cleaning the side gun, paused and searched my face with her gentle gaze. "Breathe through the urges, honey," she advised.

"Why is genocide never the answer?" I muttered back. A hint of a smile touched Gretchen's lips before she turned away. I took a deep, fortifying breath and walked toward the booth Ian had picked. To my surprise, the blond was sitting across from him. I got even closer and saw that they were holding hands across the table. Jesus, was he blackmailing her or something?

I forced down the automatic insults and poured them both coffee. Steam rose toward my face. "What can I get you this morning? Do you need a menu, ma'am?"

"We don't get a lot of newcomers here, so they don't usually bother with menus," Ian told the woman. He focused his dishwater brown eyes on me, and they had a strange gleam to them. "Did you hear the news? I went and got hitched while you were away. And Bella is an amazing lay, let me tell you."

"Oh, Ian," his new wife said, covering her red cheeks. She was smiling, though. Now I noticed the small diamond shining on her finger. It hardly drew focus away from the violent dip of her shirt, though. No wonder Ian liked her.

The man in question was sneering at me, still waiting for a response. I gripped my pen so tightly it hurt. "And I can't tell you how much I would rather swallow battery acid than talk about your sex life."

Bella's jaw dropped. Well, so much for keeping my mouth shut. Just as she started to respond, Ian took her hands back and squeezed them. The ring he wore was a gaudy, golden band with rubies. "Don't worry, honey, that's just Fortuna's way. She's a little rough around the edges. We're working on it, though, aren't we?"

This was apparently to me. Before I could say something that would make Mrs. O'Connell run for the hills, Ian ordered their breakfasts. I scribbled in the notepad, ripped it free, and walked away to the sound of her furious whispers.

Once I reached the kitchen window, I shoved the order into Cyrus's queue. Bea was there, leaning against the wall with one hip, her arms crossed. She watched Ian and his bride with narrowed eyes. She must've overheard his announcement, because she muttered, "Any woman willing to marry him deserves a sympathy card. Or an appointment with a good psychiatrist. Did you ask them... Fortuna? Are you okay?"

Dishes clinked in the background and the hum of conversations filled my ears, and it was all so loud, too loud, as though someone had turned a volume knob all the way up. I grabbed my head. A beat later, the voices started. There were dozens, no, hundreds. Shouts and whispers, fury and sorrow. They filled every part of me and left no room for my own sense of self. Pain. Pain. Pain. I dropped to my knees. A jolt ran through my body at the impact, but that was nothing compared to the onslaught of voices. "Help," I tried to shout. But it was lost in the chaos. Did I even say it out loud? I couldn't think, couldn't breathe, couldn't move—

Suddenly someone was there, someone solid and alive. Hands cupped my face, and a familiar voice broke through the pandemonium. Low, soothing, everything. *Collith.* How did he know? He always knew.

"I'm her husband," he told someone. The words weren't gentle; they were fierce. But they came to me from a widening distance.

"They're so loud," I whispered, squeezing my eyes shut. I

still clutched at my head as if my hands alone could keep it all out. "Make them stop. Collith, make them stop."

He lifted me into his arms. There he murmured instructions, quiet fragments that didn't find their way through the noise of pain. I clung to him. I buried my face in his neck, finding comfort in the familiar scent. I wasn't coherent enough to be terrified of this. Part of me was aware we were moving, leaving the bar. An engine came to life—I couldn't hear it over the onslaught, but I felt it—and I knew I was sitting in a leather seat. Warmth touched my skin.

There was a sense of passing time. Minutes or hours. The thoughts of a thousand faeries steadily drained at my sanity.

He's fucking her right now, just behind this door. He doesn't even care that I know. Oh, God, I hate him so much. I hate him so much I could kill him.

No, I can't wear the red one. They've all seen it already.

Jeremiah was a bullfrog, was a good friend of mine. I never understood a single word he said but I helped him a-drink his wine. And he always had some mighty fine wine...

Mmmm. Yes, that's it, scream for me. Louder, please.

Then a voice I recognized. Somehow it spoke over the rest, soothing and composed, like the turn of a page. "Look at me, Fortuna. Open your eyes... yes, that's it. Okay, now listen. You can shut them out."

"H-h-how?" I croaked. His features were blurry at first, but they began to come into focus. Over the throbbing pain, I desperately grasped at reality, using my mate as an anchor. Gradually I discovered that Collith held my face in his hands. They were rougher than I thought they'd be, the palms hardened by callouses. These were not the hands of a weak king.

Oh, God. Yes, yes, yes. Right there! Oh, God, I'm close.

Where is that fucking slave when I need her?

Should probably put another log on the fire soon...

"Imagine a wall," Collith instructed, putting a halt to my distant observations of his skin.

For once, I obeyed him without hesitation. Within a second the wall in my mind was so tall that the top touched clouds. The entire structure was made of unyielding, unending cement. I stood on one side, and all the faeries I'd seen at Court stood on the other.

It worked.

The voices were still there, but they were muffled. Muted to the extent that I could hear my own thoughts again. The shooting pain gave way to a dull ache. At least it was one I could function with, though.

At some point I'd closed my eyes again. When I opened them, I discovered Collith's face disconcertingly close to mine. Neither of us said anything. Instead, we allowed silence to fill the space between us. Gradually, I realized that we were admiring each other.

At this proximity, Collith's otherworldliness was even more obvious—his skin was too flawless and his irises too intricate. I couldn't help noticing, once again, the flecks of gold within his hazel eyes. His nose and jaw were so sharply cut, as though they'd been taken directly from a piece of art and brought to life. My gaze kept moving, taking in more details, and halted on the points of his ears. They poked out from beneath his silken hair. When had I stopped noticing them? When had they stopped being a reminder of what he was and just become part of... Collith? His scar, too, had ceased to exist during my reflection.

Then I found myself staring at his mouth.

We haven't kissed since Olorel, I thought suddenly. Ridiculous that after what I'd just experienced, this was the first thing that popped into my head. Heat spread through my cheeks. Feeling exposed and vulnerable, I finally broke our stare. Where were we, anyway? I twisted in the seat and peered out the windshield.

The Unseelie King had taken me home. A few yards ahead

was my house, with every curtain drawn and the path covered in fallen leaves. *No one welcome,* it seemed to shout. To our left was the copse of trees Collith and I had married in. Beyond that, the trail that would eventually lead to the Unseelie Court. A place where even Nightmares screamed.

Memories hovered at the edge of my thoughts and I surpassed a shudder. "I can't go back, Collith," I said without looking at him. The voices of all those faeries sounded like a bee flitting around in the backseat—a steady hum. My temple throbbed and I pressed my fingers against it, trying not to wince. "Not right now, at least. I need to make sure Damon is okay first."

"That's not why I'm here."

Now I did look at him. Collith's expression was back to its infuriatingly neutral state, so I couldn't gauge his sincerity. "Then why?" I asked, frowning. I'd been sure the only reason he showed up at the bar was to call me out on staying in Granby for so long.

"Because your welfare is important to me," he answered simply. "Do you need anything?"

Oddly enough, the kind words made something inside me snap. I reached for the handle, found it unlocked, and got out of the car. Collith did the same. The vehicle turned out to be an old Volkswagon—definitely not what I'd imagined for a faerie king. I slammed the passenger door shut, then got my coat from the backseat. When I straightened, slamming that door, too, Collith and I faced each other over the hood. Cold air nipped at my skin. "Don't do that," I snapped.

Collith tilted his head and a lock of hair fell over his eye. The result was devastating. "Do what?"

"Pretend to be the good guy. The perfect guy. We both know it's not me you give a rat's ass about; it's whatever you can use me for. The reason you married me in the first place. What is that, by the way?" I added. A muscle moved in his jaw. *Gotcha,* I thought. "Yeah, that's what I thought. You know what I need, Collith? I need you to leave me alone."

"Is that really what you want?" he asked, his voice self-assured and confident. Such a faerie.

I'd started walking away. Gravel crunched beneath my tennis shoes. "I'm done with your games, Collith," I called over my shoulder. "No more riddles, lies, half-truths, secrets. That's your world."

Just as I faced forward again, Collith materialized in my path. I let out a startled yelp and reared back. "It's yours, too," the faerie countered. A breeze ruffled his hair. "Leaving the crown behind didn't undo your coronation."

This response did make me pause. Because, no matter how much I wanted to deny it, Collith was right. I *had* made promises. I'd looped metaphorical chains around my wrists and walked into a cell with my eyes wide open. Collith had even tried to advise me against pursuing the crown.

It was the only way to save Damon, I reminded myself. Despair still crept in like a shadow creeping over the bedroom floor. Really, in the end, it hadn't been a coronation that had rescued my brother from the fae. I'd found that old ritual in a book and challenged Jassin for Damon's freedom. The trials could've been avoided altogether.

This realization made me want to abandon my hard-won queenship even more. I couldn't fight Dad's voice, though, earnestly telling me that honor mattered. I could still see him in my mind's eye, kneeling in a slant of sunlight, looking at me with his gentle eyes and soft smile. *We are hunted because of fear and hatred, Fortuna. But a creature of integrity is much harder to kill than one who deserves it, don't you think?*

In that moment, I knew I was going back to the Unseelie Court.

But I couldn't actually tell Collith he'd won; he held too many advantages as it was. Skirting around him, I tested the door and found it locked. Good. At least Damon wasn't making it pathetically easy for another faerie to whisk him away. Laurie had mentioned his witch's protective spell would probably be temporary, so I was trying not to depend on it. "Are people asking questions about why I'm gone?" I asked Collith, squatting to search for the spare key. It was under one of these rocks...

"No one at Court knows you're here—when Lyari has orders, she follows them to the letter. All they've been told is that you're in seclusion. Of course, there are rumors."

Found it. I stood and the key slid in without resistance. I put it back in its hiding spot before opening the door. Inside, the air was dark and stale. I swallowed a sigh, stepped over the threshold, and turned back to Collith. It occurred to me, then, that he might be expecting to continue our conversation inside.

He waited patiently for me to speak. For what felt like the millionth time, I struggled to find the right words around this faerie. "If we're going to do this, rule together," I clarified, "then you need to give up some of your secrets. A partnership doesn't work if one of us is completely in the dark."

At this, Collith's mask slipped a little. I glimpsed the uncertainty hidden beneath, just a glimpse, before he'd managed to tuck it away again. "I know," my mate said.

He'd managed to surprise me once again. Nonplussed, I looked back and forth from him to the house. I held the coat tighter, like it was a lifejacket and this moment was made of roiling ocean waves. "Do you, uh, want to come in?" I asked after a few seconds. *Why do I feel like a sixteen-year-old asking a boy to come over for the first time?*

"I'd love to." Collith smiled. It was such a rare sight that I openly stared. Thankfully, he stepped past me, providing a few precious seconds to regain my composure. I closed the door behind us and my gaze darted instantly to the couch. There was no sign of Damon, which meant he was probably catching up on sleep. The werewolf was gone, too, out on another hunt no doubt. My rapidly-dwindling checking account couldn't supply him with the amount of meat he needed to sustain himself.

"Would you like anything?" I asked Collith awkwardly, leading him into the kitchen. I tossed the coat onto a chair, then moved to fetch a glass. The headache seemed to have done away with my appetite, but I was painfully thirsty.

As Collith followed, he didn't try to disguise the fact that he was studying my home. I hadn't had any guests, not once, in all the time Damon had been missing. Bea showing up the night of our return had been a shocking anomaly. I resisted the urge to clean as I went. "Water? Coffee? I think there might be some orange juice in the fridge..."

"No," Collith murmured. I made an amused sound and filled the glass with tap water. I drank deeply, filled it a second time, and drank again. When I lowered the cup, I saw that Collith was frowning.

"What?" I asked.

"Did I do something funny?"

I stared at him blankly for a moment. "Oh! When I asked you if you wanted anything, you just said 'no.' Most people say 'no, thank you.' It was strange, you of all people sounding rude."

"Of all people?" Collith echoed.

"Yeah. I mean, you're so polite. No, like, you never seem to lose your...your composure," I explained, fumbling over the words. "It's really annoying, actually. You're one of the most cool-headed... okay, why are *you* laughing now?"

Collith's shoulders were shaking from barely-contained mirth. I had never used the word *enchanting* to describe something in my entire life, but the sight of Collith Sylvyre laughing was. Before I could command him to stop—and put an end to the fluttering in my stomach—Collith got a hold of himself. "Because you're adorable," he said, as if that was a proper explanation. "Watching you try to give me a compliment was like seeing you eat something sour. But you're right. I should've caught that. I haven't spent much time in the human world since taking the throne. I used to switch between the two without much effort at all. It'll take me a few trips to get back into practice."

I glowered. "It wasn't *that* funny."

"I assure you, it was. Now, what would you like to know about me?"

He asked the question so freely, so openly, that for a second I thought I'd misheard. The Lord of Shadows offering up his secrets? Just like that? With effort, I leaned nonchalantly against the counter, glass in hand. "Let's start with something easy," I suggested, hoping he couldn't sense my eagerness. "Like, how did you get to the bar so quickly? Can you really teleport?"

"Yes. My kind calls it sifting, actually. But that's not how I was there when you needed me; I've been spending my spare time here. Bonding with the entire Court has driven queens insane in the past, so I wanted to be there for your transition, whenever it happened. Thankfully, you have extraordinary control over your mental faculties; most don't learn how to block that quickly."

He offered the fun tidbit up about past queens without any pause or falter. His relaxed manner was encouraging enough that I dared to keep going, making a silent note to think about his revelation—the fact that he'd been lingering in Granby for my sake—later, in private. "What are your other abilities?" I asked.

Collith inclined his head. This question was a little harder for him, I could tell from the way our bond tightened, almost like a fist clenching. Nothing showed on his face, though. "You've already seen the heavenly fire," Collith said. "I can also manipulate someone else's mind—only one at a time, mind you—to see what I want them to see. It's different from glamour, since the illusions are not just limited to my appearance. Then there's the 'teleporting,' as you call it, which is how I was able to come to you on the night we performed the mating ceremony. A handful of powerful fae still have that ability. You've probably read the bible stories where angels appear to God's chosen, yes?"

I didn't respond; my already-crowded mind was filling with a memory. There was Laurie, playing the part of a browbeaten slave, but even then there'd been signs of his true self. A glint in the eye, a tilt to his lips.

No other faerie matches his power, he'd told me when I asked about Collith.

Because he has more of it, or because it's different?

Both.

I pulled myself back to the present, where I was standing a few feet away from possibly one of the most powerful faeries to ever walk the earth. Suddenly I was very, very glad he was an ally and not an enemy. "Is that everything?" I asked, refocusing on his angelic face.

Collith met my gaze. There was no trace of hesitation in him as he answered, "That's everything."

Another silence fell between us, and the only sound to break it was my cell phone, dinging with a text. The sound was muffled; I must've left it in my coat pocket. I would bet everything I owned that it was Bea.

With that thought, I started the process of making fresh coffee. I'd need some caffeine before I could come up with an explanation for my boss. Not only about why I had gotten married without telling anyone, but also for why Collith carried me off like a knight in shining armor this morning. *Oh, that. I just have a little brain tumor. It definitely doesn't have anything to do with a permanent bond to a Court of wicked faeries.* Was this really my life now?

"How are you so powerful?" I blurted, desperately trying to keep a rush of anxiety at bay. With my back to Collith, I shoved a filter into the machine. "Most faeries only seem to have one special ability."

"How are you so powerful?" Collith countered. Again, he had a point. I poured some grounds into the filter, then lifted the back lid and dumped my cup of water inside. I jammed the BREW button with my thumb, probably a tad rougher than necessary.

A few seconds in, the coffee machine started to gurgle. With my back still turned to Collith, I stood on my tiptoes to pull a cup from the cupboard. It was one of Mom's; Dad gave it to her for Christmas. It had been his last one, since the Christmas after that, they were both dead. In black, block letters it read, *I never asked to be the world's best professor, but here I am, absolutely killing it.* I finally faced the faerie standing across from me. As though he could sense my agitation—hell, he undoubtedly could—Collith gave me a small, encouraging smile. I cleared my throat and asked, "Are you sure you don't want some coffee?"

"Sure. Black, please," he said. Nodding, I moved to get another mug. One of Damon's, this time, made of undecorated green glass. Neither of us attempted conversation while coffee dripped into the pot. I was oddly nervous, unable to string my thoughts together or manage any kind of small talk. After a minute of unbearable quiet, I poured and slid the mug across the island.

The Unseelie King caught it with graceful ease. He gazed down at his drink, wearing an unreadable expression. "I do have a request to make of you," he said eventually.

I waited for him to go on. Instead, Collith wrapped his hands around the mug, as if to warm them. *He's nervous, too,* I realized. Now that I saw it, I felt it, subtly drifting down the bond like a draft. "What is it?" I prodded.

He lifted his head. "I'd like you to come back to Court for a few hours. Tomorrow night."

Just a handful of words, but they had the ability to set my

heart racing. In the space of a blink or a sigh, I was back in that watery tomb, searching the black surface for a ripple or a wave. This gave way to images of dirt passageways and I found myself within sight of a creature with ragged nails, pointed teeth, and sallow skin. The wendigo chased me into the dark, where I drew up short at a wooden table surrounded by redcaps. Their greedy fingers dug into Shameek's unrecognizable corpse. Just as I was about to scream, they shifted shapes and clothes, becoming elegant fae without bloodstained mouths or scarlet hands. A crowd. I was in that throne room, holding my father's knife and staring down at Damon, who then morphed into the stranger I actually had killed. A stranger whose name I hadn't even bothered to learn.

I think I'm going to be sick.

I didn't realize I'd said this thought out loud until Collith was there, a cool presence at my side, holding back my hair. The voices trapped at the back of my head became just a little louder —I was losing my grip on that image. Fear swelled in my chest. *Wall. Wall. Wall.* I reclaimed the mental picture so fiercely that I knew it would probably appear in my dreamscape that night.

At some point, I'd gripped the edge of the counter and leaned over the sink, where the mess would be easier to clean if it happened. God, though, I didn't want it to. Not in front of Collith.

A few seconds ticked by, and slowly, I straightened. "I think I'll be okay," I managed. My stomach quaked.

Collith released my hair but lingered. "I know you will."

Buying myself some time, I went to the fridge and got the milk. I added that to the cup in front of me, then moved to fetch some sugar. "What's so special about tomorrow night?" I asked finally, stirring the sweeteners in. The spoon made a clinking sound. The motions were habit, a way to keep my hands occupied, because now I felt far too nauseated to drink anything.

Collith returned to his stance on the other side of the island, as though nothing had transpired. "The Tithe," he answered. "It's the first Sunday of every month. There's a small feast and the bloodlines make their contributions to the crown. As this will be your first appearance as queen, your presence is highly anticipated."

There was another pause as I absorbed his words again. Suddenly the kitchen felt too small. Too dim. Hoping I didn't looked as panicked as I felt, I picked up my coffee mug. "Do you mind if we drink these in the living room?"

Collith studied me. "Not at all," he said quietly. Relieved, I hurried into the next room, and he followed suit. I set the coffee down near my usual spot and walked from lamp to lamp, turning on each one, until there was a serene glow. It made the furniture look a little less shabby, I hoped.

But why did it matter so much what Collith thought, anyway?

Collith settled on the couch, a respectful distance from my spot. I sank down next to him and glanced at the TV, wondering if I should turn that on, too. No. That would make it even more awkward. As yet another silence wrapped around us, Collith scanned this room, too. I looked at everything with him. Most of my belongings had come from Bea and Gretchen, garage sales, or the local thrift store. Compared to the elegant furnishings I'd seen in his rooms, it all looked faded and tired.

At the thought, I raised my chin. This was my home—the first place I'd ever lived and put together by myself—and I was proud of it.

"Tell you what," Collith said, oblivious to the inner battle I'd just fought. "Let's play a round of Connect Four. I still remember how to play, I think. If I win, you have to attend the Tithe."

He must've noted the stack of board games resting atop the bookshelf. I quirked a brow, ignoring the anxious way my stomach flipped. "And if I win?"

"If you win, then I'll leave you alone. No more hovering, no more checking in, no more 'pretending to be the good guy'."

This I hadn't expected. For some reason, I'd thought the bet would be sexual in some way. Now I knew that's what I had wanted. Not this complicated outcome that forced me to realize the idea of Collith disappearing from my life was... unpleasant. Holy shit. Did I actually *like* having him around?

As the Unseelie King waited for a response, I avoided him and acted as though I were considering it. I took a calm sip of the coffee, which turned out to be way too sweet. Secretly, though, my heart quickened. *Wait. This is a faerie you're talking to*, I thought. Jassin had outmaneuvered me once with double meanings and treacherous words. "That's all well and good, but how long would you leave me alone, exactly?" I challenged.

"Until you deign to summon me again." Collith's gaze was steady. He was telling the truth. There was no way I could know for sure, of course—not without using the mating bond—but I believed him. Buying more time, I stood to retrieve the box. The pieces moved within the cardboard as I carried it back.

If I didn't accept the bet, it would reveal the confusion I felt about him. The Fortuna I'd once been, so certain in her hatred of Collith and faeriekind, wouldn't hesitate. For some reason, the thought of him knowing the doubt I felt about those old feelings caused a stirring of panic.

So I sat on the edge of the cushion and began setting up our game. Halfway through, my gaze flicked up to Collith, who stared back impassively. "Red or black?" I questioned.

"Ladies' choice."

I smirked and began pulling the darker pieces toward me. "Well, whoever has the black ones goes first, so your gallantry just cost you an advantage."

Collith shrugged. "The first move hardly matters. It's the final choices that truly count."

"How eloquent, Your Majesty." I pressed a hand to my chest

and fixed adoring eyes on him, the same way I'd seen so many female courtiers look at this beautiful king. "I am awed by your wisdom. May I kiss your feet?"

Something mischievous stole into Collith's expression. "Not my feet, but I have something else you can kiss."

The air caught in my throat. I wasn't a creature that blushed easily, yet for the second time that day, I felt heat steal into my cheeks. Collith didn't offer an apology like I thought he would. Instead, he kept that hazel gaze on me and his expression intensified. I couldn't look away. All at once, I remembered his words from the day we'd become mated. *I suspect a celibate existence is not for either of us.*

My core clenched and heated. It had only been a handful of days since he'd touched me in the bathtub, but right now, it felt like weeks. I wanted to feel his hands on me again. I wanted to feel those sinful lips against mine. Would it really be so wrong? It was just sex.

I will never love you.

The words I'd flung at Collith, just nights ago in that shadowy room, hadn't only been for him. They'd been for me, too. A promise. A reminder. There was so much he'd withheld from me and so much he hadn't done right. Blinking, I turned away from him and abruptly ended the connection between us.

A spark of frustration flitted along the bond. It quickly burned to nothing, leaving that road between us dark and cold.

Without any comments or fanfare, we started playing. However simple the concept of Connect Four, though, we took our time with it, as if it were a game of chess. Collith acted like every decision he made with his pieces was life or death. Always a king, even when his throne was nowhere in sight. I found the silence unnerving, but witty banter or more questions seemed out of place. Once in a while, one of us reached for our mug of coffee and drank.

Outside, the day continued to brighten. Damon slept on and the werewolf didn't return.

The board was two thirds of the way full when I saw it. An opening, no, two—Collith had left three of my black pieces unguarded. And right next to it, there were three red pieces stacked atop each other. My hand hovered at the top, moving over the length of the board so he wouldn't know I'd seen either of the opportunities. The stakes of the game pounded at me with the tenacity of all those voices, still crowding at the back of my skull, bouncing off bone like echoes off a cathedral ceiling.

I'll leave you alone, he'd said. Those four words made me feel as though I were standing on the edge of a cliff. What awaited at the bottom? Did I even want to leap? My pulse was unsteady and I prayed Collith wasn't listening to it. I didn't know enough about fae hearing. More questions for later... if he was around to ask them.

The thought caused so much inner turmoil that my answer seemed pretty obvious.

I didn't give myself a chance to doubt or reconsider. Casually, hoping Collith really hadn't spotted it, I bypassed the two obvious choices and dropped the piece I held on the other side of the board.

That could be the biggest mistake you've ever made.

Collith had been waiting for this. With a flourish, he dropped his fourth and final piece into place. "Connect Four!" he announced, flashing a triumphant grin, as though the stakes had been entirely different. Twenty dollars or a simple kiss.

I pretended to scowl. "I don't think you're supposed to shout the name of the game if you win."

"But it's much more satisfying this way," Collith said with a wink. I just smiled, still worried about the consequences of the choice I'd just made, and started putting the pieces away. Collith's smiled dimmed. He moved to help, moving preternaturally fast. Once we were done, he took the box and stood. "Well, I supposed I should go."

"Oh." I stayed where I was on the floor, hands lying limply in my lap. "Okay."

Collith hesitated. He shifted from foot to foot, making the pieces slide in the box he still held. "Unless... unless I should stay?" he ventured, looking for all the world like an uncertain date instead of an immortal, formidable ruler.

And there it was, no matter how much I wanted to deny it. Warmth. Light. *Relief*. I *did* want him to stay, which was exactly why I should've sent him far and away. The words stuck in my throat, though. After a few seconds, I lifted one shoulder in a shrug. "Well, usually these things are best two out of three," I said, sounding as if I didn't care one way or the other.

Apparently it was enough for Collith. He came back to me, and this time he settled on the other side of the coffee table, making our circumstances feel more intimate somehow. The light of a nearby lamp cast a golden glow over him. "Well, then, prepare to face defeat," he said, his tone light and teasing. Deliberately trying to pull me out of the darkness he knew I was in.

As Collith started setting up a new game, I traced his features with my gaze. The seconds passed, marked by my heartbeat, pounding too hard and too fast. "I think I already am," I murmured. It seemed that no matter how hard I fought against feeling anything for this faerie, I was still losing.

Collith glanced up, his expression distracted. "Did you say something?"

Quickly, I shook my head. I felt his eyes on me as I joined his efforts in putting together another round, but I kept mine firmly on the pieces. "No, nothing. Nothing at all."

CHAPTER EIGHT

*S*omething was deeply wrong when I entered the dreamscape.

A hurricane raged over that distant sea. Wind howled over darkened plains, so angry that it was unrooting the wildflowers. Petals blew past as I struggled toward the cottage, which suddenly seemed much farther away than it usually did. All I could think was, *Oliver. I have to get to Oliver.*

Halfway down the path, it started to rain. The pinpricks of water felt like needles sinking into my skin. I bent my head and kept going. The pain was so distracting that I couldn't begin to question why this was happening, only that it was.

After a few long, terrifying minutes, I reached the cottage. None of the lights were on inside, but I could hardly turn toward the cliff, much less check to see if Oliver was sitting on its edge. I managed to slip inside and gasped as the door almost crushed me. Walls shook when the door slammed shut.

My gaze swept the room. The floor was covered in random debris—glass, paper, paint, dishware—every cupboard was open, and in the middle of everything, Oliver knelt with his hands limp in his lap. The windows behind him were wide open and the curtains billowed violently. I rushed over to wrestle the frames back into place. Once I'd managed that, I dropped to the rug in front of Oliver and grabbed his face. Water dripped off me. "Ollie, what the hell is this?"

When he still stared at something over my shoulder, his eyes glazed, I dug my fingers in. "Hey, look at me. Ollie, *what's wrong?*"

"They're gone," he finally mumbled. I was leaning so close that even the chaos outside couldn't snatch his words away.

"What's..." I started. I trailed off in a burst of realization. It was the paintings, no, the heartbeat of this house—they'd vanished. The mess had kept me from noticing. Where those bursts of color had once been, leaning against walls, hung over the fireplace, tucked away behind pieces of furniture, there was only emptiness. If Oliver's reaction was this strong, it must mean the change was permanent.

A pang of loss hit me, so acute that I couldn't imagine what Oliver felt. All those sun-dappled nights we'd spent with those canvases... all those hours I'd watched the bristles of a paintbrush rise and fall, a smile curving my lips that was both mesmerized and content...

Blinking rapidly, I turned back to Oliver and realized that my hands still cupped his face. I gentled my grip and whispered, "I don't understand what's happening. Why are they gone?"

"They were... they were my windows..." Oliver lowered his head. A shudder went through his body. It was as though he couldn't hear me, couldn't feel me, couldn't think of anything besides the gaping hole in his chest.

I rubbed his arms, feeling at a loss on how to comfort him. This was all so new and frightening. "Your windows?" I pressed when he didn't go on.

Oliver's throat worked. It started to seem like he wouldn't be able to respond, but after a few seconds he finally answered, "They were my windows to the outside. To your world."

To my world?

In that instant, I did understand. Oh, what a fool I'd been. What a cruel fool.

Whenever Oliver painted, I looked at his work and saw a pretty picture. A bridge, a desert highway, a bicycle leaning on its kickstand. But for him, those pretty pictures meant so much more. It made complete sense. He was forever trapped behind a glass, forced to exist on the other side of everything. He painted these things because he would never truly know what it was to experience them, and this was a way to imagine it or have a part. It's what I would've done. It's what *anyone* would've done.

And now that was gone.

Guilt roared through me like a tsunami. I closed the distance between us, pressing my forehead to Oliver's. This was my fault, somehow. Something I'd done had caused a shift in his world. My voice was hardly more than a pained whisper as I asked, "What can I do, Ollie?"

This time, he didn't reply. He looked at his hands, lying there so empty and without purpose. There was still paint around his fingernails. I scratched at it absently, needing to move in some way. It came off in flakes, leaving Oliver's skin clean and color-less. I didn't like it.

Gradually, everything stopped. The wind, the rain, the groaning walls. Quiet settled like a thick fog.

"You can drink with me," Oliver said at last, answering a question I'd forgotten I had asked. His voice was hollow, his eyes dull. Never, in all our years of knowing each other, had I seen him like this. Fear filled my lungs and made it difficult to breathe.

When I didn't say anything, Oliver disentangled himself from me and got up. His golden hair stood on end, as though he'd been gripping it in his fists. He went to the kitchen, opened a cupboard, and revealed rows of liquor bottles he'd probably just conjured.

I stayed where I was, oddly apprehensive. "Ollie, I'm not sure—"

"Don't, Fortuna. Not right now." His voice was hollow. Without looking at me, Oliver poured a shot and tossed it back. His other hand gripped a big bottle. Clear liquid sloshed within it. A thought slithered through me as I watched. *Does he blame me, too?*

The air grew colder with every passing second; bumps raced along my skin. For the first time since arriving, I took stock of what I was wearing. Yoga pants and an oversized T-shirt— exactly what I'd fallen asleep in.

Feeling helpless, miserable with self-loathing, I finally got to my feet, too. Oliver didn't so much as look up. After a beat of hesitation, I approached the stone fireplace. It hadn't been unlit in all the time this dreamscape existed—now it stared up at me with gray, forlorn eyes. Fortunately, there was a tin of kerosene next to the wood pile. I added a generous amount, then reached for the box of matches. One vicious strike later, a tiny flame spurted to life between my fingers. The entire process was a welcome distraction, I thought.

I dropped the match, feeling as though everything was happening in slow motion. Sparks scattered over tinder. Kneeling, I blew on it gently and brought it to life. Once those bits of light became flame, I sat back and studied the different colors flickering in its depths.

All the while, Oliver drank.

I didn't join him, but I didn't try to stop him again, either. The only sounds in the cottage were a strange symphony of clinking glass, mournful gusts of wind, and the crackling of fire over dry wood. Only when the soft clinking had gone silent did I glance over my shoulder. I went still at the sight that greeted me.

Stars were visible through skylights that hadn't been there a moment ago. Oliver rested in the center of the bed we usually shared, looking like a ghost in the moonlight. His head was tipped back, his gaze cast upward. The bottle rested on the floor beside him, considerably less full than it had been at the beginning. Oliver's arm dangled over the edge of the bed, almost touching that gleaming glass, but not quite.

I abandoned the fire and crossed the room on timid feet. Oliver didn't react. I sank down on the mattress, unable to take my eyes off him now. I'd caused the pain that was currently ravaging my best friend. "Ollie?" I whispered.

"Over the years," he said, as soft and distant as the sky he was looking at, "I've wondered why any species bothers to love the stars. They burn so briefly, then fade so permanently. Is the bliss and the beauty worth the absence and the sorrow, Fortuna? Well, if anyone asked me, I'd tell them what I know."

Apparently, Oliver was a philosophical drunk... and something told me he wasn't really talking about stars. I adjusted the blankets until they covered him, knowing it was an empty gesture even as I did it. He didn't sleep or dream. Still, it helped both of us. The pretending. "And what's that, Ollie?" I asked over the sound of my heart cracking.

On top of the blanket, Oliver's hand curled around mine. Once again, he didn't respond. Not at first, anyway. The fire burned down to smoke and embers. The chill returned, gleeful as it raced over the two of us and started eating us alive. Even then, I didn't rise to revive the flames. I watched over my friend, just as he'd watched over me my entire life. His eyelashes fluttered.

"Here is what I know," Oliver murmured finally, his drowsy face raised toward the heavens. "That the first thing we always do on a dark night is look up. Always."

The pace Adam set was grueling.

However passionate I felt about what he was teaching me, I kept losing focus. It was Sunday, October 6th, which I was painfully aware of because of the upcoming Tithe. It was my first day off from Bea's since getting back from Court. It was, however, Damon's first day as a busboy.

When he finally woke up, I told him about Bea's offer over our sad bowls of Cheerios. He'd taken the announcement of his brand-new employment without comment. Part of me had hoped for something, even a flash of anger, but my brother knew exactly how to exact his revenge. He looked back at me without expression and, after a few seconds, turned away to get dressed.

After dropping Damon off at the bar—to my everlasting shame, it had been a relief to make him someone else's problem for a few hours—I parked in the lot at Adam's and headed inside. He'd been working on a truck, but when he saw me, Adam flipped the sign to CLOSED and pulled out some exercise mats. Just like last time, there was no one else in the shop. His deafening heavy metal music stirred my blood and drowned out my thoughts as we began.

I'd had the inevitable conversation with Bea, since the last time she saw me, it seemed like I had been experiencing a psychotic break. To make matters even more complicated, Collith apparently announced to the entire bar that he was my husband. I couldn't exactly tell Bea the truth, so I'd lied about who Collith was and how our relationship had formed.

When I finished speaking, Bea just gave me a disappointed look. She'd *known* I was lying to her.

Now I was ready for something to utterly occupy my thoughts. I also didn't want to think about Oliver, vanishing paintings, or distant stars.

For the entire first hour of our training, the vampire had me do exercises to strengthen my grip. Being Fallen, I was stronger than the average human, but not by much. After that, he guided me through different jujitsu techniques. I hadn't worked this hard since my gymnastic days in high school. Soon enough, sweat dampened the back of my shirt. It felt fucking *good*. Adam continually barked instructions and corrections at me like a drill sergeant. "Protect your neck, Sworn. No, don't use your arms to power the movement. Keep your breathing even."

He was in the middle of showing me how to use his weight against him when suddenly he dropped his arms and straightened. "Why'd you stop?" I demanded, impatiently swiping at my forehead with the back of my arm.

Adam nodded at something behind me. His wife beater was riding up his back from the movement we'd just gone through, revealing unforgiving muscles and smooth skin. "I think he's here for you," my instructor said.

On instinct, I followed the direction of his gaze. The sight of a tall, darkly dressed faerie standing there made my stomach flip. I'd been so focused on the lesson that I'd completely missed Collith's arrival. Now I noticed how the bond—or at least my side of it—trembled.

In the next instant, I remembered his reason for being here and glanced at the clock hanging over the office doorway. Almost sunset. I'd been avoiding the time on purpose, fruitlessly hoping this moment would never come.

"Are you ready?" Collith asked. Straight to the point, then. Guardians flanked him on either side, one of them a stranger and the other Nuvian. My eyes met the Right Hand's for an instant and his lip curled with obvious dislike. Our last encounter whispered through my mind. *How much do you know about wolves, Nuvian?*

The memory buoyed me.

Collith was still waiting for a response, though, and my

mood sank again. I made a vague gesture and mumbled, "I just can't leave right now. Damon isn't—"

"You can't avoid it forever, Fortuna."

Watch me, I thought mutinously. But Dad's lessons were never far from mind; he would remind me that I made a promise. I felt myself deflate. "Okay. Fine. I'll meet you at the house. I have to give Damon a ride back from the bar. Bea wanted to start him off slow, see how things go, so his first shift was just a couple hours."

You're babbling, Fortuna.

But Collith just nodded. He bowed and went to the door. As he left, a gust of frigid air blew inside, a relief on my hot skin. Then they were gone, as silently as they'd come.

Adam had watched the entire exchange without comment. I turned back to him, feeling exposed and uncertain. He wasn't blind; he would've seen Collith's ears and that damn crown. Besides Damon, no one knew about the drastic changes that had occurred in my life. I didn't know how to begin explaining everything or whether I should even tell the truth about it all.

"Not what I expected," was all Adam said. My brow lowered in confusion. Expected? He'd known about Collith?

Oh. Right. The Granby rumor mill.

"Which part?" I asked with a sigh. "The fact that he's a faerie or a king?"

"The fact that he's a skinny, long-haired priss. I thought you liked your males covered in oil and sporting a buzz cut."

My lips twitched. "You're a good guy, Adam."

"Yeah, well, don't tell anyone. Got a rep to maintain." The vampire turned away, effectively ending our training. Panic grabbed at me with its unrelenting, spindly fingers. I wondered if Adam's heightened senses could detect it. I moved to put on my sweatshirt and tried not to think about what I was about to do. As I stalled, Adam finished dragging the mats into storage and went back to work on the car.

"See you soon," I said near the door. Adam made a noncommittal sound in response. He didn't look up from the engine. Shocking he was still single, really. I stepped out into the windy afternoon, instantly inhaling the fresh air, and struggled to find the determination and endurance that had sent me underground the first time. I gazed across the street at Bea's and saw the scene of my second encounter with Collith. Slamming the door as I stormed outside, his confident pursuit. It had been windy that day, too. Tendrils of hair streamed across my face as I fought him. *No bargain. Not ever.*

If a time comes that you should feel differently, all you must do is say my name.

He'd always been so certain. As though he'd had some kind of guarantee that I would eventually end up right where he wanted me. I tried to summon a semblance of indignation or resentment, but now I remembered last night. Felt the soft glow of those lamps as we played game after game of Connect Four. Talking. Laughing. *Trusting.*

I hunched my shoulders and ran across the street, trying to outrun a sudden whisper of fear.

The bar was busy when I arrived to pick up Damon. I greeted Gretchen and avoided eye contact with Ian, who sat with his new wife toward the back. Angela and Ariel were hurrying back and forth from the order window. Damon was in the kitchen, nearly standing back-to-back with Cyrus. The sight of him showered and dressed, talking and moving, was one I took a mental snapshot of so I could remember it again and again. "Ready to go?" I asked, reluctant to interrupt.

At the sound of my voice, Damon's expression instantly clouded. He nodded, reaching back to untie his apron. Cyrus glanced between us. He didn't ask questions or reveal any curiosity, but I knew he noticed the strain. Despite people's assumptions, he didn't miss much. I mustered a smile for him, waved, and followed my brother out.

I didn't attempt a conversation during the drive home. Instead, I held the steering wheel in a white-knuckled grip and followed Oliver's advice. Avoidance wasn't working, and I couldn't face the Unseelie Court like this, so I replayed his words and committed them to heart. *Close your eyes. Picture the worst possible outcome. Be cruel to yourself. Spare no pain. Do this again, and again, and again. Until one day, you find yourself immune to it, and the fear no longer controls you.*

Damon started to get out. "Wait," I said. He glanced back at me, his hand on the door. "I have to go back to Court tonight. For—"

"—the Tithe," he finished. His eyes were dark and haunted. "I lived there for two years, remember?"

An apology hovered on the tip of my tongue, but I didn't speak it. I wouldn't apologize for killing a monster. For becoming one in the process of saving him. "Trust me, I remember," I retorted. Guilt expanded in my chest, making it difficult to breathe. "I should be back soon, but if you need anything, send a text. I'll have Lyari bring my phone to the surface every hour to get a signal."

"Don't bother." Damon got out of the truck, hunching his frail body against the cold, and disappeared into the house.

Just as I started to do the same, the mating bond shifted. I twisted in my seat, instinctively looking toward the tree line. Collith stood there, seemingly alone. I got out and locked the truck behind me, then walked toward him. Collith's focus was on the door my brother had gone through. "He's grieving," he said as soon as I was within earshot.

I wrapped my arms around myself and followed his gaze. A light flicked on in the kitchen and cast a square of brightness onto the dying lawn. "I know."

"Do you?" I sensed Collith looking at me now. "Because it feels like you're blaming yourself for everything that happened."

"Stop spying on what I'm feeling."

There was an unexpected smile in his voice as he answered, "Never. Shall we?"

When he started walking away, I cleared my throat. I was still wearing the yoga pants and sweatshirt I'd trained with Adam in—there was a strong possibility that I reeked of sweat and fear. Making the fae endure my stench was a heartening image, but I might feel more confident acting like their queen if I showered beforehand. "Uh, are we getting ready there?"

"Yes. There should be a bath waiting for you." Collith retreated into the forest, so light-footed that the leaves hardly made a sound as he passed. Though there were so many questions to ask, neither of us spoke. I followed him through the shadows and fading light, absorbed in noting landmarks and turns.

As we walked, my mind drifted, despite my best efforts. People were always saying how autumn was such a beautiful time of year. Really, though, autumn was decay. All those colorful little leaves falling out of the trees. So pretty, so lovely... but it was still death. Give me spring or winter any day.

A little farther into our hike, I noticed a glint through the naked branches. My thoughts on seasons dissipated. Something was moving alongside us, I realized. For a heart-stopping instant, I thought it was another wendigo, just like the last time Collith and I made this journey. I faltered, straining to catch another glimpse, and our pursuer stepped within my line of sight. Thank God. I nearly sagged with relief. It was the Guardian I'd seen at Adam's shop earlier. His glass sword gleamed in the twilight. They must've been following from a distance. Why? To give us a semblance of privacy?

"Fortuna? Is everything all right?" Collith asked. He'd stopped walking.

No. I jogged to catch up. "Yeah. Fine."

Soon after that, we reached a small clearing. I recognized it immediately. There was the narrow opening in between some rocks. The moss that had been dangling over it was long gone, and now it looked like a gaping mouth, ready and eager to consume. Collith stepped into the darkness without hesitation. I stayed outside, shifting from foot to foot. It was suddenly hard to breathe.

When Collith realized I wasn't behind him, he reemerged, concern drifting down the bond like a fragrant breeze. He took one look at me and closed the distance between us, daring to cup my face in his hands. "It will be different this time," he told me quietly. He pressed our foreheads together, as though physically trying to lend his confidence.

I should have known he'd guess at my thoughts. Or maybe he just heard every single one. An automatic, sarcastic response rose to my lips, but I swallowed it. I wanted to finish this and leave as soon as possible. But... I couldn't seem to pull away. I grabbed the front of Collith's shirt and inhaled the familiar scent of him. It made me think of an herb garden. *This means nothing*, I told myself, reluctant to open my eyes. Maybe, if I lied enough times, the lies would become truth. *Nothing.*

The Unseelie King didn't add more. Didn't offer another pretty lie or a dressed up fantasy. After another few seconds, I found the will to detangle us. "What should I expect? Will this be like Olorel?" I asked more sharply than I meant to, reaching up to tighten my ponytail.

Collith watched me with his infuriating, unwavering calm. "Most of the evening will be similar. There's some food, some dancing. Then we sit in our fancy chairs and listen to people talk."

I took a breath. "Okay. Let's get this over with."

My mate smiled a little and, this time, I plunged into that gaping maw without any hesitation. Collith followed silently. Nuvian and the other Guardian appeared, swords drawn, hurrying to flank us. If any faeries thought to harm or intercept us, they'd find the way efficiently barred. It was the first time since my coronation that I truly felt like the Queen of the Unseelie Court. Two weeks ago, I'd had no enemies besides faceless hunters or vague notions of someone wanting a Nightmare's heart. Now, I had more than I could count.

Well, if I was going to die soon, I might as well have some fun until then.

CHAPTER NINE

When we arrived at our rooms, Lyari was waiting outside the doorway. Exactly where I'd left her days ago. I entertained the thought that she hadn't slept or eaten in all that time, just because I liked the idea of her suffering. Or so I told myself. The truth was, Lyari had grown on me a bit.

"Thank you," I said to her as we passed, expecting no response. Which was exactly what I got.

The door closed behind us with a soft click. Collith was already dressed for his part, apparently, because he just went to the desk. "Take your time," he said kindly, uncapping a pen. There was a stack of fresh-looking documents resting in front of him. Curiosity flitted through me, wondering what those papers meant, the weight they carried, but now wasn't the time for questions.

As promised, the bathtub was waiting. Steam rose from the water. As I undressed and stepped in, I kept glancing toward Collith, remembering the last time I'd taken a bath in his presence. But he didn't turn his head or speak while I washed myself. I couldn't deny the tiniest feeling of disappointment.

Afterward, wrapped in a towel, I approached the wardrobe with a sense of dread. *Laurie.* He wouldn't be here to help unless I used his true name again. Considering how much I was already tied to him, though, I decided to manage on my own. I opened the doors and surveyed my options for a minute. The hangers slid along the pole with a hissing sound. Eventually, I just pulled a gown off its hanger. Better not to give myself a chance to over-think it. My selection was strapless, made of a color that was something between orange and beige. The bodice was glitter-ingly beaded in a pattern that was flowers or swirls. Impossible to tell, really. I let go of the towel—Collith still made a point of appearing absorbed in his work—and stepped into the contrap-tion. I tugged it into place and wriggled around until the fit felt right. The skirt swept along the floor, ensuring my feet were hidden.

Noting this, I slid my tennis shoes back on. *The easier to kick you with, my dear.* I pictured the crowd of faeries that had attended my coronation. If any of them were planning an assas-sination or kidnapping attempt, I'd use every weapon at my disposal. Including the brand-new moves Adam had taught me.

I was about to turn toward Collith and announce my readi-ness when I remembered the last part of Laurie's preparations. Oh, right. Hair. It was still slightly damp from the water. I wasn't about to summon a slave, but I had no clue how to braid. There were no styling irons, much less electricity to use them. After a beat, I went to the wardrobe and found a fresh pair of socks. I abandoned one and tore a hole in the other. Then I put it at the end of my ponytail and rolled it up to effectively create a bun.

Better than nothing, I thought. When I finally faced Collith, he was watching me with a fathomless expression. The bond was strangely still. I opened my mouth to ask him if I looked okay, but he stood from the desk before I could speak. "You're missing a few pieces," he said, moving to the wardrobe. He reemerged holding the crown and the sapphire necklace. Honestly, I kept forgetting it existed. The latter he left on the bed, probably giving me the choice to wear it or not, but the crown he placed on my head. The sticks made a slight creaking sound. I gazed up at him, waiting for flattery or encouragement, as Laurie had done. Instead, Collith brushed a kiss along my cheek, his cool lips leaving a trail of ice and fire. My insides heated.

"Last but not least..." Collith reached into his boot and held out my father's pocketknife. I went still at the sight of it. The last time I'd seen this knife, its blade had been covered in a stranger's blood. Blood that I'd thought was my brother's. I stared down, torn between gratitude and repulsion. After a few moments, the former won. I accepted the knife and tucked it down my dress and into my bra. It nestled securely between my breasts.

When I glanced up, thinking to thank Collith for the unexpected return of it, his gaze lingered on my fingers, which still rested along the dress's neckline. Images whispered through me. Steam rising from bathwater. Nails digging into tree bark. A head thrown back in the dark.

My breathing quickened from a combination of desire and fear.

After a moment, hoping Collith couldn't sense how much he'd affected me, I retrieved the necklace and dropped it around my neck. It was lighter than it looked. I fingered it, and the jewel flashed in the firelight.

"Thank you for doing this," Collith said, his gaze steady on mine.

I shrugged and watched those hazel eyes drop to my bare shoulders, then even lower. Seeing his desire made my own core start to throb. Thankfully, my voice revealed nothing as I responded, "Hey, you won fair and square."

Collith's delicious mouth curved into a knowing smile. *He*

figured out that I let him win, I thought suddenly. I gripped the sapphire harder and its facets dug into the meaty part of my palm. "I certainly did," was all he said, though. With that, Collith went to the door, opened it, and stepped aside. My face felt hot as I lifted the heavy dress and forced myself forward.

The temperature instantly dropped in the passageway. Though there were other Guardians present—Úna being one of them, I noticed with some distaste—Lyari instantly took a position close to me. She still didn't say a word, but I felt... safer with her so nearby. A fact I wouldn't admit to her in a million years.

Once again, our entourage made the journey through all those dirt passageways. The path was wide enough for Collith and I to walk side-by-side, and at some point, I took his arm without even noticing. Soft waves of pleasure warmed the bond. For once, we didn't walk in silence; Collith pointed to various doors and told me who lived behind them. He recited names and connections without faltering. I couldn't help but be impressed.

All too soon, though, earth became stone and the colorful mural loomed over our heads. We made for that distant doorway. This time I didn't let myself pause or hesitate; Collith and I went right in.

As with most other occasions I'd been here, there was a good-sized crowd waiting. They were obviously waiting for our arrival, as the moment we stepped over the threshold, the buzz of conversation increased tenfold. All the faces turned in our direction looked like something out of a painting. *Where's Waldo?* I searched for Arcaena and her twin, but there was no sign of them. At least, not that I could see from this poor vantage point. I couldn't squelch my curiosity surrounding what the arrogant, once-powerful female was like now that she was mortal.

"I hope you're hungry," Collith murmured. "Apparently the head cook went out of her way to dazzle you. You weren't queen yet during Olorel, so this is her first chance to make an impression."

"I don't know whether to be excited or terrified," I muttered back, involuntarily tightening my hold on him. Collith began nodding to certain individuals in the crowd as we walked. The path didn't lead to our thrones as I expected, but rather a long table to the far right of the room. Two chairs had high, intricately-carved wooden backs, and I knew without asking they were for us.

The throne room had once again been prepared for a special occasion. Oversized glass candelabras stood throughout the space. Someone had installed clay pots along the walls, too, which held enormous white flowers that created a floral scent in the air. The buffet was more elegant than it had been before, adorned with linen tablecloths and silver dishes. Musicians played from one of the corners, each of them elegantly dressed, their instruments shining. Someone had put in a lot of effort here.

It was then I noticed the fae themselves.

Where my dress was fairly simple, these faeries had adorned themselves in gowns heavy with intricate knots and braids and skirts and sleeves that were entirely made of near-transparent lace. Their faces were painted white to match, and I felt as if I were in a swarm of spirits, spinning all around in a dizzying array. I knew I was staring as we reached our table. One of the Guardians reached for my chair, but Collith hastened to beat him to it. He pulled it out for me and flashed a small, secret smile, as though we were in this together. Maybe, for once, we were.

Within seconds of sitting, Collith was approached aside by a courtier with shrewd eyes and milky skin. The stranger bent over and spoke quietly in my mate's ear. In the meantime, Lyari situated herself so close to my chair that I could feel the chill rolling off her. I almost told the guard not to bother—

swords would do no good here; words were the weapon tonight.

Hoping to deter anyone from talking to me, I twisted to face her. "Why so much white?" I asked impulsively. Just then, a line of slaves emerged from that great doorway, each of them holding something. Steaming plates, chalices, platters of roasted animals. My stomach rumbled at the sight, reminding me that I hadn't eaten all day.

"They create a different theme every month," Lyari said, her disdain obvious. It was the first time she'd spoken since my return to Court and the sound of her voice was startling. I followed her gaze toward a female dressed almost entirely in white feathers as she added, "Can you guess what tonight's is?"

For a moment, I frowned with incomprehension. A few seconds later, I put the pieces together and forgot entirely about my hunger. Saw the faeries, their clothes, their makeup, anew.

Me. It was me.

Dresses the females wore were eerily similar to the wedding gown Laurie had chosen that first night. The males were pale imitations of Collith as he'd been that day, with those shining leather pants and high boots.

A slave bent over me, putting my focus back to the food. She set a plate down and retreated before I could thank her or ask for a name. Rich scents teased my nostrils, distracting me from the guilt. Pork and melted cheese and rich beer. Even if I liked beer, which I didn't, I wouldn't dare steal a sip; females were already giggling from its aftereffects and the males were becoming sloppier by the minute. One even shoved his hand down a drooping neckline. His partner didn't exactly protest—there was just more laughter, more shining teeth.

I'd eaten in the Unseelie Court without negative conse-quences before. Maybe the superstition about its food and drink carrying madness was exactly that. After all, they'd already disproven the stories about their inability to lie. Hesitantly, feeling eyes on me, I speared a piece of meat and lifted it to my mouth.

"Well met, Queen Fortuna," a rumbling voice said. I tilted my head, setting the fork down with a clinking sound. A faerie stopped in front our table and I recognized him instantly. Tarragon. He bowed deeply, his jewelry making a sound like falling rain. He wore no shirt, just a pair of loose, golden pants. Even more of his tattoos were on display, and they were truly works of art. There was a heron on his arm and a sun on his shoulder. A herd of elephants walked along his waistline and a waterfall poured down his ribcage. The lack of shirt also revealed that this faerie had a hard, defined stomach.

"Well met," I replied. My tone made it clear I didn't mean it. Whenever I saw Tarragon's tranquil face, I thought of his part on the council that had sent me to a whipping post.

"We've not had the pleasure of seeing you in Court recently," he added, oblivious to the rage simmering within me. Collith sensed it, though, and he touched my knee beneath the table. His cool skin had a strangely calming effect. After a few seconds, the red haze ebbed away and I could see clearly again. I sat straighter and struggled to remember the last thing he'd said. Yes, right, about not seeing me in Court.

Unfortunately, neither Collith nor I had thought to weave a story of why I'd been in our rooms for so long. Now I couldn't seem to come up with a single one. "I've been... doing a lot of reading."

"Well, we are fortunate you've chosen to grace us with your presence again. I hope your seclusion has come to an end." Tarragon reached across the table, palm extended. I felt my eyebrows rise—most creatures didn't offer their hands so freely to a Nightmare. Calling his bluff, I put my own out, and Tarragon took it without hesitation. Was he hoping to gain my favor?

His fears whispered through me, tasting of metal and frost.

There was an image of glinting, sharpened needles. Strange, then, that he was covered in tattoos. Was he a masochist or just braver than most creatures?

I took my hand back and regarded him with more interest now. The music went on and on, bows sliding over strings and voices rising in harmony. *Play this smart, Fortuna. There are probably dozens of faeries listening.* The Tralees had hired an assassin to kill my brother, which meant no one could know where he was or that I'd been gone. Following my trail would lead them back to him. I pretended interest in the orchestra as I said, "We'll see. I haven't exactly been in a partying mood. Or need I remind you of what this Court put me through?"

"How does your father fare, Tarragon?" Collith interjected.

Tarragon gave him a serene smile. He tucked his hands behind his back and stepped back from the table, providing me with some much-needed space. "Same as ever, Your Majesty. His consistency is both a blessing and a curse, as you well know."

"Tarragon's father is a very vocal supporter of the Court's slave trade," Collith explained when I glanced at him questioningly. "Ettrian is also the head of his bloodline, which means there are many standing behind him."

"And you?" I asked, pinning Tarragon with my gaze. "Where do you stand?"

Dismay shot down our bond, but I ignored it. Tarragon, however, was as unruffled as ever. "I stand wherever my new queen tells me to," he said with another smile. It was such a fae response. *Kiss ass,* I thought. But maybe I could use that to my advantage someday...

I had a sudden suspicion that, though his expression hadn't changed, Tarragon knew exactly what I was thinking. A sort of... amusement filled my head. Maybe a hint of admiration, too. *It's the bond,* I realized. The one I'd formed with these creatures as a result of my coronation. My grip on that mental wall had eased somewhat during our conversation, apparently allowing a bit of insight through. Interesting.

Before I could say anything else, the dark-skinned faerie bowed. "Until we meet again, my queen," he bid. I made a noncommittal sound, which he took as permission to retreat. Doubtless the entire Court would be speculating about our exchange for the next week.

And what did my dear mate think of it? As I turned, I caught Collith eyeing my untouched food. "Better take a bite," he said, "or the cook will be offended."

"Wait a second. Would this be the cook that I encountered during my second trial?" I demanded. I saw her in my mind's eye, screaming at a human child. The next time I'd seen that child, she had a fresh cut on her lip. Collith didn't answer, which for him, was answer enough. Ice formed in my veins. Calmly, I took the stein of beer and upended it over the plate in front of me. Collith heaved a long sigh. He signaled to a nearby slave holding a pitcher of wine.

"Lyari," I chirped. She appeared instantly at my side and I flashed her a bright smile. "I'd like you to return this to the royal cook, please. Oh, and make sure to tell her that if she ever lifts a hand to a kitchen worker again, I'll be personally paying her a visit."

She quirked a brow, accepting the ruined plate from me. "Probably unwise to piss off the one preparing your food, Your Majesty."

"Good thing no one ever accused me of being wise, then."

Lyari's lips twitched just before she pulled back. A moment later, Nuvian's sword clinked as he bent down. One of his dreadlocks tickled my bare shoulder. "The bloodlines grow restless, Your Majesties," he muttered. Dislike for me practically radiated through his skin.

Collith nodded. He tossed back his newly-filled glass of wine, then stood. He turned to me and the wordless question shone from his eyes. Was I ready? A memory roared through my mind like a bad dream—that cat o'nine tails coming down again. And again. And again. Suddenly it was difficult to breathe, much less speak. I hoped it didn't show on my face as I got to my feet, too, pushing the chair back with such force that its legs screeched across the flagstones. The volume in the room lowered and faces swung toward us again. Collith extended his arm. Wondering why I'd ever agreed to this in the first place, I took it.

We left the table and its delicious-looking contents behind. My stomach made a forlorn sound, and I thought wistfully about the frozen pizza in my freezer back home. Hopefully Damon hadn't eaten it...

At the front of the cavernous room, our thrones awaited. The twisted roots of Collith's and the shining flames of mine. Death Bringer stood on one side of the dais and the Tongue on the other. They looked like dark harbingers. With every step closer to them, my anxiety heightened. Collith tried to send me wordless encouragement through the bond, but I was holding onto the image of the wall so fiercely that only bits came through.

For the first time, Collith and I ascended the steps together. A taut silence fell over everyone like a blanket of glittering snow. We faced our subjects for a moment—God, there were so many—then sat in our great chairs. In that moment, it hit me how much I hated this room. How much I hated *them*. But most of all I hated how not even my thoughts were my own; they could probably hear every word screaming through my head. Once again, I made a valiant effort to picture the wall.

I assumed Collith would make a formal announcement, as he had during Olorel, and I glanced over at him expectantly. His removed expression made me shiver; he was once more the faerie king that had watched my tribunal without a word of protest. God, how I'd hated him after that night. Instead,

Nuvian was the one who stepped forward and sent his voice into the crowd.

Enochian was clearly not his first tongue; his pronunciations were clipped and his address brief. Within seconds, he returned to his place beside Collith, holding the hilt of his sword with a white-knuckled grip. With that, the Tithe began. One by one, faeries approached the empty floor in front of us. They bowed, said something formal, and Collith expressed the Court's gratitude. A Guardian came forward to accept the offering. Each one was different, which I hadn't been expecting. A jewel. An ancient weapon. One even handed over her overpriced cat.

I recognized each face straight away—these were the same individuals that had made vows of fealty to me. The heads of the bloodlines or a descendent standing in for them. Collith had mentioned it, I remembered now, but the detail had slipped my mind during all the other things we'd talked about. This time, I made an effort to remember every single faerie that stood. The knowledge could come in handy someday.

After an hour, Collith leaned over to whisper in my ear. "We're nearly through," he told me. His cool breath still smelled like wine. "All that's left are the disputes. It will be different from your tribunal, since there's no need to summon a council. When a conflict is brought forth on the Tithe, the participants are acknowledging they'll accept whatever decision you and I make. Most prefer this, as I've established a reputation of being fair, while many of the old ones like their entertainment. There's never many disputes, though. Three at the most."

I turned my face so no one could watch my mouth. The action brought our faces much closer than I'd expected. "Thanks," I murmured. Torchlight on either side of us made the amber flecks in Collith's eyes brighter. That stubborn curl of his had slipped free of the crown and rested against his temple. Instead of responding, Collith's gaze dropped to my lips. It was just for an instant, but apparently that was enough to make my core clench. With effort, I faced the faeries standing at the edge of the dais. My mate did the same.

There were three of them, two males and a female. Their ages were impossible to discern, but two obviously came from an older bloodline—their clothing was antiquated and modest. The other male radiated an arrogance I'd come to expect from fae. He wore a button-down shirt, chinos, expensive-looking loafers, and a fleece vest. In other words, he looked like a complete douche.

"Why have you asked for this gathering? In English, please," Collith asked, sounding entirely composed.

The tallest of them stepped closer. His hair hung to his waist in a dark curtain. "I am Kailu of the bloodline Shadi," he said. His nostrils visibly flared as he turned to the other male.

"And I am Reptar of the bloodline Cralynn," the other male declared.

Kailu's voice wavered with barely-controlled violence. "This... male before you attacked my daughter. We found Daratrine in our rooms after... after he'd gone. Her clothes were torn. Her bruises were so severe that they took several hours to heal. She might've had a cracked rib as well."

"Your precious daughter has been coming to my room every night for weeks," Reptar retorted, rocking back on his heels. "She's even more experienced than I am. I assure you, Your Majesties, I didn't touch this one's virtue. Someone beat me to that a long—"

The girl's father rammed into him from the side, sending them both to the ground. Nuvian and Úna both moved with preternatural speed to intervene. I'd half-risen, thinking to do something myself, but Collith rested his hand on my arm. "This is what our Guardians train for," he said quietly. It irked to do nothing, but I sat back down, trusting that we'd have the final say in this.

During all the commotion, Daratrine had started trembling.

My gaze kept returning to her as Kailu jerked out of Nuvian's grasp, scowling. I saw Reptar wink at Úna, who let him go with an expression of disgust. While the males were preoccupied, Daratrine raised her tear-streaked face toward us. "He forced me, I swear it," she said. "He—"

"Why would I force you when I could have a thousand more beautiful, more willing partners?" Reptar countered, tugging his shirt back into place. He fixed his gaze on me and a faint, suggestive smile curved his lips. "She's just a child, my lady. Surely the word of a—"

"That's enough."

Everyone went still at the sound of my voice; even Collith's fingers froze on his armrest. I stood again. I was starting to learn this particular game, and I knew Collith would look weak if he tried to stop me. As I suspected, he remained silent when I left the throne. I felt like a dog that had just chewed through its leash—every step was a rush. My dress dragged behind me as I descended the uneven stairs.

Once I reached the flagstones, I walked toward Reptar with some sway to my hips. His gaze glazed over. His mouth opened, but he seemed unable to speak. I stopped just a handbreadth away and studied him. Then, in a deliberate snub, I put my back to Reptar and focused solely on the girl. Gently I asked, "How old are you?"

Daratrine's expression was a mixture of awe and terror. "F-f-fifteen, Your Majesty."

So young. Why did the monsters always hunt them so young?

Because that is when they are most vulnerable, a voice whispered within me. An image flashed like a camera, momentarily blinding. I saw myself, cowering in that bed, listening to my parents being torn apart and eaten. I relived seeing a hulking shadow and a glimpse of red eyes. Then I was on my knees, next to my dead father, adding tears to all that blood. I clutched at his hand

and begged him not to leave me alone. To come back. But of course he never would.

I came back to reality, blinking slowly, and happened to glance toward the first row of faeries. Something in the room had shifted. There was stark fear in their eyes. I could feel it, too, emanating strongly down the bonds that tied us together.

They'd tasted my fury. They sensed the danger.

Imagine a wall, Collith had said. I pulled that image back to me, squeezing tightly like a child with a teddy bear. I would not lose myself to these creatures. I was still Fortuna.

When I turned back to Reptar, he had regained some of his composure. My heart felt like a lump of ice. I took another step closer; he could touch me now, if he so dared. "What do you fear, faerie?" I purred.

He gave no answer, but his throat visibly moved as he swallowed. Apparently he had enough sense to forego lust for fear. I circled him slowly, trailing my finger across his collarbones, then along his back. Every inch of him was rigid. My veins hummed with anticipation as I stopped in front of him. The faerie resisted the pull of my face, choosing instead to focus on the hem of my skirt. His fear was mine, regardless of where he looked. It had an unpleasant flavor, like fruit that had gone bad. Above all else, he feared being ugly. Oh, how I longed to add some scars to that pretty face.

That wasn't my plan, however.

As with most species, Nightmares had a few tricks up our sleeves that weren't known among most Fallen. Our parents had made sure to teach me and Damon every single one, despite how young we'd been. Dad said it took a lifetime to learn restraint and control, and it was never too early to start.

One such trick was that Nightmares could find fears... and we could give them, too.

I wasn't sure if Collith or, hell, the entire Court could see what I was doing, but for once it didn't matter. Not for this. I cupped Reptar's chin and forced him to look up. In an instant, my gaze ensnared his. *Child's play,* I thought disdainfully. He was good at acting the monster, but when it came to being a victim, he was unskilled. This male had never known what it was to be afraid or fight for his life.

That was about to change.

With the tiniest of mental pushes, I was in his head. I found his bedroom easily, as it was where he spent a majority of his time. Within seconds, Reptar stood naked before me. When he realized this, it excited him. His mind was so susceptible that he didn't even question why the queen was in his private chambers or how we'd come to be here. We stood a few feet apart, and I moved to close the space between us. I was still wearing my heavy gown from the Tithe.

Reptar watched my progress in a way that a hunter might watch a deer from his stand. His gaze was bright, even more so in the light of the fire that crackled beside us. I didn't break eye contact as I rested my palm on the center of his chest, then pushed. Reptar fell back onto the bed, surprisingly graceless for a faerie. He breathed heavily, the length of him raised like a flag. His stomach bunched as he sat up.

Briefly, very briefly, I thought of Collith and my vow to be faithful. It was easy to shove back into the shadows. I focused completely on Reptar and settled my weight on top of him. I then proceeded to ride him until his cock strained against my dress. The male moaned beneath me. Several times he tried to yank my underwear down, but whenever his fingers brushed against the lace, I grabbed his wrists and pinned them down. Eventually, Reptar settled for burying his fists in my skirt to quicken our rhythm. Smiling indulgently, I reached down and grabbed hold of his hard length. He nearly came then and there.

"Not yet, not yet," I whispered. "Hold on just a little longer, baby. Don't you want me?"

Reptar grabbed the back of my head, making a fist so tight in my hair that it actually hurt, and tried to pull me to his mouth. I resisted, trying to hide an annoyed wince. "Take off your dress. I'm going to fuck you so hard, you won't be able to walk for a week," he growled. His hot breath touched my cheek. It smelled like rancid meat.

"Mmmm. Sexy. Before we do that, though, there's something I need to tell you."

"And what's that?" he whispered, our mouths nearly touching.

I made a sound deep in my throat and let him hear the anticipation in it. "Just that... you're never going to hurt anyone else again."

I didn't give the faerie a chance to realize what was happening. I tightened my grip and squeezed his cock so fiercely that Reptar squealed like a stuck pig. It was into this I channeled my power, my essence, my darkness. Everything he felt—all that lust and excitement, stemming from that hard, throbbing thing I held—became tainted with fear. Reptar couldn't fight me; the onslaught of terror was too much. It was everything. He'd forgotten I was even there, still holding his soft dick. He just laid there, mouth opening and closing, his entire body rigid.

Only when I felt light-headed and drained did I step back and end the illusion.

We were back in the throne room. Reptar, who'd fallen to his knees at some point, didn't move even now. His eyes were so wide the whites in them smothered his irises. I struggled to reorient myself. My head pounded as I looked up.

The crowd didn't make a sound. Not a whisper or a cough. I smirked tiredly and turned to Kailu and Daratrine. "He'll never be able to have sex again without experiencing pure, paralyzing terror. Is this good enough, or would you like to explore a different consequence for his actions?" I directed the question more at Daratrine than her father.

Still, it was Kailu who appraised the faerie. I followed his gaze to Reptar. The faerie was still pale with shock, and there was no trace of that self-importance he'd worn like a cloak. If he didn't pull out of it soon, I'd probably broken his mind.

I knew that, if it had been me, I wouldn't be satisfied until he was dead. But apparently Kailu and I were very different creatures. After another moment he said, his voice tight, "It is enough."

Our eyes met. He gave me a subtle nod, so slight that no one but his daughter and I would be able to see. It seemed I had at least one supporter in this nest of vipers. I nodded back, then returned my focus to Daratrine. She was still gaping at Reptar. I couldn't tell if she was horrified or exhilarated, and my head hurt too much to explore the bond between us. "Remember," I said, my voice low, the words for her alone. She jerked toward me, blinking rapidly. "You're only a victim if you let them break you."

"We are in your debt, Your Majesty," the young faerie whispered. I thought about correcting her, but in this game, I had no way of knowing if I'd need their help someday. In the end, I just gave her a small smile.

Without warning, Nuvian said something in Enochian. The sound of his voice was so abrupt that I jumped. *Really should learn how to speak the language,* I thought with a flash of annoyance. As the Right Hand finished posturing, Collith joined me at the bottom of the dais. That telltale muscle twitched in his jaw. He didn't offer his arm this time, which revealed the extent of his agitation—no small detail would go unmissed by our subjects.

Walking side by side, the distance between us as noticeable as an ocean, Collith and I made our way to those great doors. Halfway there, the musicians started to play again. "Okay, what's—" I started, but Collith shook his head. I pursed my lips as the familiar heat of rebellion burned through me. I obeyed no orders. I answered to no one.

Yes, but maybe you've proven that point enough for tonight.

Collith couldn't usually be pushed into talking, anyway. I gritted my teeth and decided, however unnatural it felt, to wait.

Near the doors, a long-faced faerie tried to approach me. His eyes were bright with adoration. No, obsession. Lyari moved in a blur to intercept him, and the male called my name as we passed. *It's not real,* I wanted to tell him. *What you feel is just magic. Fantasy. Power.* But I didn't want to encourage his fixation, so I kept my eyes ahead and didn't falter.

It wasn't until we'd completely cleared the throne room and were well into the passageway that Collith finally broke his silence. "What happened back there?" he asked. He'd never spoken to me in that tone before. Sharp. Furious.

A flicker of surprise went through me, but I pasted on a mask of indifference. Nuvian and the other Guardian would be able to hear every word. "Why bother asking? Didn't you see it?"

"It seems you're a quick learner. Your mental block was so thorough that even I couldn't get past it," Collith answered. This made me smile with secret pleasure. He saw it and his expression darkened. His face went in and out of shadow with each torch we passed. "Tyrants do not sit long on their thrones, Fortuna."

With that, my satisfaction dimmed. "Oh, okay, so I'm a tyrant now?" I snapped. Of course, that was the moment I finally tripped on my dress. I paused to snatch up the skirt.

"I could use my abilities to get results," Collith said as though I hadn't spoken. He stopped alongside me, forcing our guards to follow suit. By this point Lyari had caught up, as well. "I've chosen another path. It's not my hope to be well-liked—no ruler in history has had the support of every subject—but they do respect me. There's a difference between having power and being powerful."

I started walking again in an attempt to have this conversation without an audience. The effort to maintain some dignity was a bit impeded by my armful of shiny dress material. "He was a *rapist*, Collith. Why don't you save this lecture for a time when it's actually applicable?"

For the first time since I'd known him, Collith let his temper get the best of him. Guess I'd finally figured out how to push his buttons. "My mother had a saying," he said doggedly, keeping pace with his long-legged strides. "'If your throne is made from the bones of those you stepped on to get there, don't be surprised when their ghosts come knocking at the door.'"

"Interesting. Most mothers go with, 'If you don't have anything nice to say, don't say anything at all.' Is there something you're—"

Suddenly the guard in front of us halted. Collith stiffened beside me. Alarmed, I followed his gaze. But it wasn't the sight of Laurie that made my stomach plummet like an elevator and the skirt to fall out of my arms. It was the faerie standing beside him. "I brought someone to see you, Your Majesty," the King of the Seelie Court purred. "She says the two of you are old friends."

"Sorcha?" I whispered.

CHAPTER TEN

"𝓘 had to see it for myself," Sorcha said by way of greeting.

Her voice was just as I remembered. Dripping honey and purring kittens. Just like that, I was in high school again, watching those black-rimmed clocks in each classroom, counting down the seconds until I could see her again.

I'd told Sorcha things I hadn't told anyone else. How much I resented Emma for trying to replace my mother. How badly I longed to wear my own face whenever I spoke to the other students. How I daydreamed about someday opening my own veterinary clinic.

And she'd just batted me aside like a gnat flitting around her mimosa.

Dimly I realized that Sorcha was talking again. With effort, I pulled free from the past. "...word reached me of Queen Fortuna, Conqueror of the Leviathan, Challenger of the Fearless, I thought to myself, no, it can't be the same quiet, withdrawn little Nightmare that I'd known," the golden-haired faerie crooned. A tear-shaped diamond quivered against her forehead, strung there on a silver chain. The rest of her was clothed in a modern, white suit, a stark contrast to the girly clothing she'd once worn. "Yet here you are. The crown suits you, old friend."

"You're no friend of mine," I said, finding my voice. Laurie's grin widened; he was taking far too much pleasure in all this.

Sorcha, in turn, pouted. Her skin was smooth as a china doll's in the flickering torchlight. I should've known the instant I saw her for the first time that there must be a catch, like an apple so lovely it couldn't be anything but poisoned. Nothing was that perfect. "Have I done something to offend you, Your Majesty?" she questioned. So innocent. So pure.

"Yes," I said shortly. "You're breathing."

"Have you received an invitation to this Court?" Collith interjected, ever the diplomat. One of our guards shifted and his glass sword flashed. "Your unexpected presence here could be seen as—"

"Why, of course. All due respect, I've been at this a bit longer than you, kingling." With a flourish, Laurie unrolled a piece of parchment. Meanwhile the temperature had dropped in the narrow passageway; I suspected no one had dared to interrupt the Unseelie King in a long, long time. I didn't need a magical bond to know that our guards were displeased.

Laurie smirked, stoking the flames I sensed within my mate. He offered the parchment to Collith, but before the Unseelie King could move, Nuvian stepped forward. Tension filled the passageway like water. He took the paper and presented it to Collith, who scanned the writing silently.

"Who issued it?" I snapped, unable to wait a second longer. Which faerie was I about to track down and drown in his—or her—own terrified piss?

A few more seconds ticked past. At last, Collith handed the missive back to Nuvian. That muscle in his jaw ticked once again. Good thing he was immortal, or I'd worry about him dying of an ulcer. "Ayduin of the bloodline Tralee," he answered at last. Belying his countenance, his voice was cold and even.

While the first name meant nothing to me, I recognized that bloodline instantly. *Arcaena's twin.* Realization struck, hotter than any bolt of lightning, and I swallowed a string of cuss words. If Ayduin had found out about Sorcha, it meant he was digging into my past. Which also meant that if he didn't already know about Bea, or Gretchen, or Cyrus, he soon would. A sharp, chilling truth settled into my bones.

Ayduin had to die.

"He was most eager to return the honor you bestowed upon his bloodline during your coronation," Laurie told me with a wink. I struggled to listen to his words; my heart was pounding hard and fast. All I wanted was to run back to Granby and make sure the few people I loved in this world were safe. Suddenly, all my history with Sorcha was a mere annoyance, rather than an actual player in this deadly game. "When this one requested my permission to visit the Unseelie Court, I couldn't resist tagging along to observe this special reunion."

Out of the corner of my eye, I noticed that Collith's frown had deepened. Doubtless because of the familiar way Laurie addressed me. If the Seelie King had been within kicking distance, I might've given in to the urge. "I'll have to properly express my gratitude," I said through my teeth. Lyari stepped closer to me, her boots making a slight sound in the dirt. Probably readying herself if I acted rashly. Not an entirely unreasonable assumption, since that's exactly what I wanted to do.

"We were just about to retire for the evening," Collith said. He moved closer, too. "Lady Sorcha, perhaps you should—"

"Might I have a word, Queen Fortuna?" Laurie interjected. It was the second time he'd dared to interrupt. Now each one of the guards unsheathed their swords. The glass made a brief singing sound, and for an instant, the air was filled with a strange sort of music. Undaunted by the glint of weapons, Laurie's gaze bored into Collith's. A taunting smile curved his lips as he added, "Privately."

Pressure built in the air. Any moment now, there would be a detonation, and I had no way of knowing who would survive it. Or who I actually wanted to.

"It's fine," I said swiftly, resting my hand on Collith's arm. I felt everyone notice the touch. "Lyari can stay with me. Isn't that right, Your Majesty?"

Laurie lifted one shoulder in a shrug. His eyes gleamed like melted silver. "Hardly necessary, but if you insist."

"I do."

Something indefinable drifted down the bond. It was warm and soft. It matched, I thought, what I saw in Laurie's eyes. *Admiration.* My stomach fluttered. I didn't know where to look. Just when I started to turn to Collith, Laurie pulled his gaze from mine. He focused on the female still standing beside us. "Lady Sorcha, have you ever seen the Mural of Ulesse? Even I must admit that it's quite extraordinary."

Her blue eyes darted between me and Laurie. I watched carefully for any reaction, but whatever she felt about being dismissed, Sorcha kept it hidden. "I have, but it's been many years," she said. "I imagine it's been added to since my last visit. Your Majesty, would you be so kind as to escort me?"

Once again, Collith was trapped between his need to maintain appearances and his devotion to tradition. I glanced at him, feeling his frustration, but his lithe profile was neutral. "Of course," he murmured. He didn't look in my direction as he stepped forward and offered his arm to Sorcha. She accepted without any of the hesitation I'd shown Collith on numerous occasions. They walked past and she winked at me. I briefly considered punching her in the face, even going so far as to picture it, and I knew it wasn't my imagination when Collith quickened their pace.

Within seconds they were swallowed by the earth. Laurie waited until every last faerie—other than Lyari, of course—was out of sight to pull something from his jacket pocket. Between two fingers, he held out a folded piece of paper. "Here's the information you requested," he said. His voice was different now; it was no longer edged with broken glass and small razors. This was the faerie I'd befriended, here in this dark place, wearing pretty gowns and painted faces.

"You needed a 'private word' to hand this to me?" I snapped, taking it. Our skin brushed. It was only for an instant, but that was all it took. His vibrant, sweet-smelling power assailed my senses. This time, there was something erotic in the way it affected me. Grateful for the dress, I squeezed my legs together and hoped he didn't notice the slight movement.

Seemingly unaware of his power—or maybe far too accustomed to it—Laurie rocked back on his heels and grinned. "Oh, no, not at all. But I did need to torment Collith a little."

"Why? I thought you were oh-so-loyal to him." Apparently, I'd stumbled upon another secret, because Laurie said nothing. He was as adept as Collith in shutting down when it came to telling truths. I rolled my eyes and unfolded the paper. An address was upon it, written in harried, nearly illegible handwriting. The town was surprisingly close to Granby. I frowned. "What—"

"The werewolf, silly thing. You asked for help in locating his pack, yes? Well, I held up my end of the bargain. Remember that." Surprising me, Laurie bent and brushed a kiss along my cheek. His lips were warm. However light the touch, it left a blazing path. I opened my mouth but nothing came out.

Laurie was gone, anyway.

It took my mind a moment to process that, in the space of time it took to blink, the faerie king was no longer there. Then, bracing myself for questions, I turned to Lyari. She stared back at me. Her skin glowed like a pearl in moonlight.

"You're full of surprises," was all she said after a few long, stilted seconds. Her green gaze darted to the space Laurie just vacated. "Did I understand correctly? You made a bargain with the King of the Seelie Court?"

"I make bargains with a lot of people," I countered, trying to hide the panic her words awakened. Avoiding her eyes now, I shoved the piece of paper into my bra. If I started thinking about how I'd tied myself to not one, but *two* faerie kings, I might start to regret it. And regret, I'd learned, was a flavor I was particularly averse to. I already got a healthy dose of it every day. Whenever I looked at my brother—

Shit. Damon.

All at once, my urgency returned in a rush. I grabbed Lyari's arm without thinking. "I need you to sift!"

She stepped back as though my hand on her was an affront. I tried to let go before her fears reached up through her skin, but it was too late. "...beg your pardon?" she said. It sounded like we stood on opposite ends of a raging sea, trying to shout through distance and winds. I put all my focus into unlatching my fingers, one by one. But the rest of me was falling. Through darkness, through pain, through water.

And right into Lyari's worst fear.

This isn't right, I thought wildly. Her worst fear wasn't supposed to be so accessible. Yet here I was. Just as it had been with Collith the first time I explored his mind in those dungeons, the scene was unusually vivid. Instead of flavors or images, I was inside a memory.

It was night. Of course it would be; only the most terrible things happened after dark came. Yes, there were disasters in the light of day, but the most despicable things, the things no one wants to see or get caught doing, those happened at night. Just like this one. When I took in my surroundings and spotted Lyari, I stiffened.

There she was, as a child, huddled beneath some ragged-looking covers. Someone—very clearly an adult—rested beside her. I stepped forward, clenching my hands into helpless fists.

There was nothing I could do, as this was an event that had already happened. In the next moment, though, a sound floated to me. Sobbing. There wasn't shame in that voice, no, it was despair that trembled around us. I frowned and drew even closer.

To my surprise, it was a woman in the bed. She bore an uncanny resemblance to the Lyari I knew now. Her mother, I realized. It had to be.

Lyari's young, soft voice floated through the air now, like lyrics to her mother's mournful song. She spoke in Enochian, but somehow, I understood the words. "Mother, it's me, Lyari. You're not there anymore. It's over. The battle is lost."

Silence descended upon them. Lyari's thoughts whispered through the room, through me, as though they'd been weaved in the very fabric of this moment. She looked at her mother, nestled against her chest as if *she* was the child. After a moment, Lyari felt a cold finger curl around her heart. What if this happened to her someday? What if she were so broken that she couldn't even remember those she loved? What if she were trapped in a bad memory?

Get out of my head!

Lyari's enraged scream tore through the air. *Guess she finally resurrected her mental wall,* I thought dimly. An instant later, there was a shoving sensation, or maybe more like a gust of wind hitting me. The memory blurred as I tumbled away.

I opened my eyes and immediately felt sucked into a swamp of disorientation.

It was me. More accurately, it was my body, standing a few inches away and staring back. Despite getting thrown out of the memory, I was still in Lyari's mind, at least partially.

Her thoughts blared like the horn of a semi. She was torn between flying at me in a rage or restraining herself. She was curious about the Nightmare, this new queen. Fortuna was unapologetic. She was vicious. She was brave. Despite what

Lyari had been taught about the lesser races and her own opinions, she was starting to *like* me.

The thought struck a chord within me. Guilt. I hadn't intruded on purpose, but it was still an intrusion. This time, I was the one who sought to end our bizarre connection. *Wall. Picture a wall.* I put myself on one side and Lyari on the other. I held onto the image so fiercely that everything else faded away.

When I opened my eyes again, all was as it should be. The Guardian was rigid where she stood, glaring at me, speechless with fury. My tongue was coated in flavor. It made me think of candle wax or a burnt wick. Both associated with that dim room where Lyari used to lay with her mad mother.

For both of our sakes, I didn't acknowledge any part of what just happened. "That vanishing thing Collith does," I clarified shakily, returning to the conversation we'd been having before the... interruption. "He said other faeries can do it, too. Are you one of them?"

"Yes," Lyari bit out, clearly still trying to decide whether or not to unsheathe her sword. The answer surprised me. Collith had mentioned that, of those who still had the ability, they were considered more powerful than most.

Logically, I knew that everyone had a story, a part of themselves they kept hidden, but until that moment I'd never considered what Lyari's were.

"You should be so much more than a Guardian. Why are you hiding your power?" I asked. It was meant for myself more than her. My mind explored the question like fingers over a Rubik's Cube. An instant later, I made an involuntary sound of frustration. "Fuck, no, we'll have to talk about it later. Right now, I need you to check on my brother. No, on second thought, stay with him until I can get there. He shouldn't be alone."

Lyari didn't move or speak. I didn't need to be in her head to know what she was thinking. *Why should I do anything for you?*

My first instinct was to remind her of the vows she made.

But I resented my own vows, and if Collith were to ever use them as leverage, I'd probably find a way to work around them out of spite.

Tyrants do not sit long on their thrones, Fortuna.

Annoyance burrowed in my stomach. When had Collith become the voice in my head, guiding me between right and wrong? As if he was the authority on morality. Even so, I decided to try sincerity.

"I honestly didn't mean to see your past," I told the beautiful faerie still glaring daggers at me. "I think my bond as your queen enhances what I can do as a Nightmare. It's all very new and I'm going to figure out how I can control it. Soon. Right now my brother could be in danger. I don't have a lot of allies or people I can trust. I know you and I didn't exactly get off on the right foot, and I accept part of the blame for that. I mean, I did spit in your face, so I probably would've hit me, too. But I'm hoping we can get past all that and... both benefit from this situation. There has to be some perks being the queen's Right Hand, doesn't there?"

I paused, but Lyari's face didn't change. What else could I say? I didn't exactly have a generous amount of patience, and as the seconds ticked by, the last of it evaporated. "Okay, new plan. We'll just spend every second together from now on. I'll braid your hair and do your makeup. Oh, maybe we could even go shopping in—"

Lyari's form shimmered. "Dear God. I'll go if it means you stop talking," she snarled. A moment later, I stood alone in the passageway.

She hadn't asked where Damon was, or how to find the house, which probably meant the Guardians had been keeping tabs on us. I didn't know how I felt about that.

As I lingered there, silence filled my ears. It was a strange sensation after being surrounded by faeries for the past two hours. I immediately wondered how I could take advantage of this. A visit to the mysterious camera room, maybe? A peek inside the royal treasury? Or perhaps even a visit to Ayduin...

No. Get home first, make sure Damon was okay. The rest could wait.

Just as I made my choice, a sound echoed down the tunnel. Like a frightened deer, I froze. I strained to see something. Anything. Further down the passageway, the darkness didn't move. It didn't *feel* empty, though. I pressed against the wall and held my breath, listening for more. The utter silence was unnerving; in this part of the maze, there seemed to be no doors or fae about. Usually there was the occasional cry or moan.

It was nothing, Fortuna. You've let them get to you. Despite this thought, I continued to wait, sweat breaking out in my palms and over my lip. Memories screamed through the stillness. Grappling fingers. Clacking teeth. Throaty moans.

Losing whatever rationality I had left, I turned to run.

Strong arms caught hold of me.

I didn't need to see his face to know that it was Collith. As his familiar scent drifted around us, I didn't struggle—truth be told, I'd sensed him just a moment before he arrived. The more time we spent together, the more aware I was of his proximity. It was a constant presence in my head. There were brief instances it was smothering, and I yearned to break free, but in moments such as this, I suspected it was the only thing keeping me sane.

"I felt your fear. What did he do?" Collith whispered, cupping the back of my head. His breath stirred my hair as I rested against him and allowed his scent to become everything. A small, hushed part of me was aware that I'd grabbed hold of the waistband on his jeans. My knuckles brushed against his bare skin.

Collith said my name. There was a question in it, somewhere, but I couldn't think straight enough to find the answer.

All at once, my head cleared and I saw how I was fingering

the button of his pants. I pulled back. "Oh, Laurie didn't do anything. I just got a little... spooked."

I was about to pull back when I noticed that Collith had gone very, very still. My mind scrambled backward, reviewing everything we'd said, and I realized that I'd called the Seelie King by his nickname. A connection that definitely couldn't have been made in this passageway, mere moments ago.

I was so focused on what to say that I forgot to step out Collith's arms. His grip tightened as I spoke in a rush. "Before you say anything, yes, I've met him before. But I had no idea who he was until a few days ago."

Collith absorbed this. I could sense him grasping at the threads inside him, tying them back into neat knots. Always composed. Always in control. "And how did your paths happen to cross?" he asked eventually. The lovely face staring back at me was familiar now. This was the creature that walked through black markets and made twisted bargains. He calculated risks and learned facts, then proceeded to use them for his own ends.

Like marrying a Nightmare.

"He was waiting in my room the first night you brought me here," I answered, matching Collith's cool tone. We'd stepped away from each other without my even noticing. The spots on my body where his hands had been were painfully cold. "He pretended to be a slave."

At this revelation, Collith's control slipped again. His rush of feeling was so violent that it burst through whatever dams he'd built. The surge roared down our bond. Pain, anger, confusion. Collith kept his gaze on the path in front us—a futile effort at concealing his reaction—as he replied, "That does sound like Laurelis. I should have warned you. I didn't think he'd be so bold. He's the one who helped you with the makeup, isn't he?"

Without warning, Collith started walking. It was so abrupt that I had to break into a jog to catch up, which was no easy feat in a dress. "Maybe a little," I admitted, talking to the back of his head.

Though I couldn't see Collith's face, I could hear the icicles dangling off his next words. "You know, I thought I smelled him once. I told myself I was imagining things."

I didn't trust myself not to say something that would make things worse—I still needed him as an ally. As we got closer to the surface, the tunnel widened, making it possible to walk alongside each other. I moved into the space, trying to think of what to say. The silence felt dark and bottomless. I snuck a glance at Collith, and his profile seemed to be made of stone.

A few minutes later, we reached the cave opening, and Collith finally turned to me again. Moonlight fell across his face and cast part of it in shadow. Plumes of air left his mouth with every exhale. His eyes seemed black. In that moment, he looked more fae than ever before. What I found even more frightening was how it didn't bother me as much as it should've. As much as it used to.

To make out his features better, I shifted so we both stood in the gap. Naked branches reached for me like crone's hands, forcing me to step even closer. His cool breath touched my cheek. Just like that, my body awoke in a burst of heat and sensation. I couldn't deny, even if I wanted to, how much I wanted him.

"If I advised you to stay away from Laurelis, would it be a waste of breath?" Collith asked huskily. His tone suggested he knew what my answer would be.

The question broke the spell hovering around me. I turned, hoping he couldn't see or sense my disappointment, and took a few steps into the clearing. For a moment, I considered telling Collith about the bargain I'd made with the other king. How Laurie had only helped me in exchange for knowing whenever Collith was in danger. How he'd been helping Collith from the moment I'd met him. Even going so far as to test me, when I'd found the Unseelie King sleeping in his throne after Olorel.

Whatever their quarrel, either Laurie was the guilty one or he'd long been over it.

"It's not like I have much of a choice. He usually comes to me," I said finally, facing Collith again. Why didn't I want to tell him the truth?

"Usually?" Collith repeated. Thinking of how I'd summoned Laurie in Nym's chambers, I just shrugged. My mate's jaw clenched. When he spoke, the parts of him that had softened were locked away again, secured with a lock I didn't understand. "I make an effort to maintain some semblance of humanity, Fortuna. Your new friend does no such thing. He is unpredictable and much better at politics than I am. Meaning he's better at deceit. You will never truly know where his loyalties lie or what his intentions are."

"Well, tell me how you really feel," I quipped, trying to lighten the mood.

Collith's brow lowered. "I just did."

"No, I wasn't... never mind." I bit my lip to hold back a laugh. Now was definitely not the time. I glanced upward, and through the gaps in the trees, a crescent moon smiled back. I refocused on Collith. "You don't need to walk with me. You've probably got some ruffled feathers to take care of. Besides, Lyari is waiting at the house. I sent her to—"

"—check on your brother," Collith finished. Of course he'd made the same connection I had about Ayduin digging into my past. That road would eventually lead him to where I lived. Where Damon lived.

Urgency swelled in my veins, like a river after a storm. "Yeah, exactly. So I'll talk to you... later? Soon?" I felt like a moron. What was the right way to say goodbye to someone that was somehow a king, an enemy, a mate, and an ally all at once?

Amusement flickered in Collith's eyes. The tight-lipped,

furious faerie of minutes ago was gone. "Heaven help any creatures that dare to get in your way, Your Majesty."

The words felt like a caress, and I ran without saying anything in return, for fear of what it might begin. What it might reveal.

I felt his eyes on me right until I vanished into the trees. After we were out of each other's sight, I slowed to a walk—it was hard to do anything in this dress. I'd been in such a rush to get home that I'd left my real clothes in Collith's room. *Damn it.* There was no way I was going back now. Maybe I would send a message through Lyari and ask him to drop them off. At least I still had my shoes.

The journey home was uneventful. I used my cell phone for a flashlight—it was warm from being tucked inside my bra all this time—and kept it directed at the ground to avoid notice. The autumn air was a relief against my skin, compared to the underground throne room, which had been filled to the brim with fae. The hum of their voices, making threats and giving promises, vowing wars and suggesting bargains, was now replaced with sweet stillness. It had been too long, I thought, since I'd walked through the woods on my own. I had let the goblins take this from me. No more.

Near the line of trees that stood as a boundary between lawn and forest, I came across a dead deer. It rested on its side and the flies had already begun their work. Thankfully, the air just smelled of dead leaves and distant snow. I stood over it and noted that a bullet wound made the deer's flesh pucker. I frowned at this—the season opener wasn't for another week, which meant someone had been hunting illegally. They'd probably lost track of the deer and decided to come back for it at first light.

Squatting, I reached to close its eyes. A slight rustling sound disturbed the quiet as I straightened. I stiffened and reached for the knife.

At the same moment, my werewolf stepped into the open.

"Oh, thank God." I nearly sagged with relief. The wolf didn't move to greet me, but a whine left his throat. His tail moved in the subtle beginnings of a wag and his eyes were bright, not with hunger, but vitality. A handful of days away from Court was already doing him wonders. A rare, happy smile curved my lips. I resisted the urge to pet the wolf's head when I passed, reminding myself that he wasn't a dog.

Soon there came the soft sounds of him following. However foolish it might be, knowing the wolf was near made me feel... safer. I crossed the yard, my hem darkening with dew, and tried the door. Locked. The lights were on inside, though, so Damon must've been home. There was no sign of Lyari, either.

These facts should have sent me into a panic, imagining the worst, but instinct guided me around the house. My theory was confirmed when I rounded the corner and found Damon kneeling in what used to be his garden. Something lodged in my chest at the sight. It was almost possible to imagine the past two years hadn't happened. That my brother hadn't been snatched by a faerie in the middle of the night and whisked away to the Unseelie Court. That he hadn't learned what hate was.

Lyari stood a few yards away, still and silent. Our eyes met for a brief moment. She gave me a subtle nod, and I nodded back before returning my gaze to Damon.

He hadn't done anything to fix his garden's neglected state yet—the dirt was unturned and dead plants still stuck up from the soil. It was too late in the year, anyway. Something had hold of him, a memory or a thought. I couldn't see my brother's face, but seconds brushed past and he didn't move.

Eventually, I must've made a sound, because Damon's head turned. His brown eyes found me in the shadows. His expression wasn't disappointed, exactly—it was as though he'd known better than to hope—but something darkened. I watched him take note of the dress I still wore, his attention lingering on the sapphire. To my surprise, Damon didn't ask about the Tithe. Instead, he stood up and said, "We need to go back to Denver."

It took a moment for my mind to accept the random statement or that I'd even heard correctly. Then I blinked at Damon and scrambled to think of a reason for going back. Most of our classmates had probably moved away. Our adoptive parents didn't live anywhere near there, since they'd moved when Dave retired. All that awaited us was bloody memories and fading ghosts. "Why?" I asked finally.

Damon avoided my gaze. His T-shirt fluttered in a breeze. "I have a... feeling. I just know that's where we need to be right now."

"Since when are you clairvoyant?" I asked with a frown. Alarm bells clanged through my head. Were his abilities changing, just as mine had? I'd been so busy surviving that I hadn't been able to give it much thought. Now I did. There had been a moment, during the trials, that I'd touched Shameek and I'd seen one of his memories. Yes, it had been rank with fear, probably the reason I'd stumbled across it... but that wasn't how my power worked.

Then there was those tortuous few seconds with Lyari, when I'd been witness to the moment her worst fear was born. My power was simpler than that. Skin-to-skin contact, a flash of intuition that revealed some phobia, and a flavor on my tongue. That was it. How it had always been.

"...not clairvoyant," Damon was saying. I blinked, then made a herculean effort to focus.

"Okay, you're not clairvoyant. Then why on earth would..." A new idea occurred to me. "Wait. Is this about Savannah?"

"No. I swear that it's not. Just... please, Fortuna."

It was the way Damon said my name. As though he was made of glass and the wrong response from me would cause him to shatter. Maybe this was an opportunity for us to talk more, I thought. We'd be stuck in a car together for a couple hours.

"Fine. I need to talk to Bea first, and see if yet another trip will be what it takes for her to fire me. If not, I'll go. But I'm going to complain the entire time," I added.

I'd hoped this would make him laugh, but my brother just turned away. Frustration dug a hole in my stomach. I watched him walk toward the house while I remained in the bones of his garden. I knew that if I went with him, I might say something I regretted.

I turned toward Lyari, a bitter joke on my lips, but she had disappeared. I knew she hadn't gone far, either from the annoying bond we shared or that niggling sense of being watched. Between her and the werewolf, no assassin was going to succeed here.

Clouds shifted overhead, allowing more moonlight to peek through, like a mischievous child that didn't want to fall asleep. I grabbed the shovel Damon had left behind, thinking to put it away. Something occurred to me, though, and I paused. An owl hooted in the distance as I stared down at the shovel, its head gleaming silver. A few seconds tiptoed past, then I started retracing my steps toward the trees. The werewolf trailed after me.

Within a minute, I was back at the spot I'd found the deer. It hadn't been moved or taken. It rested at the edge of the forest, a shell of its former self. I couldn't bear to leave this creature that once ran through the trees more wild and free than a star. Not to the indignities of rot or skinning.

Beneath that waxing moon, I pulled the deer deeper into the woods and buried it.

CHAPTER ELEVEN

$\mathcal{L}$ightning and thunder woke me.

I opened my eyes to the ceiling, feeling Oliver fade away to that part of my mind I could never reach in consciousness.

During our time together, he'd made a painfully obvious effort at normalcy. We went swimming and watched some old movies with pizza slices in our hands. It was different, though. *He* was different. My loving and vibrant best friend had been replaced by a pale and quiet stranger. The one time I tried to broach what happened on my last visit, he turned from me and said, "I can't, Fortuna. Not even for you."

Today, if all went well with Bea, Damon and I would be returning to Denver. That was my focus. That was within my power to accomplish.

And if I was going to beat the breakfast crowd, it meant getting out of bed ten minutes ago. Holding onto this purpose as though it were the rope, I was Alice, and the black hole was below my dangling feet, I left bed with an eagerness I hadn't felt in years. The sky flashed as I grabbed my towel and hurried toward the bathroom. This time, I anticipated a werewolf would be stretched out across the threshold—I jumped over him in the dark and went on my way.

I couldn't help but notice the door to Damon's room was tightly closed. Either he was still sleeping or he didn't want me bothering him. The message in that cheap, patterned wood was clear. *Stay away. Leave me alone. Don't come near.*

Sadness drifted closer, like a tentative ghost, but I turned my back on it and continued on. I showered and dressed in record time. The air smelled of lilac shampoo and coconut body wash.

Back in my room, just as I finished brushing my damp hair, voices drifted down the hallway. I frowned at the werewolf, who lifted his head and blinked at me with his yellow eyes. His lack of alarm was reassuring. I left the weapons drawer untouched and went to investigate.

Lyari and Collith sat at my kitchen table.

Apparently, I needed to command the Guardian to leave my side in order to shower or change—it was clear she'd done neither. Next I glanced at the male sitting beside her and realized his eyes had dropped to the sapphire around my neck. I fought an irrational urge to cover it. *I'm wearing this for safekeeping*, I meant to say. Something held the words at bay. Perhaps the possibility that he'd ask why I wasn't wearing the crown then, too. For that, I would have no answer. "Coffee?" I blurted instead.

The corner of Collith's mouth twitched. "Please," was all he said.

In that instant, I couldn't help but notice he was wearing modern clothing again. Collith Sylvyre was just as alluring in jeans as he was in leather pants. A simple but form-fitting dress shirt covered the rest of him. The brown material made his eyes more green than hazel. His hair gleamed like silk.

"Black, right?" I asked. My cheeks felt hot. I didn't dare meet Collith's gaze. The werewolf's claws clicked against the linoleum as he walked over to the corner and laid down. "Lyari, how do you take your coffee?"

"I don't depend on caffeine for my energy," she said. Her voice was flat. Her eyes shifted between the window and the doorway, always moving, always checking.

"Lots of cream and sugar, got it. I'll make sure it's as sweet as you."

I grabbed another mug and set it on the counter with a thud that managed to sound chipper. Collith's face gave nothing away, but the bond brightened with his amusement, like a porch light streaming through some summer evening. As I went about making a fresh pot, he turned so Lyari was only able to see his profile. *Why do you have to antagonize her?* his expression seemed to ask.

Because it's fun, mine said back. The small machine made a gurgling sound. I poured three cups, replaced the pot, and reached for the cream. "So what brings you here, dear husband?" I asked, dumping in so much that the coffee was almost white.

Thunder growled through the walls. I set a mug down in front of Lyari, and Collith accepted the one I held out to him. "If you're going to see the pack, you'll need backup," he said bluntly. Getting a straight answer from him was so unexpected that, for a moment, I just stood there without comprehending his words.

When I did, though, I frowned in annoyance. The only way Collith could've known about my private conversation with Laurie was the Guardian who'd been there to overhear it. It meant that I couldn't completely trust Lyari. Regardless, I'd be foolish to turn down Collith's offer.

I picked up my own mug and walked to one of the doorways. I looked back at Collith. "Can I talk to you for a second?"

"Of course."

Lyari had half-risen from the chair, about to protest, I imagined. I glared at her. "Lyari, I command you to go take care of yourself. Shower, put on some clean clothes, sleep. Come back when you're back at full strength. Understood?"

Any other day, she would've given me the rough side of her tongue. Not in the presence of her precious king, though. "I understand," she ground out. As if to remind me of how she felt about my position over her—she hadn't had a chance to react to my invasion of her privacy, either—the faerie held her mug over the sink and slowly dumped out the coffee I'd made.

And here I was, thinking maybe we'd started to feel civil toward each other. Silly me.

With a taunting smile, my Right Hand shimmered out of view. Any irritation her antics might've caused was overshadowed by the impending conversation with Collith. Wanting to stay occupied, I hurried back to my room and pulled an old suitcase from the closet. Once it rested on my bed, splayed like an open book, in went a pair of jeans. These were followed by a maroon hoodie that my mom had loved. The front of it read UNIVERSITY OF DENVER in white letters. Collith had entered quietly. He looked on from where he leaned against the wall, arms crossed loosely over his chest.

"Why do you want to come?" I asked without looking in his direction. The faerie's cool presence filled this small space, making it impossible to forget he was there. "To protect your investment?"

He could've asked me why I cared or why this mattered. It was kindness, I suspected, that he didn't. "If that's what you'd like to believe, fine, we can go with that," my mate said simply.

Despite the challenge in this response, his voice was soft. Caressing. Taken off guard, I turned toward him. Big mistake— Collith had stepped closer without my realizing. I felt the connection between us, a subtle crackle traveling like a current. Now my hand formed a fist to stop myself from tracing the edge of that jaw, from discovering the feel of his hair and skin.

"We're leaving at noon," I told him. My voice sounded uneven. "Well, that is, if Bea lets me. I'm heading to the bar to explain everything in person."

The Unseelie King had started bending toward me, but after I spoke, he stopped and pursed his lips. The tiny movement just drew my attention to his mouth. "I'll probably need more time than that. If you really need to leave that soon, summon me when you get to the pack, please, or a little before," he said.

I forced my eyes up to his. "Fine. No problem. I'll see you later, then. Will you fill Lyari in on the plan, when you see her?"

I didn't wait for Collith's response. Feeling like a coward, I grabbed my keys and rushed into the hallway. "I'll be back soon," I told the werewolf. His unhappy whine followed me out.

High above, the clouds were nearly black. I put my head down against the wind and got into my truck. It wasn't until halfway to town that the storm hit. Rain lashed against the windshield and sent the wipers into a frenzy. Cautiously, I drove down Main and took my time parking in front of Bea's.

The conversation with her went as well as could be expected.

"Denver, huh? If I ask you why, are you just going to lie to me again?" she asked without looking up. Her desk was covered in payroll paperwork. I felt the line between us, which I'd been drawing with every half-truth, evasion, and outright falsehood, get a little thicker.

"It's for Damon. I don't even know why, exactly. I think he's hoping to get some answers there."

At this, Bea heaved a sigh. She adjusted her grip on a pen and finally glanced at me. The lamplight made her gray braid glitter with silver strands. "Maybe he's not the only one that'll find something. Fine, you can take the time. I'll make changes to the schedule so your shifts are covered."

Something in my chest loosened. "Thank you, Bea. Really."

She waved me away. "Yeah, yeah. Be safe and send me updates."

"Done and done," I said, wishing for the thousandth time that I could embrace her without all the consequences.

I said my goodbyes to Cyrus, Ariel, and Gretchen. Angela shot me a glare, of course, and Ian leered from his usual booth. Did he ever, like, actually do police work? After that, I stopped at Adam's to see if he had time for a training session. His business partner was there, for once, and they were elbows-deep in an engine. I left without a lesson and fighting a sense of restlessness.

When I got home, the van was gone. Strange that I hadn't passed Damon on the road, I thought. Worry fluttered in my stomach. *Don't panic just yet, Fortuna. Maybe he needed something from town. Maybe he needed to get out of the house.*

The morning crawled past. Eventually, it stopped raining and the sky's mood lightened enough to allow sunlight through. Ten o'clock arrived. Eleven o'clock lingered. Noon came and went. I called Damon over and over again. I sent texts that went from casual, to angry, to hysterical. My knee jiggled no matter what I did. Dishes, laundry, vacuuming, scrubbing the toilet. The truck was already loaded with my suitcase and a cooler for the motel room. Every time I walked past his spot on the couch, the werewolf fixed his bright eyes on me. He didn't need the ability to speak in order to communicate his worry.

All the while I was having flashbacks to two years ago. Had Damon been taken again? What if the assassin found him? Between bouts of panic and reason, I kept thinking, *Never should have sent Lyari away. Never should have let my guard down.*

I was literally dialing the sheriff's office when there came the squeal of bad brakes. I rushed to the front door just as Damon shut it behind him. "Where have you been?" I snapped, forgetting that I'd vowed to be calm. "I told you we were leaving at noon."

Damon didn't look at me. He scratched his head—he needed a haircut so badly—and slipped down the hallway. Too thin, he was still too thin. He made hardly any sound as he walked. I stood there, fidgeting some more, and debated whether or not to stomp after him. Before I could decide, Damon came back out wearing a backpack. He brushed by me again and headed outside, leaving the door open. This time I did follow him.

"You can't do that to me, Damon," I said.

Silence permeated the yard as he moved to put his bag in the backseat. Before he could, the werewolf leapt past him and into the backseat. Damon only faltered for a moment. "He's coming to Denver?" my brother asked.

I locked the house up, climbed into the driver's seat, and slammed the door a tad harder than necessary. After a brief hesitation, Damon got in the passenger side. "Yes," I said shortly, digging in my pocket for the folded piece of paper. "Which reminds me, we need to make a stop along the way. Will you plug this address into Google Maps?"

Damon frowned. He didn't reach out to read or take the paper. "What kind of stop?"

Once again, the well of patience inside me went dry. Its bottom was nothing more than wet clay and slimy walls. With a single flick, I tossed the paper into Damon's lap. "From now on, you will tell me when you're leaving the house and where you're going," I said. "If I'm not around, you will call or text me. I know the past two years were hell on you, and that's bound to have some effects, but they weren't exactly a party for me, either. So you don't get to disappear and make me relive it all over again. Got it?"

He turned his face toward the window. There was nothing to see that he hadn't already seen a million times, but apparently he'd rather look at grass and trees than me. "Sure."

"Nope. You have to look in my eyes and say, 'I got it.' That's where we're at now."

Now Damon faced me, his dark eyes flashing. Oddly enough,

I preferred his ire over his indifference. "I got it," he said through his teeth.

"Fantastic. Now read the goddamn address and put it into Google Maps."

I could practically hear the profanities burning through Damon's head as he obeyed. He yanked out his phone and scrolled to the app, drawing my gaze to his nails, which had been chewed so much the skin looked red and raw. I immediately looked away and cleared my throat. Weapons. We'd need weapons.

I felt Damon go still when I took the Sig Sauer P365 out of my ankle holster. I'd bought it a couple years ago, shortly after he went missing. While I was infinitely less helpless than most, there was something comforting about sleeping with a gun in your nightstand.

Without a word, I checked the safety and shoved a new magazine—I'd emptied the last one during target practice—into place. It gave a satisfying click. I put it in the center console where it would be more accessible.

I was not a gun person. In fact, more often than not, I felt an aversion to them. It was probably my Fallen blood, what with its natural tendency to avoid technology. But a gun would've come in handy at the Unseelie Court, and I wasn't going to make that mistake again.

What had Damon asked again? Oh, right, about the stop we needed to make.

Laurie's words chose that moment to ring through my head. *Werewolves are unpredictable, little Nightmare. Best keep your distance. Especially from a pack.* Now it was my fear that tainted the air, and I started the truck quickly, hoping Damon hadn't sensed it.

As we left our little house behind, I held the steering wheel with a white-knuckled grip and finally answered, "It's the kind of stop that requires bullets dipped in holy water."

CHAPTER TWELVE

*a*n hour into the drive, so close to Denver we'd already seen several signs for it, we had to stop for gas. Even after the pump handle popped, though, I lingered there against the truck. I couldn't deny—even from myself—that I was avoiding being alone with Damon. He'd been utterly silent so far, and there was no radio station or podcast in the world that could drown out his resentment.

While I had no regrets about killing Jassin, the constant reminder of that night wasn't exactly fun for me. This, I realized, was probably part of Damon's punishment. He would never let me forget.

"So be it," I muttered, ignoring the strange look a woman shot my way. I glared at her. She walked past an SUV parked at the pump on the other side of ours, drawing my attention to it.

Through the concrete pillars, I could see into the backseat. A boy and a girl sat there, clearly siblings, judging from their similar features. The boy must've been playing some kind of game, because his head was bent, all his focus on something below my line of sight. Suddenly he jerked upright, scowling, and said something that made his sister laugh. As I watched, she ruffled the small boy's hair. He shoved her playfully in response.

My eyes stung. I blinked, over and over, trying to banish the pain. With a brisk movement, I removed the nozzle and put it back into the holder. Then I turned my back on the other vehicle and got back into mine.

As had been the case since we left Granby, Damon had his knees drawn up to his chest, his face turned toward the road. "I don't want to visit a werewolf pack after dark," I told the back of his head. "We'll have to stop at a motel tonight. Are you hungry?"

His continued silence didn't surprise me. Fine. Gas station food it was. I grabbed my wallet, ran inside, took some random snacks off the shelves, paid the pimply boy behind the register, and ran back.

There was a motel down the road. I drove for thirty seconds or so, then pulled into the tiny parking lot. Damon waited in the truck while I checked us in. The desk clerk was a woman with a smoker's voice and cropped red hair. She handed me an old key and mumbled, "Take a right. Go up the stairs. Can't miss it."

What is your werewolf policy? I almost asked. This seemed like the kind of place that didn't care about an enormous wolf in one of its rooms as long as the bill was paid. I wordlessly accepted the key and exited the shabby lobby.

Damon noticed me come out and reached for his things. The werewolf made a whine of excitement. He jumped out the instant I opened the door. I grabbed the gun and shoved it back into its hiding place. Then, with my suitcase in one hand and a plastic bag full of food in the other, we climbed the metal stairs. Our room was smack dab in the middle. Damon stared at his shoes and fidgeted as I set everything down to unlock it. The wolf panted.

The door creaked open like a horror movie, and instantly, cold fingers reached for us. Though I was Fallen and more insusceptible to low temperatures than a human, it still bothered me. Frowning, I threw my burdens onto the closest bed and went to investigate the heater. The dial was turned to OFF. I released a breath of relief and cranked it as high as it would go.

Once that was done, I searched for something to use as a bowl. *Should've thought of it when I was packing.* The ice bucket! I grabbed it and filled it at the sink. Then I brought it over to the werewolf, who'd taken it upon himself to smell everything in sight. I couldn't imagine they were all pleasant smells. Once he saw the water, though, he forgot his investigation.

"Are you going to hunt later?" I mused out loud, watching his shaggy head lower. "How long can you go without eating, anyway?"

The wolf's ear flicked. It was the only sign that he'd heard me at all. Now I looked around at the faded motel room. It was so quiet that I could hear voices through the wall. Apparently, our neighbors were trying to decide who got the last of their cocaine. The werewolf's tongue made lapping sounds as he drank his fill. Damon walked back and forth, trying to get a signal on his phone. Who did he have to text, I wondered?

I sank onto on the bed I'd inadvertently claimed—the springs squeaked—and sighed. Our sad dinner was spilled across the bedspread beside me. I ripped the silvery wrapper off a Pop-Tart and took a bite. "Still hate me, huh?" I asked around a mouthful of artificial flavor.

The words floated in the space between us in the form of white clouds. Damon gave up on a signal and focused on pulling food out of the bag. It was as if the movements were the whole of his universe. It became apparent that once again I would receive no answer.

The seconds kept ticking by, and I imagined Nym's clocks, those ever-moving hands. The image of those siblings at the gas station also lingered in my mind. "Well, hate me all you want, I guess," I said finally. "No matter how much you piss me off, I'll always love you."

This affected him, at least. In his following silence, I sensed my brother's grief, his fury, his confusion. "I'm going to get ice," Damon muttered after a few seconds. He didn't even give me a chance to respond—with those empty words, he was up and out the door. The wolf bolted from his place on the floor and managed to slip through before it closed.

The Pop-Tart had turned to ash. I forced myself to finish it, then put the other half back into the plastic bag. Clenching my hands into fists, I bowed my head and strove to breathe evenly. *I will not cry, I will not cry.*

"Maybe you should've let me pick the accommodations."

"Jesus Christ, you scared me," I gasped, turning to Collith. My heart felt like it was a marathon runner, lurching at the sound of the starting gun, pounding toward the opposite horizon. The solemn-faced king stood in a corner of shadows, watching me.

"I know I said to use my name when you reach the werewolves' den, but I thought I would check on you in the meantime," he said without preamble. "There's still an unaccounted for assassin, after all."

I didn't believe him. Didn't believe that an assassin was the only reason he'd come. But he'd shown me several kindnesses over the past few weeks—I felt like I owed him some of my own. "Where are your guards?" I searched the room as though Nuvian would be hiding behind the bed. "What do they think of you leaving Court so often without protection?"

"They aren't far," Collith admitted, stepping closer. "They're just getting better at pretending to give us privacy."

Of course. I wasn't sure why it disappointed me that Collith hadn't left the Guardians behind. Whatever he was to me, or whatever there was between us, he was always a king. First and foremost. "How kind of them."

The bond quivered. When Collith spoke next, his voice was soft and surprisingly tentative. "Actually, Fortuna, there is another reason I'm here. I wanted to ask... that is, the thought occurred to me... may I join you tonight?"

My heart immediately responded, picking up speed once again. Whether it was from fear or excitement, though, even I couldn't tell. Maybe the two were too closely aligned when it came to Collith.

"Okay," I said. Maybe he hadn't allowed himself to expect anything, because I caught a glimmer of surprise. Now that I was looking at him, I couldn't pull away. I studied this faerie yet again—the slant of his nose, the curve of his jaw—and enjoyed his subtle beauty.

"Shall I fetch a towel?" Collith offered.

"Uh, what? Why?"

"To wipe off the drool on your chin, of course."

Heat rushed to my cheeks. I threw a pillow at Collith, which he dodged effortlessly. When he straightened, I saw that he was smiling. It happened so rarely I found myself staring yet again. "Hold up, did you just make a *joke*?" I teased.

Collith ignored this. He perched on the edge of the bed, close to me, and raked his hair away from his face. The ring he always wore flashed in the light. "What would you like to do, my lady?" he asked. "Watch a movie? Go for a stroll?"

I fiddled with my shirt sleeves. "Don't judge me, but I was thinking of going to bed—I want to get an early start. The sooner Damon can find what he's looking for in Denver, the sooner we can go home."

"I could never judge you," Collith said, getting up to press the light switch. Darkness flooded the room, but yellow light from the parking lot filtered through the curtains. Collith's dim outline moved toward the bed as I hurried to get under the covers. "When I was a teenager, I used to sleep past noon every weekend. It drove my mother insane."

I liked hearing about this side of him. It was foreign and thrilling to picture my reserved, mysterious mate in the human world. Growing, changing, becoming. It made him less... frightening.

The mental image dissipated at the sound of Collith's clothes whispering against his skin. *He's taking his shirt off*, I realized. I told myself we weren't in high school. A guy taking his shirt off shouldn't get me hot and bothered. But my heart didn't get the memo—it felt like a car with sabotaged brakes. Careening out of control. About to crash.

My thoughts cut short when the floor moaned and the covers lifted again. Collith's weight made the mattress dip. The sheets made a rustling sound as he got comfortable. Once Collith had gone still, he was silent. I still needed to brush my teeth, but I didn't move.

I laid on my back, hands folded on my stomach. It probably looked as unnatural as it felt. Could faeries see in the dark?

This isn't the first time you've slept next to each other, I reminded myself. It was still so new, though, that I felt like a live wire.

I tried to concentrate on something, no, *anything* else. Once I managed to untangle my thoughts from Collith, I remembered that my side of the bed was beside the window. If I turned, just a little, I was gazing up at sky. The moon hung up there like a bright Christmas ornament.

Cool fingers brushed mine.

In an instant I forgot the moon existed. I looked down at our joined hands, my breathing too hard. I was very careful to avoid Collith's eyes. Had Oliver ever made me feel this way? I probably would've remembered if he had. What made this faerie different? Was it just lust? Or maybe it was the part of me that had always felt out of place, responding to someone else who felt the same?

Slowly, Collith let go of my hand, only to trail his fingertips along the underside of my arm. The sensation it created was unsettling and arousing, somehow. Without thinking—my body was starting to take over, now—I raised my gaze to his. Desire and fear warred within me. Even now, Collith didn't say anything, and he just stared back with those eyes that saw too much. He was letting me make the choice, just as he had last time I'd let him get close. What if I did let something happen? What if I did open this door?

It meant acknowledging that I felt something for him. Letting him inside my head. He would see everything. The best and worst parts of me. What if it changed his own feelings? And after... what came after? Would he expect us to spend every night together, like a normal married couple? Would I be able to close my mind again, claiming some semblance of privacy and self?

"You could ask me, you know," Collith murmured, startling me. His fingers didn't stop their tortuous antics. Up and down, skimming my skin as though it was the glassy surface of a lake.

I licked my lips. "Ask what?"

"All those questions rolling around in your head. You could ask me, every single one, and I'll try to answer."

"You haven't exactly been forthcoming before now," I reminded him. It was a reminder for myself, too. I had vowed there would never be anything real between us. Not after the way he'd forced himself into my life, or stood by during the tribunal, or remained silent so many times when one simple answer could've spared us both so much pain.

Collith didn't try to deny it. "I'm working on that. In fact, I'll prove it. Ask me a question and I swear I'll answer."

His offer made my heart quicken for a different reason now. For the first time, the door to Collith was open. I'd lost count of how many times my mind had burst with confusion, curiosity, or frustration around him. Usually it was all three at once. Here was a chance to bring at least one of them closure.

There were hundreds of things I could've asked him. About

why he'd killed the previous king, about his history with Viessa, about his feud with Laurie. A new one popped into my head, though, and it wouldn't relent.

"What's your biggest regret?" I asked. Immediately after I said it, a frown pulled at my mouth, more from consternation than the solemn nature of the question.

"I can't answer that."

His expression didn't hold any shame or regret. My stomach dropped. Had I seriously been duped into trusting a faerie? Even worse, *this* faerie? *Fortuna, you moron.* Life had taught me a lesson about them, long ago, and I'd been a fool to forget it. I jerked my arm away and spoke in a hiss. "You just said—"

"I'd have to show you."

At this, I paused. The rising tide of fury evaporated into mist. "Oh. Okay."

"Would you mind if we waited for a better time? It's... complicated," Collith concluded. The request sounded sincere enough. Still, suspicion hovered. Was he just trying to avoid answering the question now in hopes I'd forget about it? I nodded. Collith appraised me. "I know it's not exactly fair, but will you tell me yours?"

"My biggest regret?" I clarified.

"Yes."

Part of me wanted to say, *I can't answer that.* Just to jam Collith's own medicine down his throat. The other part of me couldn't help but actually think about it. Just as I had a hundred questions, so I had a hundred answers. I could randomly choose one and it would be truth. I regretted not waking up sooner the night my parents were murdered. Letting Damon be taken by a faerie. Killing the Leviathan. Failing to save Shameek. Murdering a human.

Every single one would burn like acid in my mouth.

"Right now?" I turned on my side and faced Collith. "In this moment, my biggest regret is how you and I started."

Either Collith didn't notice my specific wording or he didn't care. It was the truth, and that was all that mattered. Understanding softened the lines around his mouth. The bond tying us together flared with color and sensation. In that next moment, we were remembering it together. I felt his mind alongside mine as the memories trickled past.

The cold bars of a cage gripped in my fists and the confident hum of Collith's voice—the afternoon we'd met at the black market. The smell of damp soil and the vivid green of trees all around—the night we said our vows. A whip coming down, over and over—the moment I banished Collith from my heart forever. Our beginning, our middle, our now.

"I wish I'd met you at that bar," Collith whispered. "I've actually imagined it. Some alternate universe in which random business brought me to Granby, and I had an inexplicable craving for a cheeseburger."

"You walk in and see… Angela," I said, trying to lighten the mood. Collith cracked a smile at the mention of my rude co-worker. "She keeps shoving her boobs in your face every time she puts something down. You're so desperate for a new server, so desperate for escape, that you switch booths. Into my section."

"You're rude to me at first. Because it's you. But I'm so unflappable—"

"Unflappable? Seriously?"

"—that I eventually wear you down. You agree to meet for coffee the next morning."

Despite myself, something in me responded to the warmth in Collith's voice. "And I do. You're not a vague, arrogant asshole."

"You're not a prejudiced, snarky brat."

"We stay until well after our drinks are gone. I have a white chocolate mocha," I finished softly.

Collith smiled again. I noticed how it made the corners of his eyes crinkle. "It doesn't get more specific than that. So it *must've* happened."

Beyond our cocoon of dark pasts and shrouded futures, the wind strengthened. It made the flimsy walls of the motel groan. Collith dared to run the edge of his finger down my cheek. My eyes closed of their own volition, enjoying the touch. It was such a new and addicting sensation. "Fortuna," he said. Just my name. My eyes fluttered open and met his gaze.

We met halfway.

Just as we were about to collide in a mindless burst of tongues and heat, Collith drew back. He cupped my jaw in a hold that managed to be firm and gentle at the same time. I started to say something—probably about to embarrass the hell out of myself—and he kissed the corners of my lips, teasing me, then moved on to my cheeks, eyes, nose, and forehead.

My mouth was the last. Collith brushed his lips against mine. Once. Twice. On instinct, I opened my mouth, seeking more. He complied instantly, and we tasted each other for the first time since that hazy makeout session at Olorel. God, he was a good kisser.

A few seconds later, though, I was the one to pull away. I cast a reluctant glance toward the door. "Damon could…"

Collith cocked his head. His eyes went distant. "He's in the parking lot. Talking to someone on the phone."

"Oh. I didn't realize you could…" I tapped my ear lamely.

After I said this, I felt Collith's soothing essence slide along the bond, trying to find me. Somehow I knew that he was trying to determine whether I was uncomfortable. If *he* made me uncomfortable. "We don't have to do anything," Collith said after a notable pause. "I'm happy just being near you."

"Why?" I couldn't stop myself from asking. "You barely know me, Collith."

He picked up his pillow and repositioned it. When he laid back down, part of him was in the patterned glow coming in through the curtains. His eyes were alight with gentle humor. "At the risk of incurring your wrath, I would actually disagree with that statement," he said.

"You bastard," I whispered back. Then, catching Collith off guard, I grabbed the waistband of his pants and yanked him against me. This time, there was no slow build-up or skilled teasing. We made out like two teenagers on prom night.

Every second, every kiss was a brick flying out of the wall I'd built. Caught up in Collith, I touched him without restraint. He wore no shirt, making it easy to trace the lines on his stomach, drag my hands around to his back, and run my palms up his arms in equal turns. I delighted in the feel of his bare skin. Reveled in how hard his body was and how sharp the ridges of his muscles.

Suddenly I could feel them—the Unseelie Court. Their shrieks of elation and excitement filled my head. I should've been mortified. But I was drowning in sensation. In him. "Put that wall back, love," Collith breathed against my chest. I arched back, trying to urge him on, but he wouldn't move from that spot. I let out an inpatient sound and squeezed my eyes shut to focus.

A wall. It was so long that the ends disappeared into the horizon. This structure wasn't brick, it was concrete, with barbed wire along the top. Anyone who tried to climb over it would be cut and caught. Couldn't dig, either, because a witch had cursed the earth beneath.

I opened my eyes. *There, I put the wall back, are you happy?* I was about to say. When my gaze met Collith's, and I registered what he intended, those words vanished.

In the brief time I'd been rebuilding the damned wall, Collith had moved down the bed so that his mouth poised over the apex of my thighs. His capable fingers undid the button on my jeans in a single movement. As we stared at each other, the heat within me kept going lower and lower. I gave him a single nod, and as Collith's eyes turned to emerald fire, I lifted my hips to help him remove the pants completely.

The sound of them hitting the floor was stark. I didn't take my focus off Collith. His breath, touching me softly, was torture. Slowly, one at a time, my knees fell to the side in a blatant invitation. Need overwhelmed any shyness I might've felt otherwise.

He accepted it.

Just the first touch of his tongue nearly sent me over the edge. My head tipped back. I clutched the sheets as though they were the only thing keeping me grounded. I didn't know whether to beg for more or plead with him to stop.

More. Definitely more.

I'd no sooner finished the thought when the heat building within me imploded.

A mindless cry shattered the air. Mine, I knew in some distant part of me. The wave of pleasure kept going, and going, and going. There was something different about this orgasm. More powerful. Maybe because this was no dream, no event happening inside my head. For a few seconds, all I knew was the sensation sweeping through my body. I felt blind.

Afterward, I just laid there, feeling dazed and drowsy. Collith made his way back up the bed and I shifted onto my side to face him.

The moonlight could reach my mate now. It revealed the hills and planes of his face and torso... but it wasn't enough. Something came over me—I couldn't have defined it if anyone asked—and now it was my turn to reach for a button. For a few seconds, I just toyed with it. My knuckles brushed the skin just above his hard cock. Collith was very, very still.

I surrendered to the impulse. Once the button was free, my gaze flicked up to Collith's. In a wordless request, I tugged at the zipper. A faint smile curved his mouth as he complied by taking his jeans off. He managed to make something that should've been awkward into a moment rife with anticipation. "The briefs, too," I heard myself murmur. Collith took those off without comment. Afterward, he didn't reach for the blankets to cover himself. He just stretched out beside me, unembarrassed and without expectation.

His body was so different from Oliver's, who was the only other male I'd seen completely naked. Leaning close, I traced Collith's collarbone, then did the same to the bars of his ribcage. No matter how intriguing the rest of him was, however, I was always drawn to his face. When our eyes met again, I reached up and touched his scar. He flinched. I expected him to retreat, but he stayed where he was, looking for all the world like a statue in a garden. "You're beautiful," I told him.

In response, Collith shifted so he was on top of me. His elbows caged me in. When I made no protest, he lowered himself enough so that we were skin to skin. The sensation of his full weight was heady. As though he were claiming me. Saying, without words, that he was going to have me in any way he wanted. I couldn't get enough of touching him. My hands tangled in Collith's hair, over the curves of his shoulders, down his hard arms, around to his smooth back. Slowly, he began to rock back and forth. His hardness pressed down, taunting and teasing.

When I felt like I was on the verge again, I slid my hand down between us. Collith raised himself a little to give me better access. I trailed my fingers along his velvet length, all the way up, until I reached the tip. Collith's breathing changed. Smiling, I moved my hand back down to grasp him fully, and adjusted until I could feel him poised against me. I was so wet that all it would take was a single thrust.

I wondered if his thoughts echoed mine. Were we really about to do this?

Footsteps sounded on the walkway outside.

"Shit, Damon," I hissed. Collith was already rolling away and hurrying to put his pants on. He moved with preternatural speed. By the time Damon opened the door and lifted his head, we were the picture of nonchalance. Collith sat in a chair against the wall, and I was tucked in the bed, knees drawn to my chest. I was winded, breathless, like I had just run for miles. Collith must've turned on the TV as I rushed under the covers, because voices blared from the speakers, hopefully hiding the sound of my ragged gasps.

Oh, God, where were my pants? Could Damon see them?

My brother took in the scene before him. The rumpled bedspread. Collith's naked torso. The pointed distance between us. Despite our efforts, it was painfully obvious he'd interrupted something. The hilarity of the situation suddenly struck me and it was all I could do not to start giggling hysterically.

When the silence became too long, I turned down the volume—if Damon asked me what we were watching, I honestly wouldn't be able to tell him—and casually asked, "Who were you talking to on the phone?"

My brother just ducked his head and hurried into the bathroom. We listened to the faucet squeak as he turned it. The sound of him brushing his teeth seemed strangely loud. Collith and I both looked at the TV, but I wasn't sure either of us actually saw what was happening on its screen. After a minute or two, Damon came back into the room, wiping his mouth, and got into the other bed. He gathered the blanket around himself like a shield and turned on his side, effectively putting his back to me. To us.

Well, at least he'd stopped treating Collith like a God.

I finally processed what we'd been watching—Miss Congeniality. The brightness and the noise was too much for me after I'd just had a thousand faeries crammed inside my skull. I reached for the remote. "Hey, do you mind if I turn this off?"

"Not at all. Although I do love a funny Sandra Bullock movie as much as the next faerie."

I appreciated Collith's attempt to ease the tension. I showed it by pulling him against me once he'd gotten settled again. Bedsprings creaked as Damon did the same in the other bed.

Taking advantage of the dark, Collith pressed his lips to my shoulder. It felt oddly intimate. "Good night, my gorgeous wife," he whispered. "By the way... I love the sounds you make when you come."

Glad he couldn't see my red face, I pulled the comforter so it was up to my chin. "Sleep well, Collith."

He noticed the use of his name; the slow heat of pleasure spread down our bond.

I'd never get any sleep if this kept up. I pretended to be focused on getting the pillow fluffed just right, but the girlish flutter in my stomach didn't go away. Of their own volition, Oliver's slurred comments about stars crept through my mind. *They burn so briefly, then fade so permanently.*

"You smell wonderful." Collith's voice was velvety with sleep.

His fingers curled around mine. I turned toward him, thinking to have a hushed conversation—maybe I could substitute a different question in place of the one I'd already asked. But the words hovering on my lips faded when I saw Collith's eyes were closed. I didn't look away. As I watched, the tension eased out of his body, like an ice cube melting. He was asleep.

That was when Oliver whispered to me again, almost as though he was lying right between us. *Is the bliss and the beauty worth the absence and the sorrow, Fortuna?*

I made an annoyed sound and shifted on the thin mattress. Moonlight fell across my face and I turned toward the window.

While Damon and Collith slumbered and dreamed, I laid there and stared up at the stars.

CHAPTER THIRTEEN

*S*leep eventually did claim me.

It felt like my eyelashes had turned to stone, weighing down my eyelids. Through that dirty glass of our motel room window, the stars turned into luminescent blurs, then faded into darkness.

I'd been coming to Oliver's dreamscape for years, and arriving in the meadow was as familiar as breathing. But this time, I opened my eyes and... everything I knew was gone. The long grass had vanished, along with the trees. There were no cliffs or open skies. No house or gently-lit windows.

Instead, there was a world of vibrant color and demanding noise. I saw a carousel, a photo booth, rows and rows of those games that were impossible to win, stands that promised deep-fried food. I could smell the offerings from where I stood and my mouth was already watering. Lights glowed neon through the night's shroud, declaring the names of rides. *The Wild Thing. Monster. Power Tower.* Music blared through the air. The peak of a roller coaster towered over everything.

As I took it all in, something small and warm lodged in my lungs, making it difficult to breathe. *Oh, Oliver.*

As though the thought summoned him, I heard footsteps behind me. I turned and watched my best friend close the distance between us. He looked thinner, somehow, though that couldn't be right, since he didn't exactly need to eat or drink to survive. A gray sweater hung on his frame, and his jeans looked looser than normal. But his golden hair shone like a halo and his eyes—normally a chocolaty brown—were nearly amber in this vibrant setting.

"So what first?" Oliver asked with a wide grin. I tore my gaze from him and stared at what he'd created again, my thoughts churning like bubbles in a current. Oliver stopped beside me, rocking back on his heels, hands in his pockets. He practically glowed with pride. "If I know you at all, you'll want to go on the—"

"Roller coaster," I managed finally. "Definitely the roller coaster."

In response, Oliver took my hand, his grip warm and firm. In wordless agreement, the two of us sprinted toward a walkway that led to *The Wild Thing's* gate. As we flew up the ramp, the moon stared down on us, surrounded by wisps of clouds. Oliver followed my gaze upward and frowned. In the next instant the clouds were gone, and thousands upon thousands of stars lit up the black expanse of sky. It was so beautiful that I found myself staring again. Oliver tugged at me with a satisfied glint in his eye. "Let's go," he said.

Unlike a ride in the real world, there was no line. We walked right past the person wearing an official-looking shirt and approached the waiting coaster cars, their plastic sides gleaming green. I was jittery with excitement; I couldn't remember the last time I'd been on a roller coaster.

We got into our seats, and Oliver helped me with the buckle before I could even reach for it. In doing so, his fingers brushed the bare skin at my waist—I was wearing a tank top that had ridden up when I sat—and I couldn't deny the pulse of longing that his touch sent through me. Our gazes met. Everything else became white noise.

Suddenly the line of cars gave a jolt, and I scrambled to grab hold of the bar in front of us. With that, we were moving. A clicking sound poked the silence like it was paper, and I tried not to dance with excitement. The cars climbed and climbed. I turned to look behind us. The fair was just distant bright dots now. I could feel Oliver watching me, his eyes unwavering, his lips curved into a smile he thought I didn't see.

Then, between one blink and the next, pink light washed over us. We'd reached the top. Up here, where the air should be so cold that it numbed us, there was only a balmy wind. For one shivering, surreal instant, we were part of the sky. Sinking with the sun. Weightless. I stared at the sliver of remaining light and felt something like peace.

The cars lingered at the peak for just a moment more... and then plunged.

I raised my arms in the air and screamed. The coaster flew around a curve and around a loop. I threw my head back and laughed, exalting in the feeling of abandon. There was nothing else but this sensation, like being tossed by a wild wave.

I'd forgotten what it was like to shrug off my burdens. To forget things like grief and responsibility. Oliver had given that back to me.

The ride ended too soon.

When I opened my eyes again, words of thanks on my lips, I saw that he was smiling. We sat in the car even after it had fully stopped. I kept a white-fingered grip on the bar, not trusting myself to have free hands. My best friend looked far too sexy with his wind-swept hair and glittering eyes. "What would you like to do next?" he asked, seemingly unaware of my inner turmoil.

I looked down, absorbed in fixing my tank top. "Why don't you choose?"

To this, Oliver's lip twisted in thought. We climbed out of the car, his hand on my waist for unnecessary support. The metal walkway made hollow sounds as it guided us back to solid ground. Oliver had something in mind; I could tell by his continued silence. Once we reached the path, he cupped my elbow—another unnecessary touch—and veered to the left. We walked together, our hips bumping, and this time I wrapped my arm around his waist. He dropped a swift kiss on the top of my head. Neither of us spoke. Maybe we both sensed the tightrope beneath our feet—one misstep and we wouldn't survive the fall.

A few seconds later, we arrived at the rows of games. More smiling employees stood by, waiting to hand us whatever we needed. Grinning like the child he'd once been, Oliver rushed up to the closest one. "Let's see what you've got, Sworn," he said.

I accepted a basketball from the man that looked suspiciously like Zac Efron, who I'd had a crush on during my middle school years. "Care to make this interesting?" I asked Oliver, quirking a brow at him.

"What did you have in mind?"

"If you win, I have to... read one of those books you're always trying to force on me." My nose wrinkled at the thought. Last month he put *Great Expectations* in my lap during a perfectly nice nap.

This made him laugh. It felt like I hadn't heard that sound in ages. "Done," Oliver said, taking a basketball of his own. "And if you win?"

A hundred silly possibilities flitted through my mind. There was one at the back, though, hiding in shadow. When I took hold of it and pulled it into the light, I sobered. But it was the one I wanted. "If I win, you have to pick up a paintbrush again," I answered softly.

If he'd been a faerie, I would've worried about the wording of such a bargain. If he'd been a faerie, he would fulfill his end by simply picking up a paintbrush, then putting it down a moment later. *Well, you didn't say I had to paint with it.*

But Oliver was no faerie. He was just... Ollie. Though my words dimmed the mood a little, he didn't get angry or upset. He just looked at me, holding the ball between his palms, a hint of sadness in his eyes. Within moments, he had it tucked away again. "All right. But you'll have to actually beat me first," he pointed out with an air of skepticism.

I rolled my eyes. "Just throw the ball, you ass."

He did. Then I did. We went through the motions over and over again, until our arms were sore and the game lost its thrill. All the while, we exchanged teasing insults and light-hearted taunts. Music echoed in my ears, along with the *click-click-click* of the roller coaster every time it made its climb. Oliver ultimately won, of course, even though I *had* been trying. He would know if I weren't. At least I'd planted the idea in his head, I told myself. Knowing that I wanted him to paint again might be enough to lead him back to the canvas.

Radiating smugness, Oliver informed me that I would be reading *Moby Dick*. "Kill me now," I groaned in response.

We left the game behind in favor of the one next to it. The hours passed. We tossed balls, darts, and water guns. Then, when it was close to the time I would have to leave him again, we ate. No, we gorged. We had corn dogs, caramel apples, funnel cakes. Everything and anything until my stomach ached. Oliver, however, seemed to have no limit. Even after I'd had too much, he dragged me to another stand. There was a spot of powdered sugar on his upper lip, but I didn't tell him or wipe it away. I liked seeing it every time I looked at him, a reminder that he was happy again. Even if it was only temporary.

"What next?" Oliver asked again once we'd tried every fair food in existence.

The idea of another ride made me nauseous, so I pulled him toward the photo booth. We ducked inside. As I sat, Oliver slid the red velvet curtain back into place. The seat was plushy and welcoming. He settled beside me and leaned toward the screen to look at our options. "Let's see… we can be on a beach… on a stage… in a living room…" he murmured.

"Doesn't matter to me," I said, watching him.

Oliver pressed the screen, opting for no background, and hurried to sit back. He put his arm around me as numbers counted down in front of us. Three. Two. One. The flashes came one after the other. Oliver continued to be extraordinarily unrestrained. He laughed and made faces and kissed my cheek. He smelled of cotton candy. I tried to stay focused, be in the moment, but my gaze kept going to his face. Admiring. Hoping. Worrying.

When the machine stopped, we stood and got out. The curtain whispered against my skin. Oliver reached for the pictures that had already printed and dropped into the slot. He looked them over and snorted. "You're so serious," he said, pointing to the last image. That was usually what I said to him. I peered over his shoulder to see. Oliver was looking right at the camera, his teeth gleaming in a smile, but the lens only caught my profile. I was staring at my best friend as if someone was about to take him from me.

No. My mind instantly rebelled against the thought. He was right here, warm and solid and unchanged. I hadn't lost him.

"Fortuna?" Oliver was looking at me now. His brow lowered with concern.

I forced another smile. "I'm great. Just tired."

Before I'd even finished speaking, the meadow replaced everything in sight—the rides, the games, the food stands—until it was all familiar again. It was still night, but the wide moon hadn't moved or changed, and it lit every corner of the dreamscape like a lamp. A large oak creaked and twisted into being behind me. As it finished growing, I plopped to the ground without hesitation. Oliver settled beside me with more grace. Movement drew my gaze to the sky, and I watched a flock of birds migrate past. They were huge, with white feathers that rivaled the moon in their luminescence.

Vines and leaves sprouted from the ground beside us, growing and stretching up and up until it was a bush. Small red things nestled within it. It wasn't until Oliver plucked one free and held it out to me that I realized what they were.

"Strawberry?" he offered. As he spoke, a checkerboard appeared between us, resting on a flat stone.

"Why, thank you." Lazily, I leaned back and traced my mouth with it. I had no desire to actually eat the small fruit; I was still so full from the stands. A drop of sugary-sweet water hovered on my bottom lip. My tongue darted in and out, absorbing the taste.

"I'm sorry," Oliver said suddenly.

Somehow I lost my grip on the strawberry and it went rolling through the grass. I frowned at him. "Sorry for what?"

He moved one of the checker pieces. I still felt the lingering high of running through the empty fairgrounds, though, and couldn't really concentrate on what he was doing. "For how I've been acting. I know it worried you," he said.

I hesitated. Something kept me from meeting his gaze. I tipped my head to stare at the sky again. "Did they come back? Your paintings?" I dared to ask.

"No."

That single word encompassed all the anguish he still felt. The anguish he'd been so careful to hide from me tonight. Without looking at him, I reached for his hand. Oliver let out a small sound, the quietest of sighs, and held onto me as though I was the one slipping away.

To my delight, I realized the constellations I had always been so bad at finding were suddenly moving. Orion held up his shield against a hulking foe, bracing himself. The clash was soundless and riveting.

But I still saw it when something moved in the trees. Something tall and quick. I jerked upright, frowning. "What was that?"

Oliver's face turned toward the trees for just a moment. His fingers clutched another checker piece, despite the fact that I wasn't paying the least bit attention to the game. "A deer, I think," he muttered.

"You think?"

"Come on, you're not even making this difficult." To soften the words, Oliver smiled again, teasing me.

The warm glow that had been infusing me all night was fading. Why was he lying to me? What was he hiding? I gently pulled my hand out of his and stood. "I better go, anyway."

Oliver didn't argue, but the stars sparked like dying light bulbs. "Do you want to take these with you?" he asked.

"What do you—" I started, then my gaze fell to his open hand. He held our pictures from the photo booth. I looked at them, saw the reversed expressions, and felt the flutter of agitation within me again. Though I kept fighting it, the feeling wouldn't leave me alone.

"Thanks. I'll see you tomorrow," I said with a weak smile. I slid the pictures into my pocket.

He tried to smile back, but I couldn't lie to Oliver; he knew something was wrong. "See you tomorrow, then."

As I walked away, the light of the stars went out completely. When I reached the spot that I always arrived at, I glanced back. Oliver stood there in his black meadow. He wasn't watching me, though—he was looking up at the empty sky. As though he were picturing the world beyond it. Longing for it. A world I'd forgotten to imagine him in since...

Since I met Collith.

CHAPTER FOURTEEN

I woke up being spooned by the King of the Unseelie Court.

In spite of his natural coolness, it was surprisingly comfortable. The sheets and the blanket were warm, creating a perfect contrast. I closed my eyes again, content to linger in the nest we'd made. Damon snored softly from his bed. It had been so long since we shared a room that I'd forgotten he did that. The sound brought back a dozen childhood memories and feelings. To avoid them, I shifted to my other side and put all my focus on Collith.

Morning light tiptoed through the curtains. It reached for his face as though it was naturally drawn to beauty. His scar—a mark I'd once thought startling and ominous—gleamed pink and silver. His eyelashes were dark and thick. The outline of his lips was so perfect and tempting. And how could someone have such smooth skin?

As the seconds ticked by, the drowsiness I felt was replaced by increasing... panic. Not of Collith, or Damon waking up and seeing us, or the unknowns of what waited ahead. No, what I found most terrifying was how much I liked it. How much I wanted to stay right there, in the circle of his arms.

Slowly, trying not to wake him, I pulled away and got out of the bed. The room hadn't warmed up much overnight—goosebumps rose all over my bare arms and legs. I swallowed a curse and searched for the pants Collith had so skillfully removed last night.

They were on the floor in front of the nightstand. I pulled them on, wincing at every sound I made, and shoved my hands into the pockets to tuck them in. There was a grainy lump in the right. I frowned and pulled it out. When my fingers uncurled, shimmering ashes drifted to the floor. *What the hell?*

I mentally reviewed the previous day, trying to figure out where the ashes could've come from. What they could've been. I wasn't typically in the habit of keeping anything in my pockets, since whoever had designed them didn't have practicality in mind. I never kept receipts...

Then a thought hit me. It felt like a blow to my chest, winding me, creating a helpless blaze of pain.

These were the jeans I'd worn at the fair last night.

In my mind's eye, I saw Oliver's outstretched hand. Saw the splash of color nestled in his palm. *Do you want to take these with you?*

"It's not possible," I whispered, staring down at the mess on the floor, unable to process what I was seeing. Those ashes couldn't be the remains of the pictures Oliver and I had taken in the photo booth. They just couldn't.

"Fortuna? Is everything okay?"

I jumped at the sound of Collith's voice. He watched me from bed, his head propped up in his hand. A lock of hair had fallen into his eye. My thoughts raced in a million different directions. The wall I'd built to keep out the Unseelie Court trembled, dangerously close to collapsing into a heap of dusty rubble. "You know, I forgot to check the oil yesterday," I blurted.

Collith's frown deepened. I edged toward the door. "I better do that before we get back on the road. Are you... coming? In the truck, I mean?"

He was still watching me much too closely. "Yes, if I'm welcome."

"You are," I chirped. "I'll be back in a bit. Feel free to use the shower and all that. What's mine is yours, after all, right?"

You're babbling again, Fortuna. My face felt hot as I turned away, grabbed my coat, and opened the door. When it swung open, a needle-filled wind greeted me, causing pinpricks of discomfort. I looked down, half-expecting to find the werewolf stretched across the threshold. The walkway was empty. I closed the door behind me and raised my gaze to the trees. They stood beyond the road, tall and lit from within from daybreak's glow. Maybe he wasn't coming back this time. I told myself it was probably for the best. It also meant we wouldn't have to put ourselves in the midst of a werewolf pack today.

I hurried down the stairs, zipping my coat as I went, and made a beeline for the truck. It was covered in a layer of frost. I debated letting it run for a while, but I didn't know this area or these people. A running vehicle with the keys inside was probably begging someone to steal it. Maybe I'd just sit in the cab for a while. Not to avoid Collith or Damon, of course. Sighing, I unlocked the doors and reached inside to pop the hood. I also grabbed a napkin from the glovebox.

Once the hood was propped into place, I pulled out the dip stick. The parking lot was still and quiet. Normally, this would give the worries in my head an opportunity to hiss and haunt, but there was something soothing about the mundane task in front of me. I thought of nothing else but the movements of my hands, which were fast reddening from the cold.

"Are you cross with me for the Sorcha incident?" a voice asked right next to my ear.

I straightened so quickly that my head knocked into the

hood. The pain was there and gone like the flash of a bulb, but I still rubbed it and glared at Laurie, letting that serve as an answer. He sighed as though my grudge was incredibly inconvenient. The black leather coat he wore creaked as he crossed his arms. "She's not worth the energy it takes to be upset, darling."

Before I could respond, a door opened above us. My gaze flicked up, just to see if it was Collith, but it was a man coming out of another room. He had dark stubble and an angular jaw. When I saw him, my heart and lungs froze.

A second later, I realized it wasn't who I'd thought. This man was alive, for one, and he was much burlier. Though I relaxed slightly, it took another moment to remember what I'd been doing. Checking the oil, right.

Laurie didn't miss a thing. "Did you know that human?" he questioned, inclining his head. The wind picked up again, pushing against my truck. It moaned.

"No. He just reminded me of... someone." I wiped the stick clean with the napkin. Laurie leaned his hip and shoulder against the side of the vehicle, a very clear statement, even if he didn't say a word. I focused fiercely on hood I was closing in an effort to avoid any flashes of memory. "The human I killed. During my third trial."

Silence answered this. I risked a glance at Laurie, who was appraising me. A strand of his white-blond hair blew across his face. With a swift, pale finger, he flicked it away. "Let me ask you something, my young, lovely queen," he said in that silken voice of his. "When you are in a room with a murderer, there are only two kinds of people. One is the killer. The other is the murdered. Which one would you rather be, at any given time?"

I glared at him as I shoved the dip stick back. "Laurie, that's not—"

Once again, something moved on the walkway of the motel, and I couldn't stop myself from looking up. Lyari glared back and descended the wobbly stairs.

"How did you know where I was?" I asked as she drew near. Truth be told, I'd forgotten that I had ordered her to come back until it was too late to do anything about it. I didn't exactly have her cell phone number.

"His Majesty came to Court a few minutes ago to address his duties. He told me the name of this... establishment." Lyari said the word like it was filthy. Her gaze darted to Laurie, but if she was surprised or displeased to see him, she didn't show it. She planted herself near me unceremoniously, one hand resting on the hilt of her sword. It struck me, then, that at some point I'd stopped viewing her as a threat. With Lyari at my back, I felt undeniably safer.

Judging from the tightness of her jaw, the feeling wasn't mutual.

Apparently there was some kind of bell or alarm everyone could hear but me. In the next minute, both Damon and the werewolf appeared. My brother threw his belongings into the back, then got into the backseat without a word. He'd left the door open, and our furry guest took advantage of this to claim a spot, as well. The wolf must've known we were close to his old pack, because his fur practically vibrated with anticipation. I couldn't deny the relief that spread through my chest at the sight of him. Clearly I was getting attached to this damn creature. *Not smart, Fortuna.* We were literally on our way to reunite him with his true family.

I glanced at Laurie, curious what he thought of all this. Throughout every new addition, he'd been uncharacteristically quiet. He stayed where he was against the truck, still and observant.

Collith was the last to arrive. He wore my backpack, which looked unnatural on him, somehow. He closed the office door with his back still to us. I knew the moment he smelled or sensed Laurie—his entire body tensed, as though he were a string on an instrument—and then he twisted to find the faerie.

Even though there was an entire parking lot between us, his voice lashed out like a whip. "What are you doing here?"

Laurie shoved his hands in his pockets and straightened, shirt whipping in the wind. "I'm here to help Fortuna, of course."

My mate's face was a thunderstorm. He came toward us, every step a promise of violence. I watched his shoes, uncertain of whether I should intervene. The air was thick with a history I knew nothing about. I held the truck keys too tightly; ridges along a key's edge dug into the fleshy part of my palm. Just as Collith opened his mouth I heard myself blurt, "Did you check us out?"

His grip was dangerously firm around a paper coffee cup in his hand. He noticed the direction of my gaze and handed it to me with a terse, "Yes."

The coffee's warmth immediately seeped through the paper. There must've been a fresh pot in the lobby. Doubtless Collith had paid for the room, too. The gesture affected me more than it should have. "Great. Thanks," I said. Thankfully, my voice sounded normal. "I guess we should get going, then. Is anyone hungry? We could swing through a drive-through or something."

Without another word, Collith set my bag into the cargo area and moved toward the passenger seat. He shut the door, buckled himself in, and pulled out his phone. For him, it was a surprisingly aggressive move, and his message was loud and clear. *Stay away from Fortuna.* Laurie smirked as he climbed into the back. Collith acted as though he didn't exist.

For a few seconds, I could only stand there and stare at the scene before me. I was about to get into a small vehicle with two faerie monarchs, a brother who loathed me, and a traumatized werewolf. It seemed like a lethal combination of ingredients that was sure to explode in my face. Lyari moved so she stood beside me. "You realize that vehicle has become a ticking bomb, yes?"

she remarked. Maybe reading minds was another ability she'd kept hidden; I'd have to ask one of these days.

For now, I took a brief, fortifying breath. Timidity wasn't my style and I'd be damned if a couple of faeries changed that now. "Then it's lucky I have you to protect me, isn't it? Also, sorry in advance about the smell. I tried to give Wolfie a bath once and he almost bit my head off. It helps if you breathe through your mouth."

"Delightful," I heard Lyari mutter as I closed the hood. I circled the truck and climbed into the driver's seat. After a moment, I heard her open the door. Laurie grumbled as they all shifted to make room for her. From the corner of my eye, I saw Collith's mouth curl in a vindictive smile. It was so unlike him that I was tempted to check whether a shapeshifter was trying to pass itself off as my mate.

Trying to hide my agitation, I drank some coffee and opened Google Maps. I selected the address Damon had typed in yesterday. As our route loaded, I put my coffee in one of the cup holders and shoved the key into the ignition. The engine rolled over with a reluctant series of sounds; neither of us were fans of the cold, apparently.

"My dear, we should really discuss what you're going to wear when we visit the wolves. I'm the reason she always looks so fabulous at Court," Laurie told the wolf conspiratorially. I didn't grace this with a response as I turned the wheel and got us back onto the county road. The Seelie King's nose wrinkled. "Goodness, what a *smell*. We should make an appointment for you at the groomer's, my good man. We'll tell them you're a Husky."

"Does he have an 'off' button?" Lyari demanded.

Laurie quirked a brow at her. "Should a request for silence pass Queen Fortuna's lips, I'll never speak another word. After all, I've seen her naked. It's impossible to deny her after such a magnificent experience."

Collith stiffened.

I almost slammed on the brakes. There was a car behind us, though, and I had no interest in killing everyone to make a point. So I met Laurie's gaze in the rearview mirror and made my voice steel and venom. "Listen to me closely, faerie. I'm not playing your games right now. It's obvious that you're here for Collith just as much as you're here for me, so drop the act and stop using our friendship to provoke him. And Collith, whatever happened between you two, put it aside for now. We have no idea what we're heading into and you were right about my needing backup."

As I spoke, my power filled the cab. It contained a plethora of smells, each one from someone's fears who sat in this confined space with me. Damp soil, sweat, perfume. Seemingly unperturbed, the Seelie King's eyes glittered. "I like the fire-cracker version of Fortuna," he observed. "Are you this assertive in bed?"

I glared at him. "I just told you to knock it off. Don't forget that I can have you pissing your pants in five seconds, *Your Majesty*."

"I dare you to try, Firecracker."

Jealousy spiked within the bond. "Is it your intention to alert our presence to every creature that resides in these mountains?" Collith asked sharply.

Laurie flashed him a brilliant smile. "Nope, just the wolves."

Collith's nostrils flared. Okay, it was time to try a different tactic. "What is the difference between werewolves and shapeshifters?" I asked quickly. "I've always wondered."

There was nothing subtle about the topic change, but Collith made a visible effort to regain control of himself. "When a shapeshifter becomes another creature," he began tightly, "it maintains the mental faculties from its true form. It also doesn't possess all of the traits the shape should have. A werewolf, when it changes, is mostly animal in how it thinks. It does have the abilities a wolf would—enhanced hearing and smell, incredible speed, etcetera."

Laurie opened his mouth, prepared to make some kind of snarky comment that would rile Collith, no doubt. My hand flew for the volume knob, and I cranked it up so high that whatever he said was drowned out by Post Malone. The wolf's ears flattened against his head and Lyari was scowling. Damon stared out the window as though there were a movie playing on the other side of the glass. I ignored everyone's discomfort and relaxed for the first time since leaving that warm bed Collith and I had shared.

The address wasn't far from the motel. Forty-five minutes later, after a stop for fast food and a bathroom break, GPS led us down a driveway that hadn't been tended to in a long time. The tires of my truck rolled and bumped over tree roots and potholes. At frequent intervals, there were signs warning us this was private land and trespassers were not welcome. No one acknowledged them.

I drove a little over one mile until we reached a cabin. The small structure looked just as neglected as the road leading up to it. The siding was a combination of caulk and dark logs, but it was all rotting. There was exactly one window and one door, from what I could see, and the grass around the cabin was dead and overgrown.

Everyone else clambered out the moment I shifted gears and killed the engine. Collith and I lingered in our seats, though. I wasn't sure why. The shivering silence wrapped around us like cloaks. Collith gazed at the horizon, seeing something I couldn't. Knowing Collith, he was probably plotting or planning, hoping to prevent the thousands of ways this could go wrong. Without looking at me he said, "I'll ask again. If I gave you a piece of advice, would you listen to it?"

I lifted one shoulder in a shrug. "Depends on the advice, I guess."

Now Collith focused on me. He had an excellent sense of dramatic timing, I thought. The intensity of his hazel eyes felt like a physical touch. "I know it's not your first instinct, but it would be wise to play nice today," he said. "These Fallen are just as dangerous as you and me. More so, as they can slice your throat open in less than a second. You may also want to avoid mentioning that a faerie from our Court took him—a war with the wolves is the last thing we need."

Or is it? I wondered, pursing my lips speculatively. *War equals a lot of dead faeries.*

Collith sighed. "I heard that, Fortuna."

"I don't want *you* dead," I protested. The admission startled both of us. Collith's eyes were suddenly far too bright as he watched me. I cleared my throat and reached for the handle. "We better get going. The pack could be miles into these woods, and I don't want to be caught out here after nightfall."

Collith nodded, and before he could say anything, I opened the door. The burst of fresh air was liberating; it felt like I'd been underwater for the last hour. I dropped to the ground, breathing deeply. The others had scattered. Laurie was talking on his cell—I really had to ask him who his service provider was—and Damon was kneeling in the dirt. Knowing him, he was probably curious about the quality of the soil.

Several yards away, the werewolf paced at the edge of the trees.

"There's no one inside," Lyari announced, walking toward us. She must've gone up to the cabin while Collith and I dallied. "But there's a trail. The wolves have used it recently."

At this, I hesitated. What if they were hunting?

Footsteps sounded behind me. I glanced back at the small gathering that had formed on the driveway. Collith, Lyari, Damon, Laurie, and the wolf. However unhappy they were with me or torn by other loyalties, the sight of them hardened my resolve. We were more than a match for any oversized dog that tried to eat us. "Someone with sharper senses than mine should probably take the lead," I said.

A king down to his bones, Collith immediately walked past me. I moved to follow and heard the others do the same. Our strange party cut through the front yard and around to the back. The branches of the trees beckoned to us like emaciated hands. The woods had not been kind to me recently—stolen brothers, goblins, and wendigos were never far from my mind—and it went against every instinct to approach. Hoping no one else noticed the instant of hesitation, I hurried after Collith, who had already plunged into the thicket. After me came Laurie, then Lyari, then Damon, then the wolf.

"I like the view from back here," the Seelie King murmured in my ear. His warm breath tickled. I elbowed him in the gut and kept moving, smiling at the sound of his pained grunt.

The trail Lyari mentioned wasn't difficult to find; the way had been traversed so many times that it had become bare, packed earth. The farther we went, the more this changed. Soon we were trying to make our way over thick and slippery mud—it was a good thing I'd worn my hiking boots. The ground made sucking sounds with every step, as though it were reluctant to give me up. No one spoke, which felt strange. Ominous. I arched my neck back to gauge how much daylight we had left. The sky was a deep, periwinkle blue. It hung like a curtain over the treetops. A hawk screeched overhead. It flew in wide circles, searching for prey.

As the morning marched into afternoon, I longed more and more for gloves. I exhaled on my fingers to bring feeling back into them. At the same time, my gaze fell on the wolf, who'd left his spot on the trail to stalk through the trees. Though it was difficult to tell beneath a layer of fur, the lines of his body seemed rigid. It occurred to me, then, that maybe it hadn't been anticipation I'd been seeing back in the motel parking lot. Now the way his hair stood on end seemed borne from dread.

Unease stirred in my stomach, like waking hornets in a nest.

"Fortuna," Collith said. There was something in his voice that made me snap to attention. But he wasn't looking at me. I followed his gaze and almost stumbled.

Two figures stood in the path.

It was a male and a female. The latter only had one arm, and on the other side of his body was a dangling shirt sleeve. His hair was long and greasy. A beard covered half his face, making it difficult to make out his features. What skin I could see was covered in faded scars. Despite his missing limb and ragged appearance, every inch of him was muscle. If there were a poster child for werewolves, he'd be it.

In contrast, the female was only what anyone could describe as mousy. Chin-length brown hair, black-rimmed glasses, and nondescript clothing. If she were standing next to me, I knew she would barely reach my shoulder. I was about to turn from the girl when I met her gaze. Those eyes pierced me, gray as slate and shining with intelligence. I should've known better than to dismiss her—every moment of my existence as a Nightmare was a reminder of how misleading and meaningless appearances could be.

The two of them were clearly waiting for us. As we got closer, a scent teased my senses, a combination of sweat and bonfires. All the trepidation I'd been hiding behind a wall of bravado and good intentions burst free. These were real, honest-to-God werewolves. They had a pack, which meant numbers we didn't have. They knew these woods. As Collith had said, they could form claws between one blink and the next.

"Easy, Fortuna," Laurie muttered. If he could smell my fear, it meant they could, too. I tried to breathe more evenly.

As we stopped a few yards away, the girl glanced at the wolf we'd brought. Her eyes went wide. *They must've spotted us earlier, though. Why is she surprised?* I thought with a frown. Then it hit me that she hadn't seen him in months—possibly years—and the wolf hadn't exactly been treated well during that time. Doubtless he was as changed as Damon had been when I first found him. As the girl quickly masked her reaction, I experienced a strange sense of kinship with her.

I'd expected the male to speak first, but instead, the girl addressed us. "One of our wolves recognized Finn," she said by way of greeting. "Astrid wants to see you. She's got some questions."

Finn. His name is Finn. I barely heard the rest. "Sure," I managed. Apparently she'd expected Collith to be our spokesperson, because that disconcerting gaze of hers returned to me and assessed anew.

The male was quicker than he looked. While I'd been distracted by his companion, he had crossed the space between us and reached for me. I caught a glimpse of the erection straining against his jeans before Adam and Dad's lessons came alive. I danced out of his reach.

My werewolf growled a warning and cold fury radiated down the bond. I heard Lyari's sword slide free of its scabbard just as Laurie materialized at my side. Suddenly I found myself surrounded by a small but formidable army. "What was that?" I asked calmly, more for everyone else's benefit than my own.

The male wasn't as foolish as he seemed—he stood very, very still now. But he didn't take his eyes off me and the bulge in his pants didn't shrink. My effect as a Nightmare was particularly potent on the weak-minded.

"He's just looking for weapons," the female explained. She addressed all of us with undisguised interest. "It's standard procedure."

"Standard procedure?" the bigger wolf echoed, a note of mocking in the words. He started to reach for me again.

"You don't want to do that," I said coolly. More sounds of warning erupted from the creatures around me. When my power filled the air, as it had done in the truck, they quieted.

This time, the silly wolf ignored any instincts that might've been whispering through his head. The instant his fingers wrapped around my wrist, he was mine. I smiled as he stared into my eyes, quickly realizing his mistake. Like the first hit of a heady drug, his fears fogged my mind. The flavor of something gritty and cold came to me, as well. Dirt. This tough-looking wolf was afraid of the ground. Finding himself beneath it. Being surrounded by it. Getting buried in it. And now, just like the rest of my victims, that's exactly what happened to him.

Instead of my face, the wolf saw his horror as reality. His eyes were wide and vacant. The fear already threatened to break his mind. I found it fascinating how differently each creature responded to my abilities—some froze, like this werewolf, and others physically reacted to the illusion.

"Whatever you're doing to him, stop it," the girl snarled. Before I could respond, still riding the high, Collith's gentle presence brushed against the wall in my mind. He didn't move, didn't speak, but it was jarring. I blinked and mentally withdrew. The big wolf instantly dropped to his knees, gulping in huge breaths of air.

I smirked down at him. "Sorry. Just standard procedure."

"It's times like this I wish I'd packed an engagement ring," Laurie remarked. Everyone ignored him.

I turned toward the girl whose name I still didn't know. She was openly staring at me. There was something in her eyes that I couldn't define. Not fear, or curiosity, or admiration. "What are you?" she breathed.

She was going to figure it out sooner or later, so there was no point in trying to hide it. If one of her packmates went after my heart, I'd know who to blame. "I'm a Nightmare."

There was a pause. Whatever the girl thought of this, though, she kept hidden. Her and Lyari had a lot in common—maybe if everything went well here, the two of them could go out for cocktails.

"Look, if you don't let us do a pat-down, Astrid will send more wolves. They'll be a lot scarier than us, too. It's that simple," the girl told us. No one spoke. She sighed, and the sound was much older than she looked. "What if I search the Nightmare and Clark does everyone else?"

I glanced at the other werewolf, who'd recovered from his terrible ordeal and stood silently, killing me a thousand different ways with his eyes. Moments ago, they'd been brown. Now they shone an unnatural blue.

"Fine," I said. The girl must've been anxious about keeping Astrid waiting, because she approached with no regard for the circle of uptight bodyguards around me. She made a sharp gesture to indicate that I should raise my arms. As I did so, I almost elbowed Laurie in the face. "Guys... it's getting a little hard to breathe here."

Both Collith and Laurie instantly moved away. My mate's face looked as though it was made of stone, while Laurie still seemed to think this was all a game. Our gazes met for a brief moment and his bore a twinkle that belied his earlier words of warning. Clark had begun to search him, and Laurie murmured something that made the air rumble with his growl.

My own experience was far less dramatic. With movements that were both brisk and fluid, the girl patted and ran her hands down the length of my body. It was only a matter of time before she found the gun, and the thought of not having it only heightened my anxiety. "Is it usually below you to do this?" I asked, more from curiosity than disparagement. It also might've been a futile attempt to distract her.

"My aunt has strong ideas about pack hierarchy," the girl answered tonelessly. So she was the alpha's niece. I wasn't sure what that meant in terms of her privileges or power—Mom's lessons on werewolves had been pretty generalized—but something told me this young wolf had ideas of her own.

"I'm Fortuna, by the way," I said on impulse.

The girl paused again. I could feel her debating whether or not to respond. "Cora."

I forgot whatever I would've said next; the alpha's niece had reached my ankles now and her fingers skimmed over the gun. I waited for her to pull it free. But Cora didn't hesitate or falter. She straightened, nodding at Clark to indicate I was clean, and stepped away.

Though I kept my gaze on the ground, I frowned in confusion. There was no question whether Cora had felt it—the gun's hard edges were impossible to miss. What was I missing here? Why would this wolf trust an outsider she hadn't even met before? It felt like I'd stepped onto the board of a new game and didn't know the rules.

A minute later, the thick-limbed male finished his searches, as well. He held several knives in one hand and an intricate sword in the other. My guess was the entire lot belonged to Lyari, who now wore a murderous expression. Her delicate-looking muscles were bunched, as though she was about to launch herself at the werewolf.

Subtly, knowing she would catch the movement, I shook my head. Lyari's eyes flashed with resentment, but she made a visible effort to calm.

Without comment, Cora turned and let the sleeping forest swallow her. I hurried after her, knowing everyone else would follow suit. My werewolf—no, Finn, I silently corrected—kept so close to me that his fur brushed against my hand every few feet. It was no longer a question that he was afraid; I could feel it. Taste it. It had the flavor of chewing tobacco.

We walked for at least another two miles. At some point, the trail ended. I'd been too busy searching the dead foliage for glowing eyes to notice. I was also unprepared when a mountain rose up and cast the world into shadow. Logically, I knew it was impossible, but it seemed to come out of nowhere. Like the wolves had conjured it. I shivered, though the chill shouldn't have bothered me, and concentrated on the steel against my skin for reassurance. Cora had let me keep the gun for a reason... and I suspected it was because we'd need to defend ourselves. What were we walking into?

My heartbeat felt like a hollow, gigantic drum. I knew everyone except Damon could hear it, but I couldn't seem to slow it back down. Not without taking some sort of precaution, at least, to offer myself comfort in this situation I'd put us all in.

Collith, can you hear me? I ventured, unsure if I was doing this right. During the trek, our positions in line had shifted. My mate was now toward the front, just behind Cora. His head tilted, the barest of indicators that, yes, my words had reached him. I still hadn't figured out how to let Collith past my wall and keep the other faeries out, so this was probably his only way to respond. *If things take a bad turn, I want... no, I need you to get Damon out. Will you do that for me?*

I watched him closely, but he didn't give any sign that he'd heard or agreed. Shit.

In the next moment, I forgot about whether my words reached him, because Cora stopped.

She stood aside, her gray eyes fixed firmly on the ground. Everything about her body language set me on edge. "Through there," she muttered. It wasn't clear who she was talking to, but her meaning was obvious enough. Firelight filtered through the trees. Night was already coming this way. In an hour or so, the sun would be gone, along with the last of my nerve. Finn's increasing distress had been like sandpaper, rubbing my mind raw. More than once, I'd considered turning back. Something told me our guides wouldn't let that happen peacefully, though.

One by one, we each passed Cora. Where the light broke through, Collith held a thick branch out of the way, almost as though he were holding a door open.

We emerged into a clearing, of sorts. Trees were still scattered throughout. One side was a towering rock wall that was covered in graffiti. From a cursory glance I spotted what I guessed to be lyrics, the names of bloodlines, and hundreds of paw prints. The word Lycan was everywhere. There was an enormous stone lodged against its base, the top of which was flat, for the most part. A solitary female stood there, looking out over the werewolves that had gathered. It was immediately obvious she was Astrid.

She was also the one I'd seen in Finn's mind when I'd touched him for the first time.

The alpha was made of sharp angles and sallow skin. She wore thick, dark eyeliner that made her irises look black. Her nails were painted, but the polish was chipped and faded. Like Clark's, her jeans were tight and stained. Her hair was scraped back into a ponytail and it was apparent that she was balding. Every inch of her looked like a poster warning off against drug abuse.

These were not the regal, free creatures I'd been imagining for Finn. The food in my stomach felt like a hard lump. I looked down at the wolf walking beside me, wondering if I'd betrayed him by coming to this place.

Like Clark and Cora, the pack had obviously been waiting for us. Their expressions were closed off and the only sound was wind stirring the treetops. There was a narrow path through the crowd. As we made our way toward Astrid, I had flashbacks of arriving at the Unseelie Court. That hadn't exactly ended well for me.

Something small and smoldering flicked through the air—a cigarette. It landed at my feet. "First things first," Astrid said, drawing my gaze back to her. There was a drawl in how she spoke, the syllables drawn out and softened. "How did you find us?"

I halted in front of her, legs planted, instinctively putting on a show of confidence. Agitation still thrummed through my body, though. I felt like a minnow in a tank full of sharks. *No*, I reminded myself. *They are the minnows.*

I met the alpha's gaze—her eyes were red-rimmed, the veins thick as the lines in a child's coloring book—and didn't flinch as I said, "We had some help."

She made the assumption I'd hoped she would, in that my werewolf had led the way. Laurie had probably procured the address from a pack member, and I had no doubt there were harsh punishments for traitors.

For the first time since we'd entered the clearing, Astrid turned her attention to Finn. She hopped off the rock, despite the considerable height, and landed with preternatural grace. I fought the instinct to step back, but Astrid's attention never wavered from Finn. She squatted so she was at his level, making me think of an insect with her too-thin legs and pointed elbows. A strand of greasy hair fell against her jawline. I watched closely for a reaction. Joy, disbelief, or sorrow. While there was nothing in her Astrid's eyes, her movements spoke volumes as she ran her palms over Finn's fur. There was something sensual and possessive about the simple touch.

A shiver wracked Finn's body, and I didn't think it was from pleasure. Pain suddenly radiated through my jaw and I realized that I was grinding my teeth. I knew that if Astrid didn't pull her hands away from him in a few seconds, I was going to do something that would shatter this precarious peace.

"Finnegan Protestant of the pack Alma, show me your other face," Astrid ordered suddenly, straightening. Something ancient and powerful echoed through her voice. Though it was directed at Finn, other pack members shifted their feet or made sounds of discomfort.

My wolf fought her command at first—I could tell from the way his muscles clenched—but the transformation began after a few seconds. Finn got down on his belly, whimpering like a kicked dog. As he writhed, I tried to think of something I could do to help. I came up empty. A hand wrapped around mine, more to console than restrain, I thought. I didn't look to see who stood beside me; the entirety of my focus was on Finn. Rivulets of blood flowed through the dirt he rested upon. Bones cracked and tendons snapped. The sounds coming from his throat changed to anguished cries that were undeniably human. I caught a glimpse of skin. Smooth, bloody, and brown.

Though the sight made my stomach churn, I still couldn't tear my gaze away. An elbow appeared amongst all that torn flesh. Eventually, after several agonizing minutes, the transformation was complete. A male shivered on the ground, curled into a fetal position. He had curly dark hair, a long nose that looked like it had been broken several times, and an angular jaw. Not handsome exactly, but there was an inexplicable beauty about him. Maybe it had nothing to do with his face and everything to do with the way he immediately searched for me, just moments after that unimaginable pain had ripped him apart.

Our gazes met and I saw that his eyes remained yellow. It was probably permanent from remaining in his animal form too long. He would never be able to appear amongst the humans again. Well, not without colored contacts, at least. Werewolves didn't have the ability to cast glamour.

Astrid stepped in front of Finn, effectively cutting us off from each other. "Thanks for returnin' him," she said to me, sounding anything but grateful. "I'll see to it that you're rewarded for your trouble."

Nothing about this felt right. Finn was so afraid of his alpha that her memory lived right beneath his skin. Frowning, I turned my gaze to the wolf peeking around her leg. *Is this what you want?* I tried to ask without actually saying it.

The werewolf didn't answer, but what I could see of his expression was lined with misery. That was enough for me. "Don't worry about it," I said slowly, knowing I was about to endanger every creature in this clearing. "I think he's coming home with us, anyway. So, really, it's me who should be thanking you. For turning him back, I mean."

Tension thickened in the air. Nostrils flared and teeth flashed. When I refocused on Astrid, her ears were undeniably longer than they'd been. Claws had sprouted from her fingers. Erring on the side of caution—she could be on me in an instant, if she gave in to the urge—I bent and pulled the gun out. The alpha's gaze flicked down. When she saw my weapon, surprise and fury sparked in her eyes. I knew Cora would pay for her kindness. No matter what I did here, someone was going to get hurt.

"Let me be very clear here," Astrid said. Her words were accompanied by the sounds of skin ripping and limbs snapping. Lyari appeared beside me, and if I'd had any hopes of getting out of this without trouble, they died at the sight of her. "In this moment, you got two choices. You can hand the *loup garou* over to us now. Or you can try resistin'. It probably won't go well for you, but if you do manage to escape, you'll be announced an enemy of the pack. We got numbers throughout the world; there'll be no end to the runnin'. When we do catch up with you, your death will be long and painful."

Halfway through her brief speech, I'd looked upward, catching the movement of some colorful bird. When Astrid was done, I waited a few seconds, then looked at her again. "I'm sorry, while you were talking I was trying to figure out why you think I care," I said with raised brows. Behind me, Collith sighed.

"You should care because he's *mine*," Astrid snarled, a vein throbbing in her temple. Finn growled at her. She moved in a blur, kicking him with such ferocity that he went flying. His spine rammed into a tree, and werewolf or not, I knew he'd be in pain from the blow. My grip on the gun tightened. Finn pushed himself up, moving slowly, pieces of bark clinging to his skin.

"Oh, fuck, lady." At the sound of his voice, we all turned in Laurie's direction. He unfolded his arms and cracked his neck, as though he were warming up. The weak sun shone down on him. He looked like a hero from the stories, so incandescent and untouchable. "You pretty much just guaranteed Fortuna is going to do the exact opposite of what you want."

Astrid seemed to realize a second after I did that he was moving to stand at my side. Damon and Collith drew closer, as well. My brother's expression was a mask of terror. Why hadn't I told him to stay in the truck?

The air practically crackled with the promise of violence now. Astrid must've sent some kind of wordless communication to the rest of the pack, because in the next moment, our small band was surrounded on all sides. Finn was still near the tree he'd struck and I didn't like the distance between us. I tried to catch a glimpse of him as the majority of Astrid's followers completed their transformations. Trapped as we were, we had no choice but to watch. I couldn't help feeling a bit of awe as the gruesome show unfolded.

Magic, or power, was something I had always taken for granted. Something that had always been there. But watching the wolves change form reminded me of how strange and beautiful it really was. We all had abilities lurking beneath our skin, just waiting to come out. Like a friend or foe that lived inside our bones.

Astrid reappeared once most of them stood on four legs. I kept my gaze trained on her. Since I hadn't been able to make skin-to-skin contact with her yet, I'd have to resort to more human means of defense. A hush filled the clearing as we waited for someone to make the first move.

Of course it was Astrid.

Instead of attacking me, she went after Finn again. He hadn't been able to reach us through the throng of bodies, and he was completely on his own as the alpha kicked him in the gut, ribs, and face. He didn't defend himself. Instead, my werewolf just curled into a ball.

A sound of fury tore from my throat. Suddenly I was moving, shooting every creature that got in the way. Like a well-oiled machine, the faeries took out ones I missed. Collith must've been preparing while Astrid talked, because blue flames filled my vision. Laurie focused his silver eyes, and whatever illusion he wrought made his victims tear into the wolf closest to them. Lyari must've managed to keep a dagger hidden from Clark's seeking fingers—she stabbed and slashed as though it were an extension of herself. Damon stayed in the circle they'd formed, and as I watched, his arm flew out to touch a werewolf that was still trying to change. My brother's eyes went hazy, just for a moment, and the female he'd touched began to shriek. *What do you know,* I thought distractedly. *He's a Nightmare after all.*

Little by little, we fought toward the trees. Toward Finn.

Finally, a werewolf shifted, and a path opened to him. The alpha hadn't relented, even as her comrades met our magic and blade. She'd resorted to stomping on Finn's head. He hadn't lost consciousness yet, since he was still huddled inside himself, but he had to be close. Blood pooled on the ground near his face. "Did you really think you could leave?" Astrid spat down at him, breathing hard. "Turn your back on this pack? Make me look weak? You are *nothing.* Worthless. By the time I'm done, you won't even—"

"Hey, Astrid!" I called. Her head swung in my direction. Before Astrid could so much as blink, I lifted my gun and shot her in the knee.

The alpha's scream made me believe in the existence of banshees. It rang through the treetops and made the sky crack. Astrid buckled—to her credit, she didn't collapse—and gripped the wound with both hands. Blood gushed between her fingers. She lifted her head and fixed her newly golden eyes on me. "I'm going to kill you," she hissed.

I grinned. "You'll have to get in line, bitch. Collith, would you grab Finn? I think he needs some help."

As Collith moved to comply, I lifted the gun again, expecting a surge of wolves to stop him. Apparently Astrid thought the same, because when no one moved, she released an enraged howl. "What are you *doing*, you fucking morons? Kill them. Kill them *all*."

A boney male toward the front dared to speak. "Astrid... they're gone."

Her head swiveled so quickly it was a wonder her neck didn't snap. She scanned the area we'd been standing, looking through each of us, and then the rest of the clearing. I frowned with bewilderment. *What's going on?*

When I happened to glance past him, seeking an explanation, Laurie winked. My confusion cleared. Of course. The Seelie King was shielding us from view.

"Find them," the alpha bellowed. Her mouth was half-changed. The shape of it was still human-looking, but the teeth were all wolf. I couldn't hold back a shudder. In a wave of fur and snarls, the pack crashed into the woods. Astrid, Cora, Clark, and two other wolves I didn't know stayed behind.

Time to go, Collith mouthed at me. Damon was staring at Astrid with an inscrutable expression. I touched his arm, trying to get his attention without making a sound, and he jerked away as though my touch burned. Gritting my teeth, I nodded toward the trees. Laurie was already walking away, his footsteps so light, they hardly made the leaves stir. Damon began in that direction, too, not bothering to look back. I reminded myself that it had been little more than a week since he'd made his vow of eternal hatred. It would be sad, really, if he caved so quickly.

No time to think about that now. I turned to Lyari, wanting to make sure she followed us, and saw the Guardian was gone. *Oh, fuck.* I frantically searched the crowd, a horrible suspicion taking hold. My fear was confirmed when I found her. She made her way toward Clark, weaving and slipping through the were-wolves. Some of them had already sensed something amiss; I saw a wolf lift its snout. Lyari didn't notice; she was too intent on the sword in Clark's grasp.

There was too much distance between us. I'd never reach her in time.

I had no choice but to drop the mental wall I'd constructed.

The onslaught of voices—whispering, laughing, plotting, fucking—felt like a hurricane tearing through my head. A moan threatened to escape me, and I bit my lip so hard I tasted blood.

Leave it, I shouted, throwing the words toward Lyari. I had no idea what I was doing. It seemed to work; the Guardian twitched at the sound of my voice in her head. Her face, pale and round as the moon starting to appear above us, sought mine. Our eyes met, and for the first time, hers were pleading.

My mother gave me that sword, she said. I heard what she didn't say—that Lyari's mother had given her that sword either before she went mad or in a rare moment of lucidity.

The fae sensed my presence now. Dozens of them seized the chance to communicate with me. Bargains and promises swelled in my skull, threatening to make it shatter. It was easy to understand how other queens had broken from this particular brand of magic. I could feel Collith there, too, trying to help. Urging me to move.

I will make sure you get it back. You have my word. But right now, I order you to leave it and run, I screamed at Lyari.

Whatever progress I'd made with her shriveled like a flower in frost. The female glanced back at Clark, making no secret of the fact that she was still considering the retrieval of her beloved weapon. If she did, they would know we were still here. The entire pack would hear the commotion and come running. We could keep fighting, but they had numbers. Eventually they'd overpower us or land a well-timed blow. If Lyari gave our presence away, she'd be signing our death certificates.

I looked back at Collith, another terrible idea forming in my head. He stared back with obvious mystification. He hadn't overheard the exchange between me and Lyari. For an instant, I hated him. Hated that he'd made his inner wall so insurmountable that he had no idea what we were capable of.

But I did.

It felt like something inside me cracked as I faced Lyari again. She was still wavering, trapped between her nostalgia and our destruction. I felt, more than saw, her take one more step toward Clark. Any lingering indecision evaporated. I closed my eyes and reached into the darkness, allowing myself to become part of it. Part of *them*.

The pain subsided almost immediately, as I was no longer fighting against the bond connecting me to Court. I sifted through the mass of minds, feeling like a child again, clumsily learning magic at my father's knee. It would be easy, so easy, to forget who I was and what I was doing. Insanity breathed down my neck. I was a snowflake in a blizzard or a drop in the ocean; I needed to rebuild the wall *now*.

Not yet, I thought desperately. *Where are you?*

Then, by sheer force of will—and perhaps a bit of luck—I found her. Lyari. Her presence was strong. I couldn't describe how I knew, even to myself. There was just an… essence. It was all her own. I felt myself grimace as I attempted to grasp it. At first, I pictured wrapping my hand around a vague object. Nothing seemed to happen. Next I imagined myself plunging into Lyari like a possessing spirit. Looking out from her eyes. Forming words she hadn't commanded herself to say.

When I opened my eyes again, Lyari was standing utterly still, looking like painted clay rather than a living being. She'd been just about to reach for the sword. I stared at her, hardly able to believe that I'd actually succeeded.

Thinking of what I was about to do next, I tried to memorize this moment. Later I would want to remember what it felt like, existing as a creature that hadn't committed one of the most vile acts possible. I let out a long breath. I could feel Collith finally coming toward us, radiating urgency and concern.

And then I took Lyari's choice from her.

This was why there were Tongues. *This* was why every fae ruler was bonded to their subjects. Not only to detect subterfuge, but to squash it, whenever and wherever it scuttled out of the dark. My control over Lyari was absolute; she didn't even have the capability to panic or despise me. I'd stripped her free will away as simply as removing jewelry. *Walk,* I thought. She did. From an outsider's perspective, nothing would've seemed amiss—Lyari moved with her usual grace and her expression was bland.

Collith still knew something was off. His eyes were dark as he followed us. I didn't release my hold on Lyari until we were well into the woods, though. The faerie slowed to a halt. She blinked rapidly and a line deepened between her perfectly-arched brows. *She doesn't know,* I thought wearily, putting the wall back. After a few seconds, the din of the Unseelie Court faded into a distant hum. Lyari glanced back at me, frowning, asking the question with her eyes.

I didn't answer. But it was only a matter of time until she put it together.

The sharp tang of bile filled my mouth. I rushed from Lyari and Collith to escape their prying gazes. Once I was out of their sight, I bent beside a thick pine tree. God, my head hurt. *Get up, get moving,* I thought. We didn't have time for weakness. Despite this, I couldn't bring myself to move. Not even when nothing came up. After a minute or two, a familiar summery scent warned me I wasn't alone. Boots appeared within my line of vision. "That's quite an ability you have there," I managed, holding onto the tree with desperate fingers. My other hand still gripped the gun.

"There are *some* perks to being friends with me," Laurie

agreed. "But I won't be able to hold onto this illusion. It's bigger than most and I'm using my own energy to feed it."

Scraping at the recesses of my endurance, I faced the silver-haired king. The world tilted. "It's at least three miles back to the truck. How long can you give us?" I asked unevenly.

"Guess we'll see, won't we?" He grinned, but it was a pale imitation of his usual smile. I could already see the toll his magic was taking on him. Somehow I knew he didn't want my pity, just as I didn't want his. Maybe we had more in common than I'd thought, this faerie and me.

"I guess we will," I said, stepping away from the pine tree. "Where are the others?"

"They're heading back to the vehicle. I told them we'd catch up."

I nodded wordlessly and Laurie moved to lead the way. With that, we hiked back the way we'd come, our pace crueler than before. The sun was not on our side. It sank quicker than usual, as if to taunt us. I concentrated on the ground to avoid tripping over something, resenting my inability to see in the dark.

The only time Laurie spoke was to let me know his power was completely sapped. Without his illusion protecting us, I felt jumpy and vulnerable. Over and over again, I thought I saw something in the corner of my eye. A flash of fur or bright eyes. When I mustered the nerve to look, nothing but leaves and shadows looked back.

At last, after what felt like hours, I recognized a fallen tree. We were close to the cabin now. Mere yards away from my truck, where Collith, Lyari, and Damon were waiting. A burst of fresh adrenaline went through me and I broke into a run. "Fortuna—" Laurie began to hiss.

A stick snapped.

The sound was too jarring to be paranoia. I froze, knowing that if it was a wolf, we were dead. If Laurie was too weak to continue his illusion, it probably meant his ability to sift was gone, too. I stopped breathing as I turned.

Cora stood between two trees.

I didn't speak, for fear another werewolf was nearby. Cora didn't say anything, either. She watched me with those gray eyes. Within their depths, I saw that light again. The one I hadn't been able to identify when she witnessed my power. This time it was even brighter, and suddenly its name was so obvious, I wondered how I'd been confused.

Envy.

In that moment, I saw Cora for what she was. A young, scared werewolf trapped beneath Astrid's thumb. "The only power she has is what you give her," I said quietly, knowing the girl's sharp ears would still hear.

For a few seconds after I spoke, none of us moved. I could've sworn I heard our three heartbeats, there in that brown pocket of forest.

Then, never taking her eyes from mine, Cora stepped aside.

Part of me wondered if this was a trap. She'd already defied Astrid once by letting me keep the gun, though. Chances were this opportunity was genuine, and I wasn't about to look a gift horse in the mouth. I made a sharp gesture to Laurie, and he hurried past without a second glance. I didn't follow—not until I was sure everyone else was safe. Seconds later, I heard the truck roar to life. The wolves must've heard it, as well, because the silence shattered with a chorus of bays and howls.

"Go," Cora growled. Her eyes were now the same gold her aunt's had been.

With the sound of the pack's fury ringing in my ears, I ran.

CHAPTER FIFTEEN

*W*erewolves may be fast, but my truck was faster. Soon we'd put enough distance between us and the pack that I stopped watching the mirrors. I slumped in the passenger seat. The adrenaline in my veins had faded, leaving me a drained husk of who I was when this all started. The gun was safely tucked in the glove box, resting from a job well done.

Only a minute or two had gone by when Laurie leaned forward. "That went wonderfully, didn't it?" he chirped.

I rested my temple against the window and watched the landscape blur past. I could sense Lyari staring at me and pretended not to notice. "Well, I haven't made any really bad decisions lately. I was getting bored," I said without any of my usual force.

"Be sure to send me an invitation to the next party. I'll make sure you're dressed properly for it," Laurie added. Before I could reply, he vanished. *He sure regenerates quickly,* I thought with a pang of jealousy. Laurie's lovely smell lingered, ensuring Collith wasn't going to relax anytime soon. Silence hovered through the cab. I knew there was a lecture coming—it was only a matter of time. But I wasn't going to hurry it along.

The Unseelie King's voice was tight when he finally asked, "Where am I taking you?"

I glanced at Finn in the backseat, who was pressed against the door. His eyes were squeezed shut and his expression scrunched in obvious pain. He was also completely naked. More than anything, I wanted to take him to a hospital. But Fallen had a blood type no human doctor would recognize, and when the werewolf started to heal, they'd have even more questions.

Damon, on the other hand, looked good. Really good. There was color in his cheeks and his gaze was clear as he tracked our progress into the city. Using his powers against that werewolf had apparently reinvigorated him.

I still couldn't bring myself to glance toward Lyari.

"The first hotel you can find," I told Collith eventually. "But we should stop at the store first. I want to get some bandages for Finn. He's lost too much blood already."

No one responded. We were all in agreement, then. I shifted in the seat, trying to get more comfortable, and willed sleep to come. It didn't.

Just as dusk succumbed to darkness, I saw it. Lights. They spread across the landscape like a constellation. A sign flew past for an upcoming exit and a Walmart sign towered in the distance. Collith turned on the blinker without comment.

Collith pulled up in front of the entrance and turned on the hazard lights. Four pairs of eyes watched as I dropped to the pavement and went inside, annoyance flickering through me. *This weird day needs to end.*

The florescent lights and human noises felt like a dream. It was hard to wrap my head around the fact that while we'd been fleeing through the woods, life had gone on, blissfully unaware of the danger just miles away. Struggling to adjust to this reality, I moved through the store. It was busy, and more than once, I edged around a human standing in the middle of the aisle. I remembered that it was early yet. Folks were just getting off work.

I found the bandages next to the pharmacy counter. I grabbed the first package I spotted, along with a pair of sweat-pants and a T-shirt. I rushed through the checkout line and jogged back to the truck. Collith had remained near the doors, as though he were ready to make a quick getaway if the need arose. Maybe he wasn't as okay as he seemed, either.

When I opened the back door, Finn got out and knelt at my feet. I was so startled that the protest I'd been about to make died. He really, really needed to put some clothes on. We were lucky no one had seemed to spot him yet.

"For the rest of my life, I am yours," the werewolf said hoarsely, bowing his head so I couldn't see his expression. Or his pain. *His voice is deeper than I imagined it*, I thought absently.

He wasn't the first one to express such a sentiment, but he was the first one I believed. "I appreciate it, Finn, but the last thing you need is another mistress. How about belonging to yourself for a change?" I suggested, sounding as exhausted as I felt. After a moment, I set the bag of clothes in front of him.

Finn didn't move. For both of our sakes, I got on my knees, too. His head snapped up. He watched with wide eyes as I tore the box open and started to wind bandages around each of his gaping cuts. Astrid had been thorough in her beating; the only parts of him not bruised or bleeding were his feet.

I finished securing the last bandage and sat back on my haunches. There were still some left in the box, thankfully, since I could already tell he'd need fresh ones later. Before I could speak, Collith cleared his throat. "Would you mind if I drove again? The practice is good for me."

I saw right through him—he thought he was sparing my pride by making the request about his needs instead of mine. I wasn't nearly as proud as he seemed to believe. "Knock yourself out," I said, getting to my feet as though I were an old woman, full of creaking bones and old wounds. I couldn't remember ever feeling this tired. Collith held the passenger door open for me and I got in without a word. Slowly, hesitantly, Finn dressed in the new clothes, then did the same on his side.

For the third time that day, we got back on the road. We had to be close to a hotel, but Damon and Finn fell asleep quickly, lulled by the truck's rumble. As my brother's snores drifted through the air, Collith launched into his inevitable lecture. "I told you to play nice," he said. Though his face was neutral, our mating bond pulsed with frustration.

I didn't move or look his way. "I did."

"Fortuna, you shot the alpha of a werewolf pack."

Did we really have to do this right now? My head was still pounding and all I wanted to do was sleep for the next twenty-four hours. "Well, she deserved it. Not sure how great your memory is, but she was beating Finn to a pulp when I put that bullet in her. Plus, she wouldn't shut up," I snarled.

"I don't believe she was speaking at the time your gun came out," Collith said dryly. For whatever reason, though, he let it go. I knew he also wanted to ask about the strange moment between me and Lyari, but she was wide awake behind us, an audience to every word. I was safe... for now.

It felt like the conversation was over, so I said nothing else. I focused on my hands like I was fascinated by them, stretching my fingers out, watching the way the skin around my knuckles stretched and thinned. "Is something wrong?" I heard Collith ask.

"It's not in me to play nice," I said abruptly, still looking down. "Not when I see people like Finn or Damon being treated how they were. It's not who I am. Please don't try to change who I am."

I wasn't sure what Collith found more surprising—my honesty or my usage of the word 'please.' He didn't respond for a while. I counted the seconds, wanting to avoid the memory of

Astrid's foot connecting with Finn's face or the vacant way Lyari walked through the trees. Twenty seconds passed. Thirty. Fifty. At the minute mark, Collith spoke. His voice was soft and final. "Okay. I won't."

"Okay." I turned away, back to the window. I repeated, more quietly this time, "Okay."

The trees were behind us now and Denver waited ahead. I couldn't help looking in the side mirror, though. The forest had gone from brown to black. I'd learned the hard way what creatures and terrors hid within, and now I could add one more to the list. Astrid was out there somewhere, healing and making plans. However weak she'd appeared, there had been strength in the way she told me of the pack's reputation. I had no doubt whatsoever that she'd already sent a wolf to track us.

No matter which direction I turned, there were enemies waiting. Wanting my brother, wanting our hearts, wanting me. The thought made me sit straighter. My mouth hardened into a determined line. I glared into the darkness and dared something to come out.

If the other monsters thought I was going down without a fight, it would be the last mistake they ever made.

Within minutes of checking in, I found myself alone in the motel room.

Finn slipped away while we grabbed our bags, probably to hunt or heal. If I had seen him leaving, I probably would've tried to intercept. Damon was taller and thinner than Finn, so his borrowed clothes didn't exactly rest naturally on the newly-transformed male's frame. Once I added his glowing eyes and an angry werewolf pack to the equation, I kicked myself for taking my attention off Finn even for a second. At the front desk, I kept glancing at the doors, hoping he would walk through.

The boy checking us in—his nametag read DAN—slipped me his number when handing over the room keys. My first instinct was to throw the sticky note back in his face. Instead, something drove me to just shove it in my pocket, sighing. "Thanks. Have a good night."

"You too," Dan squeaked. Puberty was a bitch.

The moment we reached the room, Lyari blinked out of sight. She didn't even bother with an explanation. I knew it was out of character for her; I'd had to forcefully dismiss her last time.

Damon was next to leave. He set his bag down and mumbled that he was going to see some old friends from high school. I argued, pointing out that we should stay together. My brother walked out before I'd finished the sentence. I was too tired to shout at him through the wall.

Then, finally, Collith. With a regretful smile, he told me there was a matter at Court, so he had to go, as well. "Summon me if there's any sign of danger," he murmured. I just nodded. I didn't even care that he was going; all I could think about was dropping onto that dirty, flowered bedspread. Collith touched my cheek, more brief than a breath, and winked out of sight.

Oddly enough, I didn't move toward the bed once he was gone. Now that I was alone, I felt restless. Disjointed. My gaze went to the windows, which were covered by hideous curtains. I crossed the room and pulled them open, one by one. The sound of the sliding rings was the only one in the entire motel, it seemed. I stepped close to the glass and looked out.

We'd gotten a room on the second floor again. However shabby it was—there were open electrical wires which sparked when I turned the lights on—it had a good view of the mountains. I leaned my temple against the window, wishing I could open it, and admired those distant peaks, standing like soldiers against the night.

I nearly screamed when my cell phone rang. Scowling, I

yanked it into the open. The screen brightened with an unknown number, but I recognized that area code. *Granby.* "Hello?" I hurried to say, panicked, my mind diving off a cliff. Someone was going to tell me that Gretchen was in the hospital or Cyrus had gotten burned at the stove. Why else would I be getting a call from a strange number?

"Fortuna, is that you?"

My eyebrows shot up with surprise. I was still looking toward the mountains, but now I didn't register them. "Bud? How did you get this number?"

"Why, your brother gave it to me, of course!" the old man replied. He was Granby's best and only lawyer. He'd moved from Texas decades ago but his accent only seemed to get thicker with age. "Damon and I have been playing some phone tag, so I thought I'd try you. I just wanted to make sure I had the spelling of your name right, since he's leaving everything to you. You can never be too careful when you're dealing with will stuff, as I'm sure you know. Now, is that F-O-R-T-U-N-A?"

I held the phone harder against my ear, certain I'd heard incorrectly. A child called for his mother in the hallway, his voice echoing off the walls. "Hold on, did you say 'will stuff,' Bud?"

"Well, yeah. Didn't your brother tell you?" He sounded worried now.

I forced out a laugh. "Sorry, yes, of course he did. I just forgot. It's been a long day and driving always makes me drowsy. And you did spell my name right."

"Thanks, sweetheart. Damon mentioned y'all were spending the week in Denver! That should be fun."

"Thanks for being so careful with this, Bud. Please call me if you have any other questions."

"Will do. Take care, now."

After he'd hung up, I lowered the phone slowly. Well, now I knew why Damon had been so late coming home yesterday afternoon. He'd been paying a visit to Bud's office.

Our parents had left behind a sizable life insurance policy. Damon and I got half when we each turned eighteen. It took twenty years to declare a missing person dead, so my brother's two-year disappearance hadn't affected his ability to receive it. If Damon was bothering to do anything with his will, it was because of that money. But why now? Why the urgency before this Denver trip?

"How long are you staying here?"

This time, Collith's voice was right behind me, so close I could feel his breath. All I had to do was shift, I knew, and the back of my shoulder would be touching his chest. "That was fast," I commented, hoping to distract him from the way my heart stuttered.

"I was motivated." His soft exhales toyed with my hair. I let myself pretend, just for a moment, that it was his fingers. "You didn't answer my question."

For a moment, I had no idea what he was talking about. "Oh, right. I have no idea how long we'll be here. Until Damon gets some answers, I guess," I said. My voice was a frozen lake, covered in a dusting of snow; he couldn't see to the depths below. I pushed thoughts of Damon and wills aside, focusing solely on the scent that was Collith.

Collith responded, but the words were lost in a burst of noise. I flattened my hand against the window and couldn't hold back a sound of pain. Something was going on at Court. The voices rose into a crescendo. I made my mental wall thicker and taller, but some of the chaos slipped through. One of the bloodlines was furious that a descendent had mated with a faerie of the Seelie Court.

I didn't care. I just wanted them to be *silent*. I pulled away from the window—leaving behind a sweaty imprint of my fingers and palm—and rubbed my temples. I added more bricks, more stones, more cement. The wall was a mass of various materials, haphazardly built.

"How badly does it hurt?" Collith asked. It felt like his voice came from a distance, but he hadn't moved.

"Like someone is hitting me in the head with a brick," I said shortly, turning to face him at last.

Collith tilted his head. The lamp's glow was at his back, casting a halo all around. The effect made him seem like an angel sent to save me from myself. "I can help you. There are ways to block them out."

"Would this require letting you into my head?"

"To an extent," he admitted. "You'd have to trust me."

Just as it had in my truck, the pain made me irritable. Scoffing, I stepped around Collith and walked to the farthest bed. I sat down and the springs moaned as though I weighed a thousand pounds. "I don't even know you," I told him, lifting my chin defiantly. "We met, what, three weeks ago? I trust my mailman more than you; at least he's been in my life for a few years."

"Then let's remedy that."

I frowned. What did he mean? The same moment I started to voice the thought out loud, a light turned on in my head. "Wait. Are you asking me out?" I blurted. The idea seemed outlandish, for some reason.

But Collith's gaze was steady. "If that's what you need, yes."

I gave a shaky laugh. He made the proposal so casually, so smoothly. I could almost believe that he hadn't planned it. Almost. "When?" I heard myself say. Was that really my voice? It had softened without my permission.

Collith knelt in front of me much the way Finn had earlier. Only no vows of fealty passed his lips and his expression held no pain or sorrow. Somehow, he didn't look ridiculous, though I wouldn't kneel on that carpet even if someone paid me. As I waited for the faerie king to answer, he brushed a strand of hair out of my eyes using the tip of his finger. A shiver whispered through me. "Whenever you're available," he murmured, searching my face for a reaction.

"I can't tomorrow. I'm going to track down Savannah Simonson. She's..." I hesitated. "Well, I guess she's Damon's ex-girlfriend now. I couldn't bring myself to tell her over the phone that he's back, and she deserves to know."

His finger hadn't left my skin. That single spot of cold was distracting. "Would you like me to accompany you?" Collith asked.

"Thank you, but no." I cleared my throat. "After I find her, maybe?"

"It's a date. Oh, also..." Collith plucked my cell phone away, which I'd been holding throughout our conversation. I started to tell him the passcode, but he was already typing it. He pretended not to notice my glare as he added himself to the contact list.

"I'm surprised you didn't put 'King' in front of your name," I commented, taking it back. Now that he'd stopped touching me, relief and disappointment warred inside my chest.

"I did consider using 'Darling Mate.'"

I twisted my lips to appear deep in thought. "What about 'Delusional Moron?'"

Collith's eyes twinkled. Before I could conjure another insult, he bent and retrieved what looked like a messenger bag from the floor. He must've set it down while I was looking out the window. I'd been so absorbed in watching him that I hadn't even noticed the thing... and it was right by my damn feet.

"I have something for you," Collith said, sitting across from me. The mattress made a sound like he'd just inflicted a rare, slow torture upon it. Ignoring this, he reached into the bag and pulled out a worn, faded tome. Its cover was engraved with a crest of some sort.

"Oh, yay," I said in a less-than-enthused tone. "Books. I love those."

"Don't worry, that's not all I brought." Collith pulled a Tupperware container out next. The inside was filled with steam, making it impossible to see the contents.

I dove for it. "Oh my God, I could marry you!"

"You already did that," he replied with a teasing smile. I was already popping the red lid. Inside I found a piece of fried chicken, a pile of mashed potatoes, and glazed slices of onion. My mouth immediately began to water. I half-stood, thinking to look through the bag for a fork, but Collith was waving one in my face. Sitting again, I snatched it from him and stabbed the chicken. "I know you've read a good portion of my collection, but you haven't even begun to familiarize yourself with our history. It might be good for you to know, considering you're the Unseelie Queen."

I gasped, despite the huge bite of food I'd just taken. "What? I am?"

Collith mimed throwing the book at me. I was too busy eating to respond. It wasn't until the chicken breast was half-gone that I said, sparing a glance toward him, "Look, I've been driving a lot, and the last thing I want to do right now is look at some tiny, boring words."

"How about I read to you?"

The offer made me blink. "Really?"

"What are friends for?" Collith countered. He didn't wait for my reaction to this comment and stood. I had no idea what he intended to do until he was already lying in the spot next to me, adjusting the pillows to his comfort. "This crest on the cover was Olorel's. The three moons represent his ability to travel between worlds."

"What's your bloodline's crest?" I asked curiously.

Something strange passed through Collith's eyes. "Let me read a few pages and maybe you'll find out."

"*Fine*. Sadist." I glared and shoved another piece of chicken into my mouth.

Collith adjusted his hold on the book and, without any trace of discomfort, started reading aloud from the first page. I tried to pay attention, but his intoxicating scent brushed against my senses. Unbidden, images from that steaming bath came back to me. His hand reaching over the edge, skimming along my bare leg, dipping below the water. Collith had made me come in a way I'd never experienced before, not even with Oliver.

Probably because it was real, that inner voice remarked. Damn, she could be an even bigger bitch than me.

All at once, I had no appetite. I swallowed the last bite I'd taken and set the Tupperware on the nightstand. Collith was so engrossed in what he was reading that he didn't stop until I covered the page with my hand. "That's sweet, but I'm not in the mood to listen, either," I murmured thickly.

Responding to whatever he saw in my face, Collith's eyes darkened. "What do you want to do, then?" he questioned. His voice folded around us, soft in the dim room. Slowly, he set the book aside.

What do you want to do? The question echoed through my head. I started to answer, stopped, started again. In a burst of frustration, I stood and took a few steps toward the window. The curtains were still open but I couldn't find comfort in the view anymore. The mountains were gone anyway, hidden beneath a midnight cloak.

Collith had gotten to his feet, as well. I turned toward him, trying to scrape together the courage to answer his question. When I saw his expression, though, the howling winds in my mind went still.

The Unseelie King cared about me. It was written all over his face, more obvious than the darkest of inks. Seeing it made me consider telling him the truth. That if I closed my eyes, there were a dozen bad memories waiting to rise up. Jassin's feline smile. A screaming dragon. Blood on my hands. Finding Mom and Dad's ravaged bodies. *What do you want to do?*

I know what I didn't want to do—I didn't want to think about it. Any of it. Again, I halted in front of Collith, looking up at him. My gaze dropped to his lips. *What do you want to do?* "This," I said.

Before he could ask what I meant, I wrapped my fingers around the back of Collith's head and pulled his face down to mine.

CHAPTER SIXTEEN

"*H*ere is your meat, Queen Fortuna. Rare, just how you like it."

I opened my eyes to find myself staring into a smiling face. When our gazes met, the faerie I didn't recognize bowed deeply. Before I could summon a response, he stepped aside, revealing a slave who looked as if she had limbs made of sticks instead of bones. She was on her knees, despite the stone slabs, and a covered plate rested on her head. She was literally wearing a potato sack instead of any decent sort of clothing. Beaming, somehow oblivious to my quiet rage, the faerie lifted the plate off her. As he set it down in front of me, I took stock of my surroundings and tried to hide my confusion.

I sat at a long table in the throne room. The gown I wore was red as blood and heavy as a dead body. Had I blacked out? How were we at the Unseelie Court when the last thing I remembered was falling asleep in a motel?

"Your Majesty? Has something displeased you?"

The faerie was staring at me worriedly now, a line appearing between his eyebrows. There was also a muscle twitching in his cheek that promised violence if I expressed any sort of irritation.

But he wouldn't take it out on me, no, he'd later beat the human girl and blame her for the error. His thoughts and memories whispered to me through the bond, speaking of this knowledge whether I wanted to know it or not. I needed to rebuild the mental wall that usually kept such things from me. Why had I let it down? Why couldn't I seem to summon it now?

I glanced down at the silver dome covering the plate the faerie had delivered. Along its edges, there were drops of blood. Nausea gripped my stomach. "I didn't order this," I rasped.

"Fortuna? Are you all right?"

Collith's brow wrinkled in concern. Somehow I hadn't noticed him there, sitting beside me, or maybe he hadn't been there before. As always, he was more beautiful than I wanted him to be. Maybe he would be easier to resist, then. Skin so smooth and unlined, except for those telltale ones between his eyes and around his mouth. A jaw so strong and defined, it practically begged to have a finger run along its edge. Like mine.

Unaffected by my blatant stare of admiration, Collith nodded at the plate. "Better hurry, before it gets cold," he remarked. A faerie on the other side of him said something, and he turned his back to me, responding in a low murmur. His plate held steak and mashed potatoes. There was also a small cluster of green beans.

Nothing to be afraid of, Fortuna. With this thought, I forced myself to lift the lid.

Shameek's screaming face looked up from the plate.

Figs brushed against his cheeks and chin. His face had been garnished with parsley and sauce. Horror clogged my throat. For a few seconds, I was absolutely convinced that I was about to vomit all over the plate and table. I gripped the bench on either side of me like it was only thing keeping me upright. I could feel the faeries in the room glancing at me sidelong, peeking through their lashes, or just staring outright without any trace of shame.

I fascinated them. I wasn't human, I wasn't fae, and I

wielded a power none of them could understand. They truly had no idea how I would react to this.

All of which I knew because I was in their heads as well as my own.

Though I had no desire to see Shameek's gaping mouth again, I dropped my gaze. It was what I deserved. He stared back at me with accusation in his brown eyes. It was then I remembered I hadn't even bothered to find his family, as I'd promised myself I would. My word was as trustworthy as a faerie's, it seemed.

I'm sorry, I thought at the dead human, unable to speak out loud. Collith and the others would hear. Even now I couldn't show them any weakness. *I'm so sorry. Please forgive me.*

"Your fault," Shameek whispered, startling me. "All your fault."

I screamed.

When I opened my eyes again, the scream dying in my throat, the cavernous throne room had been replaced by the walls of a motel room. The firelight, the fae, and the talking head were not even an imprint in my vision, like the colors that flashed when one looked into a bright light.

Which meant none of it had been real.

A dream. I'd actually had a dream. It had been so long since I'd experienced one that I had forgotten what they felt like. I was eight or nine, the last time it happened.

The moment I realized I was awake, my first thought was of Oliver.

The dreamscape hadn't appeared. No cottage, no sea, no best friend. I couldn't blame drugs or injuries. First the missing paintings and now this. What was going on?

As morning light streamed through a crack between the curtains, I stared at the ceiling, frowning and worrying. Every few seconds, Damon's gentle snores penetrated the stillness. Collith was already gone. If the sheets beside me weren't rumpled and there wasn't an indent in the other pillow, I might've wondered if I dreamed it all. Every heated kiss. Every unhurried touch. Afterwards, we'd faced each other on the bed, exchanging more whispered questions, and fallen asleep that way.

It had been disturbingly easy. Comfortable.

The thought bothered me and I kept going back to it. Picturing those hazy moments just before everything went dark. How the side of Collith's face—all I could see in the dim room— had looked like rolling hills. How much I'd liked the fact that he kept touching me, his fingertips so light and brief, but constant. As if he liked it as much as I did and couldn't resist the pull between us.

Oh my God.

It felt as if a shooting star soared across my mind, illuminating everything that had been hidden in the dark. Suddenly it was obvious; I should've figured it out far sooner. It was *him*. Collith was the reason Oliver was slipping away. The night his paintings vanished was the same night I'd played Connect Four with my mate. I'd gone to bed with thoughts full of him, without any of the usual anticipation for seeing my best friend.

A hard knot of certainty formed inside me. Even if there wasn't much to go on, I knew I'd discovered the cause for Oliver's torment.

I just hoped he hadn't figured it out.

I laid there, prepared to let guilt tear me apart with its invisible teeth and claws. In the next moment, though, my phone vibrated on the nightstand. Glad of the distraction, I reached for it. When I saw Collith's name on the screen, I couldn't hold back a smile. I'd seen him putting his number in, but it was still hard to imagine the King of the Unseelie Court sending a text.

Good luck on your search today, his message read. *Please don't hesitate to ask for my assistance, should the need arise.*

Right. I'd told him that I was looking for Savannah. Now my

thoughts turned to the day ahead and the inevitably uncomfortable conversation I was about to have. Deciding to just get it over with, I found her in the contacts list and pressed CALL.

After a few seconds of silence, a sound blared in my ear. A tinny, female voice droned, "We're sorry. You have reached a number that has been disconnected or is no longer in service. If you feel you have reached this recording in error, please check the number and try your call again..."

I listened to the entire thing, and all I could think was, *Shit. Now what?*

The last time we spoke, Savannah still lived in Denver, and it was unlikely she'd left. *He's out there, Fortuna. I know it. I feel it,* the witch had said to me, our connection crackling. To my eternal shame, I hadn't shared her hope. If Damon wouldn't bring Savannah the closure she deserved, then I would.

I couldn't ask her parents, since her father moved to California and her mother left them when Savannah was a child, but their old home was on the same street my family had lived on. Maybe the new tenants knew something of Savannah's whereabouts. People did that, right? Left a forwarding address in case a stray piece of mail didn't reach their new place?

It felt good to have a plan, however weak it might've been. Steeling myself for the cold, I stretched my legs and arms, each joint releasing loud, satisfying *cracks*. Just as I opened my eyes again, reluctant to leave the warm bed, a face popped into view. Animal eyes glowed in the slant of shadow.

"Jesus!" I yelped. My head slammed against the headboard.

"Sorry," Finn said. His voice was still hoarse from disuse.

I hurried to reach over and turn on the lamp. The werewolf winced and hunched his shoulders as though I were about to lash out. Suddenly, I wished I had shot both of Astrid's kneecaps. And I'd let the faerie who'd taken him get off far too easy. Maybe I would pay her a visit next time I was at Court...

Finn must've thought my quiet rage was directed at him; he

dropped to the carpet and rolled onto his back, exposing his belly. The position looked bizarre since he wasn't in wolf form.

"Oh, God, I'm sorry. I'm not mad at *you*." I shoved the bedspread out of the way and stood, wondering how I hadn't noticed him. Finn didn't move, and thinking of how he'd been there the moment I woke, I realized that he must've slept on the floor. Another needle of guilt pricked me—I had assumed he wouldn't come back until morning, just like the last motel we'd stayed at. It didn't once cross my mind that he'd need a place to sleep.

I would make it up to him. Once we got home, I'd fix up the small room we had been using for storage. Finn would have a safe place to retreat and call his own. With the softest damn bed money could buy.

Finn was still laying there on the moldy carpet. Maybe he'd get up if I wasn't around. I awkwardly sidestepped him and said, fumbling over the words, "Please don't feel strange about... about making yourself at home. You're part of this family, for as long as you want to be. Take a shower. Use the kitchenette. Watch something if you're bored. The remote is missing but there are volume and channel buttons on the TV. Oh, and that plastic bag on the counter has some snacks in it. They're from the gas station, so not exactly nutritious, but I'll go grocery shopping later. Wait, doesn't this place have continental breakfast?"

"Fucking hell, Fortuna. If I check, will you let me sleep in peace?" Damon's cross voice said from beneath his covers.

"That would be great. Take Finn," I said as I hurried into the bathroom. The warped floor creaked with every step. Dreading what I was about to find, I pulled the shower curtain aside. It was just as dirty as I'd imagined. I turned the handles and reminded myself we were on a budget. Hotel bills added up fast, and if we ended up staying here a week, it was already going to make a dent.

Still, when it took nearly ten minutes for the water to heat, I couldn't help picturing the suites at Hyatt Regency.

Fifteen minutes later, I was showered and dressed. My clothes were wrinkled but clean. I rushed past Damon, who was back in bed, and went in search of the werewolf we'd adopted. It crossed my mind, scuttling like a beetle, too quick for me to crush it, that Lyari probably should've been back by now. If she didn't return, she would be openly breaking her vow of fealty. Others would view it as an act of rebellion, and I couldn't afford to appear weak, not when I was already worried about an assassin.

In that moment, I understood Collith a little more.

I decided to exercise my American right to be in denial. I arrived at the dining room, if one could call it that, and looked for Finn. There was only one other guest eating breakfast in the big sitting room—he held a newspaper in front of his face and seemed content with a single cup of tea. Finn had settled at a small table next to the window. There was a plate of food in front of him, but it looked untouched. We'd have to fix that. A quick scan of the room showed a far counter with cereal dispensers and covered dishes gleaming silver. My stomach was already grumbling as I hurried over.

I immediately grabbed one of the simple white mugs, filled it with coffee, and dumped in cream and sugar. Then, once I'd piled my plate high with toast, eggs, and sausage—it must've been there a while, because grease had started to congeal in the pan—I sank into the chair across from Finn. I squinted in the brightness and waited for my eyes to adjust. Finn didn't speak.

"Finnegan Protestant. That's quite a mouthful," I remarked offhandedly, sprinkling salt over my scrambled eggs. Finn looked at the mug I'd set down. Ripples vibrated through the pale liquid. I shot him a sheepish smile and took a sip. "I like a little coffee with my creamer. Were you a coffee drinker? No, sorry, *are* you a coffee drinker?"

Still, he said nothing. This was a silence different from Damon's; there was no cruelty in it. Instead it held a sort of... emptiness. Like a river that had been depleted and all that remained was the dry bottom. I felt inept and out of my depth. How did one treat a creature that had been abused in his first life, only to be taken out of it and abused in the second? How did one talk to a creature that had chosen to permanently wear the skin of a wolf rather than face the pain?

Well, first, coffee. Every war in the history of mankind could've been solved with a little more coffee.

I got up and padded back to the breakfast bar. When I returned, I put a mug down in front of Finn. "Here. They made it pretty weak, but I added my own flair to it. Hopefully the amount of sugar doesn't make you puke."

Finn just stared down into the coffee as though it were a crystal ball. I nudged his fork closer in wordless urging. He picked it up, more to please me than to appease his own hunger, I suspected. We passed a half hour in a silence that was uneasy, at first, and gradually became companionable. I got a copy of the paper for Finn and browsed the news on my phone. *In Arapahoe County, a Crisis of Missing Women,* a local headline read. Doubtless it had something to do with the Fallen. There were multiple species that would enjoy taking female victims. The knot in my stomach tightened.

"I need to look for someone today," I told Finn abruptly. I stood and shoved the phone into my back pocket. "I'm planning to hit the grocery store afterwards, too. Do you want to come? Fair warning, it'll probably be a boring day."

I knew he would nod before I even made the offer. Together we brought our plates to the dish bin, then retraced the way to our room. There I pulled on a coat, found my purse, and left a note for Damon next to the cell phone he wouldn't call or text me with.

Outside, the air was a bit more vindictive than it had been

yesterday. The cold raked my skin. It was almost Halloween, I remembered as we crossed the parking lot. As a child it had been my favorite holiday; now it just meant serving more drunk people and getting shitty tips.

It wasn't true, what humans believed about some veil being thinner or the supernatural having more power. For Fallen, it was just like any other day. Well, except for whoever wanted to hunt—they'd be able to blend in a little easier. On Halloween, everyone was a monster.

At the truck, Finn's muscles bunched, as though he were about to jump in. It was impossible to imagine adapting to a human body after years of existing in a four-legged one. I pretended not to notice and slid behind the wheel, leaving the choice of where to sit up to Finn. After a moment, he got into the back. Was it because he didn't think of himself as an equal? Or maybe it was just to avoid any further stilted attempts at conversation. I started the engine, shifted gears, and began driving toward a place I never thought I'd return to.

The Sworns had lived in the South Park Hill neighborhood, a detail I'd never forgotten, but I lost my bearings halfway there and had to open Google Maps. Less than twenty minutes later, familiar houses appeared on either side. I parked close to an oak tree, and as we got out, its shadow sent a shiver across my skin. I hardly noticed—farther down the street, our old home still stood. Faded blue paint covered the front door. My mother had done that. She'd wanted to paint it red, but I couldn't remember why she hadn't. It was strange, the details that lingered in memory and the ones that didn't.

I turned toward Finn, thinking to tell him where we were. "You're Fortuna Sworn, right?" someone asked.

Startled, I swung around to find the voice's owner. A girl stood next to a car, holding keys in her hand. She wore a fuzzy sweater, white as cheeks drained of color. She was not beautiful, but her smile was so friendly that it was easy to think so. "We went to high school together, right?" I said, rummaging through my memories. "You're... Harper. Harper Danes."

She beamed. "That's me. We were on the cheerleading team for a bit, before you..."

"Before I quit," I finished, grinning. "Yeah, it just wasn't for me. I've never liked the spotlight or wearing a skirt."

Which are two strikes the Unseelie Court has against it. You know, if it weren't for all the slavery, torture, and manipulation that was already happening.

Harper tilted her head speculatively, a curtain of honey-blond hair falling over her shoulder. "Well, what about drinking? Is that for you at all?" she asked.

I pretended to consider it. "I've been known to have a cocktail or two."

She glanced at Finn, who came up behind me silently. She opened her mouth, probably to introduce herself or extend a polite greeting, but whatever she saw in his expression made her change course. Harper's smile wavered and she refocused on me. "Well, why don't you come out with the team one last time?" she suggested. "We're going dancing in a few days. Give cheerleading a proper farewell. You never gave us that."

I laughed. "I need to check with my brother, but I might be able to make an appearance."

"Great. Here, put your number in." Harper held out her iPhone. I opened the contacts app and typed my information into the blank spaces. When I handed the phone back, she pocketed it without looking at the screen. "I'll be in touch, then. So glad we ran in to each other, Fortuna! See you soon!"

The headlights of a BMW flashed as she unlocked it. Finn and I watched her get in, rev the engine, and peel away from the curb in a burst of sound and exhaust.

"She didn't smell right," the werewolf muttered as Harper turned at the end of the street. Within seconds, quiet descended over the neighborhood again.

I couldn't hide my surprise, both at the fact he'd spoken at all and what he'd said. "Harper?" I clarified, just to make sure I'd understood correctly. Finn nodded. I squeezed his arm, pretending not to see how he flinched. "Hey, she's okay, I promise. We went to school together as kids. She's just a human."

"Humans can be dangerous, too."

He said this quietly, almost like he was afraid to argue with me, and I smiled. "Well, you're right about that. But not Harper. From what I remember, her weapons of choice are spreading rumors and sleeping with her friends' boyfriends. We're not in any danger from her. Okay?"

Wearing an unhappy expression, Finn just nodded. Since my hands were tucked away now, I gave him a friendly nudge with my elbow and headed for the sidewalk. He walked behind me, rather than alongside, and I added that to the list of things we'd need to work on.

I had every intention of walking right past—Savannah's old place was still a ways down the road—when I recognized another house. Unlike ours, it had been tenderly cared for in the years since my parents' deaths. It had cheerful yellow siding with white trim, wide bay windows, and cone-shaped turrets. Someone had taken the time to hang a swing from the large tree out front. Flowers lined the path and curtains fluttered in the windows.

The Millers, I thought wistfully. They used to babysit me and Damon whenever our parents were gone. Looking back, it was likely they were Mom and Dad's best friends. But what were the chances they still lived there? Little to none, probably. Fred had always talked about moving somewhere tropical when they retired.

Just as I was about to move on, my gaze caught and held on two people sitting on the porch. It wasn't exactly warm out, but that didn't seem to bother them. Neither had noticed me yet, and I drew closer, openly staring. Could it be...?

It *was* them. My heart launched like a rocket. I didn't think to explain anything to Finn before rushing up the front walkway. At the steps, I slowed. Vines of uncertainty wound around my throat, cutting off all words and breath. They hadn't seen me in, what, sixteen years? Would they welcome such a random intrusion into their lives?

At this proximity, I could see more details. Time had clearly not been kind to Emma Miller. She was only in her sixties, if memory served, but already her skin sagged painfully. Her bones were jutting things, like a baby bird's. Her eyes were young, though, two huge blue saucers that emanated innocence despite the fact she was anything but. Even though her knees were wrinkled doorknobs and it was barely thirty degrees, she wore cut-off shorts. Somehow I still remembered that, every two weeks, she went to her hairdresser to have her hair permed and colored. Right now, it was the hue of some kind of mucus. I'd hazard a guess that she was going for blond but it didn't work out so well.

"I'll plant some next year," Fred said. However altered their appearances, his voice was just as I remembered. Low and scratchy, like a wool blanket.

Tentatively, I approached the porch steps. I waited until there was a lull in their conversation to venture, "Emma? Fred?"

The old woman turned in her wicker chair, a welcoming smile already spreading across her face. When she saw me, the smile froze. She pressed a hand to her mouth and tears spilled from her eyes, leaving luminescent trails. "Fortuna? Is that you?" she asked, starting to rise from the chair.

"Oh, no, don't get—" I started. Too late; she was already up and heading for the steps. Then she was there, standing in front of me, a ghost from the past come to life.

Emma's embrace brought a rush of memories. She smelled like my childhood—floral laundry detergent, homemade soap, and ever-burning candles. No one touched me this freely. A fact that was my fault, of course, but something about the way she didn't hesitate to pull me close made my own eyes sting with sudden, unshed tears. Seconds ticked by but she didn't pull away. I waited until my eyes felt dry before I moved. She let me go only after a gentle squeeze and a kiss to my cheek.

The moment she moved back, Fred was there, ready to wrap me in his arms. Though I had fewer memories of this man, it wasn't my first instinct to shy from his touch. Fred Miller had a kind air about him, a gentleness that was disappearing from the world. He cupped the back of my head as if I were some precious item that had been lost. When one of his phobias whispered through my mind, I couldn't deny a sense of relief that came with it. My abilities had been so strange lately. So uneven. However much I'd avoided using them in the past, this was how it was supposed to be.

Apparently Fred was not a man much swayed by fear. The flavor was slight, hardly more than a faint aftertaste, and I couldn't even place it. He was scared of heights, but I suspected that if I were to put him on the tallest building in the world, his mind wouldn't break from it.

"Will you stay and visit for a bit?" Emma asked. She made me think of a hummingbird, so frail and fluttery and bright. Fred stepped away and wrapped his arm around her shoulders. Both of them waited for my response. What had she asked? If I would stay and visit?

I was about to accept when I remembered Finn. "Shit. I mean, shoot. Actually, we were…"

He was gone.

I looked toward the truck, wondering if he'd gotten back in, but it was empty. There was no sign of him in either direction, either. I wasn't sure if I should be concerned or even frightened. While Finn seemed to have no impulse to hunt humans in his wolf form, there were a dozen other things that could go wrong with a creature of his size wandering Denver.

"Please?" Emma asked, folding her hands in a gesture of pleading. "I can't tell you how many times Fred and I have imagined this moment."

Her words made my heart ache. "I can't stay long, but I'd really like to catch up, too."

"Wonderful," Emma said with another radiant smile. With that, they ushered me up the stairs and onto the porch. There was a small table, its glass top reflecting the ceiling above, and it looked like I'd interrupted brunch. There were plates with half-eaten pieces of toast and the remains of scrambled eggs.

"You guys were eating. I'm so sorry, I should come back once you've had a chance to—"

"Honey, would you run inside and fetch the teapot?" Emma asked over her shoulder, completely ignoring me. She sat down and patted the chair next to her. As I obeyed, I cast another disbelieving glance at her bare legs. "Now, where have you been? What's brought you back to us? I want to know everything."

I gave up trying to protest—from what I remembered, Mom had once said this old woman was 'stubborn as a mule'—and sank onto the flowered cushion. "I'm looking for Savannah," I answered, zipping up my coat to hoard whatever warmth I could.

Emma raised her yellowy eyebrows. "Oh, Savannah Simonson?"

"Here's your water, dear," Fred said, the hinges of the screen door moaning. He carried over a kettle, a thin trickle of steam still coming from its spout.

"What would I do without you, Fred Miller?" Emma asked, smiling into his eyes. She accepted the kettle from him, careful to avoid touching anything besides the handle, and tilted it over some cups on the table in front of us. Water filled the porcelain hollows. As she poured, Fred moved to sit in the chair across from us. "Anyway, she's become something of a shut-in, I'm afraid. Doesn't leave her house much."

"That's strange," I said, frowning. I watched Emma place fresh tea bags into the water. It instantly turned purple. "That doesn't sound like the Savannah I know. Was she in an accident or something?"

"Not that I've heard. I saw her at the grocery store a few months back. She looked like she could use a good meal or two, but there was nothing out of the ordinary about her. I think I have her address written down, if you'd like me to find it."

"That would be great, actually. Thank you." I took a drink from the teacup she offered me. The flavor was weak; the leaves needed more time to steep. I put it down and cleared my throat. "I was surprised you still live here. Fred, didn't you always talk about moving to Arizona?"

The old man leaned back and crossed his legs. It was surprisingly graceful for someone with such a lanky frame. He didn't seem affected by the chill, either. *Maybe they have a few drops of Fallen blood in them*, I thought wryly. Stranger things had happened.

"Sure did," Fred answered, holding the end of the tea bag string. His fingers moved up and down, pulling it through the water. "Still do. But this one 'isn't ready yet.'"

His wink was directed at Emma, but oddly enough, she didn't smile back. "Well, it's lucky for me you weren't," I told her, wondering why she looked so serious. "Do you still work at the library?"

Emma seemed to shake herself. She focused her pale eyes on me—they were the lightest of blues, like the sky on a bright day —and tucked a strand of hair behind my ear. "Goodness, you've got a good memory. No, I was laid off from the library a few years back. But I've kept myself busy since then!"

"She sells her own products on websites like Amazon and Etsy," Fred interjected, sounding proud.

I blinked. When I was a kid, they hadn't even owned a computer. "Really? What do you sell, Emma?"

The old woman waggled her eyebrows at me. "Oh, erotic oils and such."

I couldn't help it. I burst out laughing. "How... how did you... get into *that*?" I asked once I'd caught my breath.

"It's a funny story, actually," Emma began. I was still smiling as I tried another sip of the tea. It was perfect this time.

When Emma finished filling me in about her new business, I had another topic at the ready. Neither of them seemed to realize what I was doing, which was avoiding any questions about me and Damon. While Fred and Emma spoke, though, recounting the years since we'd lived in Denver, I kept losing focus. My gaze wandered to the smallest details and the slightest movements. These two humans were at the point in their lives where their bones literally creaked. Their wrinkles ran deeper than any river or canyon. They had touched every part, spoken every word.

Yet she smiled at him and he looked at her as if they'd been together one day instead of one lifetime.

Halfway into my second cup of tea, I tried to glance subtly at my phone. But Emma didn't miss much. "Where are you staying?" she asked, standing up to put her empty cup on a tray. I started to rise, thinking to help, but she waved me away.

"Just a small place nearby," I said, watching her. "The Pinnacle Motel."

Fred made a sound of discontent. Emma nodded at him in solidarity. She added the teapot and a jar of honey to the tray. Next went the spoons we'd used to stir. "Well, that won't do. I think it was voted one of the nation's ten dirtiest hotels, once. You're staying with us."

"Oh, thank you, but—"

"Don't you wish *ifs* and *buts* were candy nuts, so we could all have a Merry Christmas?" she mused, grasping the handles on the tray. She didn't spare me another glance as she went to the door. "I'll dig up Savannah's address for you. Make sure to pick up your things from the motel on your way back. Fred, will you check if there are enough clean towels in the guest room?"

Her husband put his hands on his thighs and stood a little more slowly than Emma had. "Consider it done, my love. And I'll dig out that dreamcatcher you liked so much, Fortuna. Remember that thing? Any time you kids slept over, you'd fall asleep touching it. Told us that you never had bad dreams here. We tried to give it to you, but you just said that we needed to be protected, too."

I liked hearing about the girl they'd known—it felt like they were talking about someone else. Felt like remembering a life that had never belonged to me. It sounded too good to be true. "I did?" I asked.

He nodded, almost proudly, as if he were talking about his own daughter. "Fearless little thing, our Fortuna."

"Fearless? Hardly," I said with a bittersweet smile.

"Well, maybe not fearless," Fred rectified with one hand on the door handle. The wind picked up, then, and it whistled through the bare branches of a nearby oak tree. "You were smart enough to be scared of Emma's meatloaf."

I laughed as he went back inside. Once he was gone, I sat there in the wicker chair, my palm warmed by the tea. The air smelled of frost and withered leaves. Since it was the middle of the day, there were no cars in the street or children playing in yards. It was... peaceful. I wondered if I'd been wrong about a veil being thinner between worlds.

Because it seemed that I'd encountered a little magic after all.

CHAPTER SEVENTEEN

ind ruffled Finn's hair as we left city limits. Every few minutes, I glanced down at the GPS, certain it was taking us the wrong way. My grip was light on the steering wheel, ready to turn around at the slightest provocation.

Why would Savannah live so far from everything?

"Arrived," our guide announced at last. With this many miles between here and Denver, the homes were more spread out. I didn't have to search for a house number to know which one was Savannah's—there was a lone, dirty mailbox to our left, and nothing else.

No, I realized as I turned. There was a sign next to the mailbox. It creaked in the wind, drawing my gaze, or I probably wouldn't have spotted it otherwise. The painted wood was difficult to see, even in the daytime, since it was nearly overgrown by weeds. I slowed to read it. *Madame Mirielle*, the letters declared in chipped paint. Beneath this, it also advertised tarot card, palm, and crystal ball readings. Witches often used their talents to survive amongst humans, but I was still surprised.

The last time we'd spoken, Savannah was about to graduate with a master's degree in psychology.

"Are you all right?" Finn asked in his gravelly voice. He spoke so little that I still wasn't used to it.

"Yes, why?" I said. At the same moment, I noticed that we'd come to a complete stop. I shook my head, as if to clear it, and returned one foot to the gas.

There had still been no sign of Lyari.

Eerily similar to the cabin we'd seen just before plunging into a forest full of werewolves, the house at the end of the drive gazed at us with windows that looked like sorrowful eyes. The siding, which might've been white at some point in its lifetime, was yellowed and breaking. Some pieces were missing entirely. There was a swing hanging from a tree out front, though from the looks of it, I wouldn't trust it to hold my weight.

The brakes whined as we parked. "Maybe I should do this next part alone," I said without taking my eyes off that front door. There was nothing out of the ordinary about it, but I got the strange impression that it was firmly locked and visitors weren't welcome. As a response, Finn slid lower in the seat and began to fiddle with the beads on my purse, saying without words that he would remain right there. I gave him a tight-lipped smile—the best I could manage—and opened the door. My boots hit the gravel with a crunching sound. I glanced down and realized that I'd taken the keys with me. Force of habit. I started to turn, thinking Finn might want to turn on some music.

"What are you doing here?"

When I followed the voice, I saw that Savannah was standing in the doorway. Were it not for those vivid green eyes, I wouldn't have recognized her. Damon's girlfriend had always been a little overweight, but now she was painfully thin. She looked as though she hadn't slept in years, with smudges beneath her eyes and a pallid cast to her skin. Her hair, which once fell to her waist in auburn waves, had been cropped short.

I should've checked on her. I should've made sure she was okay. Out loud I called, "Hey, Sav. It's been too long. How are you?"

She didn't respond or move as I approached. Something was off, but I didn't know what. Now that I was closer, I could see how her cheekbones jutted out, like a living corpse. Just as I was about to repeat the question, Savannah seemed to awaken. "I'm okay. As well as can be expected, I guess. What about you?"

I stopped at the base of the steps and hesitated. "The answer to that is complicated. Can I come in? We really need to talk. Oh, that's Finn. He's a... friend."

Her gaze returned to me. The emptiness there alarmed me, and it felt as if I was looking down a deep, dark well. This girl bore no resemblance to the vibrant cheerleader I'd grown up with. My instincts argued with each other and created a distracting din. *There's danger here. No, no, it's Savannah. She wouldn't hurt a fly.* When the witch spoke again, all she said was, "I wish you'd called."

Despite my best efforts, I was frowning now. "I tried. Your old number isn't working."

"Right, yes. I forgot. I have a new phone. This isn't a good time, actually. I have a client coming."

She's trying to keep me out of the house. What had she gotten herself into? "No worries. Is there somewhere I can wait?" I asked.

There was a challenge in my voice, even if I hadn't meant to put it there. *You can come up with as many excuses as you'd like, honey. I'm not going anywhere.*

Savannah looked like she'd taken a bite of something sour. "My sessions are private."

I moved quickly, taking the witch by surprise, and got around her. However many flaws I had, timidity wasn't one of them. "No, don't—" she cried.

Too late.

My eyes took a moment to adjust to the sudden dimness. There was a TV on somewhere; I recognized Caillou's annoyingly high voice. Interesting choice for entertainment, but I was hardly in any position to judge. A strange smell permeated the air, pleasant one moment and revolting the next. Herbs hung from the ceiling on strings, and I wondered if they were to blame. Was this what she'd been trying to hide? That she was still practicing? But why would she think I'd care about that? Dissatisfied, I continued my appraisal of the house.

I stood in a split entryway, with stairs leading to the second floor, a hallway that undoubtedly went to the kitchen, and a living room. Every curtain was drawn and the space was lit with lamps rather than overhead lighting. To my left was probably where Savannah took her clients. The doorway was covered in velvet curtains of such deep violet that, at first glance, they looked black.

I moved toward the living room. The furniture was shabby, like mine, but that was where the similarities ended. Where I at least attempted to keep my house clean, Savannah clearly made no such efforts. Every surface I saw was littered with trash, dirty dishes, clothes, and... toys? Were they for her clients' children? I took a step forward, the floorboard moaning, and suddenly I could see the couch.

A jolt traveled the length of my spine.

A figure sat on one of the torn cushions, one arm wrapped around a stuffed animal, and the other positioned so he was able to put a finger up his nose. It was Damon. Or, more accurately, Damon as a child. His gaze was fixed on a small TV, where the cartoon played. It was as though I were standing in a memory that felt far too real. The boy on the couch had the same overly big eyes, the same thin face, the same sweet smile as the brother I once knew. I didn't need a DNA test to confirm what was right in front of me.

Damon was a father.

The floor creaked as Savannah moved to stand beside me. I couldn't take my eyes off the boy. "This..." She stopped and swallowed. She went to pick the child up, then rested him on her hip. The rings on her fingers glittered in the low lamplight. "This is my son. I named him Matthew."

After our father.

Astonishment swiftly gave way to anger. I'd never made it a secret that I didn't like children, it was true, but my brother's child would've been a different story entirely.

"Why didn't you tell me?" I demanded. Savannah set Matthew down on the floor, where a blanket was laid out and surrounded by toys. "It's not like you didn't have my number or know where I lived, so it couldn't have been a case of inaccessibility. Which means you chose to withhold the fact that Damon has a son. That I have a *nephew*."

Facing me, Savannah cupped her elbows and made herself look even smaller. "I... I didn't... "

I waited for her to go on, giving her a chance to provide a reasonable explanation, but the witch just stood there looking miserable. Whatever patience I'd scraped together blew away in a gust of hurt. "I could've helped you, damn it. We may not be flush with cash, but Damon and I have savings. I would have babysat, too. Gladly. But you didn't even give me a chance. Why, Savannah?"

Her face was pale and strained. "I'm sorry."

When she didn't go on, I focused on the child, as if the truth would be written on his skin. He was absorbed by Caillou and I could only see the back of his head. But this just made me notice he even had the same cowlick as Damon. "Is he a warlock or a Nightmare?"

Before Savannah could answer, the front door opened. Both of us turned, instinctively following the sound. Lyari Paynore's willowy frame filled the bright opening. "We need to go," she announced without preamble.

How had she found me? It wasn't like I was hiding or avoiding her, but if this faerie could find me so easily, it meant others could. Annoyed by the interruption—which conveniently hid the rush of relief I felt at the sight of her—I scowled. "Lyari, what are you doing here?"

"Like it or not, I swore a vow of fealty, Your Majesty. You'll not die on my watch," she said coolly. There was something about her countenance, though, that made the words seem false. Had this ferocious faerie actually started to care about me? I started to respond when she added, "What would become of my reputation then?"

Of course that was why she'd come. Had I actually thought we were starting to become friends? My tone was dry as I said, "While I appreciate the devotion, I don't need a babysitter right now."

"Actually, you do. There are werewolves in the woods. I saw at least two."

I paused to let Lyari's words sink in. How the hell did they find us here? Suddenly it seemed ridiculous that I was wasting so much energy caring about her opinion of me. "This is just wonderful. And here I was worrying something wouldn't go wrong..." I trailed off when I remembered that I'd left Finn outside.

Savannah spoke from behind me. "Fortuna? What's going on?"

"Werewolves. *Angry* werewolves," I said through my teeth, stepping around Lyari. My stomach lurched when I saw the truck was empty. The passenger side door hung open like a mournful wave.

I drew back and slammed the door shut, but I didn't bother locking it, since a werewolf would be more than capable of shattering their way through. Thinking quickly, I turned to face Savannah.

The witch had picked Matthew back up at some point and she held him tightly against her, as if by sheer force of love, she could protect him. "They're coming here?" she asked shakily.

"If I had known there was a child involved, I never would've come," I told her. It was the closest thing to an apology she'd get from me. "I'll stand outside and keep them distracted. It's me and Finn they want, not you. Lyari, take Savannah and Matthew out the back. Keep them safe. *Now*."

The faerie unsheathed her sword. "I'm not going anywhere. Get behind me."

"I don't need a bodyguard," I hissed, disregarding the fact I'd assigned her to be exactly that. "I need a goddamn weapon, which is why I'm going out to the truck. Your first priority is the kid, understood? There's no time to argue, so take it as an order from your queen."

Her hand tightened on the sword's hilt as if she were imagining slicing *me* in half with it. "As you wish, Your Majesty," she said. The title sounded like a curse on her lips.

I'd care about that later. Maybe. Where were my keys? Hadn't they been in my pocket? We might need them at some point. As I searched the floor, I could hear Lyari and Savannah talking to each other. A minute later, when I turned around, I was baffled to see the witch standing there. Lyari and Matthew, however, were slipping out the back door. I caught a glimpse of her flashing sword just before they vanished. "What are you doing?" I demanded, refocusing on Savannah.

She swallowed. "I might be able to help. I know a couple spells that could slow them down."

Truth be told, if I wanted to survive this, I could use the help. Right on cue, I spotted the glint of my keys. They'd fallen in the living room doorway. "Great," I said, rushing past Savannah to grab them. "Start on those while I get my gun."

There was no sign of the wolves when I stepped outside. My insides felt jittery as I hurried to the truck, opened the door, and opened the center console. Cool metal greeted my fingertips. However much I disliked guns, I already felt less vulnerable. I straightened, darting a glance toward the backseat on the off chance that Finn was hiding back there. Empty. I let out a worried breath and turned to go back into the house. At the same moment, something in the underbrush caught my eye.

Lights. Small and bright. Like fireflies.

But it's too late in the season for fireflies… the thought cut off like a cord tightening around a throat. Suddenly I knew what I was looking at. What I was seeing.

Eyes. They were eyes.

Lyari was wrong; there weren't just two wolves hunting us. I counted at least seven, all of their luminous gazes fixed on me. It may not have been a full moon, but they were still Fallen. Still creatures with supernatural speed and strength. All I had were a few bullets and an ability that required physical touch to use.

That's not all you have, that small voice reminded me. Oh, right. I had a fucking faerie king for a mate.

"Collith," I shout-whispered, slowly retreating back to the house. Adrenaline was already coursing through me, heightening every sound. A breeze. A skittering leaf. "I may need your assistance after all. Collith?"

My back touched the front door. The eyes remained fixed on me. Didn't wolves blink? I waited another thirty seconds, but Collith didn't appear. Usually he answered before I could even finish saying his name. Something within me knew that he wasn't coming. That he couldn't. Our bond was too still, a sensation akin to how lungs felt during a held breath. I'd gotten so accustomed to its gentle pulses that I instantly felt off kilter without them.

As I fumbled for the doorknob, I noticed that the glowing eyes were bigger than they'd been before. They were inching closer, closing in for the kill. The moment I realized this, I knew fighting them wasn't an option. We had to *run*.

I didn't bother with an explanation; I just reached inside, grabbed Savannah's arm, and *yanked*. She was too frightened to protest. We flew out the door and crossed the driveway one more time. I held the gun, ready to use it at any moment.

The wolves knew we were leaving; one burst from the trees just as I slammed the driver's side door shut. Savannah made intelligible sounds of panic. She sprinted past the front of the truck and around to the other side. She pulled the door closed and let out an ear-splitting scream. An instant later, the wolf leapt onto the hood and snarled. Its nails made screeching sounds on the fiberglass. Within the same beat, I turned the key —the engine came to life with its usual phlegm-filled cough— and shoved the gear into drive. I'd hoped the wolf would slide off and hit the ground, but it saw the danger and jumped off in time.

I tore down Savannah's driveway like it was a NASCAR track, and the air exploded with howls. The hunt had begun.

"Put your seatbelt on," I ordered the witch, yanking at my own. Her eyes were wide with panic as she hurried to obey. Something told me I wouldn't be able to count on those protective spells happening anytime soon. My rearview mirror filled with those unnerving eyes, staring hatefully after us. Did that mean they weren't going to chase us?

I prayed Lyari had been able to get the boy away safely. It wasn't possible to sift with him, so she must've been running. Why the hell hadn't I ordered her to take my truck? Everything was happening too quickly, too frantically. It wasn't until recently that I'd had to think on my feet with the stakes being death or survival.

Wait. Lyari had a cell phone. "Here," I said breathlessly, thrusting my phone at Savannah. "Call Collith and get Lyari's number. Keep trying if he doesn't answer. Try Damon, too. We need to warn them."

"Damon?" she repeated faintly. The phone slipped between her limp fingers and landed on the seat between us.

Shit. I'd never gotten the chance to tell her that he was alive.

"Yes. This isn't exactly how I planned to break the news, but I found Damon earlier this month. Or saved him, more accurately. He's... different now."

"Different how? What happened to him? Where has he—"

I kept my eyes on the road as I said, "Look, Savannah, you deserve all those answers. Right now, I need you to make those calls."

For a moment, it looked like she wanted to argue, but something in my face must've convinced her not to. After a few minutes, with the phone still pressed to her ear, Savannah shook her head. The glow from the radio gave her skin a sickly tint. "None of them are picking up."

"Lyari and Collith probably don't have signals. But Damon should. Try sending him a text... and let him know it's you. Maybe that'll make him answer," I muttered. Savannah's fingers visibly trembled as she started typing a message.

The witch didn't speak after that. She seemed to be absorbed in writing a novel for my brother. I kept my opinions to myself and left her to it.

We were halfway back to Denver when, to my left, I saw a flash of gray within the trees. I frowned and strained to catch a better glimpse. If the pack had already caught up with us, I couldn't lead them back to the motel. They'd find Damon.

Savannah pointed wildly. "Fortuna, look out!"

I followed her finger and comprehended there was someone standing in the middle of the road. I gasped and jerked the steering wheel to the left. In an instant, the truck was thundering off the gravel and at the line of trees. *Fuck*," I shouted.

We slammed into a tree, hard, and the airbags instantly deployed.

Sweet-smelling smoke clouded the air and my ears rang. Time slipped past me; I knew we couldn't stop, couldn't rest, but it was a battle to care. Blood trickled down my chin—a throb of pain revealed that I'd bitten my tongue. After a few more seconds, I managed to scrape my thoughts together. I looked over at Savannah, who seemed dazed but unharmed. "We need to run," I croaked. She blinked at me and I repeated myself. The witch nodded and fumbled for the door handle. We both got out of the steaming vehicle.

I scanned the clearing around us, struggling to remain alert. There was still some daylight left, but that would change soon. Nothing moved except leaves and air. The werewolf I'd swerved to avoid—why hadn't I just *hit* that asshole?—was nowhere in sight. But that didn't mean the danger was gone, not even close. It had probably gone to get the rest of the pack.

Which meant we only had a small head start.

It occurred to me that I could call the police under the guise of reporting an accident or claiming someone ran us off the road. But how long would it take them to arrive? What if these wolves didn't hesitate to take a human life? Emergency services would probably send a single squad car, and no cop would let a couple of bloody-looking women just jump into his vehicle without explanation. No, we'd have to get to Denver on foot, without involving anyone else.

I turned to bark instructions at Savannah... but she was nowhere in sight. Swearing, I circled the truck. There she was, on her hands and knees, swaying precariously. Snot and blood pooled on the leaves in front her. She'd need help to stand, damn it. It had been years since I'd touched her last, and often-times when a person went through change, so did their fears. I forced myself to reach for her delicate arms, knowing the instant I did so, her secrets would belong to me.

"No, don't." Savannah's voice was strangled. "I'm fine. Just give me a second."

"Don't you know any spells to heal us?" I muttered, fear and frustration making me bitchier than normal. I stood back and watched her struggle. Night breathed down my neck, taunting me. *I'm coming for you*, its ancient voice seemed to say. The shadows felt thick and sinister. I envisioned myself as a terrified rabbit as I twitched at every sound. When had the darkness stopped being a friend? It was just one more thing I'd lost since marrying Collith.

Once again, the air erupted with howls. *They're coming.* Maybe they'd think we were still on the road and head toward the city...

In that instant, it hit me that we were being pursued by *wolves*. I grabbed Savannah's arm and pulled her close. "We have to hide our scent," I whispered urgently in her ear. "Do you know a spell?"

She shook her head and I swallowed a curse. There was no wind, thankfully, but we'd already left a trail for them to follow. Despite popular belief, crossing a river would do nothing except carry our scent back to the ground as the water dripped off. Pepper spray, if either of us had any, just bought a few minutes. I glanced at Savannah's pockets and they looked pretty damn empty.

Getting to a populated area was our only hope. I hissed this to the witch, who panted and nodded. She got to her feet, looking far too pale for my liking. We started in the direction of Denver, using the trees for cover.

Pain climbed up my side after we'd been running a while. My lungs burned. Sweat darkened the material at my armpits and lower back. Savannah didn't look like she was faring any better. Somehow we kept going. We were lucky to have our Fallen blood, this witch and I, since a human probably would've stopped miles back.

Afternoon became twilight, then twilight became darkness. Still, we ran. An angry chorus followed us through the blue-black night. At least it answered the question of whether or not the wolves had chased us.

On the outskirts of the city, there was a billboard, covered in an image of a woman with long legs and pouting lips. We ran beneath it, briefly exposed by its lights, and Savannah whimpered in terror. I had no comfort to offer her. Crouching low, like burglars darting over city rooftops, we weaved through houses and yards to keep off the roads.

I had a plan and it was simple—get to a public place, order an Uber, and go to Fred and Emma's. The werewolves weren't aware of my history with them. They wouldn't know to look for us there. Then, once I'd had a chance to catch my breath and evaluate Savannah's injuries, I would figure out what to do next.

There was a saying, I thought, about best-laid plans and how easily they went wrong. I couldn't remember the exact wording. But as headlights flicked on, exposing dust motes dancing through the air like snowflakes, I tried to. Savannah and I slowed, then stopped. The lights also exposed the silhouettes standing all around us. Savannah bent over, gasping for air, but I made a valiant effort to remain upright.

"You're surrounded," a male voice growled, confirming what I'd already realized. It sounded as though he said the words around a mouthful of fangs. "Keep runnin' and I might forget that Astrid wants you alive."

For once I overcame the urge to say something snarky. Savannah was getting harder to hold up and I could feel her breathing against my ribcage. The harsh rhythm of her lungs had begun to slow. She was probably going into shock... or her injuries were worse than I'd realized. Either way, I needed to get her to a hospital, and I wouldn't accomplish that by pissing the wolves off even more.

When it became clear that I wasn't going to do anything

stupid, one of them stepped forward. The light was still to her back, but the female was close enough that I could faintly make out her features. *Cora.* I almost let out a sigh of relief. Then she shifted, angling her body slightly to the side, and light fell across half of the girl's face.

Any hope that she would help us again died when I saw her expression—there was something harder about it this time. That, and there was also a machete clutched in her small fists. I wondered what Astrid had done to her for letting me keep my gun. Maybe it had broken her.

"Let's go, pup," one of the werewolves called. Cora's amber eyes darted toward him. I watched her take a breath, then she looked at me again. *I'm sorry,* she mouthed, her lips moving so slightly that I almost missed it.

Then, so quickly that I didn't even have a chance to let go of Savannah, she swung the butt of her machete at my head.

CHAPTER EIGHTEEN

I came to in an unfamiliar clearing.

For once, there was no disorientation or loss of memory; the image of Cora coming at me was clear and fresh. But when I looked down, expecting to see blood and shackles, I frowned in bewilderment. My jeans and boots were gone, and someone had put me in a gown that was wildly inappropriate for the season. Now that I thought about it, though, I realized it wasn't cold. Was this the dreamscape? Where was Oliver?

I stood up slowly, worried that I'd carried my injuries into unconsciousness, but nothing hurt. I scanned the clearing again, hoping to catch sight of my best friend. Only trees and stars looked back.

When I took a step forward, I nearly tripped on the long skirt. I lifted it with an irritated huff, yet I couldn't help admiring it, too. The dress I wore was, in a word, whimsical. The material was pink and transparent, with a hard bodice underneath. The sleeves and skirt flowed. Around my elbows and waist, there were bands of wildflowers. It should've looked ridiculous, but instead, I felt pretty and... free.

Okay, time to figure out where I was. I raised my gaze from

the dress and blinked. While I'd been distracted by the dress, more details had popped into existence. Flowers dotted the grass, more colorful than bruises or graffiti. Strings of lights had been hung in the trees. Stars shone without restraint, nestled comfortably in the dark blanket of sky. Music floated through the air, more lovely and dreamy than fireflies.

Then, everywhere I looked, there were faeries. *Winged* faeries.

Since seeing the two long scars on Collith's back, I had caught myself imagining what their wings used to look like. Instead of the human cliché, in which they were formed entirely of white feathers, I'd pictured them translucent. Pale. Almost like a spider's web in the way the veins reflected light.

But reality wasn't even close to what I'd come up with. These were more like… solar flares of a star. *They were once beings of light*, Laurie had told me. It was easier to believe now. It was also harder to look away. No wonder there were so many stories and legends of angels. If creating them had been an investment, God spared no expense.

Suddenly, a familiar conscience brushed against mine, jerking me to attention. I spun in a circle, searching every beautiful face. In doing so, I couldn't help noticing more details. These faeries wore clothing meant for warm nights and summer months—material so flimsy it was nearly transparent and footwear that was more slipper than shoe. Drinks glittered in their hands. Jewelry gleamed in moonlight. There were no grisly feasts or the hulking form of the Death Bringer. Instead, there was tinkling laughter and bursts of graceful dance.

My gaze finally latched onto a lone figure, standing in the middle of it all, who stared back at me. His usual crown was gone. In its place, a silver circlet rested on his silken curls. With each passing second, our connection intensified. Collith's soul called to mine, a force more powerful than any whirling current or steady moonbeam. I didn't try to resist its pull. Neither did he.

"What is this?" I asked once we'd closed the distance between us. Of course I knew what it *was*, specifically. My mother told me about faerie revels and how dangerous they could be. Her long list of risks included losing track of time, getting whisked away, and succumbing to madness. Just to name a few.

Thankfully, Collith understood what I meant. One side of his mouth tilted up in a rueful smile. His hazel eyes reflected the starry lights that hung above our heads. "A distraction. There isn't much I can do until the holy water is out of my system."

With those words, my head cleared, as though clouds had parted and vibrant sunlight shone through. "Wait, the wolves have you, too? And they gave you holy water?" I demanded, hoping he would correct me. Admit he'd just made a bad joke.

But Collith nodded. "Put me in chains soaked in it, then forced a gallon down my throat."

I'd been planning to summon him again once I regained consciousness. Savannah was in no shape to save our asses, and my abilities weren't conducive to taking on an entire pack of monsters. There was still Laurie, of course, but something told me there would always be strings attached to his help. "Why didn't you just make a nice barbecue out of them?" I asked now, trying not to pace. There was no room to do it, anyway. Faeries were dancing all around us.

"Because they had Damon," Collith countered. "They threatened to harm him if I so much as twitched a finger. Surprisingly strategic for werewolves, don't you think? There must be more to Astrid than meets the eye."

Rage and fear rushed through me like leaves carried in a current. "Is he okay?" I asked tightly.

"As much as Damon can be. He's worried about you. He won't say it, but he is." Collith didn't give me a chance to formulate some kind of plan. "Dance with me, Fortuna."

I'd never know whether I would have accepted, because once again, Collith didn't wait for a response. In the next breath, he held me close, his palms like two spots of ice against my waist. I planted my own against his chest, thinking to push him away. But I didn't. A distraction, he'd called it. I was always focused, always fighting. Right now a distraction sounded really, really nice.

We spun, around and around, so swiftly and so effortlessly that dizziness bypassed me altogether. I gripped Collith's hand and shoulder with white fingers, but I wasn't afraid of hurting him. Not him. His presence was so powerful that it felt like a physical thing. Like strength radiated from his very bones.

When the music slowed, I looked around again, undeniably drawn to the wings, the lights, the drinks. I could touch it, any of it, and still this wouldn't be real. Acting on an impulse, I closed my eyes to listen—too often we depended on our eyes to tell us what was beautiful.

"This is a dream," I said suddenly. My eyes snapped open. The revelation about the wolves had made me forget to ask more questions about our current reality... which was exactly what Collith had intended. Tricky, tricky faerie.

The Unseelie King watched me carefully; he was afraid of what my reaction would be. "Yes."

"But it feels so real. Like..." *Like it does with Oliver,* I'd been about to say. Thinking of Ollie sent a rush of guilt through me. He'd be so worried. How many nights had we been apart now? I was losing track.

Collith must've felt something; that familiar line appeared between his brows. But I couldn't confide in him, because I still hadn't told the entire truth about my best friend. This definitely didn't feel like the right time or place. For a few seconds I floundered in uncertainty, not knowing how to finish or whether to share this part of myself.

Collith took pity on me. "That's because it is real," he said.

"I'm here. We are having an actual conversation. Both of us will remember this when we wake up."

"You're using our bond." I searched his eyes to confirm this. Sometimes it felt like I hated them; they pulled me in like a tide and I drowned every time. "How long have you been able to do this?"

"Since the moment we were mated. I didn't tell you"—Collith added this quickly, knowing it would be my next question—"because you were already scared of me."

At this, I scoffed. "I was never scared of you."

His eyes burned into mine. "Yes. You were."

The solemnity in his voice made me sober. I'd forgotten that I couldn't lie to him. Not well, at least.

Collith stopped, right there in the center of the chaos. Dancers around us merely parted and continued on with the steps and turns, as though we were a stone jutting from the sea. A fire ignited in me, stoked by the heat of his gaze. He didn't give me a chance to break away. He leaned so close that his breath teased my lips. My instincts and desires battled each other with a ferocity that stole the air from my lungs. "Fortuna, I—" he started.

Fear rushed through me, roaring like a river after the spring thaw. He was going to say something he couldn't take back, something neither of us would be able to forget. It would change everything. I put a finger on his lips and shook my head. "No, don't. Let's just keep dancing, okay?"

In response, the Unseelie King splayed his fingers against the small of my back and pulled me against him. I allowed Collith to sweep me away. In this dream, I knew the dance better than the beat of my own heart. I moved as he did, I matched every thrust and retreat, I answered each shift and sway.

Somehow, our movements began to feel sensual. Sweat gleamed on our skin. Our eyes met with fleeting, burning intensity, then wrenched away. His fingers around mine—such an innocent touch—sent currents of electricity down my arms.

I wanted his fingers to trail over every inch of my body.

We were both breathing hard now. Once again, the music started to slow. Like the end of a rollercoaster, it drew to a gradual halt. Our hands dropped to our sides. Collith and I stood there, face-to-face, our chests nearly touching. *Grab me*, I thought. *Kiss me. Claim me.*

I couldn't be the one to initiate it. Admit in such a blatant way that I yearned for him.

Maybe Collith felt everything through the bond. Or maybe he was beginning to know me, too. Instead of tearing it down or exploring its perimeter, he allowed the illusion to remain intact. He stroked my chin with his thumb, searching my gaze. I looked back, trying not to let it show that even this simple touch affected me. Slowly, Collith bent his head, and I closed my eyes.

Unlike our other kisses, this was tender.

Our mouths brushed, once, twice. The third time, Collith's tongue teased mine. Heat stirred in my lower stomach. I opened myself to him, wanting more. He tasted so, so good. Collith's hands slid around my waist, pulling me completely against him. In that instant, I could feel how much he wanted me, too. I buried my fingers in his hair, forgetting everything but this. His long fingers trailed up the side of my thigh. My core clenched in response. *Off. I want this dress off.*

I opened my eyes to search for zippers or buttons. To my surprise, the clearing was gone. We now stood in a shadowy bedroom. Floor-to-ceiling windows made up the wall to our left. An enormous bed filled the space behind Collith. "Where are we?" I whispered, automatically stepping back. The blatant power he held over my mind was unnerving.

The Unseelie King stood in a slant of moonlight, watching me intently. "My home. I bought it a couple of years ago."

Curiosity got the better of me, and I moved to the window.

Outlines of trees and mountains stood against the dim skyline. It suited him, this calm and gentle mate of mine. "How often do you come here?" I asked without turning. Collith's chest brushed against my back and an involuntary shiver went through me, as it always did whenever he was near. Nothing had been real and then, with no warning, everything was.

"Not as much as I'd like," he answered. His cool breath teased my skin. "Once a month, maybe. I come whenever things are calm at Court... or when I'm about to lose my mind."

I caught myself wondering if he'd ever brought others here. Or, more specifically, a female that now lived in the bowels of the Unseelie Court, covered in ice and secrets from the past. Collith had been so open lately; maybe he would actually answer if I asked. I was about to give in to the urge when Collith said, "Would you like to see your room?"

"*My* room?"

"Of course—you're my mate. Everything that's mine is yours, as well. It stood to reason that you should have a place of your own in our home."

For what felt like the thousandth time, Collith had struck me speechless. There didn't seem to be a need to speak anyway. Without another word, Collith took my hand in his. There was a childish gleam of anticipation in his eyes as he led me down a moonlit hallway. Everything—the floors, the walls, the ceiling—was made of rich, smooth wood. Its scent permeated the air, and I liked it. It reminded me of those nights I'd spent in the woods, unafraid and content. The nights I'd found a sense of belonging and didn't have to hide who I was.

At the end of the hall, just to the right of a tall window, there was another door. Collith opened it and stepped aside.

As I entered, I felt like a deer, timid and cautious. I looked around with disbelief and shy pleasure. It was simple, but Collith had added details that were entirely me. The beige wall behind the bed had a stencil of a sunflower on it—my favorite flower. There was a small bookshelf in the corner, and I approached it expecting more fae history or the mysteries Collith enjoyed so much. Instead, they were textbooks. *The Merck Veterinary Manual. McCurnin's Clinical Textbook for Veterinary Technicians. Color Atlas of Veterinary Histology.*

I'd mentioned my dream of being a veterinarian to him once. Just once. Apparently that was all it took with Collith Sylvyre.

My throat felt full. No one had ever done something like this for me before. Even Maureen, who'd wanted so badly for me to be the daughter she'd always dreamed of, had decorated my room in the way *she* thought it should be. Pink walls, posters of boy bands, dainty furniture. The fact that Collith had chosen the exact opposite said that he knew me better than I wanted to admit.

As though I could outrun the unwelcome rush of emotion, I hurried toward the window. Floorboards creaked beneath my weight. The view was even better than Collith's—those mountains I loved so much spread across the horizon like a painting.

Feeling overwhelmed, I turned to face the one responsible for this unexpected gift. Of its own volition, my gaze immediately dropped to his mouth. There was no point restraining myself or denying it, was there? He already knew I wanted him. Giving in, I wrapped my hand around the back of his neck and pulled him to me. Collith didn't hesitate to respond, and somehow he tasted better every time we did this. We started moving toward the bed, never breaking apart or coming up for breath. Along the way, Collith's capable fingers undid the buttons along my spine.

As we fell onto the mattress, the dress loosened.

I landed on my back. Instead of resting his full weight against me, as I'd expected, Collith braced his strong arms on either side of my head. I lifted my chin, but his eyes didn't meet mine—they were on the dress. Or, more accurately, what had been exposed from its absence. I laid there, watching Collith admire me, and it affected my ability to breathe. He was the first one—the first real one, at least—to think I was beautiful. Me, and not some false vision of perfection. It was terrifying and thrilling.

After a few seconds, Collith used one hand to pull the neckline down, down, down. The gossamer material pooled around my waist and left me topless. Then, without warning, he dipped his head and ran his tongue from navel to chest. Need exploded at the apex of my thighs. Pieces of rubble fell from the wall between me and the Unseelie Court. Groaning with impatience, I propped myself up to reach Collith's mouth again.

Gradually, though I wasn't sure who initiated it, the kiss changed. It went from something urgent and hungry to tender and exploratory. I told myself it was the moonlight or the wind whispering past the house. Collith murmured my name, no, he breathed it, as though he'd been wanting this for years instead of weeks. I felt my nipples rise and my legs go weak.

I was ready to do this. I wanted to feel Collith inside me. Right about now, I usually felt a sense of wrongness or the urge to get away. But here, with him, there was just heat.

You should probably tell him you're a virgin. The stray thought caught me unawares, and apparently I wasn't the only one.

"You're a virgin?" Collith echoed, asking the question against my lips.

Reluctantly, I pulled away. His mouth was red and swollen, and for the first time since we'd met, his eyes were hazy with desire. It took all my willpower to stay back. "Yes," I answered. "Ever since I was a baby. I was just born this way."

His eyes gleamed with soundless laughter. "Do you always use sarcasm when you're uncomfortable?"

It was my first instinct to deny it. That I wasn't uncomfortable at all; I didn't care what he thought. Something stopped me. I wanted to affect him as much as he did me. I wanted to hear him come undone, as I had in that bathtub. I wanted to see him in a way that was real and vulnerable.

I put my hand on Collith's shoulder and guided him to the edge of the bed. I was still bare from the waist up, but he watched my face with obvious fascination. "Fortuna, you—"

Once again, I silenced him with a finger to his lips. Collith acquiesced instantly. I hooked my thumbs in the dress and finished taking it off. As it puddled around me, I knelt naked between Collith's legs and tugged at the button of his jeans. The zipper came down with a sound that felt loud in the stillness. My heart pounded with anticipation. Collith was affected, too— his considerable length strained against the material of his boxer briefs. I bent and pulled his pants off.

Emboldened, I pulled the briefs down. It was the first time he'd allowed me to see him like this. His cock was long and straight. Once I'd had my fill of looking, I cupped his balls in my palms and leisurely licked the underside of his shaft. Collith's body gave a jerk, as though he hadn't been prepared for it. A satisfied smile touched my lips. I proceeded to explore his length with both my mouth and hand. Faster and faster. Harder and harder. Collith's moans traveled through my entire body.

"I don't want to come yet," he breathed suddenly. I ignored this; I was too impatient. Too reluctant to stop, even for a moment. Mere moments later, Collith came undone beneath me, the taste of him filling my mouth. His entire body quaked. I watched his face and my own body reacted at the way his eyes squeezed shut and his head tilted back. His exclamation was soft and guttural.

"Now that's what I call a distraction," I managed after I'd swallowed. I rested my chin on his knee and smiled.

Collith's hazel eyes twinkled. He sat up slightly, making the muscles in his stomach bunch, and brushed the hair back from my eyes. "I hope you realize this doesn't count as our date," he informed me.

I raised my eyebrows. "No?"

He bent over to kiss my eyelids, then my lips. "Not even close."

Smiling, I got up from the floor and sat beside him. There was a throw blanket on the end of the bed, which I dragged over and dropped around me. "That must be some first date you're planning."

"Don't build it up too much," he warned.

"Why? Afraid I'll be disappointed?"

"Always." The seriousness of his response surprised me. Before I could respond, his fingers slipped beneath the waistband of my underwear. "May I return the favor?"

I couldn't explain it, but the fervor had left me. All I wanted to do now was curl under the covers and get warm. "Would it be okay if we just... slept? Is that weird?"

If Collith was disappointed, he hid it well. His hand slid out of my underwear and settled on my hand. He gave it a gentle squeeze. "Not weird at all."

"Okay. Scoot over, then," I ordered. Collith's eyebrows flew up in surprise, but he obeyed readily enough, shifting to make room. With brisk movements, I lifted the sheets and duvet cover, then tucked them over us. I got into my usual sleeping position, resting on my side, arms tucked beneath the pillow. When Collith didn't move, I informed him over my shoulder, "This is the part where you spoon me."

The faerie king didn't say a word, but I felt his amusement. He obediently tucked one muscled arm beneath my head and the other around my waist. "Good night," I said without thinking. It seemed Collith's distraction had worked a little too well —of course it wasn't a good night. He wouldn't sleep well, or have sweet dreams, or any of the other clichés. The wolves would keep pumping him full of holy water and only God knew what Astrid had planned for me.

I kept these thoughts to myself, though, even when Collith murmured back, "Good night."

Silence draped over us. The room was so still that, inevitably, I began to fill it with worry and dread. Out there, in the real world, my damaged body was in the possession of werewolves. I had no idea what to expect or how much pain I'd be in. It was the not knowing, I thought, that was driving me toward the edge of sanity. "I don't want to wake up," I whispered.

"Don't think about that right now," Collith commanded softly. He pressed my head against his chest. The steady rhythm of his heartbeat vibrated through me.

I didn't fight him. Instead, I nestled closer and hoped he wouldn't notice. "Then what should I think about?"

"Only good things," his voice answered, rumbling in my ear.

"What do you know? The King of the Unseelie Court is a closet optimist."

Collith just held me tighter. We both knew there was a lot more in that closet he hadn't shown me. For once, the thought didn't cause stormy clouds to gather over my thoughts. Because I was only thinking of good things. A few minutes passed, and this time, they were silent and peaceful. My eyelids fluttered. Was it still falling asleep, if you were doing it in a dream?

I felt Collith gather breath to speak. I roused myself and waited. It took him a full minute to say, "May I ask you an intimate question, Fortuna Sworn?"

"It never hurts to ask. Answers, though, are different beasts altogether." Dad used to say that to me. Somehow I'd forgotten it until this moment.

Oblivious to the sudden tightness in my chest, Collith pressed another kiss to the top of my head. "How is it possible that you're still a virgin?" he asked.

"Oh, that. It's not a big deal, really. Every time I came close, it didn't feel right. Not because of the person—a lot of the guys were nice—it was always me. All I could feel or taste was their fear. I wasn't enjoying myself or excited about what we were doing. After a while, it felt like I'd waited too long just to get it over with. It started to mean something." I let out a breath. "Jesus, I sound like a sixteen-year-old. I'm not explaining this right."

Collith's chest shook with quiet laughter. "You're doing just fine, actually. I understand."

You should tell him about Oliver. Once again, the thought took me by surprise, brushing past me like a stranger on the street.

For a minute or two, I considered it. Trusting this faerie whom I had vowed to keep a distance from only weeks ago. I thought of Damon, then, and the vow he'd made. He hadn't been in his right mind when he told me those words. *For the rest of our lives, I will hate you.*

Maybe... I'd made a mistake, too.

And yet, when I opened my mouth to tell Collith about the imaginary friend that I should've outgrown years ago, nothing came out. Memories blinded me. The concern in my adoptive parents' eyes. The judgment in how other children said my name.

"Breathe, Fortuna. Just breathe," Collith said abruptly. I'd gone rigid. He trailed his fingertips up and down my arm. Little by little, I relaxed again. Then, startling me, he started to sing. The soft, lilting words surrounded me. Though I didn't understand a single one—the song was Enochian—it lulled me toward the edge of sleep.

Is it still falling asleep if I'm doing it in a dream? I wondered again.

The question followed me into darkness.

CHAPTER NINETEEN

*P*ain. So much pain.

Distantly, I knew I was waking up and returning to reality. I fought against it to avoid the bright, hot agony awaiting me. A groan escaped my lips.

Eventually, though, I had to wake up. Everyone had to wake up at some point.

A musky scent filled my nostrils, accompanied by a damp cold that sank into my bones. I lifted a shaky hand and pressed it to my forehead. It didn't help. Seconds passed in a pounding blur. Details slowly solidified.

The first thing I saw was a fly on my thigh. It moved in twitches and jerks, obviously seeking something. As I watched, it stopped and put its little black hands on my jeans. Then it rubbed them together, in a nonchalant, brisk sort of way. Whatever it discovered must have been unsatisfactory, for the fly leapt into the air. It went around and around, buzzing past my ear, and was gone.

I was slumped against a rough wall. The ground beneath me was stone. Grains of dirt were embedded into my skin. The cold lump of my gun was long gone, probably confiscated by the wolves. Savannah sat next to me, eyes closed, her arms folded across her stomach. Blood peeked out from beneath her hairline.

Certain species of Fallen—like Nightmares and witches—didn't possess the ability to spontaneously heal. Savannah needed to get to a hospital. Soon. Hell, we both did, since it was now apparent that I'd hit my head pretty hard. It was then I finally searched the rest of the space, hoping to make an escape plan, and realized we weren't alone.

The werewolves had been busy; I counted six others cowering in the dark. Two males that looked like teenagers, three more that varied in ages and sizes, and one female. There was no way of knowing whether they were human or Fallen. From the looks of them, not to mention the God-awful smell hovering in the air, they'd all been here considerably longer than me and Savannah.

Where was here, exactly? A brief glance told me that it was an underground room... except it had no doors whatsoever. Stars glittered over an opening above. *Oubliette*, I thought dizzily. *This is an oubliette.*

There must've been wolves guarding the hole, despite the impossibility of someone down here actually reaching it—voices drifted through the moonlight. They were talking about a shift supervisor named Laura and whether or not she was pregnant. Apparently most of the pack worked at a nearby manufacturer.

I lowered my chin and focused on Savannah. "How long have we been here?"

She didn't look at me. No one else did, either, though my voice was the only one disturbing the stillness. "Just a few hours," the witch said. She was even paler than when I'd first found her.

Collith was somewhere down here, too. I could feel it. Which meant that I hadn't dreamt everything that had happened between us... and that I had a promise to keep. *If you do this, I will swear a blood oath to send word if I sense he's in danger.*

Those had been my exact words to the king of the Seelie Court. I may have broken some vows and told a few lies since this all started, but I couldn't become known as a queen who didn't uphold bargains. Not to mention that breaking a blood oath would have catastrophic consequences, death being one of them.

"Laurelis." I pressed the heel of my hand against my pounding temple. "*Laurelis.*"

Minutes passed, but he didn't shimmer into sight or greet me with one of his sly remarks. Either the pack had somehow gotten to him, too, or Laurie couldn't pull himself away from his Court. It seemed that, if we were going to escape anytime soon, my only option was to touch those guards. How, though? They clearly didn't hold our lives in high regard, considering they could probably smell Savannah's blood even now. What would be enough incentive to get them down there... or me up there?

I wracked my brain, over and over. Some of the others fell asleep—deep, male snores kept the silence at bay. Savannah was fighting it, which was smart, since she probably had a concussion. A thought I kept to myself, as voicing it out loud wouldn't do her any good. I went over different scenarios that would get two werewolves to enter this filthy hole.

The night wore on and I came up with nothing. The cold was like a dream; it crept into every joint and pore. As frost crept over prison and prisoners, the moon locked into a fierce battle with the clouds. Our guards kept talking without any regard to the prisoners below. From what I was able to gather, their borders had been crossed without permission by a rival pack. If the challenge went unanswered, they could lose some of their territory, so Astrid had gone to confront their alpha.

Which meant we had a little time.

The temperature continued to drop. My two layers weren't enough. I kept my head down and imagined warmer places. Next to my face, between two jutting stones, was a spiderweb.

Its occupant was long gone, driven away by frost and cold, no doubt.

Then, between one moment and the next, sunlight reached down through the bars. *Morning*, I thought with faint surprise. For some reason, its arrival was unexpected. Night had begun to feel eternal as a vampire, sucking away at my strength. The werewolves on the surface were silent now. Had they gone? Or were they just sleeping? Either way, I knew we had to use their absence to our advantage.

Just as I started to stand, the slop fell.

Chaos erupted. Shouts bounced off the stone walls, and the prisoners hit at each other to get beneath the hole, their mouths gaping open like dying fish. I squatted next to Savannah, prepared to attack anyone who dared to come near. Most were crowded in the center, waiting for food to come through the opening overhead. They arched their necks back and stared up at that round glimpse of sky, roughened, dirty creatures. A fight or two broke out.

As quickly as it began, it was over. The bucket dangling over the hole disappeared. Two of the captives got down on their hands and knees, licking the stones in case there was a stray drop of the tasteless food they threw to us. Others drifted away, back to their corners.

One of the males didn't get up at all.

"Oh, God," Savannah whimpered. "He's not dead, is he? He can't be dead."

Her fear was strange. Since I'd touched her before, I was able to discern that it wasn't a phobia of corpses or a deep-rooted dread for death. Savannah hadn't known the prisoner, either, so it couldn't be genuine concern for his well-being. This was something else... and it was something that instinct insisted I try to understand. That I needed to understand. I frowned at the witch, my fingers itching to reach for her.

No. I was going to do this the smart way. The way my father

taught me. I moved back to use the wall for support. The pain had become a dull ache, which was easier to ignore. Easier, but not completely. I grimaced as I closed my eyes. It felt more important than ever to have control over my abilities, especially since they'd been changing. I sat there, on the unforgiving ground of yet another cage, and tried to remember everything Dad had taught me about being a Nightmare.

There is a delicacy to what we do, Fortuna. It's not as simple as putting your hand on someone and suddenly gaining complete power over them. What if you don't want to break their minds? What if you don't want them to be aware of your presence?

How would I do that, Dad?

It's very similar to meditation, actually. Do you remember what I taught you about that?

Meditation is a gradual emptying of the mind. It's about being in the present, but not keeping out every thought or shoving them away. They are visitors. A temporary being. Acknowledge them, then turn away.

Very good. Such is the nature of fear, as well. Except, rather than acting as a vessel, you carry some intent.

Intent?

Yes. A very faint one. Hardly more than a shadow. That's why it's delicate—shadows disappear when the darkness comes. You must find a balance and maintain it. Does any of this make sense, Fortuna?

Not really, Dad.

I'd never been good at meditation—it was my nature to move, accomplish, do. I hadn't bothered trying in months. Now, dredging up the instructions I'd listened to on some app, I focused on the breath going in and out of my lungs. Okay, intent. Go in with a faint intent.

Of course it was there, in the oblivion of my closed eyes, that every sound was heightened. One of the other prisoners sneezed. Two others whispered about the unconscious male and whether or not he could be eaten. Every now and then,

Savannah shifted, making scraping sounds against the stone floor.

Intent. Intent. Intent.

There was a crow somewhere in the woods; the sound of its cawing burrowed beneath my skin. Did it sense death nearby? Was it waiting for a chance to feast? No, that didn't matter right now. I was meditating. *Concentrate, Fortuna.*

When one of the prisoners broke into a coughing fit, I let out a growl of frustration. This wasn't working. Not from a lack of patience or dedication, though. I wasn't like most people, so why was I trying to meditate like them? Once again, I ignored the pain and pressed my forehead against the tops of my knees.

This time, instead of the breathing, I concentrated on the darkness.

Except it wasn't darkness—there was a subtle color to the insides of my eyelids. *Hazel*, I thought. The same hazel that looked out from Collith's eyes.

Within seconds, the turmoil inside me settled like the debris caught up in a tornado. All the background noise faded until there was only Collith's eyes and my breath. In and out. In and out. At the back of my head, so vague that it was only a shadow instead of a solid presence, I thought of Savannah Simonson's fear. I paid no attention to however many seconds ticked past. I had a firm grip on my anchor now, mooring me to the present. A flavor touched my tongue, but it was subtle enough that I wasn't drawn out of the darkness.

All at once, I knew what I was sensing. What I'd been feeling ever since finding my brother's ex-girlfriend. Savannah's terror had a thread of resignation weaved through it. A knowledge of what was to come. That alone wouldn't be enough, but combined with how she'd stared at the body with such terror, a puzzle piece finally clicked into place.

My eyes snapped open and I stared at her. "You're a necromancer," I whispered, knowing it was the truth as soon as I uttered it out loud.

Instead of looking surprised or terrified, Savannah just started chewing her lip. Her teeth visibly tore the skin. There was a sudden, feverish light in her eyes. I tensed, wondering if she was willing to kill to keep her secret.

"I thought Damon was dead... so I turned to the dark arts," she confessed. The words weren't quick or frantic. They were hushed, soft, like an isolated hill in the middle of winter, getting covered in a clean blanket of snow, flake by flake. "I couldn't imagine existing in a world without him. I did so much research, Fortuna. I was so careful. But the spell was too power-ful, and now I know that it had nowhere to go, since Damon wasn't dead after all. Its effects were permanent. Anywhere I go, if there's a body near, it rises. Back in the woods, when you were about to help me up—"

"You were worried something would rise," I finished, still too shocked to feel anything else. "And if I had touched you, I would've figured it out."

Savannah nodded, wearing an expression of absolute misery. A tear was caught in her eyelashes. She discovered a stick and dragged it across the stones with listless movements. "I know what happens to my kind if other Fallen catch wind of it," she muttered. "We're either killed for our tongues or used in the black markets. I know you would never betray me, but I have Matthew to think about now. I couldn't take any chances."

I mulled over this revelation. Everything made sense now. Why she lived so far from town, why she'd become a shut-in, and why she'd never tried to pursue a career with her degree. As I mulled over it, something else occurred to me. "A few months ago, I was in the forest with a faerie," I said slowly. "We were attacked by a thing that looked exactly like, well, *that*."

"I was following you," Savannah admitted. "I couldn't hear what either of you were saying, but I know how much you hate faeries. I figured there had to be a good reason if you were willingly hanging around one. I hoped it was Damon."

She was trembling. She was so small, so brittle. As if she hadn't had a decent meal in months. There was a bit of dirt near our feet. Using the stick she still held, Savannah pushed and prodded it until it formed a face. I swallowed a sigh and, steeling myself, wrapped my arms around the witch's frail shoulders. We didn't make skin-to-skin contact—not with so many layers on us both—but it had become instinct to avoid moments like this.

Savannah had no such instincts; she leaned into me as though I were her best friend. I looked down at the top of her head and saw the blood had hardened. She'd manage to stay awake the entire night, too. These seemed like good signs. As for my own head injury, the ache was still there. I wasn't sure if that meant anything, but it was probably to blame for why I couldn't think of a goddamned way to get us out of this.

Time was sand slipping through my fingers. The sleepless night had caught up with me. Several times, I started to nod off, only to jerk back to awareness. I couldn't rest. I couldn't stop thinking. Astrid was coming, and when she did, she'd keep all the promises that had shone from her yellow eyes.

"Son of a bitch," one of the other prisoners swore. His voice startled everyone; it had been hours since any of us had spoken. We all looked at him, but he was looking at the body in the middle of the space. "That fucker's heart just stopped beating. Now we're going to be locked in here with a rotting corpse."

Before anyone could speak, the body sat up.

CHAPTER TWENTY

*T*he witch's eyes were huge.

"How do we kill it?" I whispered urgently, edging away and consequently dragging her with me. The last time I had faced one of Savannah's creations, Collith burned it to a crisp. Now there was no Collith, no fire, and no time to build a flame.

The body—or zombie, more accurately, for that's what it was —lifted its head. Its bloodshot eyes settled on one of the teenage boys. Oh, no. Not a kid. This thing would *not* hurt a kid.

But no one else moved to intervene. I swore and shoved off from the wall. The boy was frozen in terror, watching the zombie lumber toward him. Even his friend had made himself scarce. "What's happening? How are they doing this?" I heard someone whimper. A second later, I was there, grabbing the zombie by its shoulders to pull it away.

The sound this human-thing let out couldn't be called a scream. It was something far more animal, manic, and hungry. I heard teeth clack together just as the zombie twisted away. I'd certainly gotten its attention, because now it swung around, and those unnatural eyes fixed on me. I moved back, breathing hard, and the thing slowly followed. My spine hit the wall. Savannah said my name.

Remembering the fight with the Leviathan—how it had been intelligent enough to use my abilities on—I spent precious seconds searching for a flavor or fear. But there was nothing human left about this creature. Only death and magic. "Collith!" I screamed, desperate for his strength. His fire.

Of course he couldn't come. The wolves had made sure of that.

There was no time to panic. The zombie moved faster than I anticipated—maybe the scent or proximity of flesh had given it a rush of motivation—and its nails scraped my cheek as I scrambled away. The other captives scattered like bugs whose dark hiding place had been exposed. My heart hammered as I walked backward, trying to buy time, struggling to think of how to kill this thing Savannah had created. Where were those goddamn wolves? Wouldn't Astrid be furious if they let someone else kill me?

Without warning, the zombie dove at me. "Shit!" I blurted, just barely managing to dodge it in time. However inhuman this creature was, it could still feel anger—my continuous efforts to escape its grappling fingers caused a low, bone-chilling sound in its throat.

With every passing second, the space felt like it was shrinking. As I circled the perimeter, once again forcing the others to scramble away, panic tightened around my throat like a closing hand. I realized that I needed to go on the offensive. If I just kept reacting, kept responding, this creature would kill me when I inevitably made a mistake.

Wendigo, I thought suddenly. *It's like the wendigo.*

That particular species of Fallen had died when Shameek crushed its head with a rock. But the one I faced now was no rotted corpse. Those were not brittle bones. Its skull wouldn't be so easy to shatter. I scanned the space wildly, searching for a glimpse of anything I could use.

I instantly paid the price for letting my guard down, even just for a moment.

Once again, the zombie moved much quicker than I thought it would. Before I could jump out of the way, it wrapped itself around me. The weight propelled me backward. Teeth buried into the curve between my shoulder and neck. I screamed and struck it with my fist, despite the awkward angle. The thing's head snapped to the side. During all this I'd been spinning in frantic, pointless circles. It became an advantage when I fell into the wall and my foe took the brunt of the blow. A shriek erupted in my ear.

Still it didn't let go. Just as it moved to bury its face in me a second time, I got my arms between us. Its skin was freezing to the touch. I grimaced as I gathered momentum, preparing to ram into the wall again. An instant later, I threw myself forward. The zombie released another pained scream, which gave me the strength to keep at it. But the arms tearing at me, choking me, wouldn't relent, even though its back had taken several blows.

I needed a new tactic. *Weapon, weapon, what can I use as a weapon?* I searched the area around my feet.

Suddenly, the zombie's hold loosened. The moment I realized this, I wheezed and shoved it off me. Savannah stood in the center of the oubliette, legs spread, lips moving subtly. A thin line of blood came from her nose and her small hands were fists at her sides. It took many endless, torturous seconds for the zombie to collapse in a heap.

If I hadn't been staring directly at it, I might not have noticed the wall above its head.

The stones. The two stones jutting out that a spider had once made a home in. They were probably sharp enough to do some damage or at least slow the thing down. They were low to the ground though, and this zombie was too strong to get it where I wanted it. The only way I could think of was to use the creature's hunger. Lead it to its death... again.

"Does anyone want to help me?" I called to the others, darting an assessing glance toward Savannah. She was still in the throes of her spell and kept her focus on the zombie. Something about her demeanor told me this solution was only temporary. "My plan is to bash its head in."

Nothing but cold stares or shifting eyes. Well, then. Guess I was on my own. What else was new?

Savannah lost her grip on the spell a moment later—in my peripheral vision, I saw her body give a violent jerk. She fell to her knees and threw up. Meanwhile, the zombie stirred and made a rasping sound. When it sat up, it was like an image from a nightmare. It turned its head slowly. Within seconds, those red-rimmed eyes landed on me. Not intelligent enough to be afraid, apparently, but just dumb enough to hold a grudge.

"Fuck," I sighed.

It stood up in two jerky movements, then ran at me. This was nothing like dead people in movies—the suddenness of its approach was supernatural. Not even my instincts had time to react, and as we both hit the hard ground, I was barely able to raise my hands in time. My spine collided with stone and I couldn't suppress a scream. But then the zombie's yellowed teeth snapped an inch from my nose and all thoughts of pain vanished.

Hot and foul breath assaulted me. I gagged while we wrested with each other. The zombie's furious shrieks made it almost impossible to think, but eventually I managed a panicked glance to my left, and yes, there were the two stones I planned to use. I just needed to get this thing over a few feet...

God, I was tired. So, so tired. These past few weeks had been nothing but pain and terror. There didn't seem to be any end in sight. I stared up at the zombie, thinking about how much ugliness I fought on a daily basis. Not just monsters, but enemies like hatred, mistrust, and doubt. Would it be so wrong to let go? To rest?

But if I died, so did Oliver. If I died, those slaves in the Unseelie Court would never go free.

You just have to find a little more strength, a voice urged. It could've been anyone—Collith, my father, my mother, Oliver—all that mattered was the burst of resolve that came after it.

I screamed as I bucked the zombie off. It went flying in the direction I'd angled my body, but landed just shy of the wall. Adrenaline and pain coursed through me. I didn't give the zombie a chance to recover—I grabbed two fistfuls of its hair, lifted its head, and slammed it against the stones. The zombie snarled, sounding more annoyed than agonized. I gritted my teeth and tried to do it again. But there was nothing left in me now. My grip on the zombie's head began to loosen. I braced myself for teeth and tearing.

When I let go, though, there was nothing. I began considering the possibility that I'd died when the zombie screeched. After that came a squelching sound and a loud *crack*. I thought of broken egg shells. No, it was probably the zombie. That's what I had been fighting, right? It was hard to remember...

Get it together, Fortuna. You were about to die. Someone saved you. The thought made me open my eyes. Had Savannah worked another spell?

Blood trickled through cracks between the stones. I followed it to a prone form lying below the section of wall I'd been aiming for. Before I could ask the others what had happened, a goblin stepped into the light, just a few inches away from the zombie he'd crushed. Dark blood coated his fingers.

He must've hidden in the shadows, or kept his hood up all this time, because those pointed ears were impossible to miss. The beauty that had once set him apart as fae was long gone, though. He was goblin now, and a big one, at that. A faerie that had been banished, and once banished, lost all the power and strength that came with belonging to a Court. The loss of magic also affected their appearance, warping it into something far less appealing.

Oh, he was also different in that he had horns.

This creature must've had them surgically added, for some reason. No matter what humans could find in books, or what stories they told their children at bedtime, Fallen didn't have horns. Tails, sure. Fangs, sometimes. But we drew the line at horns. It wasn't exactly smart of this fellow to have the procedure done. There were humans more perceptive than others, humans who stared long and hard at a glamour. The horns would just make him stand out all the more.

The goblin stared back and didn't utter a word. *Is he expecting something from me?* My last experience with his kind had involved getting kidnapped, held hostage in a garage for three days, then put on display at a black market. Even if this one saved my life, it didn't absolve the sins of the many.

"Thanks," I croaked, hoping the rush of prejudice I felt didn't show in my eyes.

The goblin approached slowly. He looked down at me for another moment, his expression carefully blank, then brushed past. As soon as he was tucked back into the shadows, Savannah rushed over and fell to her knees. "Fortuna? Are y-you all right?" she whimpered. Her hands were like nervous, fluttering birds as she helped me up. I muttered that I was fine and tried to subtly hide the torn skin above my collarbone. Savannah didn't notice —she just released a tiny, hitching sound that might've been a sob, and followed me back to our spots along the wall.

I winced as I sat down. A bird flew past the hole above us, sending a fleeting shadow through the sunlight. Everything must've happened in a matter of minutes, but it felt like I was years older. Why hadn't one of the werewolves intervened? Had they fled in terror and left us to die?

More time crept by. The silence was so deep, so dark, that it brought to mind the image of a bottomless well. Savannah watched me with anxious eyes, seemingly unaware of the wetness trickling from her nose. "You're bleeding," she said dumbly, staring at where the zombie had bitten me. When had I lowered my hand?

I made a sound that was supposed to be laughter. It came out as something else, though. "Yeah, that's just a side effect of being ripped to shreds. Am I about to turn into one of those things?"

Savannah's gaze dropped. She shook her head. "No. Hollywood gets more wrong than right when it comes to the undead."

"Well, thank God for small favors," I said blearily, slumping against the stones behind us. After a moment, Savannah took hold of my hand and held it in both of hers. I watched her examine it, too miserable to care that she was touching me. "What are you doing?"

"Reading your palm."

"Why?"

"Because it'll distract both of us and I'm curious, that's why."

The response was surprisingly assertive coming from her. I liked it, so I let go of whatever reservations I had. When Savannah adjusted her hold, a flash of color caught my eye. I looked more closely and saw there were four marks in her palm. They were too small to be from a knife. "You've got injuries of your own," I observed. "You had a nosebleed earlier, too. Do witches normally bleed this much?"

"You know, it's a misconception that palm reading is done with psychic powers. Really, one has nothing to do with the other. Anyone can do it," Savannah told me. I couldn't tell if she hadn't heard my comment or was just ignoring it. I suspected the latter. She stared at my palm for several more minutes. "You have such a straight heart line. It's deep, too."

It felt like my eyelashes were made of iron. Nothing sounded better than succumbing to oblivion right now. I knew there were reasons I needed to resist, even if I couldn't remember them at that exact moment. "Cool."

Savannah didn't let my lack of enthusiasm deter her. "It means that you're guarded about your emotions. The depth indicates a resilience or strength in you. Your head line tells me that you're strong-willed—"

"You didn't know that already?"

"—and it's also crossed. That usually means crucial decisions might have an important effect on your fate."

"Good thing I don't believe in fate, then. Also... don't most crucial decisions affect the future?"

I had to give her points; Savannah wasn't fazed in the slightest by my sarcasm. She went on as though I hadn't spoken. "This is line of stability. It's also called the fate line. A lot of people don't even have it, but I'm not surprised you do. For God's sake, your mother named you Fortuna. This one is deep, too. Usually this means the life will be controlled by fate." She ran the tip of her finger along each of the lines on my palm. After doing this a few times, she closed her eyes.

I watched her through half-lidded eyes, now more bemused than annoyed. After a few moments, though, a frown tugged at Savannah's mouth. I'd seen enough movies to know this was the part I wouldn't like. I was about to pull away when the witch's grip tightened. Her nostrils flared. "Someone is coming for you, Fortuna," she whispered. She was no longer reading my palm. In fact, her eyes were closed and she didn't seem to be aware that she was still holding onto me.

"Hey, maybe we should—"

"This aura is dark. The darkest I've ever seen. What *is* it?"

Unnerved, I succeeded in freeing my hand from hers. The

suddenness of the movement startled Savannah and her eyes snapped open. "I thought you said reading someone's palm had nothing to do with being psychic," I mumbled, rubbing the back of my hand as though I could remove the memory of her touch.

Savannah blinked as though she were clearing something from her eyes. Her breathing was too hard. "It doesn't," was all the witch said. She opened her fist, looking down at it, and the movement seemed unconscious. Those angry marks stood out against her pale skin.

"It was the spell, wasn't it?" I asked quietly. "The marks on your hand—they're from your nails. You used your own blood for power."

She shifted under the guise of getting more comfortable, but it effectively put her back to me. Her voice drifted to my ears. "Desperate times," Savannah murmured. "I don't know why I bothered. We're all going to die anyway."

With that, we fell silent again. Not from a lack of things to say, I thought, but because neither of us had any strength left. Savannah fell asleep after a long struggle; for hours I watched her eyes drift shut, then snap open again in an aching cycle. Finally she lost the battle. She wasn't the only one; a quick glance told me that everyone else had followed her into slumber, despite morning pouring into the hole. It took every drop of endurance inside me not to do the same. Was there any part of my body that wasn't throbbing?

I knew I was losing too much blood. All I could keep thinking was that the world's tiniest desert existed on my tongue. *Stay awake, Fortuna. Stay awake.* Someone needed to keep watch... and if I were to die from my injuries, I'd rise as one of Savannah's things.

Hours later, someone whispered to wake up. *Wake up, damn it!* I jolted back to awareness, groggy, drowsy, coming from that place halfway between consciousness and dreams. It was midday, I saw, blinking at the rays of sunlight streaming down. I frowned at the strange shadow it cast on the ground. I looked up at the opening and nearly screamed—Cora's face pressed against the bars above us.

"My aunt is on her way," she whispered urgently the moment our eyes met. "She just texted me and they're an hour out. I've done as much as I can."

"What do you mean? How have you—"

"Hey, Peter," she said, raising her voice to overpower mine. Others in the oubliette began to rouse. "Thanks again for switching with me. Laura keeps fucking up the schedule."

There was a zipping sound; Peter must've wandered off to take a piss. That or he'd been fucking someone in the woods, which would explain how he'd missed the entire zombie episode. The werewolf just grunted in response to Cora's gratitude. Then there was more silence. I waited with bated breath, my heart quickening. It had finally hit me that we were getting out of here.

Peter must have left, because there was a slight scraping sound as Cora removed the grate. Everyone else was wide awake now. When a rope fell into the center of the room, we all remained frozen for an instant.

Then everything happened at once. Savannah and I watched the prisoners reenact the scene that occurred at breakfast. Dust flying, fights breaking out, desperate cries shattering the air. One by one, though, each captive got to the rope and climbed to freedom. There were pounding footsteps as each one of them fled.

"Go," I said to Savannah when we were the only ones left. We stood at the edge of the light. "I'm right behind you."

She stared dubiously at the rope, and I made sure my expression didn't reveal that I shared her doubt. Neither of us were feeling so hot, and climbing that would require upper body strength I didn't have on a good day.

Savannah muttered something under her breath. Before I

could comment, she jumped as high as she could and grabbed the rope with both hands. It only took her a few seconds to cry out in pain. I cursed and hurried to hold her up. As she used me for leverage, Savannah's boot pressed down on the zombie's bite. I stifled a cry of my own. She climbed the rest of the way, inch by agonizing inch, until Cora's arms snaked through the hole to grab her. Something loosened in my chest knowing that Savannah was safe. Despite her lies, she was still my nephew's mother.

Seconds later, Cora came back into view and jiggled the rope. "Hurry up."

For a brief, irrational instant, I wanted to turn my back on it. Find a different way to get out of here. It irked that I'd had to depend on a wolf pup to save me. In the next instant, of course, I realized how ridiculous I was being. I grabbed hold of the rope with both hands and put all my focus into biting back an agonized scream as Cora pulled it up.

Then I was airborne. When I hit the ground, I almost blacked out then and there.

"Okay, forget climbing," Cora hissed as I laid there moaning. "Can you just hold onto the damn rope? I'm going to pull you up."

Vomit threatened to surge up my throat. I counted silently to myself, thinking of nothing but the numbers. *One. Two. Three. Four. Five.* The taste of bile faded, and Cora's question still hovered, awaiting an answer. I nodded, hoping she saw me make the movement, because I didn't feel capable of speech. With dirty, trembling fingers, I reached for the rope again.

My arms, my injuries, my very veins screamed soundlessly as Cora tried to bring me to the surface a second time. Later I would have no idea where that strength came from. In that moment, however, it didn't matter. Spots of color filled my vision. "Stop, lower the rope," I tried to say, certain I was a second away from letting go.

Thankfully, I must not have said it out loud, because Cora finished pulling me up. I collapsed to the ground in a graceless heap. Once I could breathe normally again, I straightened and tried to blink the tears from my eyes. Cora was already in motion. "Your mate and your brother aren't far. I can take you to them, but we have to hurry. *Run.*"

I bit back a groan and stumbled after her. Though she must've seen my wound and smelled the blood, Cora gave me no quarter—she ran through the trees with the speed of a wolf. My concentration was divided between keeping her within sight and holding the darkness at bay. It crowded at the edges of my vision like moss or vines. At some point, I dimly realized that Savannah wasn't with us. We couldn't wait or look for her, not when Astrid was so close. Hopefully Finn could track her, once we found him.

We couldn't have gone more than a mile, but it felt like ten. I pushed myself as I never had before, swallowing whimpers and sobs. By the time Cora began to slow, I truly was on the verge of passing out.

"They're in there," she said.

Oh, thank God. The bite on my shoulder burned. I bent over to catch my breath again and Cora practically vibrated with impatience. After another moment, I managed to lift my head.

The wolves hadn't bothered with a fancy oubliette for Collith and Damon—yet one more rundown cabin appeared through the trees. The pack must've been pretty certain of my mate's cooperation, since it didn't look like it would be difficult to break out of.

After we'd taken a few steps, Cora turned around and squared her narrow shoulders. "Before you go in, you have to hit me."

I'd already started toward the door, but at these words, I paused. I didn't even try to argue; the request made sense. Astrid would be suspicious, regardless, but if Cora was knocked out cold she'd at least create some reasonable doubt about her involvement. The girl could claim I'd forced her to lead me to this cabin. "We need Savannah," I mumbled, swaying as I scanned the area around us. "I actually don't think I have the strength to—"

A snarl rent through the air. An instant later, a werewolf burst through the trees.

He'd only just begun the transformation, and as I watched, a piece of flesh popped to the dirt. He had claws and fangs, though, which would be more than enough to tear someone open. In the next beat, Cora came at me, releasing a long howl. She was sending a warning to the pack, some part of me thought as I threw myself to the ground, avoiding her swiping claws. Air whooshed from my lungs. The most I could do was roll over. I stared up at fluffy clouds, completely unable to move or ask Cora the burning question. Was this all for appearances, or had she just been toying with us?

Death loomed over me. With a face made of stone, Cora raised her newly-formed claws, intending to bring it down and slice my throat.

Something rammed into her. Suddenly Cora was gone and the sun shone into my eyes.

A few seconds later, I could move again, and I rolled over to push myself up. Yards away, Cora was fighting with a boy, and it took me another second to recognize the teenager I'd saved from Savannah's zombie. Holy shit—he was a kitsune. I'd never seen one before, but he was halfway between forms and it was obvious. Black claws gleamed where his fingertips should've been and his eyes glowed yellow. His face had changed, too. Close-set eyes, thin eyebrows, and high cheekbones created a decidedly fox-like appearance.

It occurred to me, as a second kitsune ran at the other werewolf, that I'd risked my ass saving someone who didn't need to be saved. *Those little fuckers.*

To their credit, they were doing a good job of redeeming themselves. Werewolves had the gift of supernatural speed, but apparently kitsunes were faster—one boy was a blur as he ran around his adversary, claws lashing out again and again, leaving deep scratches every time. The werewolf tipped his head back and bellowed. Rage and pain made the air tremble.

The other, still protecting me from Cora, bounced on the balls of his feet as if he were a boxer. But it looked different from those fighters in the ring; this one's jumps looked higher, more graceful, like a dancer with hollow bones. Cora's lip curled into a snarl and her eyes glowed yellow. As if they both heard the same, soundless horn, the two youths charged at each other.

"What's all this?" a familiar voice called. Relief surged through me and I looked around wildly. Laurie stood on the other side of the two battles happening.

"You're a little late!" I shouted back. Just as I finished speaking, two more werewolves emerged from the underbrush on either side of the faerie king. They, too, were only halfway to their animal form, and the effect was disarming. No, terrifying, really. Before I could shout a warning, they ran at Laurie.

The blond faerie made an annoyed sound. He put his pale hands up, palms-out, and said something I didn't hear. The wolves slowed, wearing identical expressions of confusion, and they stared at each other. They reacted at the same moment—each of them launched forward, met in mid-air, and hit the dirt with an explosion of dirt and sound. Laurie skittered out of the way, gaping down at his arm.

"That... *mutt* ripped my jacket! Do you know how expensive it was?" he asked with outrage.

While I found the strength to stand, I rolled my eyes. "As if you pay for your own clothes."

Laurie's eyes flashed with indignance. In the blink of an eye, he vanished and reappeared beside me. "I pay for some of them!" he argued, wrapping his arm around my waist.

I hid how much this gesture surprised me and nodded toward the cabin. "The guys are in there. We need to get them out."

Laurie followed my gaze. His expression darkened. Without a word, the faerie helped me slip past all the fighting. At the door, he dropped his arm and stepped back, giving me room to enter first. As I did so, he was close behind, a warm presence at my back.

It took my eyes a moment to adjust. Sunlight poured in from behind, making the captives squint. They were all chained to a different wall. Collith looked unharmed. Finn, however, was nearly unrecognizable. My stomach churned when I saw his black eyes, split lip, and misshapen cheeks. Astrid would pay for this. Oh, how she would pay.

But… where was Damon?

I found him a moment later, a small shape in the dark. As Laurie broke everyone's chains—he hissed at the first one, leading me to believe they'd been doused in holy water—I crossed the room and stopped an inch away from my brother. I strained to see his face, his arms, his hands, praying he hadn't been as mistreated as Finn. Damon seemed to be doing the same to me. He seemed relatively unharmed, but I noted he held a rock in one trembling fist. *At least he was ready to defend himself*, I thought.

Finished freeing the other two, Laurie came over to us. His delicate nose was wrinkled, as if that alone would ward off the smell of waste and refuse. He took Damon's shackles in his hands and, with one try, yanked them apart. He didn't linger or make any comments; in the next breath, Laurie was gone. Probably off to take a perfumed bath and get a manicure.

Now that he was unchained, I held out my hand to help Damon up. He silently got to his feet and brushed past, making for the door. My hand fell to my side. I stayed where I was and watched him go. Hurt rose in me, hot and choking, like smoke from a fire.

You are the strongest person I've ever met, Collith's voice murmured in my head. I looked at him sharply, confirming what I already knew—he hadn't spoken out loud. Those words were for me and me alone.

"Thanks, Collith," I said. My use of his name brought a smile to his lips, as it always did, but he looked as exhausted as I felt. After a moment, Collith gestured that I should walk in front of him. Thinking of Cora and the kitsunes, I hurried toward the doorway.

Outside, the battles had waged on. The two werewolves Laurie had pit against each other looked like they were ready to topple over. Their bodies were covered in bites and gouges. The kitsunes were still holding their own, one fighting Cora and the other fighting the werewolf I didn't know, but something had to give. "We need to do something," I muttered to Collith, who'd moved to stand beside me.

"Unfortunately, the holy water is still in my system," he said, his fingers seeking mine, and squeezed in a silent greeting. I reminded myself that it was not an appropriate time to think about the dream we'd shared. I glanced at Cora, who was doing surprisingly well. For someone so small and mousy, she was vicious when it came to survival. Whatever her real motivation had been in helping me, she'd saved my life, and now it was time to return the favor. But I wasn't about to jump in between them... maybe I could use the chains in the cabin as a weapon...

"Gentlemen, if I may have your attention?" someone called. It seemed that everyone turned simultaneously. Another curse lodged in my throat when I saw that Laurie now stood behind Cora, a thin but wicked-looking blade pressed to her throat. In a conversational tone he added, "Shall we see just how quickly a werewolf can heal?"

"Hey," I said, feeling the focus shift to me. I kept my eyes on the Seelie King and his new toy. "She's just a kid."

"A child she may be, but that doesn't make her claws any less sharp." He lowered his chin and murmured in Cora's ear. I was close enough to make out the words. "I saw the hovel where you kept him. Collith Sylvyre, a fae-born *king*. And you dared to put him in *chains*."

His arm tensed, and I knew then that he would do it. Gladly and without regret. I was thinking too much like a human... when I needed to be thinking like a faerie. "I'm disappointed, Your Majesty," I said, raising my brows. "Death is so unimaginative."

This got Laurie's attention. "I assume you have something better in mind?" he purred.

I lifted one shoulder in a shrug. "Make the punishment fit the crime. Let them wear the chains and sit in their own piss."

He liked this. I could tell from the gleam in his starlight eyes. "Follow me, gentlemen," Laurie said now, addressing the three bleeding werewolves. "Unless you'd like your alpha's niece to die with a bloody smile."

Each one of them were stiff with fury, but they obeyed. Collith squeezed my hand again, then moved to assist the Seelie King. As the werewolves walked by, something flashed in the sunlight and caught my eye. "Wait," I said, raising my voice so everyone would hear. Laurie paused and glanced back with a quirked brow. His fingers idly spun the handle of the blade.

But I wasn't speaking to him. Not really—my focus had gone back to that sword, which one of the werewolves still held in his dripping claws. I closed the distance between us, far more wobbly on my feet than I usually was, and grasped the hilt. I made sure our gazes met as I murmured, "This doesn't belong to you."

His lip curled and his eyes burned bright with hatred. Knowing the werewolf would be able to smell any fear, I kept my gaze on his and calmly waited for him to let go. We both knew he had no choice. Slowly, claw by claw, he surrendered Lyari's sword.

The weapon was heavier than I expected, and it took a considerable amount of effort not to drop it in front of everyone. The instant I stepped back, Laurie jerked his head in a silent order. The wolf radiated menace as he walked past, and I half-expected him to whirl around and rip my head off. Thankfully, he didn't. A few moments later, all of them disappeared into the dark cabin.

I sighed and turned toward Damon. "I don't know about you, but I'm ready for a hot shower and a long..." I stopped when his gaze shifted. Something in his expression made me turn to see what he was seeing.

Lyari and Savannah stood a short distance away. *Thank God*, I thought with relief. They were safe.

"Please tell me you hot-wired a car to get here," I said by way of greeting. I didn't think I could walk anywhere, much less handle another long hike through the woods. Our lovely hosts had probably taken us back to the pack's land, which meant we were miles from anything and everything.

Before Lyari could respond—she'd gone still at the sight of the sword in my hand—Savannah moved, drawing my gaze toward her. The witch's palm was braced against a tree trunk as though she would fall without it. The whole of her being was focused on Damon. Her expression was of a starving woman who had just spotted a full plate of food, dripping with grease and sugar and salt. "You have no idea how much I've missed you, Damon. No idea," she breathed.

It was after she said this I noticed the two of them hadn't come alone. A tiny figure waddled into view, his eyes wide and curious as he took in the scene before him. Oh, shit. Now was definitely *not* the time to drop this bomb on my brother. "Hey, Sav, maybe we should—" I began.

"This is your son," she said to Damon, as though my voice were nothing more than a whispering breeze.

The only sound in the forest was chains rattling from within the cabin. Eleven seconds went by. Even now, though, Damon didn't move or say anything. Disappointment tugged at the corners of Savannah's mouth. I knew that, if I were in her position, I probably would've dreamed about this moment from the day my child was born.

She said something else, but I was drowning now and her words came to me through the deep. I blinked and her voice was normal for a moment. "...could at least say 'hello...'"

Then the world tilted.

The sword slipped from my hand as I grabbed at the closest tree. After a moment, I managed to right myself. I thought no one noticed. But as I scanned every face to make sure, my gaze met Laurie's, who was frowning. When had he come back? Where was Collith?

I realized then that my breathing wasn't right. Each inhale and exhale was ragged, as if there were glass in my throat. "Fire-cracker, are you—" the Seelie King started. My legs gave way and, just as the ground rushed up, I heard Lyari utter a low curse.

Then everything went dark.

CHAPTER TWENTY-ONE

*S*ounds were muffled, as though there was a blanket over the world.

"Someday, my lady, I would like to attend you when you're actually conscious," someone murmured. I tossed my head, trying to force myself back to awareness. There was a muted sense of urgency deep within me. A reason that I had to be awake. I was needed.

When that didn't work—I couldn't tell if the darkness was a dream or just the insides of my eyelids—I struggled to focus on the small details. Use them as a rope to pull me out of this mental oubliette.

Warm air. Gentle fingers. A voice like feathers. *Zara*, I thought. Collith must've called her to look at my injuries. We were safe, then. We'd slipped out of Astrid's grasp. My muscles turned to liquid and I released a long sigh. Sleep began to slide its arms around me again.

"I forget how young she is, sometimes," a new voice said. I imagined I could feel the heat of someone's gaze on my face.

Knowing there was another in the room gave me a fresh surge of motivation. Maybe if I just focused on one function at a time, I could bring myself back, piece by piece. My throat worked and I thought about the words I wanted to say. "You gave me something for the pain," I finally mumbled.

And then my eyes opened.

The world came into focus slowly. The first part to solidify was Zara. She stood next to an antique dresser, atop which a large porcelain bowl rested. It must have held water, because she put a damp and bloody washcloth in it. "Was I not supposed to?" she asked with a distracted frown, reaching for a pitcher. She poured water into a glass and crossed the room again, holding it out to me.

I lifted my hand, secretly worried I wouldn't be able to, but everything seemed to be working fine again. "Next time, try to avoid it, if you can."

"It's a bit tragic that you assume there will be a next time," Zara countered. I barely heard her; I drank deeply from the glass until every last drop was gone. Dear lord, how long had it been since I'd had water? At least two days. I was *hungry*, too.

Now that my vision had returned to normal, I saw that Collith and Laurie were there, too, standing on opposite ends of the room. Another glance told me that I wasn't clothed under the flowered bedspread. "What is this place? Where are we?" I asked, clutching it against my chest. Why was I constantly waking up naked since Collith had come into my life?

Zara didn't give them a chance to answer. She fixed a frosty glare on each of the two males. "See?" she asked. "It's like I told you. She'll be *fine*."

Laurie winked at me. "I merely wanted an opportunity to annoy the Unseelie King a little more. Queen Fortuna, during my next visit, I'm dying to hear how you obtained that nasty bite. Now, if you'll excuse—"

The instant he opened the door, Finn rushed in. He was back in animal form, I saw with some dismay. What if he had trouble changing back again? The werewolf put his enormous paws on the bed and regarded me with his golden eyes, as though he needed to see for himself that I was alive. "He's the one who told us to bring you here," Collith said. "You're at Fred and Emma Miller's home in Denver."

"Thank you," I murmured, reaching up to scratch Finn's chin without thinking. He leaned into the touch and a happy growl vibrated through him.

"I'd better leave before I vomit all over the nice human's floor," Laurie remarked. "Until next time, my lady. Try not to get yourselves killed in the next five minutes; I actually have things to do with my time other than saving your asses."

He didn't give any of us a chance to respond. I watched the door close, wondering why he was bothering with it at all, seeing as he had the ability to sift. Unless Fred and Emma had seen him arrive and he was keeping up appearances, which would be oddly considerate of the Seelie King.

Once he was gone, my mate moved to stand at the foot of the bed. The floorboards creaked. His fingers curled over the metal bed frame and his silver ring flashed. "Whatever he told you, Laurelis is not just here to torment me," Collith said, avoiding eye contact. "He cares about you."

I frowned and absently stroked Finn's head. "Why are you telling me this?"

"In case it was something you wanted to know." He still wouldn't look at me. Zara moved busily around the room, and for a few seconds, her footsteps were the only sound between us.

As my gaze lingered on his expression, though, it clicked—Collith thought there was something between me and Laurie. Or wondered, at the very least. I stifled the immediate urge to set him straight, since Laurie could probably still hear us and Zara was a mere yard away. I didn't want to have this conversation in front of an audience. "Can we talk about this later?" I asked, hoping he sensed my sincerity.

"Of course. I do have a previous engagement, however. Perhaps tomorrow? Please call or summon me if anything arises." Stiffly, he bent and kissed my cheek. His lips barely made contact with my skin. Great. One more person that was upset with me.

This, of course, brought Damon to the forefront of my mind, and I remembered the shattering truth Savannah had told him just before I passed out.

"Wait." I grabbed Collith's collar, preventing him from straightening. "You can't leave me here to deal with Damon by myself. He still hates me, and you're better with people, anyway. *You* go talk to him."

A soft smile touched his mouth. "What did I tell you in that cabin yesterday? Do you remember?"

His words made a memory whisper through me. *You are the strongest person I've ever met.* Collith had been sitting in chains that burned, forced to drink holy water, and still he'd lent me strength.

During my tribunal, I'd hated this faerie. I thought him weak. A coward. But would a coward place the needs of others above his own? Would a coward face a pack of werewolves just to support his mate?

When I pulled myself back to the present, Collith was already fading. I could see the wall behind him. "There should be *some* benefits of being married to you," I hissed.

"Oh, I think you know there are benefits," he murmured. Now an image brushed the edge of my mind—steam rising from water, Collith's arm plunged below the surface, my head tossed back against the tub's edge. He was using our bond, teasing me, tempting me to experience those sensations all over again.

Unamused, I swore at the space Collith had just been standing in.

Zara, apparently, found my predicament amusing; though she wasn't smiling, there was a tilt to her eyes that hinted at one. I glared at her, too, but it was halfhearted now. I knew I'd been unfair toward this faerie. If she was going to keep saving my ass, I should probably be on better terms with her. But how? I wasn't exactly great at making friends.

"I like your hijab," I said lamely. *Seriously? You couldn't do better than that?* my inner voice chided. It was the truth, but the healer would probably take it as a barbed comment.

Once again, I hadn't given her enough credit. Zara raised her raven eyebrows and replied, "I'm surprised you haven't asked me about it yet. Most of my patients do. You've heard of nephilim, yes? I was born in Syria and we moved to the States when I was nine. My parents are Muslim, so that's how they raised me, too. I discovered my ability to heal after I went through puberty. My mother told me the truth about my biological father, and once I went in search of him, I discovered the world of Fallen. That was eighty years ago now. What a journey it has been."

As she spoke, it was clear Zara was getting ready to leave. She untied the strings of the apron she was wearing and pulled it off. There was a black leather bag beside the bed, and after folding the apron, she tucked it through the unzipped folds.

"I can probably never repay you for everything you've done," I said abruptly, watching her. "Not with money, at least. Is there anything else you want?"

The faerie paused and tilted her head. "Why is this so important to you? His Majesty has taken care of the bill each time, as I'm sure you know."

"My parents raised me a certain way, too," I answered. It felt strange to speak of them so freely, but Zara had shared hers with me. The least I could do was return the favor. "Dad, especially. He taught me how to protect myself. How to survive. I'm used to being alone and I prefer it that way. Those are my bills to pay. My responsibility."

Zara's lips twisted thoughtfully at this response. She opened the door, keeping her body angled toward me. "You know, I've been alive a long time. If I've learned anything during those years, it's that no one really likes being alone. No matter what they tell themselves," she added.

I didn't know what to say, especially since I'd resolved to stop being a bitch to her. I plucked at the bedspread. "You're probably right. Am I allowed to get up?"

"Would it stop you if I said you weren't?"

I considered this. "Probably not."

"Well, there you go, then. Farewell for now, Your Majesty." With that, Zara closed the door gently behind her.

Silence draped over the room. I sighed and looked at Finn, who'd been silent throughout our exchange. "Should we hunt down some food? How much can you understand, by the way?" I asked him curiously. The werewolf just sat and stared. I wondered how the others had explained him to Fred and Emma. *Oh, Fortuna just adopted a mutant rescue dog.* Doubtless there would be more lies to remember. Heaving another sigh, I threw the covers aside and got up. Nothing I could do about that right now, but what I could do was shower, go downstairs, and take advantage of the Millers' hospitality. It felt like there was a black hole where my stomach should've been.

I reached for the door, and just as it started to whine open, I remembered that I was naked. I closed it hurriedly and spun to search the room for something to wear. Finn stared at me with those wide, unblinking eyes. "Dude, look away!" I gasped, covering myself. Or trying to, anyway. The werewolf tilted his head with obvious bewilderment. Maybe he didn't understand me, after all. Besides that, nudity was probably normal in his pack—they were always shifting back and forth. It was unlikely there was a convenient stack of clothing every time.

As I kept looking for something to cover myself with, I finally noticed my backpack. It rested against the base of the bed frame. Someone—probably Collith—had brought it in here for me. But I would have to walk toward Finn in all my naked glory to get it. Were there any other options? After a moment, my frantic gaze landed on a plush-looking robe hanging on a hook next to the vanity. I dove for it, almost tripping over the rug, and yanked it on. As I secured the ties, Finn just slid down to the floor and closed his eyes. He made a faint, content sound deep in his throat. *Must feel safe here*, I thought. Fred and Emma had that effect on people.

My brief humiliation hadn't diminished the desire for a shower. Why did I feel so nervous, though? As if I were playing hide-and-seek with someone, I poked my head into the hallway.

I'd spent so much time here as a child, but I didn't recognize anything. It was a big house—from where I stood, I could see five other doors and a set of stairs leading downward—but I seemed to have it all to myself. Not a single sound drifted up to me. I spotted a bathroom to my left and darted over to it.

The soft glow of a lamp illuminated the frilly space. On the counter, Emma had left me a pile of thoughtful supplies. Towels, lotion, a face mask, a razor, and shaving cream. There were bottles of shampoo and conditioner waiting in the tub, as well.

Unlike the motel, the water was warm instantly when I turned it on. Eagerly I took off the robe, pulled the curtain aside, and stepped in.

Beneath the pounding stream, I examined myself. To my surprise, I looked better than I had in weeks. Not only was the zombie bite completely healed, but so was every bruise, scrape, and cut I'd accumulated since my trials. I lathered every inch of myself with sweet-smelling body wash, enjoying the fact that it didn't hurt. After I ate some food, I'd be good as new. *Thanks, Zara.* I should've said it to her while she was here. Next time, I told myself.

Afterward, back in the bedroom, I reached over Finn to grab the backpack. I pulled on some jeans, a long-sleeved shirt, and a puffer vest. I was too impatient to find a pair of socks, which I suspected were at the bottom of the bag. Barefoot, my hair wrapped in a towel, I left the room again. This time, Finn followed, the sound of his nails muffled against the carpet.

At the top of the stairs, the smell of baked goods hit me in the face. I followed it, walking slowly to absorb every detail of this place I'd once known. Every wall was decorated with framed pictures. The wallpaper was striped and flowered. On either side of the carpet, the wooden floor was scuffed and fading from so many busy feet passing over. I imagined all the meals and conversations in this house, all the laughter and squabbles, and my chest filled with an inexplicable sadness.

When I reached the main floor, I immediately spotted Fred, sitting in a chair on the porch. Damon sat beside him. Fred said something, the low timbre of his voice drifting through the screen door. Still feeling hesitant, I took a step toward them, then stopped.

Finn made the decision for me. His fur tickled my wrist as he walked past, nosed the door open, and padded down the porch steps. I hurried after him, reluctant to let him out of my sight. Someone might recognize him for the wolf he actually was and get their gun.

Outside, another day was ending. A sliver of sun still lingered, but the clouds were pink as cotton candy and a sort of drowsiness filled the world. Either I'd been out for an entire day or just a few hours. "Hi," I said uncertainly.

Fred looked up with a friendly smile. They both held coffee mugs in their hands. "Why, hello, there! You gave us quite a scare, my girl. Glad to see you up and moving."

"Yeah... I'm sorry about that. Really sorry." I sat in the wicker chair next to Damon and shot him a questioning glance. I had no idea what they'd told the elderly couple about why I'd arrived bloody and unconscious. My brother, of course, just pretended not to notice and took a drink from his mug.

"Where's Emma?" I asked when the quiet felt too long.

Fred nodded in response, his eyes on the yard, and I turned. Emma knelt in the leaves, her thin arm extended. Several squirrels hopped up and plucked something from her palm. Bread, I realized when I saw the plastic bag in her other hand. Oblivious to her audience, Emma smiled and plunged her hand into the bag again, reaching for more. A breeze lifted the colorful bangs off her forehead.

Fred made a bemused sound. "She's convinced we're the sole reason they survive each winter."

After that, the three of us just watched her. I had no idea how someone with such terrible hair could manage to be beautiful, but Emma did.

The stillness ended when Damon shifted beside me. I glanced at him, wondering if he'd started to process Matthew's existence. "How are you?" I ventured.

"Why don't I make us some grilled cheese and tomato soup?" Fred asked tactfully. He pressed his palms against his thighs and stood. The process looked painful. I imagined his bones as rusty gears, turning with reluctant groans. The screen door slammed as he lumbered into the house.

I lifted my legs and held them against me. Emma's laugh tinkled through the air, probably entertained by the squirrels' antics. Damon stared out at the street, his young face so hard and pale. *You shouldn't be here*, I thought suddenly. He should've been on a college campus somewhere. Studying for exams, drinking too much at bars, flirting with some guy or girl he'd noticed in a class. Life had been unfair to him, too. His parents had died, too.

"Look, I can't imagine what it must be like, suddenly finding out you're a parent," I began. Already, though, I faltered. Fear dug a hole in my stomach—a worry of saying the wrong thing or getting rejected again. I sat straighter in the chair. Fear did not control me. "This could be a good thing, Damon. We've lost so, so much. Maybe this is a chance for our family to be happy again."

As I spoke, Emma ran out of bread. Soon she would return to the house and this moment would end. When I was finished, I risked a glance at Damon's face. No reaction, no expression, no reply of any kind. It was as if he was a statue with a heart of stone that didn't bleed or pound or hurt.

For the briefest of instants, I hated him.

Any indication I gave of the discouragement I felt was yet another sigh. I got up and went to the door.

Damon's voice stopped me at the threshold. "I've been remembering more."

I looked back, still holding the handle. "What?"

The lump in his throat moved as Damon swallowed. He kept his gaze trained on the dying sun. "About Jassin. I've been remembering more. There was so much I lost. So much that felt... foggy. Especially toward the end."

Trying not to look excited, I sat back down. *He's talking to me. He's actually talking to me,* I thought wonderingly. Okay, focus, Fortuna. "Is remembering a good thing?"

Damon held the coffee mug tighter. His angular jaw flexed, as though he were about to say something, then swallowed the words back down. This happened one more time until he managed to respond. "A few days before you came—no, maybe it was a few weeks—I got up the courage to ask Jassin what was wrong. He'd been staying away more and more, and since I measured time in his visits, I noticed. That night, he turned and looked at me. 'You are losing my interest and that is very dangerous,' he said."

A response jumped to my lips, full of indignation and fury. With effort, I locked those emotions away. "Were you scared?" I asked instead, sounding much calmer than I felt.

"Not really. I'd stopped caring about whether I lived or died a while ago, I think. There was just him."

I expected hate to fill my brother's eyes, then. For Damon to say, *And you took him from me.* Maybe it was progress that he didn't. Instead, he abandoned his chair and, wooden boards creaking with every step, slipped back inside. A moment later, I heard Fred greet him in the kitchen.

It had been too long since I'd seen Oliver. Might as well go back to bed—maybe Damon would be ready to go home tomorrow.

Suddenly the scent of soap and hot water teased my senses. A moment later, Emma sat down next to me. There was something about her expression that made me wonder if she'd overheard the conversation with Damon. Once again, I lacked an idea of what to say or how to end the silence. Emma put her hand over mine as if she sensed my frustration. I stared at her fingers, thinking that it had been a long time since anyone had touched me so casually. So lovingly.

"Whatever has gone wrong between you two, try not to worry," the old woman said. "Damon loves you too much to stay angry."

"I wouldn't be so sure," I muttered. This made Emma smile. Deep wrinkles spread from the corners of her eyes and across her forehead. Dusk made those lines soften.

It was a cool evening, but it seemed that everyone was outside anyway. A man played catch with his son in the front yard. Two women strolled down the road, pushing baby carriages in front of them. While we sat there, most of them called out greetings to Emma.

"I wish I'd had a chance to grow up here," I confessed.

"It's like any other small town, sweetheart. There's nothing really special about it."

"You're wrong," I said. Emma waited for me to go on. I gave her a small smile. "You're here. That makes it pretty damn special."

With a tender light in her eyes, Emma leaned over to press

our temples together. Her scent was all around me, and if I closed my eyes, it was like the last sixteen years never happened. "The Fortuna I knew was always so sweet," Emma said. "I see that hasn't changed."

I'm not sweet. It was an automatic response, and one that I managed not to say out loud. But I wanted to be the girl she remembered. I wanted to reclaim a piece of that life.

So I said nothing.

The sun left this half of the world, bowing graciously to the moon, and Denver was greeted by darkness. I'd tensed up, expecting it to have a sinister edge. The nighttime was kind again, though. A friend once more. A breeze meandered past, playful as a dress skirt, and the quiet was adorned with lovely sounds of life.

Soon Fred came out with the food, and the three of us ate together. Once my stomach was full and my eyelids felt heavy, I thanked them and slipped away, walking quietly up the stairs.

Finn padded along behind me. He hovered in the hallway while I brushed my teeth and washed my face. Then, together, we slipped into the room Fred and Emma had given me. The werewolf curled up on the end of the bed, and I made a mental note to buy a lint roller before we left Denver. I turned onto my side, tugged the covers over me, and closed my eyes. I was only thinking of one person now. Seeing one face in the darkness of my eyelids.

I'm coming, Ollie. I'm coming.

An unfamiliar voice echoed through the darkness.

I came out of sleep slowly at first, then awareness rushed in, flooding me with details and heightened senses. Something felt off. Wrong. The room looked otherworldly at this time of night, awash in shadows and moonlight. I was sitting upright, though I didn't remember doing so, and goosebumps covered my skin. Finn still slept at the foot of the bed, his breathing deep and uneven. He should've felt me moving. Usually, he'd already be staring at me by the time I opened my eyes. I watched his sides expand and deflate, my instincts coming alive, hissing at me like Medusa's snakes.

Something was in the house.

A voice had woken me, I recalled. A voice with threads of power woven through it. No, not threads. More like… currents.

As soon as I finished the thought, a whisper drifted past my ear. It was insubstantial and swift, like tendrils of smoke. I couldn't quite make out what it was saying. My name, maybe? I pushed the covers aside and stood up. Even when the floorboards creaked, Finn didn't stir. This should've made me nervous. My emotions were being toyed with, too, I thought. All I felt now was a mounting curiosity and desperation—I had to find the one who was calling to me.

When I stepped into the hallway, the air was thick with magic. My bare feet left sweaty prints on the hardwood floor. Was that the voice again? Listening closely, I tiptoed past Emma and Fred's room. The door was open a crack and a fan—or maybe it was a space heater—hummed within. I could hear one of them snoring.

I kept going, led by some voiceless instinct. Everything in the house seemed huddled and frightened, the shadows and furniture, the knickknacks and pictures. I crept downstairs, using the wall for balance. My eyes darted in every direction, searching for anything out of place. Once I reached the entryway, I looked toward the windows. Most of them were covered by filmy curtains, but the ones that were exposed held nothing except night and moonlight.

Something drove me outside. I left the front door wide open and drifted through the yard. At the back of my head, I knew it would be smarter to stay inside. Go back to bed. Ignore the call.

Just as I turned to do exactly that, my insides writhing in protest, the voice spoke again. *Damon*, it said. This time it was as clear as Granby's church bells.

I instinctively turned and looked up at the house—the room Damon had been given was on the right. In that moment, I knew that if I were to go up there, his bed would be empty. As I stood there, my brother's name was a handful of syllables on the wind, urgent and coaxing all at once. I let it take hold of me again, to save Damon, I told myself. My bare feet made slapping sounds on the pavement.

At the end of the street, there was an enormous park. Leaves and branches reached for me. Something prickly sank into my heel. Wincing, I bent to pull it out. The pain did something, though—suddenly I could think clearly again. What the hell was I doing out here? What was I hoping to find?

Screw this, I thought. I was going back to bed.

Something rustled nearby before I could act on my resolve. Wondering if it was Damon, I hobbled toward the sound. My sweatpants snagged on a bush when I tried to draw closer. I yanked free. The brief distraction was long enough for whatever had been in the foliage to disappear—everything was still and silent again. I paused to listen, but nothing moved. It reminded me, then, of the day Damon had gone missing. The empty bedroom. The lonely nights searching.

Fear seized my heart, squeezing so tight that it hurt.

"Damon!" I hissed. "Don't do this to me again, damn it. Where are you?"

When he didn't appear, I abandoned caution and began to shout it. My terror was swallowed by the sky. A breeze picked up, its cool touch cruelly serene. I moved deeper into the trees, shoving branches out of the way. Some semblance of self-preservation clung to me and I kept my focus on the ground, wary of encountering more thorns or barbs. My foot ached. My clothes clung to me and my breath was shallow.

Determined, I pressed on, even when my footprints became bloody.

I was just about to scream my frustration when someone appeared.

No, not someone, I thought in a daze. There was a star-like glow around their shape. As I gaped, the unearthly being started to move away. "Wait! Come back!" I shouted, running after it without thinking. But the bright creature continued on.

I stumbled again and again during the long chase. Fresh pain vibrated through my heel—I must have stepped on another thorn—but I refused to let the figure out of my sight. A cut opened on my cheek and I didn't falter for a second. Nor did I pause to wonder why I was so frantic to catch it.

At last, we reached a small lake. Its surface was covered in a thin layer of ice. The glowing thing didn't hesitate before stepping onto it. I halted at the water's edge and opened my mouth, about to give a shout of alarm. Apparently this creature didn't answer to natural laws, though—it got halfway across the lake before it stopped. Though I couldn't see its face, I got the distinct impression that it was facing me.

Without warning, the spot of brightness went out. I was so shocked, so dismayed, that I took a step forward to go after it. My foot landed in the freezing water. I glanced down, mildly irritated, then did a double take. A horrified gasp lodged in my throat.

Damon's face stared up at me.

CHAPTER TWENTY-TWO

*G*asping, I shot upright.

My gaze landed on the striped wallpaper of Fred and Emma's guest room. I focused on it, holding the bedsheets with trembling fists, and willed reality to become solid again. The dream retreated just a few seconds later. I groaned and rubbed my face. Jesus, this one had felt real. That was two times now that the dreamscape hadn't appeared. It meant that Oliver was still fading. I had to stop it... but how? I couldn't exactly do a Google search or check out a book from the library.

Both Collith and Laurie had been alive a long time; maybe one of them had garnered some kind of knowledge on Nightmares during their days on Earth. If anything, they had to know someone who did, right? While I wasn't about to tell anyone my exact reasons for wanting more control over my abilities, I clearly needed help.

God, Fortuna, don't open that *door.*

Someone cleared their throat. My head swung to the left. When I saw Lyari sitting in the armchair, I let out a deafening shriek. The faerie winced. Her fingers, which were wrapped around the sword resting across her knees, tightened until the tips were white and bloodless. As always, she wore the armor of the Guardians, though her long hair looked freshly washed. It hung free and gleamed in the morning light.

I sat with my back pressed to the headboard and tried to breathe normally. "Are you just... watching me sleep?" I managed. Thank God I'd actually fallen asleep wearing clothes for once. "If you are, we need to have a conversation about boundaries."

Lyari didn't react. She just stared down at the sword as if there was writing inscribed along its blade. "I've been observing you," she said suddenly.

I blinked. Any lingering drowsiness faded. "See, that's just not—"

"Not while you sleep," the Guardian snapped, rolling her eyes. "Since your arrival at Court."

"Oh. Okay. That makes it better, then."

"I know what you did to me in the woods," she went on. These words made my heart stumble. Lyari saw my expression and scowled, as though I'd confirmed something she didn't want confirmed. "Don't worry, I'm not going to kill you. Not after the return of my sword. That would be dishonorable, and I seek to bring prestige back to my bloodline. We were once known as a powerful family. Did you know that?"

I said nothing. Suspicion bloomed in my heart, a dark and poisonous flower. Why was she being so open? Was this a trick?

She didn't seem to expect a response. Frowning, Lyari turned the sword over, staring into the glass as though there were a carved message. "Time and time again, you make decisions that most would regard as foolish," she said. "Impulsive. Suicidal, really—"

"Okay, can you get to the point?"

"—but you don't let that stop you. Because I think you want

to do what's right, even if puts your own life in peril. Like what you did in the forest. Invading my mind? You knew there could be consequences with me, yet you did it anyway. Since then I've wondered, time and time again, what the king would've done in the same circumstances. His Majesty may have a noble soul, but he also has a heart full of fear."

I could tell this knowledge troubled her; her finely-arched brows were drawn together in thought. Before I could say anything, Lyari stood up, sheathed the sword in one fluid movement, and walked away. At the door, she paused. Now Lyari turned and looked me in the eye.

"You may not be the ruler they want... but I think you're the ruler we need," she said, sounding just as puzzled as I felt. As though she couldn't believe it, either. "Also, I put my number in your phone."

With those words, the faerie left, closing the door behind her. I laid there, stunned and disconcerted. *What the hell was that all about?*

Quiet unfurled over the room, and I became aware of sounds drifting up through the floor. Laughter. Dishes clinking. It smelled like someone had cooked. Soon, I'd go downstairs and join them. For now, though, I couldn't bring myself to move. Sunlight eased across the floor and warmed the parts of me it touched. It was almost enough to lull me back to sleep. For the first time in a long time, though, there was so much to stay awake for.

I decided to dismiss the conversation with Lyari, for now, and get dressed. After a luxurious stretch—it was a new and addicting sensation, being able to do so without any pain—I reached for my phone. There were a few texts waiting for me. One from Maureen. One from Bea. And one from an unfamiliar number. *We're going out tonight! 10:00 p.m. Keg and Cork. Don't you dare flake. You owe the squad a real goodbye.*

Harper. I'd completely forgotten about running into her on the street.

Strangely enough, the idea of going out and getting drunk sounded really nice. I typed a response and pressed the blue arrow before I could overthink it, then tossed the covers aside, eager to get ready. As I dug through my bag for clothes, my phone made the sound that meant the message had been sent.

I'll be there.

The biggest difference between Bea's bar and Keg and Cork was the crowd.

Every night, I served families, long-established couples, the sheriff and his deputies. Here, all the faces I saw were young. Beautiful. Searching. This was a place where the fae would thrive—there was the same hunger, the same exhibitions, the same perfection.

I walked in with Harper and her friends, feeling like a scene straight out of a movie. Faces and gazes turned our way, evaluating the new offerings. Harper had loaned me one of her dresses—she'd taken one look at my jeans and long-sleeved shirt and declared that she would grab one of the emergency outfits in her trunk. She'd also forcibly applied a layer of thick, red lipstick on me.

The white dress stopped at my thighs, clung to my body like a layer of sweat, and looked neon under the black lights. I thought about telling Harper that no one would be paying attention to my dress, just for the sake of avoiding the entire situation, but that would lead to questions humans didn't like the answers to.

After we'd shown our IDs to the bouncer and shuffled our way inside, I saw that most of the people here were already drunk. Or well on their way.

"There's a bar downstairs," Harper shouted in my ear. "The line will be shorter down there!"

I nodded and followed the line of girls down a narrow flight of stairs. It opened into a basement that flashed with multicolored lights, had a dance floor at the far end, and booths along each wall. There was the bar Harper had mentioned. The line was shorter, but not by much, and the girls formed an awkward cluster as we waited to reach the counter.

Since it was so loud, and we were so close together, conversation wasn't much of an option. Already regretting this venture, I glanced down at my phone to find out the time. To my surprise, there was a text from Collith waiting.

Would you like to have our date in the morning?

A smile tugged at the corners of my mouth as my fingers moved over the letters. *Sure. What did you have in mind?*

The response came less than thirty seconds later. *You'll have to wait and see. Please meet me outside of Emma and Fred's at 9:30.*

So formal, Your Majesty.

I am who I am, darling mate.

"Who are you talking to?" Harper asked.

I raised my gaze to find her watching me. My mind went blank. I'd never given thought to how I'd introduce Collith to anyone outside of the Unseelie Court. Was he a... boyfriend? A husband?

"What'll you have?" the bartender shouted, saving me.

I hid my relief and faced him. "Rum and Coke, please."

While he made my drink, and Harper leaned over the bar to tell him what she wanted, I scanned the crowd with idle curiosity. My gaze skimmed over a face, then I did a double take.

Damon was here.

And so, apparently, was Savannah. They sat in one of the booths, looking surreal in the glow that a single, dangling light bulb cast over them. Damon wore an uncomfortable expression. He nodded at something Savannah was saying. I resisted the temptation to creep close and try to hear. When I left Fred and Emma's, I'd assumed Damon was up in his room, like any other night since his return from Court. Maybe this was a good thing.

"Let's go dance!" Harper shouted. She walked past with one hand holding a drink while the other was claimed by a boy that looked like a freshman in college. I smiled and shook my head. Harper pouted, but a moment later, disappeared into the throng of dancers. The other girls must've done the same, because they were nowhere in sight.

I glanced at Damon and Savannah again. Deciding not to bother them, I gulped down some rum and watched the dancers. There was a couple just a few feet away from me. She jammed her ass against his crotch, bent over, and wriggled frantically. Jesus, I may as well have been in the Unseelie Court. They liked orgies, too.

"Penny for your thoughts. Well, actually, I'm rich. So I can offer a hell of a lot more."

I spun at the sound of Laurie's voice. My eyes confirmed what I already knew—that the King of the Seelie Court was standing behind me. Seeing him here, in the middle of a college bar, felt strange and disorienting. Like two worlds colliding. Not to mention he looked more casual than I'd ever seen him. His jeans were black and he wore a blue button-up over a white shirt. A leather watch adorned one of his wrists. "What are you doing here?" I blurted, clutching my drink tighter.

Instead of answering, Laurie put his hand on my waist and pulled me close. "I like your lipstick," he murmured in my ear. I shouldn't have been able to hear him, not in this din, but he pressed his lips against my skin and the words were crystal clear.

My first instinct was to push Laurie away. I found myself distracted by the feel of his fingers, though. Just as it had been with Collith, they were rougher than I expected, calloused and worn. These kings of mine were no cowards.

Your kings, huh? that vicious little voice asked. It threw me off balance, and I stepped back, breathing unevenly. "My love life is complicated enough, Laurie."

The faerie tilted his head. Colorful lights flickered across his face. "Who said I wanted anything to do with your love life?" he questioned.

Heat spread through my cheeks. "I may not have as much... experience as you do, but I know I'm not misreading things. Don't be an ass."

In response, Laurie spun me and pulled me back, crushing our bodies together. It was so quick that I had no time to react. "Pretty sure being an ass is hardwired into my DNA. Sorry, Fire-cracker."

"So, what, just because I'm a Nightmare, I have an excuse to walk around terrifying people? After all, it's hardwired into my DNA." I deepened my voice as I said this last part, blatantly mocking him. At the back of my mind, I acknowledged that I hadn't moved away from him.

"Why does everything have to be a debate with you?" Laurie countered, walking backward toward the dance floor. "Just grind on me, damn it."

I told myself it was the rum as I laughed. "How did you find me, anyway?" I asked, letting him guide us. He stopped beneath the disco ball, leaving my question unanswered. I felt shy, uncertain, and it probably showed on my face. Laurie didn't smirk or make one of his sardonic remarks. Instead, he trailed his fingertips down my bare arms, then laced our hands together. I watched him lift my arms and loop them behind his head. Every move was expert, smooth, as though he'd done it a thousand times before. Over his shoulder, I saw Harper give me an enthusiastic thumbs-up.

Without any hint of embarrassment or hesitation, Laurie began to dance. He was good, I discovered after just a few seconds. He wasn't overbearing or sloppy, like most of the other males in this bar. As we moved together, I became acquainted with every part of his body. The ridges of his stomach, the swell of his biceps, the dimples in his lower back. Then, two or three songs in, I felt his warm hand beneath my dress—not difficult to do, considering how short it was—and slide up. I wasn't prepared. I couldn't think. His fingers slipped past my underwear like they were made of air. A moment later, he touched me. Just a single, slow stroke. I bit my lip, trying not to moan, then remembered myself.

"Tell me something, Your Majesty," I said breathlessly, stepping back again, out of his reach. "When you look at me, what face do you see?"

Quick as the ever-changing lights above us, the desire in Laurie's eyes gave way to mischief. Holding my hands against his chest, he put his lips next to my ear and whispered, "I see... Angelina Jolie."

I couldn't deny the sense of dissatisfaction that pulsed through me. I hid it by rolling my eyes. "And here I thought you'd be original."

Unperturbed, Laurie spun me again. He caught me against him and grinned. "Okay, your turn to tell *me* something. How will you know what's right until you do what's wrong first?"

But I didn't let him bait me. I searched his gaze, unsure what I was seeking, exactly. I just knew I wanted to find more than what he presented. "Don't do yourself such a disservice, Laurelis," I said quietly, hoping he'd still be able to hear me over the music. "Anyone would be lucky to have you."

The smile he gave me was derisive. "Tell that to your mate."

"God, Laurie, why don't you just *talk* to him?" I demanded, pulling away. A girl jostled me from behind. "You know, instead of your whole lurking act? Or putting me in the middle?"

Laurie considered this. The colorful lights glinted off the silvery strands of his hair. After a few seconds he pulled me back toward him and said, "'I am very proud, revengeful, ambitious, with more offenses at my beck than I have thoughts to put them in, imagination to give them shape, or time to act them in. What should such fellows as I do crawling between Earth and heaven?'"

"Did you just quote something at me?" I asked, rolling my eyes again. "What a complete cop-out."

Laurie shook his head with disappointment. He spun me again. This time I was ready, and as I whirled back into his arms, I resisted falling completely into him. "You don't know Shakespeare? How your human education has failed you," he sighed.

My back was pressed to Laurie's chest now. I turned and met his pale eyes, and our faces were closer than they'd ever been before. I could make out flecks of blue in his irises. His breath tickled my cheek. "Can you be real? Just for a second?" I asked.

Maybe the sincerity in my voice disarmed him. The briefest of frowns tugged at Laurie's mouth, but it was gone an instant later, and he was grinning again. The beautiful faerie who cared about nothing and no one. "Very well. What do you wish to know? No, wait, don't tell me. Something about Collith."

I didn't bother denying it. We started moving again, so we weren't the only two people standing still on the dance floor, but I was too focused on our conversation to enjoy it. "I just want to know if I can trust him."

"Isn't that something you should decide for yourself?" Laurie countered. He tilted his head in a manner eerily similar to Collith. "What makes my word so trustworthy?"

"I've always trusted you, Laurie. Call it stupidity... or intuition. You haven't betrayed me yet."

"The key word being 'yet,'" he remarked. Apparently, Laurie tired of talking, then, because the movements of his body became coaxing and sensual. Every time I opened my mouth to speak, he shook his head or pressed a finger to my lips. I began to scowl. Laurie must've realized that seduction wasn't the best way to distract me—without warning, he grabbed both my hands and spun around and around. The rest of the world faded into a blend of colors and meaningless sound. I forgot to worry about Collith, or Damon, or werewolves. At some point I heard myself laughing.

I almost didn't recognize the sound.

Suddenly, there was a tug within me. All thoughts of dancing flew from my mind. It felt like I had no control over my own body as I disregarded Laurie and twisted around, searching for the other end of that string.

Collith came down the stairs. His gaze roamed the crowded space, and it took him mere seconds to find me, despite that I was surrounded by gyrating humans and ever-moving lights. He wore a pressed, white button-up with the sleeves rolled up to his elbows. Dark jeans clung to his legs and his hair had been gelled to perfection. *Sexy as hell.*

He must've caught the thought, like a feather caught on a stray breeze, because he smiled faintly. Then his gaze flicked to Laurie... and the smile faded.

Warm lips pressed against mine. I jerked to attention, and the same moment I comprehended that Laurie was kissing me, he cupped the back of my head. His tongue touched mine in a burst of electricity.

Adam's training finally kicked in, and within seconds the faerie king was on the floor, holding his groin and cursing. Everyone around us stared or laughed. "What the hell is *wrong* with you?" I snarled, standing over Laurie, my fists clenched.

Still cupping his balls, Laurie looked up at me. There was a hard glint in his eye. "Do you want a list?"

I made a sound of exasperation and looked for Collith again, but he was gone. I ran from the dance floor without another word, leaving Laurie to his own devices. Harper stood near a small table, talking with a different guy than the one she'd been dancing with. She noticed me rushing past and her flirty expression changed to concern. Whatever she said was drowned out by the new song. I shot her a reassuring smile and broke into a run to catch up with my mate. The steps were narrow and crowded; I lost precious seconds getting to the main floor.

Upstairs, there was no sign of Collith in the booths or around the bar. I glanced at the bathroom and briefly considered barging in before I remembered that Collith and I shared a bond. It was stretched taut and it felt cold. Maybe he was outside, then, if he hadn't completely sifted and gone back to Court. I edged by the line of people showing their IDs to the bouncer and hurried outside.

Wind raked at my skin as I stopped on the sidewalk just outside the bar. There were so many people, even out here. They stood in groups, smoking, laughing, talking. Cars and buses filled the street, the headlights overly bright. One of the drivers honked. While I strained to catch a glimpse of Collith, something niggled at the back of my mind.

It hit me a few seconds later—Damon. He hadn't been in the booth when I'd run past. It was possible he'd left with Savannah, of course, but worry settled in my gut now. A sense that something wasn't right. I told myself I was being paranoid, that it was good he'd actually started living. Still, when Harper emerged from the bar, I jogged over to her and blurted, "Have you seen Damon?"

She blinked. "What?"

Hysteria was crowding close; I could the pressure building inside me. "My brother. Did you see where he went?"

Harper gave me an apologetic shrug as she rummaged through her purse. Her hand emerged holding a vaporizer pen. "I'm sorry, it's been so long since I've seen Damon—I can't even remember what he looks like. I honestly had no idea he was here. What's wrong? Is he not allowed to leave your sight or something? Also, who was that hottie you were dancing with?"

I barely heard her... because I'd found Damon.

He was yards away. I couldn't see his expression since his

back was to me, but my instincts kept insisting that something was *off*. "Damon? What are you doing?" I called anxiously, starting toward him.

As I watched, he stepped off the curb in the same instant that a bus came down the street. Dread exploded into panic. I bolted toward him, but a hand wrapped around my arm and yanked me back. Harper's cloying perfume assailed my senses. A scream tore from my throat. *"Damon!"*

At the last possible second, there was a bright blur, and Damon stood on the other side of the street. Dazed but unharmed. Laurie's silver gaze met mine just before he vanished again.

It felt like my chest had collapsed from the weight of my terror. For a few seconds, all I could do was shake. I looked around once, thinking to scream at Harper for interfering, but she'd made herself scarce. Probably for the best, since in my current state, I was tempted to send her to a hell of my own making. When I regained enough composure to move again, Damon was still standing where Laurie had left him. I crossed the street, breathing shakily, and reached my brother's side. I didn't trust myself to speak as I found his phone and opened the Uber app.

"What are you doing?" he asked faintly.

"What does it look like?" I snapped back. Now that the danger had passed, I was pissed. Deeply and incandescently pissed. "Since you can't seem to stop getting kidnapped or nearly killed, I'm putting you in a car that will take you back to Emma and Fred's. They can babysit you until I'm back."

"I don't know what happened," Damon whispered, a line deepening between his delicate brows. He looked at the spot where he'd almost been hit. "I think I... I think I heard something."

I shot him an irritated glance as I typed in our location and confirmed the ride. "You stepped in front of a bus because you *heard* something?"

Damon didn't answer. He stood next to me, looking confused and troubled. Neither of us spoke again until the Uber arrived a couple minutes later. "I'll be back at the house soon," I told him flatly as the car pulled alongside the curb.

He didn't ask me why I wasn't leaving with him now and I didn't volunteer the information—I was still too livid. Damon opened the door and the driver called, "Fortuna?"

"That's me," I replied, nodding at him. "Just getting my brother home. Thank you."

As I spoke, Damon got in without any arguments. I shut the door a little harder than necessary, then stood there to watch the Uber rejoin the swarm of other vehicles. Something shimmered in the corner of my eye. I turned and caught Laurie trying to disappear again, half-transparent and silent. "Thank you for saving my brother," I said loudly. I didn't care if anyone noticed or thought I was insane. "It doesn't make up for the sexual assault, but it's a start."

The Seelie King paused, lingering between my world and his. "You need to stop doing that," he said after a notable hesitation.

"Doing what?"

"Thanking me. Have you learned nothing from your time amongst us?"

I met his gaze without flinching. "Like I said before—I trust you. Well, when you're not trying to make Collith jealous, I do."

"Then you're a bigger fool than your brother," Laurie growled. I uttered a hollow laugh in response. My legs were still quivering, a fact that he didn't miss; Laurie's expression softened. I could see it even though he was more spirit than faerie right then. "You should also know that I couldn't care less about that Nightmare. I did it for you."

There was something in his voice that made my heart ache. "I'm lucky to have you for a friend, Laurie," I said.

It was his turn to laugh mirthlessly. "I'm not sure which one of us is the bigger fool. You or me."

"What's that supposed to... you know what? Never mind. I've got bigger things to worry about right now." I scanned the crowd again. Harper had probably gone back inside, hoping to use her friends as a buffer. As if that would stop me.

"Like what?" I heard Laurie ask.

"Like where that fucking human went," I snarled.

"The one who laid its hands on you? I saw it go that way," Laurie said. He waited until I refocused on him, then inclined his head to indicate somewhere to my left. When I looked in that direction, all I saw was the parking lot next to the bar. I started to barge over, then remembered Laurie. I faltered, thinking to thank him again, but of course he was gone. There would be another chance to repay him, I knew. Harper, however, was a window closing fast.

A few seconds later, I realized that I shouldn't have worried —the human stood between two parked cars, clearly waiting for me. I stopped a few feet away from her and tried to calm myself. "Okay, I'm going to give you one chance to..." I trailed off when her face began to change.

Unlike the transformation of a werewolf, this wasn't bloody or gradual. Within seconds I found myself looking at Sorcha.

Shock seized me so tightly in its grip that I couldn't breathe. She wore a satisfied smile, and the clothes clinging to her slender curves were exactly what Harper had on.

She didn't smell right, Finn had said after meeting her. He'd tried to warn me. Tried to tell me.

"This is the part where I'm supposed to kill you," Sorcha purred, strands of her bright hair lifting in the wind. "Ayduin offered a lot of money, and after a decade of partying, my accounts are getting a little low. You get it, right? And damn, that bus was about to do the job for me—it would've been perfect. But I found myself saving you instead. Our friendship didn't mean nothing, Your Majesty. Let tonight be the proof. Oh, and don't bother looking for me."

Before I could respond—or just make her regret the day she was born—Sorcha dramatically snapped her fingers and vanished.

CHAPTER TWENTY-THREE

*S*leep crooned to me, crooking a dark and dreamy finger.

I resisted. For the first time in years, I didn't know what to expect when I fell asleep, and that terrified me. What if I dreamed of Sorcha? What if I had another nightmare? What if I found myself wearing Damon's face again?

After what he'd seen at the bar, it was unlikely that Collith would use our bond to initiate a conversation. I regretted that I'd never learned how to do it myself. I tossed and turned, unable to push away any thoughts or worries. Sweat beaded my skin.

From his place at the end of the bed, Finn watched me and whined. He'd spent the evening with Emma, and she must have bullied him into taking a bath, because a floral smell clung to his fur. It teased my senses as I battled with myself through the night.

At last, around 5:00 a.m., the darkness won.

I arrived at the dream with closed eyes. A childish part of me wanted to stay like that, for hours and hours, until it was time to wake up. But curiosity was stronger—I took a breath, as though I were about to jump into a cold pool, and opened them.

I was on the roof of a skyscraper.

There was a smell in the air, something rich and sweet. Following it, I turned. A few yards away, with the dimming skyline as a backdrop, a table awaited. It was covered in a linen tablecloth, gleaming dishes, and a silver plate. Candles flickered in a breeze. The ground was littered with sunflowers—my favorite—and more half-melted candles. I glanced down and saw that I wore a designer gown made of glittering gold.

At the table, Oliver stood beside one of the chairs, dressed as I'd never seen him before. He looked like a model that had stepped out of the pages from some fashion magazine. God, it felt like I hadn't seen him in years. As I gaped, greedily drinking in the sight of him, he lifted the cover over the silver plate, revealing two steaming steaks. "Medium rare, just the way you like it," my best friend said with a grin.

Still awed and confused, I approached. After the encounter with Sorcha, who I probably hadn't seen the last of, this was a delicious distraction. "Wow. Did you make this yourself, or did you make it appear?" I managed.

Oliver raised his eyebrows. "Which answer would impress you more?"

"Definitely cooking it yourself," I decided, settling in the chair he'd pulled out. "You know I can barely pull off a box of mac 'n cheese. Which would mean you did this in *spite* of me."

He laughed. The sound was so warm and familiar; it felt like coming home. "There are a lot of things that I can do that you can't, Fortuna," Oliver reminded me.

I twisted my lips and considered this. "I think I'm offended."

"Don't be," he laughed, moving to sit in the other chair. Oliver glanced down and adjusted his tie, which had started to come out of his jacket. A second later, he realized that I was just sitting there observing him. "What are you waiting for? Dig in."

"With pleasure," I said, smiling, choosing not to acknowledge the second half of his comment. It would open a door that I wasn't ready for. There was so much to tell him, like about the werewolf pack or the discovery that Damon had a *son*, but I couldn't relive it all right now. Instead, we both lifted our utensils and started to cut the meat. I put the first piece on my tongue, and the flavor gave me the urge to weep. Moaning, I hurried to take another bite. I'd missed this—missed Ollie—so much. A piece of myself that I hadn't realized was missing settled back into place.

With anyone else, in a setting like this, the quiet would be unsettling. I'd feel the need to fill it with words, no matter how meaningless or dull. With Ollie, though, it was a relief. As I chewed, my gaze flitted around the rooftop again, taking in all the thoughtful touches he'd added. A sense of unrest crept over the contentedness I'd just been feeling, covering it like ivy on a house. I set my fork down and watched Oliver for a moment. "Hey... what is this?" I ventured, feeling my forehead wrinkle. "I know it's been a while since we've seen each other, but you acted differently last time, too. At the fair. Is this about the paintings?"

Oliver set his fork down and looked at me. Candlelight flickered over the faint dusting of freckles on his nose. His lips pursed, and he didn't respond right away, as though he were struggling with what to say. I knew when he reached some sort of decision, because his expression seemed to harden in resolve. "In case it wasn't clear, I'm in love with you," Oliver told me.

I frowned at his tone. "I love you, too."

"No. That's not... I'm trying to..." He released a short, frustrated breath. Panic bloomed in my chest, its petals curling over my heart. "I love you the way a man loves a woman, Fortuna. I want you to be mine, the same way I'm yours. I know I can't offer you a conventional life, which kills me, but I'm offering what I have. Devotion. Partnership. Friendship."

Most women longed to hear words like this. But as my best friend sat there, watching me with his dear, familiar brown eyes, all I felt was pain. If he'd said these things to me before Collith came into my life, maybe it would be different. Maybe I could've completely disregarded that he was a dream. Fuck normality.

But one of us had to cling to reality. The fact of it was, Oliver hadn't said those things before I married Collith. No matter how much I loved this man, real or not, there were a handful of sins I was trying my damnedest not to commit. Adultery was one of them.

Like a coward, though, I delayed giving him the answer lodged at the back of my throat. "Why are you telling me this now?" I managed, holding the handle of my knife tightly. I couldn't bring myself to meet his gaze any longer, see the hurt that was inevitably coming. I focused on the candle instead.

When he answered, Oliver sounded more resigned than in pain. "Because I know I'm running out of time," he said, hardly louder than the breeze slipping past us. "That faerie bastard is trying to take you from me. I would regret it for the rest of my existence—however long that may be—if I didn't at least tell you the truth."

"Ollie..." I forced myself to look up. *Don't make me say it. Don't ruin everything.*

A sad smile curved his lips. We both knew there was something urgent about this truth, something unavoidable, like the next breath of air. "We should probably keep eating, huh?" he asked. "Don't want the food to get cold."

In all our years together, I could count on one hand the number of times I'd seen my best friend cry. "Ollie, what's wrong?" I asked stupidly, reaching across the small table to touch one of the tears, as though to prove that it was real. His unhappiness was a bitter taste in my mouth.

He leaned into the touch and covered my hand with his.

"Every day, just a little bit more, I feel you forgetting me," he murmured.

My first instinct was to deny it—I had loved Oliver for so long that it was impossible to imagine a world without him—but the words stuck in my throat again. He used to be my only friend. He used to be the reason I was able to go through the motions of school or work. Every night, I'd close my eyes and urge sleep to come, eager to see his face. Feel his touch. Hear his laugh.

Things were different now. I had met Bea, Gretchen, and Cyrus. I had rescued Damon. I had married Collith. I had befriended Laurie. I had reunited with Emma and Fred. Then there was the giant werewolf that followed me everywhere. I wasn't alone anymore, and the painful truth was, I *had* been thinking about Oliver less. His vanishing world was proof of that.

Unable to face him, I got up from the table, waited for him to do the same, then wrapped my arms around his middle. I pressed my cheek against his chest. He hesitated only for a moment before putting his arms around me, too. We stood like that for a long time. Somewhere in this make-believe world, wind chimes tinkled.

At last, I spoke past the apprehension clogging my throat. "Ollie, if you could be granted one wish, any wish at all, what would it be?"

I knew what I wanted him to say. I knew what I needed to hear. Something along the lines of, *I want my freedom. Let me go. Release me.* But what if he wanted to be with me more? How could I justify moving on when Oliver would never be able to?

Oliver pulled back to look at me. His expression was solemn and there were still tears in his eyes. I didn't think he was searching for anything, really. He was just looking. "I'd wish for you to be happy, Fortuna. That's it," he answered simply.

I didn't just hear the truth in his words; I could feel it. Petals flitted by, twirling through the air like the ballerinas. "Ollie, I—"

He silenced me with a kiss. It was rough and anguished and I could taste the salt in his tears. I responded instantly, squeezing my eyes shut. My hands tangled in the material of his shirt. Somehow, I was opening my mouth and Oliver deepened the kiss. I gasped. His hand formed a fist in my hair. I put my hand on his chest, a halfhearted attempt to end the moment, and he crushed it between us. I lost the distinction of where I began and he ended.

Collith. You're married to Collith.

My passion drained as abruptly as it had consumed. It took Oliver a moment to realize that I'd stopped kissing him back. When he did, he pulled away, frowning. I breathed hard, my lips swollen and my emotions overflowing, spilling everywhere. I saw his face and my heart broke all over again.

"Fortuna…" Oliver began. His voice sounded strange, as though someone had their hands around his neck. He didn't go on.

Just as I opened my mouth to speak—make an impossible attempt to repair this thing that was broken beyond repair—something yanked me out of the dreamscape. I flew backward and into the sky, the skirt of my brilliant dress flapping violently.

The last thing I saw was Oliver falling to his knees, his shoulders shaking with soundless sobs.

I woke up ready to destroy whoever had intruded on the dreamscape.

But my room was empty. Well, empty except for Finn, who must've been in the throes of a dream himself. His eyes were squeezed shut, his breathing harsh and erratic. Sunlight poured

K.J. SUTTON

in through the window. After my own eyes adjusted, I saw my cell phone was simultaneously ringing and vibrating on the nightstand. Its sound was piercing—enough to steal me away from Oliver. There was no one to blame but myself for the interruption, then.

I tried to ignore the damn thing and yanked the covers over my head. As soon as it stopped ringing, though, it started again. Someone *really* wanted to talk to me. Pushing myself up, I squinted at the clock. The numbers glowed red. 10:22 a.m. I frowned with incomprehension for a moment. I was forgetting something... there was a place I had to be soon...

Oh, shit. Collith. I was supposed to be on a date with Collith.

Now I checked my phone. Yes, it had been him calling. *Son of a bitch.* As I tumbled out of bed, causing Finn to wake up from the burst of movement and noise, memories began returning. The dance with Laurie. Damon's brush with death. Harper's face shifting until Sorcha looked back at me.

No time to think about any of that. I had to put some clothes on.

Then my phone started ringing again. Cursing, I snatched it up and blurted, "I'm coming!" into Collith's unprepared ear. Fuck. I owed him *so* many apologies. Why hadn't he just sifted into my room when I didn't pick up the first five times he'd called?

Thirty seconds later, I was passable in jeans and a wool sweater. I didn't even care that Finn had seen me naked. As I rushed down the stairs, I typed a message to Lyari. *Please watch over Damon if you can. I'm going to be busy for the next few hours.* It showed that she'd read it less than five seconds later. She didn't respond. I halted in the entryway and snatched up one of my boots.

"Good morning," a cheery voice said. I jumped at the sound, then turned and finally noticed Emma and Fred sitting in the living room. A fire crackled in the grate. Fred held a newspaper and Emma lightly grasped a pair of knitting needles. Even though she was looking at me, her motions never faltered. It looked like she was making a blanket.

"Good morning!" I said back in a rush, standing there with one boot clutched in my fingers. "I'm heading out to meet a friend and I'm already—"

Emma waved her hand. "Go, go. We'll be here whenever you come back... *if* you come back."

She accompanied this with a wink. I just snorted in response, and I heard Fred chiding Emma as I pulled my boots on. I went in search of my coat next. It hung haphazardly on my shoulders as I grabbed my purse, settled the strap on my shoulder, and finally dashed into the crisp fall air. I took out my phone to call Collith again...

...and drew up short at the sight of him in the street.

He leaned against a lamppost, legs crossed at the ankles. There was a book in his hands, and he turned a page with the soft, absent touch of someone deeply in thought. "Hi," I said breathlessly, pulling a strand of hair out of my mouth.

Greeting me with a polite smile, Collith pushed himself upright and tucked the book away. Once again, he was wearing modern clothing. He looked just as good as he had last night. His shoulders seemed broader than usual, clad in a quilted bomber jacket. His jeans were artfully torn and he wore suede shoes. "Hi, yourself," he replied. In the morning light, his eyes were almost green. "Are you ready?"

The word thrummed through my veins. I knew I was over-thinking it, but his question felt alive with meaning. I opted not to answer, for fear Collith heard something in my voice, and accepted his arm. We started walking along the sidewalk, which was unexpected, since I'd assumed we would be driving.

"So where are we going?" I asked, wondering if Collith was

going to bring up what he'd witnessed last night. The kiss between me and Laurie.

"I thought we'd walk to a coffee shop I found. It's close by."

"A coffee shop?" I echoed, unable to hide my surprise. I wasn't sure what I'd been expecting, but I found myself instantly warming to the simplicity of his suggestion.

"Yes," Collith said firmly. "Not only will the casual setting make it easier for you to flee, should you have a terrible time, but I happen to know that you like coffee."

I smiled, becoming more relaxed by the second. "You've been paying attention."

Something in Collith's expression shifted. His gaze intensified. It occurred to me, just then, that I'd never truly smiled around him before. Not a genuine, unrestrained smile, at least. Feeling self-conscious, I studied the tips of my shoes as we walked. "Is everything all right?" Collith asked, saving me. "It's not like you to be late."

"Totally fine," I chirped guiltily. There was another pause, this one a bit stilted. I thought about lying, but it was pointless with someone who could feel your every emotion. Not to mention I still heard Dad's voice every time I tried. Collith quirked a brow at me. *You may as well tell me, because I'll find out sooner or later,* the action said. I sighed. "Fine. I sort of forgot about our date, okay? Don't be hurt, please. Last night went later than I thought it would."

The Unseelie King stopped, pressed a pale hand against his chest, and closed his eyes. As I watched, a single tear slipped from the corner of his eye and trailed down his face. Standing there, he looked like something straight out of a painting. I burst out laughing. "How did you do that? The tear?" I managed.

"I was involved with a drama program for a while," he answered, smiling now. "I think it was in middle school."

I kept forgetting that he'd been raised in the same world as me. That he'd lived among humans. It was difficult to wrap my mind around. Not because it was so out of the ordinary for Fallen to make a life, hiding in plain sight, but because Collith was... Collith. How had those kids not taken one look at him and known he was something more?

"Tell me more," I said, feeling like an addict. Every answer was a small rush. "Where did you go to school? Where were you born?"

Collith stopped again. "I would, but we've arrived."

I followed his gaze. We stood in front of a medium-sized white house. There was a black and yellow OPEN sign out front. Beyond this was a wraparound porch. Plants and twinkling lights hung everywhere. Another sign hung above the walkway read, QuinceEssential Coffee House. "It's cute," I said with another smile. It didn't hurt that I could smell the coffee from here.

With a disarming grin, Collith led me up to the door.

A bell jangled as we entered. Inside, it was eclectic and colorful. There were several different rooms we could choose from to drink our coffee. Collith and I approached the counter, looking for all the world like any other couple. I loosened my scarf and scanned the menu. Collith nudged me with his shoulder. "What would you like? This is a date, remember, so I'm paying."

"I'm surprised you don't already know," I said with a smirk. Apparently, my mental walls were still holding.

Collith quirked a brow, then gave his attention to the barista, who was waiting patiently for us to order. "She'll have a white chocolate mocha, please, and I'll take a double shot of espresso," he requested.

I realized what he was doing. What he was recreating. It was the date we'd imagined together, laying next to each other in a dingy motel room. I could still feel the scratchy sheet against my cheek and see the glow in his eyes.

You agree to meet for coffee the next morning.

And I do. You're not a vague, arrogant asshole.

You're not a prejudiced, snarky brat.

We stay until well after our drinks are gone. I had a white chocolate mocha.

Oblivious to my train of thought, Collith gave the employee a twenty-dollar bill. She typed on her screen and a drawer popped open. She moved quickly and handed back his change. Collith pocketed it and turned to ask me, "Where would you like to sit?"

After a brief deliberation, I settled at a table next to a large window. The chairs were painted red and the tabletop was covered in chalk drawings. Collith slid into the chair across from me. He didn't give me a chance to feel awkward or start second guessing this outing. "I was born in Portland," he announced, picking up the conversation where we'd left off earlier.

I blinked. Once again, he'd taken me off guard. "Oh? Portland, huh?"

"Indeed. My mother chose to settle there because she knew a small caste of fae living in the city. We rented a small house in the woods. That's where I met Laurelis. It was an accident, as the best things often are. We grew up together." A fond smile accompanied the words.

I was feeling so comfortable with him that I didn't think about the words that came out of my mouth next. "So did I miss the part when he did that to your face?"

That smile instantly vanished. Collith's eyelashes cast shadows over his cheek as he looked down. I caressed his features with my gaze. The dark hair that curled over his shirt collar. "Like all of us, Laurie wanted power," he said slowly. "One day, we were trying to best each other, showing off our abilities. I don't think Laurie had realized how strong I'd become. Stronger than him, even. When he finally saw the truth, his emotions got the best of him; he lost control and tried to kill me. I stabbed him and fled. Since he was a prince of the

Seelie Court, it was as good as an act of war. Mother brought me to the Unseelie Court for protection. The king wouldn't let any harm come to a faerie in his domain; it would've made him look weak. She knew he would protect me."

I wanted so badly to ask more about his mother. But I'd already made that mistake once—it'd had the effect of a closing door. "Why did you kill the king? Where does Viessa fit into all this?" I asked instead. Once again, though, I'd pushed Collith too far. Those familiar shadows crept into his eyes. *Damn it.*

Just as I knew he would, Collith withdrew. "A story for another day."

The barista called out the names of our drinks, then, and Collith rose to retrieve them. When he returned, he sat down and asked me about my foster parents. The topic change seemed deliberate and final. Since he'd already answered some questions, I didn't fight him on it. I wrapped my hands around the mug to warm them and told him about the complicated woman who'd raised me.

An hour passed. People came and went, the bell over the door jangling every time. The espresso machine hissed as it steamed milk and ground the beans. Soft, acoustic music played overhead. All the while, Collith and I sat there, taking turns learning about each other. Occasionally, one of us laughed or nodded. It was the first date I'd been on that I truly enjoyed.

I also told Collith about what happened the previous night. The unwanted kiss, Damon's near-fatal step into the street, and Sorcha's deceit. "I was going to check on him this morning, but then I woke up late," I finished, looking down into my mug. The mocha was long gone, and all that remained was a brown ring at the bottom.

Collith understood what I was trying to say. "So you need to get back soon," he interpreted, pushing back from the table. I looked up at him, trying to gauge if he was upset, but the warmth in his eyes never wavered. Without another word, he went to the door and held it open. I reached for my coat, which was draped over the back of the chair.

I'll walk you home, Collith said as I came up to him. Except he didn't say it out loud. I didn't need to ask why—using our bond felt good. Natural. Intimate. Since the moment it weaved into existence, I'd fought the connection between us, hurting both of us. Letting Collith in felt like releasing a long breath I'd been holding.

Together, we stepped back outside, and it took me a moment to comprehend that it was snowing. I raised my face toward the sky, smiling in delight, and tiny cold spots bloomed and faded on my cheeks. When I looked back at Collith, curious to see how he felt about the snow, he was staring at me rather than the beauty all around us. In that instant, I saw it again in the depths of his gaze, the bizarre and heady truth. Collith truly did care about me. This wasn't a marriage of convenience or a game to him.

And in that moment, I couldn't deny it anymore. I wanted him back. I wanted to touch his skin. I wanted to feel his hands on me.

For once, desire was stronger than fear. I reached up and slid my fingers through the silken strands of Collith's hair. My other hand pressed against his chest. I didn't allow myself to feel self-conscious, and my bravery was rewarded when the corners of his eyes crinkled in an unrestrained, genuine smile. Giving me a chance to pull away, Collith leaned down and brushed his mouth across mine. I didn't move. He teased me by doing it again. Too brief, too light.

I growled—the sound made his smile grow—and stood on tiptoe to wrap my arms around his neck. My chest and thighs flattened against his. I kissed him like we were saying goodbye. As though we'd never meet again and this was our last chance to taste each other. I consumed him with every moment of denial or restraint I'd ever endured over the last few weeks.

Collith got an erection right there in the light of day, standing on a sidewalk, just outside a busy coffee shop. I felt myself smile in his mouth.

Collith's cell phone rang into the stillness.

I was about to tell him to ignore it when he uttered a low moan, sending a wave of heat down to my core, and reluctantly straightened. My lips felt warm and swollen as I glanced at the screen, curious in spite of myself, and saw Nuvian's name. Collith raised the phone to his ear, his gaze lingering on mine. "Yes, what is it?" he murmured. The greeting seemed abrupt for him. I explored our bond and realized that he hated this interruption just as I did. A warm sensation spread through me.

Then Collith's expression shifted and his spine went rigid. His eyes finally broke away as he searched the gray horizon, seeing something I couldn't. "No, that won't be necessary. I'll be right there."

"Let me guess," I said with a rueful smile as he hung up. "You've been called back to Court."

A shadow passed over Collith's face, and it felt as though our kiss had been a dream. It didn't seem possible that everything could change so quickly. "I'm sorry. A tribunal has been demanded," he told me.

Tribunal. The word yanked a memory back on cruel, biting chains, screaming its way through my mind. *Bloodstains on the Death Bringer's hood. Pale fingers curled over an armrest. Great, twisted roots of an ancient tree. Hands bound. Leather handle. White-hot pain.*

During my tribunal, no one had fought for me. No one had demanded my truth. I met Collith's gaze again and felt something determined in mine. I wanted to check on Damon, yes, but going to Court now could mean saving a life. "Isn't this the sort of thing I should be at, too?" I asked.

Collith didn't reveal the surprise I knew he must've felt. "Yes, actually. I was going to spread the word that you weren't feeling well."

"I appreciate that, but the fae are going to think I'm some delicate flower. We can't have that." I started to take a right, going back in the direction of Fred and Emma's, then realized I actually had no idea where we were going. "How will we get there? The door I know of isn't exactly close."

Yet another smile hinted around Collith's beautiful mouth, and I caught myself wondering how I could coax it to life.

"Have you ever been to a tiki bar?" he asked.

CHAPTER TWENTY-FOUR

*T*o my disappointment, we didn't actually go *in* to the tiki bar. I wouldn't have minded an afternoon cocktail. For a moment I gazed up at the painted white letters—Adrift, the place was called—a bit wistfully, until Collith tugged on my hand, urging me to keep moving. With long-legged strides, he walked past the gray building, down to the street corner, and eventually led me into an alley.

"Is this the part where you murder me?" I muttered as he kept going. Collith didn't bother responding.

At the back of what I assumed was Adrift, he stopped and glanced back at me.

"Do you remember what I taught you about expectations?" my mate questioned. *The trick is to expect more*, he'd said to me outside the passage to Court. That was the first time I'd ever stepped foot into the ground. If it were possible to travel through time, I would go back to that moment. I would warn the person I'd been.

But time travel wasn't possible, and all that remained was going forward. I squeezed Collith's fingers involuntarily as we walked toward a gray brick wall. This entire scene reminded me of Platform 9 3/4, and a thought flitted through my mind, a burning ember of curiosity. If I focused too much on that image, would I find myself on a train to Hogwarts?

A question, I thought when I noticed the tense line of Collith's shoulders, best saved for another time.

I was trying to make light of the fact that I was about to reenter the Unseelie Court. Again. Maybe Damon wasn't the only one with a death wish, I thought darkly. Then we passed through the brick wall. Memories of the dirt tunnels had invaded my mind, and when I opened my eyes, we stood in one of them. Nuvian was waiting, of course. His braids gleamed like burnished wood. When he saw me beside Collith, his blue eyes darkened with displeasure. I winked at him.

"How much time do we have?" Collith asked his Right Hand. At the same time, he silently offered me his arm.

"None," Nuvian said shortly. "The bloodlines have already gathered. It's been too quiet; they're bored."

Collith's lips thinned. The arm beneath my hand tensed. He nodded once, a jerky movement, and we began walking. More Guardians appeared, coming out of the shadows like they'd been born into darkness, and flanked us. I had a sense of déjà vu as I listened to their light footsteps in the dirt.

"Stop right there," a familiar voice ordered, bouncing off the uneven walls. I obeyed, more out of surprise than compliance, forcing Collith to do the same. We both turned to watch the Seelie King approach our party. He was dressed resplendently today in a black and silver tunic. The pants he wore were so tight that absolutely nothing was left to the imagination. I darted a nervous glance at my mate. There was a torch to the left of his head, and its flickering glow fell across his face, revealing his working jaw and blazing eyes. In that instant, I saw the truth he was trying so hard to hide. *You still love him, too,* I thought with a pang.

"What's going on?" I asked, trying to make my voice neutral. Why did it feel like someone had shoved a knife into my gut?

Laurie drew close and scowled. He didn't seem the least bit concerned that most of the Guardians were now touching their swords. "You're not going dressed like *that*. Have I taught you nothing?" he demanded.

I glared at him. "Look, this really isn't—"

"Say another word and I'll stop by that dirty little bar you work at. You can be sure I'll introduce myself to every single human in your life. When they ask how we know each other, what should I say, do you think?"

"For the love of God." I shoved past Laurie and went back the way we came. I didn't look to see who followed, but I heard them. No one asked if I knew where I was going; though I radiated agitation, my steps were firm and certain. Turn after turn, passage after passage, I never faltered. Five minutes later, we came upon a carved door I was starting to know better than the lines on my own palm. I pushed it open and stepped inside. Draped prettily at the foot of the bed was another one of Laurie's gowns.

Before I could take in the intricate details, there was a scuffling sound behind me. I whirled around just in time to see Collith slam Laurie against the wall, his hand wrapped around the other faerie's throat.

"If you ever touch her without her permission again, I will skin you alive," he said. His calm tone belied the rigid way he held himself, as though it were taking all his self-restraint not to follow through on the threat.

Laurie smiled into Collith's eyes. Even though they were talking about me, it felt like I wasn't even there. "What makes you so sure I didn't have her permission?" he asked silkily.

Collith's grip tightened. "Did she say the words?" he growled.

To this, Laurie quirked a brow. "Did I say the words when you fucked me?"

"*Okay*. Wow. You know, I think you've both made your point." I crossed the space and lodged myself between the two males, flattening my palms against their chests to use as leverage. But Collith was like a tree, decades old and firmly rooted. My first instinct, as always, was to use violence and fear. Then, in my mind's eye, I saw us standing on that icy sidewalk, snow drifting down. I could still taste him—the rich, bitter flavor of espresso.

After a moment, I met Collith's gaze and sent everything I felt for him down the bond. The result was something glowing and gentle, floating through darkness, like a firefly or a spark. Collith met my gaze and slowly stepped back. I smiled at him and something in him shifted. As though he'd made a discovery in the depths of my eyes.

"Now that we've gotten *that* out of the way," Laurie drawled, tugging at the bottom of his tunic, "let's get you ready, Queen Fortuna. Shall I assist you with the gown?"

Collith snarled. Laurie held up his hands in a gesture of surrender, but it was somewhat negated by his impish grin.

For fuck's sake. I turned my back on them and gave my attention to the dress. Nuvian had said we didn't have any time, so I didn't waste any more of it. Someone had brought a privacy screen since the last time I'd been here; I picked up the dress and hurried over to it.

This creation was lavender and gold. Its sleeves were filmy and floating, stopping at my upper arms. The bodice was some stiff, white material. It began as a straight line across my chest and ended in a V at my waist, revealing every inch of leg I possessed. Climbing up the length of everything, though, as if they grew gold instead of green, were flowering vines. The skirt ended around my feet like a dramatic waterfall.

As I stared at the floor-length glass—the mirrors Laurie kept ordering to Collith's room were getting continually bigger—the Seelie King appeared behind me. I turned toward him and began to say something, but he started applying lipstick, effectively silencing me. He went on to do the rest of my face, his manner brisk and efficient. I stood still and endured it, since there was little point in arguing. As a final touch, Laurie slid two golden combs into my hair.

Once again, I tried to speak. Before I could, Laurie gripped my shoulders and turned me around. He put his face next to mine. "Do you see that creature?" he whispered at our reflections. I frowned. "There, it just moved! It's in the mirror, I think, trapped there by some curse or spell."

Now I rolled my gold-lined eyes. "Laurie—"

"No, hush, or you'll scare it away. Tell me something, my dear. Would you say the creature in that mirror would ever deign to be controlled? To cower before something so insignificant as tradition or a little bloodshed?"

"Okay, what exactly are you getting at?" I demanded. But in the second it took me to face him, the faerie was already gone.

I really, really hated it when he did that.

The creature in the mirror stared back at me, her brows raised as if to say, *What are you waiting for?* Reminding myself that an entire room of faeries awaited us, I lifted the skirt and turned away. The dress whispered as I emerged from behind the privacy screen. Collith stood near the door, now wearing his crown and a shining sword. "Somehow, you outdo yourself every time," he murmured. His gaze began at the combs in my hair and ended at the hem of the dress, leaving a trail of fire in its wake.

It was difficult to speak. I cleared my throat and said, "This is all Laurie's doing."

Collith's eyes never left mine as he shook his head. "No, actually, this is all you, Fortuna Sworn."

Compliments usually rolled off me, but not this one. It

started as a spot of warmth in my chest and spread down, all the way between my legs. It was terrifying how much this faerie could affect me without even trying. "My phone," I said suddenly, looking toward the pile of clothing I'd left. "I need to have it, in case Lyari texts, but this dress doesn't exactly have pockets."

A smile hovered around Collith's lips as he bent and found the phone in my abandoned jeans. "Allow me," he murmured, putting it into his own pocket.

"Thanks. We better get going, huh?"

"Yes, we should." As he passed, heading for the door, I caught a twinkle in his eye. Collith knew exactly what I was doing, then. I pretended to be oblivious, and he held it open as though we were going to prom together. I hurried by and stepped back into the passageway, avoiding his gaze the entire time.

"Would you like your weekly report, Your Majesty?" Nuvian asked stiffly, standing across the path, his back close to the dirt wall. Two torches flickered on either side of him. Instead of my eyes, he looked at my forehead. I had a flash of remembrance, the real reason he loathed me, and saw the illusion I'd put him in. The gigantic werewolf and the canopy of trees all around. The roiling sky and the spreading stain on Nuvian's pants as he'd wet himself.

I looked at Nuvian's face now. His hatred for me simmered just beneath his skin. "My weekly report? What is that?" I asked, trying to hide my regret. I'd probably acted a little too rashly when I'd done that to him.

This earned a barely perceptible nod. "Yes. It is typical of those in my role to inform the king and queen of any unusual activity every seven days."

Nonplussed, I glanced at the other faeries in the tunnel, taking in their remote expressions. "Sure, I guess."

In the same monotone way, Nuvian began. "One of my spies

witnessed Lyklor of the bloodline Sarwraek purchasing arsenic. Previous to this, he had been overheard on multiple occasions that he wished the queen dead for her slaying of the former Jassin, also of the bloodline Sarwraek. I have informed Her Majesty's taste tester and he will continue taking every precaution. There are no further developments at this time. Also observed by my informants, Renestrae of the bloodline Cralynn has vowed to avenge her brother and assassinate Queen Fortuna. I have ordered for her to be watched at all hours but there are no further developments at this time. Next we have—"

"I think that's enough for now, Nuvian," Collith said, moving between us. I wondered if my shock was evident to him because of the bond or because it was all over my face. I had a taste tester? Faeries had been trying to kill me? Looking far too serene, Collith extended his elbow. I was used to the routine now and took it automatically. I waited for the Guardians to close in, which they did, of course.

Like some kind of small, creepy parade, we all started in the direction of the throne room. The air was so still that even the torches seemed subdued. I swore I could hear the flames whispering to each other. *Do you think she'll survive? What if the assassin was looking for her instead of Damon?*

"So... will the heads of the bloodlines get involved again? Stand council for you like they did last time?" I asked, disturbing the silence like touching the surface of a glassy lake.

Amusement drifted down the bond as Collith shook his head. "No. Their role on the dais came to an end the moment you were crowned."

"Do we know anything about the tribunal?"

"I'm afraid not." He studied me for a few seconds. "Would you like to hear of the time a tiger was loose here in Court?"

My eyebrows flew to my hairline. "A *tiger*?"

For the rest of the way, Collith talked, and despite our audience I couldn't contain a laugh or two. Then the tunnel fell away and a vibrant ceiling loomed overhead. What was it called again? The Mural of Ulesse? I stared up at it until we passed through the doorway, thinking that if the paintings truly depicted the history of the fae, I should come back and study them.

Reluctantly, I turned my gaze to what awaited ahead of us. As with every other occasion I'd been in this wretched room, it was too full. The fae either needed to make it bigger or start selling tickets to these things. We began the journey from the gaping doorway to the great tree on the other side. It felt endless. Collith played the game effortlessly, nodding at certain courtiers, while I pretended not to care all those eyes were on me. I felt them, though, like tiny pinpricks of ice on my skin.

Our thrones waited up ahead. Collith's was made of roots and polished wood, while mine gleamed silver, made in the shape of dragon and flame. A seat that I had paid for in blood. So much blood.

My mind shied from the memories.

We climbed the dais steps—there were five, I counted them in my head—and faced the long path we'd just walked. Without delay or fanfare, Collith and I sat. It was then I noticed two faeries standing apart from the rest. One of them clutched a tiny bundle in her arms.

Collith had seen them, too. "Why have you asked for this gathering? In English, please," he added, just like last time. I knew it was for my benefit.

The smaller of the faeries—the one holding a child—moved closer. Her eyes were wide and tormented. She wore clothing I might choose in my life as a human. A sweater, jeans, and tennis shoes. Her hair was long and dark. It hung over one slender shoulder in a braid. "I am Calaso of the bloodline Ettrian. I suppose I'm the one who asked for the tribunal."

Now the other female stepped forward. There was a haughty tilt to her chin and her eyes burned with emerald fire. She wore diamonds on her fingers and a dress made of feathers. "I am Isarrel of the bloodline Daenan," she announced.

Collith indicated that the first female should continue. She trembled and said, her voice breathy, "I had my daughter two months ago. My neighbor and friend, Isarrel, helped me through the difficult pregnancy. I didn't know it, but every time she went out in public, she pretended that she was pregnant, too. After I had Farryn and started going out again, I discovered rumors circulating that I'd stolen her baby."

"That's because you *did* steal—"

"You'll both be able to speak your piece," Collith cut in. The onlookers had begun to speculate amongst themselves. All their voices sounded like a hum, as though this were a hive instead of a hole. At the sound of the Unseelie King's voice, a hush fell. Collith waited until it was completely silent to nod at Calaso again. "Go on, please."

She visibly swallowed. "I told everyone Farryn is really mine, that I carried her myself, but because I was never seen while I was pregnant—I was so nauseous that I could barely get out of bed—most of our community seems to believe her. A few days ago, I opened the door to a mob. Someone tried to physically take her from me. I told them that I would let our king determine who's telling the truth, and that I would cooperate with whatever he decided."

Isarrel said nothing this time, but there were tears in her eyes. Her hands were clenched into small, white fists. I caught her glance longingly at the baby.

Once it was clear that Calaso had finished, Collith leaned forward and rested his elbows on his knees. His hands formed a steeple below his chin. Though I wanted to watch his face and try to discern which direction he was leaning, I kept my eyes on the two females, gauging their expressions and their stances. It occurred to me that I could force the truth from them, using my abilities as their queen, but that was probably frowned upon. I was already on too many shitlists in this place.

All at once, Collith straightened, gripped the armrests, and angled his body toward me. "I would like to know what Queen Fortuna thinks," he said. Surprise rippled through the air, and every gaze in the room turned to me. The attention felt like a physical weight on my body. I resisted the urge to slump down. I didn't know whether to be grateful to Collith or annoyed. Eventually I decided on the former, since I was the one who'd requested to attend this tribunal.

All right. Here goes nothing.

Butterflies erupted inside me as I looked down at the faeries. For once, I didn't say the first words that popped into my head. I held the armrests of my chair with light fingers, knowing no detail would go unnoticed. I tried to think slowly and methodically. Every action, especially those of a queen, had consequences. Whatever I said next could result in a new addition to the Mural of Ulesse.

The wisest people I knew were my parents. What would they say in this situation? What lessons would they remind me of?

Minutes passed. No one dared to pressure or urge me into a decision. My thoughts continued to wander and explore. At last I said, my tone cold and final, "Kill the child."

Somehow, though there wasn't a single sound in the room, it went even quieter. Both of the faeries stared at me. "I b-beg your pardon, Queen Fortuna?" Calaso stammered.

I raised my eyebrows, hoping the sweat clinging to my underarms, palms, and lower back wasn't obvious. "Did I stutter?" I asked coolly.

Through the mating bond, I felt trickles of worry and bewilderment. Still, Collith didn't move to intervene. He had decided to trust me.

When the king remained silent, Nuvian unsheathed his sword and stepped forward. His training ensured that no emotion showed on his face, but I was his sovereign. I still felt the fog of distaste and resentment clouding his mind.

"Please set the child down on the stones," he said to Calaso, whose entire body was shaking violently. She kept looking from Nuvian, to me, to Collith, as if one of us would tell her it was a lie or a joke. We all stared back at her, stone-faced and silent. Calaso clutched the baby to her chest, breathing raggedly, then bent over. An eternity went by as she set it down onto the cold floor. A thin wail shattered the stillness. Calaso backed away, her face twisting as though her heart were being ripped out of her chest. Isarrel was so pale that she looked more like a corpse than fae. Still, she did nothing to stop the proceedings.

Nuvian shifted so he was standing over the baby. Just as he raised the blade, tensed to bring it down, Calaso screamed. She threw herself across the tiny lump. "No, please, no! Isarrel can take her! She can have Farryn! Just, please, I beg of you, don't—"

"No one is going to hurt your baby," I interjected, loudly enough that my voice echoed. Nuvian immediately stepped back and sheathed his sword. He didn't look relieved, exactly, but it showed in his movements somehow. I focused on Calaso again. "You may take her home. This dispute is over."

Once again, both of the females stared at me. "W-what?" Calaso rasped, tears gleaming on her cheeks.

Isarrel's confusion swiftly gave way to tight-lipped fury. "I, too, demand an explanation, Your Majesty."

I ignored her and gave Calaso a kind smile. "She's clearly yours. Only a mother would rather see her child raised by someone else than come to harm."

The faerie stood up, cupping the back of her daughter's downy head. Her expression was dazed, like she was afraid this was all a dream. I knew the feeling. After a moment, I followed her lead and got up from my throne. The entire Court, seeing this as the dismissal it was, burst into sound. There were cries of outrage and worship. Some called me names and others shouted praise. I glanced back at Collith to make sure it was okay to leave. His head moved in a subtle nod. Hand in hand, we descended the stairs and made for the small doorway off to our right. Our small battalion followed in a surge of graceful movement and glittering swords.

I knew another lecture was coming. Thankfully, Collith waited until we were in the passageway. "That was…" he began.

Steeling myself, I turned around and met his gaze. We were still holding hands. The moment I realized this, I tried to pull free. "Look, I know it was risky—"

"*Incredible.*"

I blinked. My mind struggled to catch up with my ears, and when it did, the din behind us faded away to nothing. "Wait. You're not mad?"

"Mad?" Collith repeated, squeezing my fingers. He didn't seem to care that the Guardians could hear every word. "No. Hardly. How could I be angry when you were more of a ruler in five minutes than I've been in five years? You're the sort of queen legends are formed around."

I had been admired by hundreds, adored by thousands, but it all paled in comparison to praise from Collith. I cleared my throat to disguise the rush of sensation pooling between my thighs. "I was just lucky to have a mom who passed on what she knew. I remembered a story from the bible that was somewhat similar to what happened in there."

Before Collith could reply, sounds of a new commotion reached us. I turned and saw one of the Guardians point his sword at a human's chest. She was starving, her skin clinging to bones rather than fat and muscle, but she stared up at him defiantly.

"Stop! Let her through," I ordered.

The girl looked at me, then, and though I'd guessed her to be fifteen or sixteen, those eyes were ancient. Her dark hair looked like it had been cropped short with a knife instead of scissors. "I want you to see something," she said. No explanation or introduction.

I frowned. "Who are you?"

At this, the girl lifted her chin. She had two swords crossed beneath her throat, and yet she seemed completely unafraid. "My name is Annika."

During my time at Court, I had observed many interactions. It was how I'd learned that slaves, rather than giving their own names, always stated who their master was whenever a faerie demanded identity. Her answer, however simple it sounded, was a rebellion against them. Proof that the fire inside her hadn't been snuffed out.

"What would you like to show us?" I asked.

In response, the girl turned away. I understood we were meant to follow. As I moved to do exactly that, I felt incredulity emanating from our guards. I wondered what bothered them more—that I was actually interacting with a slave or stooping so low as to humor her request.

But humor her I did, paying no heed to their traditions or small ways of thinking. The girl had clearly been here a long, long time; she wound and wove through the maze without a second of hesitation or uncertainty. Our procession followed her for at least ten minutes. Wherever we were heading, it was a corner of Court few used or bothered to go. The dirt wasn't so packed down, the torches were fewer, and there were no carved doors anywhere in sight. It became so narrow that everyone was forced to walk single file.

If Annika hadn't stopped, I never would have found the room. Not in a million years.

It didn't even have a door. The opening was so tight that Collith and I both turned sideways to get in, and the Guardians had no choice but to remain in the passageway. When I straightened, my head brushing the low ceiling, I saw it was nearly the same size as my closet back home. The smell hit me an instant later, and I resisted the urge to cover my nose. The space held just one twin mattress, which rested on the ground. A girl laid upon it. It took me a few seconds to recognize the child I'd given a pair of shoes to—she was still wearing them, in fact. I'd never learned her name. Why hadn't I learned her name?

She'd clearly been beaten. Her eyes were both swollen shut and her lip had split open. Blood caked her hairline and her arm was wrapped in stained towels. She was either asleep or unconscious, because she didn't react to the sound of voices.

"When he actually spared a second to notice her, our master thought she stole the shoes from one of the other courtiers," Annika told us in a shaking voice. It didn't shake from pain alone, though—there was rage, too. "He couldn't be bothered to kill her outright. Instead, he just clapped her in chains and used her for entertainment at his next party. By the time they were done with her, she was—"

"That's enough," Collith cut in, his voice harsher then I'd ever heard it. The firelight coming from the tunnel made his eyes an otherworldly green and highlighted the hard, determined line of his body. "You've made your meaning quite clear."

"Her meaning?" I repeated faintly, still staring at the body on the that thin, moldy bed.

Annika turned her glare on me and said, accusation sprouting from every word like thorns, "We thought you were going to save us."

Guilt and remorse clogged my throat. I felt like such a fraud, standing there in all my finery while these children wore rags and faced brutality every single day. "I... I didn't... I've been..."

"Fortuna."

At the sound of Collith's voice, I turned. He held out my phone with a grim expression. I took it and glanced at the screen. A text from Lyari waited, which meant it must've been sitting on my phone before we even got to Court. Dread buried its splintered fingernails into my gut. I hurried to type in the passcode and open the faerie's message.

It's your brother. Get here now.

Feeling like I was caught in a net, I glanced from the bed to the door. I couldn't leave now. Not like this. Then Collith gripped my shoulder and said under his breath, "Go. I'll take care of this."

"What does that even mean?" I snapped, feeling my nostrils flare.

"It means, I'll take care of it. For now, all you need to focus on is getting back to Denver and Damon."

But that would mean depending on you, I wanted to say. *Leaning on your strength. Trusting your choices.*

In the end, I didn't say anything, because I'd made my choice. In the face of tragedy or shame, humans often claimed they didn't have one. But they do. We do. We just didn't like the options or how it made us feel.

Without another word to Annika or the others, I left the room. Two Guardians detached from the wall and followed me. I didn't look at either of them. Instead, I kept my eyes on the path ahead, letting my feet lead the way.

Just as I turned the corner, a sound echoed down the passageway. I faltered as I tried to place it. When it happened again, I realized that Annika was sobbing. Collith said something, his voice a soothing hum.

Somehow I knew, though I couldn't see them, that the person I called my mate had taken the girl into his arms. A king that held his subjects while they cried. It didn't sound real, even in my head. It hadn't been long ago that I thought Collith was a monster.

Now I wondered if I'd been the monster all along.

CHAPTER TWENTY-FIVE

I bolted from the Uber as if it was on fire.

Lyari was waiting on the front porch. Fred and Emma weren't in their usual spots, which meant they'd probably gone somewhere. Good. As soon as the car pulled up, Lyari moved, and we met on the lawn. She answered the question before I could ask it. "He woke up and walked out of the house. Didn't even put on his shoes," the faerie said. "I did my best to slow him down, so he'll have a few bruises tomorrow."

"Where is he?"

In response to this, Lyari turned her head, looking down the street. I followed her gaze. There he was, a frail silhouette at the end of the street. I broke into a run to catch up, sunlight spilling across the road like liquid gold. Damon had to hear the pounding of my shoes against the pavement, but he didn't turn or speak. His movements were slow and dazed. He wore an empty expression I had never seen before, as if he were dumbfounded or someone had drained him of everything.

"Hey," I started, reaching out to touch his arm.

"You're wasting your breath," Lyari told me just as my fingers made contact. She walked on the other side of Damon, keeping pace without any effort. "I yanked at him hard enough to dislocate his shoulder and he didn't even flinch."

"Okay." I dropped my hand, but I couldn't stop staring at him. Seeing Damon's eyes wide open and vacant like that made it difficult to breathe normally. I sounded shaken as I said, "Let's see how this plays out, then. The last time this happened, he stepped in front of a bus. I can't guarantee one of us will be there to stop him a third time. Collith? Can you hear me?"

My mate materialized within moments. I thought about summoning Laurie, too, but quickly dismissed the idea. He'd come in handy a few times, perhaps, but he was already too involved in our lives. If I closed my eyes, I could still feel his hard kiss in the basement of that bar.

Collith walked alongside us. "Is this sleepwalking?" he asked, frowning at my brother.

Remembering the bus incident, I shook my head. Damon had been wide awake when I'd seen him just minutes before that. "I don't think so."

"He reeks of magic. Can't you smell it?" Lyari asked, looking over at Collith. Her eyes widened, as if she'd just realized who she was talking to, and she quickly lowered her gaze.

He was too absorbed in the scent to notice. His nostrils flared, testing the air. "You're right. I can't quite place it, though. It makes me think of... seaweed."

I inhaled quietly, trying to detect what they were smelling, but there was nothing.

None of us spoke after that. The sky darkened as we followed Damon from block to block. Street to street. Neighborhood to neighborhood. We walked past buildings with bright open signs in the windows and groups of people standing around doorways or cars. This was not a dream, and we were not invisible anymore. Anything could go wrong and humans could see the unusual behavior my brother was exhibiting. I kept forgetting to breathe or unclench my jaw in an aching cycle.

After two hours of walking, we arrived at another high-scale neighborhood. Behind some of the houses, a lake glittered. *It's the same one from my dream*, I thought. No, I realized in a burst of intuition, not my dream. That was why, in the last one, I'd been wearing Damon's face when I looked down into a reflection. The magic affecting *him* must have touched me, that night, and I'd seen what Damon was actually seeing. This was all about him, somehow.

Damon hadn't stopped, but it seemed we'd finally arrived. Still wearing that vacant expression, he made his way up a sloped lawn. The house was modern, a structure of white surfaces and abrupt edges. Every window was dark... but the front door was wide open in a voiceless invitation. Why were we here? Why hadn't Damon snapped out of it yet?

Collith vanished and reappeared so he was in front of my brother. He entered the house first, doing so without knocking or trying the doorbell, which probably meant no one was inside. Damon did the same, and I followed close behind, my instincts shrieking to grab him and *run*. The only sounds, as we crossed the threshold, were our slow footsteps and an insistent wind.

The foyer was pristine, along with every other room we glimpsed or walked through. I expected as much, seeing the outside, but there was something almost eerie about how perfect it all was. Every piece of sleek, modern furniture was deliberately placed, and I had a sense that whoever owned them would know immediately if something had been moved.

Oddly enough, many of the walls and floors were bare, so when we came upon a wall of pictures, it was impossible not to pause and take notice. Each one was in a black frame and it was obvious most had been professionally taken. Right in the middle, there was a portrait of a couple.

In the image, the man was attractive but severe. He looked directly at the camera, standing ramrod straight. His eyes were a steely gray. A woman, presumably his wife, sat in a chair slightly in front of him. Simply put, she was stunning. Her hair was dark as a starless night and it hung to her waist in waves. I'd never seen eyes like that—such an unnatural, piercing blue that they looked like colored contacts. The rest of her was slender and pale. Breakable.

"Recognize either of them?" Collith asked.

I shook my head. "No, but doesn't she look—"

Lyari hissed our names.

Damn it. I broke into a run. I'd gotten so distracted by the picture that, while we'd been staring at it, Damon must have kept going. Collith and I made for the French doors, which gaped open like an unhinged jaw. As we crossed the patio, I instantly saw the cause of Lyari's alarm.

My brother was walking straight toward the lake.

I faltered when I saw the Guardian hanging back. Why wasn't she trying to stop him? Recovering, I ran even faster, desperate to avoid that freezing water. When I got my hands on Damon I was going to shake him, demand why he'd dragged us out here, ask what could possibly...

I froze when I saw the water nymph.

In fairy tales, they were called sirens, and now I understood why. She crawled out of the depths and onto shore, intent on my brother. She made an eerie sound that wasn't quite singing, but it was alluring nonetheless. From the waist up, she was completely naked. Her tail wasn't made of pretty green scales like *The Little Mermaid* depicted. Instead, it was silver, and there were sharp things jutting out from it, like knives or barbs.

There was no time to doubt my own eyes or the creature's intentions. "Damon!" I screamed, running to him. He didn't turn or falter. Reaching him, I jerked his arm so hard I feared I had dislocated his shoulder. Damon didn't even cry out as he fell. He simply pushed himself up—his skin was so slick with sweat that I lost my hold—and began walking into the water.

The siren retreated, her eyes gleaming with triumph. Any second now she'd grab his ankles and pull him under.

A renewed sense of fury gave me strength. Panting, I seized hold of Damon's waist and pulled him away again. As my brother went limp, his weight made us topple.

The collision cleared his mind. Damon blinked at me, frightened and perplexed. "Fortuna?"

"Run!" I ordered, looking wildly over my shoulder. There was just enough time to see him obey before the creature turned her churning eyes on me.

"Fortuna," she breathed. I tried to avert my gaze, but she'd trapped me in her thrall. She reached out with webbed fingers, caressing the patch of ankle visible above my shoe. Her voice—as cold and dark as the depths she came from—absorbed into me and made my center clench. I gasped, all thoughts of escape going cloudy.

"Collith, help," I heard myself whisper just before everything became wisps and breezes.

"Do you want a taste, Fortuna?" the siren purred. She lay there on her belly like a worm, but I had never seen something so beautiful, so achingly lovely. Her ribs poked out, her ears were pointed, and her breasts round and perfect. "Do you desire a touch?" she crooned.

Her power was so overwhelming, it didn't cross my mind to feel guilt or anger. Swallowing, I couldn't even bring myself to nod. "Yes. Please. Yes."

"Come closer," she begged. More tears pricked my eyes, and I couldn't bear to hear that agony, that need in her wet tones. Without hesitation, I followed her into the water. She kept backing away, evading me. I grew frantic and the water lapped at my waist. Some distant instinct—or maybe it was a voice—brushed my mind, but I disregarded it. It wasn't her, so it didn't matter. I was so enchanted that when my heel slipped on a stone and I found myself utterly submerged in the water, I didn't react. It closed around my head, the lake so deep that my feet didn't touch ground.

Blindly, I held my arms out, trying to find the siren. Freezing hands brushed mine, and I grabbed hold. Her skin was slimy but I hardly noticed. She wrapped herself around me, arms and fin, and kissed me. I gasped, water rushing into my lungs. Still, I didn't care. Her tongue caressed mine, and I felt her pulling off my clothes. I helped her, exploring the siren's body with my own hands. She ground against me, reaching down, down, to use those long fingers of hers. I arched, my body racking with pleasure. The numbing water was killing me, filling my lungs. It didn't matter. Nothing mattered but her.

Once again, a voice trickled through my thoughts. It was a small stream at first, then a river that washed everything else away. *Come back to me, Fortuna. Fight her influence. You're stronger than her.*

I couldn't quite place it. Couldn't remember who the voice belonged to... but I could see him. An image wavered in front of me, a faerie with hazel eyes and a beautiful smile, on the rare occasions he let me see it. He was the one I wanted to be touching. Because he was my mate. That was real.

And this wasn't.

With the realization, the pain came back. A burning in my lungs. *I'm drowning.* Despite the agony roaring through me, I felt my mouth thin into a determined line. I wasn't going to die like this. My father had taught me better.

Conveniently, I was already touching the siren. Without any delicacy or skill—already I could feel my sense of self slipping away again, the haze of lust closing in—I tore through her mind like a rabid dog on a carcass.

I was faintly aware of the siren screeching. Usually my victims didn't even feel me. I clawed past her phobias and quiet fears, those subtle flavors and feelings, all the way to the fears that were scars on her very soul. These were the memories and rooms.

I stopped in one of them. It was a bedroom in the white house we'd gone through; even in here, the most intimate of spaces, there were no rugs, colors, or knickknacks. The siren sat on the low bed, her back against the cushioned headboard. Her human glamour was intact, hiding the pointed teeth and silver fin. Her body was covered in a silky, lavender nightgown, and one of the straps had been torn.

There was a shuffling sound, and it jerked both of us to attention. The siren watched a man move out of the shadows— the same one from the portrait we'd seen in the house—his footsteps slow and measured. There was a leather belt in his hand, and he wrapped it around the other, then unwrapped it, making sure to draw her attention. "I will give you one chance to answer truthfully," he said. His voice somehow matched the decor in the house; it made me envision white walls and dangerous edges. "Did Andrew Parker touch you this morning, just after the pastor finished a sermon on the sanctity of marriage?"

The siren tried to make herself smaller. She shook her head frantically. "It was just my shoulder, Ethan. He was asking me if I felt all right, since he'd noticed me swaying during the—"

"You will never humiliate me like that again." The hollow-cheeked man stopped at the foot of the bed. His eyes were dark with intent. Before he could touch his wife, I rushed out of the room, unwilling to watch the rest.

As I returned to my own mind, I shoved away the compassion that threatened to replace my fury. I erected yet another wall, this one between me and any soft emotions. I had a weapon now and nothing would stop me from using it.

Above all else, the siren feared her husband.

Back in the water, I had utter control over her now. Her mind was mine, all the way down to the brain matter. I felt a vicious smile curve my lips as I twisted it against her. When the siren opened her eyes again, she saw her husband cutting through the water. His hair floated around his head like a black halo and his empty eyes were fixed on her. The siren's hands jerked away from me as she recoiled, a stream of bubbles bursting from her mouth. She vanished into the depths... and my smile instantly died.

Air. I needed air.

I fought for the surface, kicking my feet, flapping my arms. We'd gone deeper than I thought. I wasn't going to make it. Just as my vision started to go dark, though, I broke the surface. My lungs greedily sucked in a long, deep pull of oxygen. I fought to stay afloat and stay conscious.

Turning, I caught a glimpse of Collith and Damon on the shore—Collith was holding my brother back, grimacing as he struggled to keep his grip. No wonder he hadn't been able to help me. And there was Lyari, farther back, her eyes dull and her jaw slack, clearly under the siren's spell. Couldn't blame her for not helping, either, then. I swam toward them with arms that felt heavy as bowling balls.

An eternity later, my feet touched solid ground. I knew if I collapsed now, I wouldn't be able to get back up. I used the last of my endurance to take five more steps. I was still in the water, but it was only ankle-deep, and I hit the wet sand without another thought.

Colorful spots flashed over the world like a disco ball. Beyond that, all I could see out of my right eye—the other was submerged in water—was a black sky and the distant brightness of a house window. More time passed. A few minutes, a few hours, I had no idea. I just laid there and enjoyed the air going in and out of my lungs. The fog of the siren's voice began to clear from my mind.

Just as I was about to call out, wondering why no one had spoken yet, someone stood over me. I didn't have the strength to see who it was, but Lyari's voice drifted down a moment later. "I failed you, Your Majesty. I heard her song and fell sway to it. You should kill me."

I managed to look up and watch the faerie kneel. With a bowed head, she presented her sword, her meaning clear. "Stop that," I said wearily. "I wasn't exactly immune, either. Should I be executed?"

Her eyes flashed with annoyance. Her grip tightened on the sword. "Of course not."

"Well, there you go, then. Will someone help? My legs feel a little shaky." A moment after I made the request, fingers wrapped around mine, lending me enough strength to stand. I glanced up, thinking it would be Collith. When I saw that I actually held Damon's hand, a shock went through me.

He didn't meet my eyes and let go the instant I was upright. I glanced around, wondering where my mate had gone, and found him standing next to the water. He held the back of the siren's neck, no doubt to keep her from slipping away. She'd exchanged her fin for legs, and I wondered if she'd intended to attack us again. Why else would she leave the water?

Irrelevant now, I thought. This creature had some explaining to do, starting with why she'd targeted my brother.

I didn't realize I'd spoken out loud until Lyari said, "She was probably after the boy's heart."

"But why Damon? How did she know he's a Nightmare?" I directed the questions at the siren, but she wouldn't lift her head. The ends of her hair dripped. She held herself as far from Collith as possible, which was impressive, considering he had such a firm grip on her.

Lyari got back up and sheathed the sword. Judging from her expression, my Right Hand wanted nothing more than to put it through the creature's chest. Lyari returned her gaze to me, as if she were afraid that looking at the siren too long would tempt her to do exactly that. "Makes sense. He would be an easier target than you, Your Majesty," she said.

"Do you recognize her?" I asked Damon, and he shook his head. I frowned. "Then how did she—"

Without warning, the siren started to laugh. Unlike her song, the sound was harsh and grating. It felt out of place beneath the wide, serene moon and gently lapping waves. "No, you wouldn't remember me, would you?" she rasped. "No one does. That's how he wants it."

"Who?" I demanded. Now that I wasn't under her influence, I was able to notice more than her body. She was painfully thin and almost every part of her was decorated with bruises. My thoughts traveled back to the memory I'd found during our struggle in the water. "Your husband?"

In response, the woman opened her mouth and released the loudest, strangest noise I'd ever heard. I felt the undeniable pull of magic. Collith wrapped his free hand around her throat, cutting it short. With that, the strength seemed to go out of her. The woman sagged and began to sob.

"Fortuna," Collith said, his voice soft. "Why don't we go inside? We should find you some clothes."

It hit me, then, that I was standing there stark naked. My own clothes were long gone, most likely sitting at the bottom of the lake. At least I still had my shoes. I nodded, covering my chest at the same time. No one was looking at me, though. Damon's gaze was carefully averted, and Lyari was eyeing the siren as though she was still considering killing her.

My cheeks flamed as I hurried by them. Still holding onto the siren, Collith followed me. He drew uncomfortably close—I could feel his arctic breath on the back of my neck—and it wasn't until a few seconds later that I figured out he was trying to shield me. "Thank you," I said without turning, knowing he'd still hear it. We reached the patio and my drenched shoes left footprints on the concrete.

"You're welcome." Collith's voice was neutral, but I could feel the waves of protectiveness coming from his side of the bond. Warmth spread through my stomach as we walked inside. *The bedrooms are probably upstairs.* I hurried through the living room and toward the stairs. After what the siren had put my family through, the least she could do was lend me some clothes.

I reached the top and realized that Collith wasn't following. I looked for him, frowning, and saw that he'd stopped in the living room. He wore a strange expression as he said, "I'll stay with the siren. Lyari, would you accompany Fortuna upstairs?"

I fought the urge to cover my ass. "Hang on, where's Damon?"

"Your brother decided to wait out front, farther away from the siren's influence," Lyari told me. My rapid heartbeat began to slow again. She reached my side and I only hesitated for a moment, my gaze darting toward Collith again, before we padded down the hallway. The carpet was white and plush. I poked my head into every room until we found the master suite. I barely spared a glance for the enormous bed and glittering chandelier; my main focus was the closet.

Holy shit. In the doorway, I stopped short. These people had more clothes on one rack than I'd owned in my entire life. For a moment, I could only stare, then I remembered I was naked and jolted into motion again. I walked past the sparkling dresses and elegant blouses and, at the far end, spotted a shelf of exercise clothing.

"I still don't get how the siren knew about Damon," I called to Lyari, pulling on a tank top with a built-in sports bra. There was a zip-up hoodie hanging up next to the shelf, and I yanked it free. "The timing is so weird. Forget about the fact that we don't advertise what we are—Damon had just gotten back home. We weren't in contact with anyone from Denver."

Lyari appeared in the doorway. She turned slightly, giving me some privacy as I pulled on a pair of yoga pants. "Who knew your brother had returned?" she asked.

I thought about it as I rummaged through drawers in search of socks. Everyone in Granby knew, because of Angela's big mouth, and everyone else in the world knew thanks to… "That fucking *newspaper article*," I spat, forgetting the socks. My hands clenched into fists.

Uninterested in my problems, Lyari held a framed photograph up that had been resting on the nightstand. It was the man from the portrait downstairs, standing in front of a sign that read, Cooper Funeral and Cremation Services. "Apparently, her husband owns a funeral home."

This shouldn't have made me pause, but it did. Damon. Song. Funeral home. Just like that, my mind made another connection. The puzzle was so simple, but we hadn't been in possession of all the pieces. "That's how she was originally planning to get Damon's heart," I said slowly. "She made him step in front of that bus, remember? It would've been easy to get into the funeral home her husband owns and help herself. Easier than a confrontation, at least. But when we kept interfering, she got desperate."

Hearing myself say her vile plan out loud made my heart rumble with rage. Suddenly I couldn't believe that I'd left her mind intact. I left the closet and headed for the hallway. Lyari was right behind me, almost frantic in the way she moved, and I knew it would be a long time before she forgave herself for losing to the siren. I descended the stairs, mentally flipping through the most painful ways to kill her.

Collith was in the living room where we'd left him, tending to a gaping cut on the siren's shoulder. It was obvious the wound wasn't fresh, but I should have noticed it earlier. Maybe the siren's magic still lingered somewhere within me, clouding the way I saw her. "Is everything all right?" Collith asked cautiously, noticing my flinty expression.

I stopped a few feet away from them. I didn't need proximity to finish this. "Considering this *thing* just tried to kill my brother, no, it's not," I answered. Behind me, Lyari's sword rang as she pulled it from the sheath.

My voice gave nothing away, so Collith must've felt my cold fury through our bond. "She's a victim, Fortuna," he reminded me, letting go of the siren's arm. He got to his feet. I noticed that he moved as if I were a wild animal, snarling and about to pounce. "Desperation drives people to do ugly things."

I looked past him to fix my gaze on the siren. "And what's going to stop her from trying it again?"

"Nothing," she hissed, baring her teeth at me. "Nothing will stop me from trying again, and again, and again, until I'm either dead or chewing on your little brother's heart."

I launched myself at her, in both mind and body. The siren shrieked and reeled back. Then Collith was there, standing between us, his expression unafraid. In that instant—just like that one after the third trial, when I had briefly considered killing Damon—I thought about breaking Collith. Tunneling through his brain and bursting out the other side, leaving him a drooling husk.

Wait. No. I didn't want to hurt Collith.

The darkness inside me felt like a physical thing. It was too big, too uncontrollable. "What's happening to me?" I whispered, more to myself than him. I hugged myself as if that alone could contain the inner chaos.

"Your power," Collith said, reaching to hold my face between his hands. "You're changing, so it stands to reason that your abilities are, too. But you're pushing them away, fighting them, disrupting the balance. Listen to me, Fortuna. Look at me. Your power is fear, yes, but fear isn't always ugly or dark."

"What the hell are you talking about?" I asked between my teeth. Nightmares woke children in the night, crying and screaming. They haunted humans as they went about their days, like a shadow or a cold breath. It was nothing *but* ugly and dark.

"Isn't fear what drove you to save Damon?" Collith challenged. "That he was frightened or being harmed? And I know it's what sent me here to protect you, to leave my throne and my people behind when nothing else has managed to tear me away before."

The darkness writhed and roiled, trying to break free of its cage. "You think I'm ashamed of what I am? I'm not. Trust me."

"Ashamed, no. Frightened? Yes. Which is why you're struggling so much now that there's an imbalance."

Flavors burst on my tongue; I recognized them from my time in the siren's mind. It could only mean that, as Collith and I had been speaking, my powers had worked their course without any prompting from me. Truly afraid now, I focused on Collith and gripped his wrists fiercely. "Spell it out," I demanded. He was obviously trying to make a point, but the power was like a storm in my head, building and thickening, making it difficult to think of anything else.

Collith pressed his forehead to mine. His scent surrounded me and, just like that, some of the tension eased from my body. "Fear is a seed, my love. It can grow from pain or anger… or it can grow from something else. Love. Hope. You are not a monster, Fortuna Sworn. Concentrate on the good, take it into you, and let the rest go."

It's not that easy, I tried to say. Letting go would mean leaving the siren unpunished. After everything she'd done—sinking her claws into my brother over the past week, drawing us here, coaxing Damon in front of a bus, almost drowning me—I wanted to pillage through her mind like it was a candy store.

Collith must've heard my thoughts to some extent, because he pressed against me even harder and whispered, "Holding onto anger is like drinking poison and expecting the other person to die. Choose mercy, Fortuna."

A hundred cutting, sarcastic responses waited on the tip of my tongue. Then a sound shattered the glass sphere that had formed around us and I forgot them all. Collith turned around, and in doing so, put the siren back into my line of sight. She was crying; the racket came from her. I clapped my hands over my ears and saw that everyone else had done the same. I glanced toward the windows, expecting the neighbors' lights to flick on. But nothing happened. How was anyone sleeping through this?

After another few seconds of this, I stepped closer to the siren, intending to slap her. She sensed the movement and raised her face toward me. A gasp caught in my throat, and all the darkness drained from me like I was a broken glass.

It was those eyes. Those pink eyes that whispered her secrets to anyone who cared to listen. *I am in pain. I need help.* I remembered her now.

She'd lived on the same street as us, before my parents were killed. I'd see her sometimes, getting the mail or taking a walk. She had been a slender thing with neat hair and white knuckles as she clutched at a purse strap, a book, or an umbrella handle. Once or twice, as we walked past each other, she'd glance at me through her lashes. And I glimpsed the whites of her eyes, tinted pink in those moments, a wordless cry for help. But I'd been too young, too naive.

Looking at the siren now, I realized that whatever glamour she'd been wearing was gone. Like all Fallen, this female was not as she appeared at first glance. She didn't have creamy skin, but the wan complexion of someone in suffering. The bones in her wrists and knees were tiny and pronounced.

Seeing these details, presented with the undeniable truth of what she'd been through, calmed the brewing storm within me. I couldn't hurt her now. I even understood why she had wanted to be fearless.

If only her plan hadn't involved eating Damon Sworn's heart.

"If you ever try to hurt my brother again, I *will* kill you," I warned the creature, realizing after I'd spoken that I still didn't know her name. But I didn't want to know it. Didn't want to humanize her even more when it was very possible I'd have to kill her.

"Maybe you should anyway," the siren whispered, as if she knew what I was thinking. "Anything would be better than this. Consider it a mercy, if that eases your conscience."

"Do us both a favor and get help," I growled, burying my nails into my palms. The pain grounded me. Without another word to her, Collith, or Lyari, I withdrew and retraced our steps through the house. I knew that if I didn't get out, leave that instant, I might succumb to the blackness inside me.

When I emerged from the front door, I saw Damon on the sidewalk. The world slowed as, for a terrible moment, I thought the siren had already kept her promise. Was I about to watch him step in front of the next car that drove by?

The world creaked back into motion when Damon glanced back at me and said, "I ordered an Uber for us."

The tightness in my chest loosened. "Oh. Thanks. Wait, didn't you leave Fred and Emma's in your pajamas? You don't even have shoes on. How do you have your phone?"

Damon turned his face in the other direction, suddenly preoccupied in spotting the Uber. "There's a YouTube video that I play on repeat every night. It's called 'heartbeat sounds.' I'm still used to falling asleep on Jassin's chest."

I couldn't tell if he was confiding in me or trying to deepen the wound between us. "How far away is it?" I asked after a minute. It was a cowardly choice, but I didn't have the strength to battle Damon right now.

He looked at his phone. "Five minutes."

I nodded. After another moment or two, Lyari appeared on my other side. We all waited there, on an empty street in a brightly-lit Denver neighborhood, and didn't say a word. It was that time of night when it felt like we were the only people left on Earth. Collith exited the house a couple minutes later, and he stayed silent, as well. Whatever he'd talked about with the siren had seeped into his skin. He looked... sad.

The car soon arrived, its brakes squealing into the stillness. Damon got into the front seat, leaving me, Lyari, and Collith to get cozy in the back. I found myself sitting between them, my shoulders brushing against each of theirs with every turn the driver took. The woman I once was would've cared. She would've cringed with every touch. Now I just struggled to stay awake; being in a car always lulled me to sleep. It had also been one hell of a night.

"Have a good night," our driver said, startling me. My eyes snapped open. When had we stopped? Disorientated, I looked around as Collith and Lyari got out. We were back in South Park Hill; Damon was already disappearing inside Fred and Emma's house. Now that the way was clear, I scooted out, thanking the gray-haired man behind the wheel as I went. Once I stood upright in the cool air, he pulled away from the curb.

"Lyari, go home," I called to the Guardian, who was nearly to the porch steps. She turned, an argument poised on her lips, but I raised my eyebrows at her. Lyari vanished with a murderous expression.

I turned back to Collith, suddenly feeling vulnerable. I could still feel his hands on my face and hear his voice telling me that I was afraid of myself. "May I walk you to the door?" Collith asked before I could say anything. Those hands were in his pockets now. Safely tucked away where they couldn't do any more damage or make me question everything I knew.

To his question, I just nodded, and we started forward at a slow pace. The stillness drew my thoughts back in. Something had been bothering me, taking the form of a quiet but insistent voice at the back of my head. "You know, while we were in the Uber, I kept going over this whole night. Trying to figure out what, exactly, happened under the water, since so much of it is a blur. And it occurred to me that you didn't even blink when you heard the siren's song. Lyari even succumbed to it. It's just got me wondering—do you have *any* weaknesses?" I smiled to show Collith I was joking. Kind of.

"Of course I have weaknesses. Of course there are times I am vulnerable. But all of them are tied... to you," Collith said quietly. He cleared his throat and added, as if he didn't want to linger on that none-too-small revelation, "There's a legend about those who can hear her song, by the way. Do you know of it?"

I climbed partway up the porch steps, then turned to face him. We were the same height now. "No. Enlighten me."

"They say the ones who are lured by her have undecided or unclaimed hearts. They don't know who they love or whether they want to entrust themselves to another creature. And... the ones who are deaf to her sweet nothings are wholly and pathetically lost to another."

"Pathetically, huh?" I asked softly, feeling that warmth again. When Collith stepped closer, his eyes asking the question, I met him halfway. We kissed as if we'd known each other for years instead of weeks. His taste banished the memory of the siren's mouth. The wrongness of what I'd felt for her was burned away by the heat I felt for Collith. Once again, I forgot the promises I'd made myself to resist him forever. Or maybe I just didn't care about them anymore. I buried my fingers in his hair and stood on tiptoe, reveling in the sensation of his body crushed against mine.

After a time, Collith reluctantly drew back. His hands slid down to my waist, leaving a tingling path in their wake, and our breathing sent clouds into the air. I closed my eyes and tried to keep the memories of this evening at arm's length. A few images still slipped through. "Why didn't you come upstairs?" I asked suddenly, pulling back to peer up at Collith.

That small line appeared between his brows. "What?"

"Back at the siren's house," I clarified. "We went inside for clothes, and instead of coming with me, you sent Lyari up. Why? It's not like you hadn't seen me naked before."

His eyes cleared as he understood. Collith wore one of his serious expressions as he searched for the right words. "Because... it will be your choice," he said after a long pause. I felt his struggle, the soft pulses of unrest that came from his side of the bond. "It has to be. When you and I are finally together, there can be no confusion about it. Whether or not you truly wanted me."

When, he'd said. As if there was no uncertainty that we would, eventually, be one instead of two. I let out a breath, hoping he couldn't feel my own inner battle raging. "How is it that you can be so kind to me, again and again, but you can watch everyone else suffer?" I whispered, meeting Collith's pained gaze. In case he misunderstood my meaning, I sent an image down the bond like a paper ship along a stream of rainwater. The slave girl with dirty, bare feet, staring up at me with hope in her eyes.

Before Collith could answer, his phone sounded. His head dipped as he looked at the screen. I already knew the Unseelie King was leaving when he looked up to give me a rueful smile. "I'll be back as soon as I can. I'm needed at Court for a couple hours," he murmured.

I returned his smile, knowing he could probably see the frustration in it. "Oh, you'll be back, huh? Are you inviting yourself into my bed? That's a little presumptuous."

"You may have a point. Leave a light on, then. If I arrive and see that your window is dark, I'll assume you'd rather spend the night alone." Collith slowly released his grip and walked backward. With every step, he faded more from view, until I found myself staring at an empty sidewalk.

A sigh seeped out of me as I jogged up the porch steps and

tried the door. Thankfully, Damon had left it unlocked; he must've thought to ask Emma or Fred where the spare was. I stepped inside and turned the dead bolt behind me.

Finn was waiting at the bottom of the stairs, his fur bristled with agitation. "Everything is okay," I told him, hushed, not wanting to wake Fred and Emma. The werewolf didn't make a sound, yet somehow I could sense his disapproval for leaving him so long. I finally took off my icy shoes and socks. I crept up the stairs barefoot, with Finn following, of course, and into the bathroom. I washed my face, brushed my teeth, and went to climb into bed. I still wore the clothes I'd taken from the siren's closet, but they were clean and comfortable, so why not? Finn curled up next to my feet, as was becoming our habit, and promptly fell asleep. I stayed awake to wait for the Unseelie King. The light beside me glowed soft but bright.

An hour crawled by. Two. I kept sleep away by looking at pictures of dogs in nearby shelters. Despite my efforts, however, I felt my eyes continually drifting shut. Then I remembered that Oliver would be there, waiting in my dreams, and I'd be leaving him for Collith whenever the faerie deigned to show up. Guilt, an emotion that was becoming all-too familiar, drove sleep away like wolves chasing a fawn.

Another hour passed. Collith didn't come, but a text did. He must've gone all the way to the surface to send it, I thought distantly. *Got held up,* it read. *I'll make it up to you.*

I put the phone back on the nightstand, unable to deny a sting of disappointment. After switching off the lamp, I closed my eyes and waited for the healing wave of sleep to wash it away. My veins wouldn't stop humming, though. I tried switching to my other side. Fluffing the pillow. Kicking off the covers.

When I heard the telltale moan of the stairs, a sound of relief left me. Emma. Maybe she'd appreciate some company. I abandoned the rumpled bed and crept into the hallway with Finn on my heels.

There was no one in the kitchen when I arrived. Frowning, I poked my head into the living room. Furniture and shadows stared back. I checked the front porch next, recalling that Emma used to have the occasional cigarette. But when I looked out, the chairs were empty. I stood in the foyer, trying not to jump to conclusions. *I'm sure Emma is fine.* Finn sat down, watching me, and his tongue lolled out. I scowled at him. "Think you could help a girl out with those supernatural senses of yours? Where did Emma go?"

Finn's attention shifted. Following his yellow gaze, I noticed the back door was open. A slant of moonlight fell across me as I approached it and pulled the screen open. The hinges squeaked. When I stepped into the open—Finn pushed past me, adamant about not getting left behind again—and searched for Emma's familiar shape, my gaze landed on Damon's thin profile instead. He looked out at the lawn, but I suspected he wasn't really seeing it.

Hardly daring to breathe, I joined him on the swing. It swayed from my movements. Damon didn't say anything, but he didn't leave, either. Finn's nails clicked as he wandered to the other side of the porch, sniffing everything along the way. After a moment I gazed upward, hoping to catch the sun cresting that faraway skyline. Predawn light made everything seem surreal.

"I finally put it together," I said, squinting as my eyes adjusted to the sudden change. I was so tired, and all I wanted to do was sleep, but something about this felt important. "Bud told me you went to see him about your will. That you wanted to make sure everything went to me, in the case of your death. I didn't see the pieces, though, until the siren asked me to end her life. 'Anything would be better than this,' she said. You knew what you were walking into. You knew she wanted to kill you. This was supposed to be your suicide."

"Yes," Damon said hoarsely. He didn't hesitate or try to hide it. In that moment, I wanted to hit him. It was irrational and cruel, maybe, but I did.

Instead, I put my arms around him and leaned my temple on his shoulder. Damon didn't hold back. He didn't lean into me. But he didn't push away or move, and that was something. It was. I thought about taking advantage of the quiet to ask Damon about his conversation with Savannah. There was a little boy out there with his eyes, and despite everything else that had happened, the issue of Matthew remained unresolved.

I couldn't bring myself to say anything else, though. Not right now. Instead, I pressed even closer to Damon. We passed some time like that, connecting in the smallest of ways. But Nightmares knew better than anyone how much impact a single touch could have.

"Fortuna?" my brother ventured at last, his voice vibrating through me.

I didn't move. The sun was almost here. Any moment now, it would arrive to coax the world into waking. "Yeah?" I said back.

"Let's go home."

His words made me smile. We didn't even have a vehicle, since mine was totaled somewhere in the woods, but... home. That sounded nice. "Okay. Let's go home."

CHAPTER TWENTY-SIX

ONE WEEK LATER

*a*ir hissed through Adam's teeth as he exhaled.

His expression was twisted in pain, but he didn't let it weaken him. I couldn't suppress a small, satisfied smile. We had been sparring for twenty minutes now, Adam landing so many blows that I'd definitely be sore tomorrow. The fact that I'd managed to touch him meant I was getting better at this.

As Adam recovered, we kept circling each other on the exercise mat. My adrenaline was high, my eagerness to win overwhelming. With every step, I could feel my bare feet leaving behind sweaty imprints on the plastic.

Then I saw Collith a few yards away, leaning against the wall, silently observing our antics. How long had he been standing there? As always, he looked *good*. Today he was dressed in Court attire, a black shirt that had feathers along the shoulders, dark pants to match, and shining knee-high boots. I wondered whether Collith had a stylist of his own or if this was all him.

Suddenly, the movement so swift I didn't have a chance to

block it, Adam knocked me to my feet with one swipe of his leg. I scrambled back up, scowling. "You're not paying attention," he informed me. Shadows danced over his features, cast by the dangling light bulb overhead.

"Yes, I am."

"Prove it."

I knew he was expecting an attack, so I restrained myself for a few moments. Then I feigned to the left. Adam anticipated that it was a trick. He didn't anticipate that it actually wasn't. I reached him and jumped into the air, jabbing his neck with my elbow, and while he staggered I dropped to the ground and yanked at his firmly-planted feet. He fell. I immediately leapt out of reach, readying myself to go on the defense.

Adam moved in a blur, standing again before I could blink. Instead of coming at me, his focus went to the clock. "Well done. I need to get started on some stuff," he said in his toneless way.

Just in case it was a ruse, I stayed as I was, tense and crouched. "Okay. Mind if I stop by in a couple days?"

Adam turned away. He walked past Collith without acknowledging him. "Fine by me. We'll work on the sword next," I heard him say before he went into one of the side rooms. He kicked the door shut and its slam echoed through the garage.

His response gave me a rush of anticipation. My interest in swordplay grew every time I saw Lyari's, gleaming at her hip, its wicked edges winking at me. Smiling again, I straightened and retrieved my purse from a lawn chair in the corner. This time I'd brought a hand towel, and as I approached Collith, I pulled it out to dry my sweat-drenched skin.

"What are you doing here?" I asked, knowing he would feel my soft pleasure. We'd seen each other a few times over the past week—coffee twice and dinner once—but Collith hadn't spent the night or offered any explanations for why he'd flaked on me in Denver. Asking him for one was like trying to push the wind; it only parted around me or rushed away.

Collith's eyes followed the towel's progress. The heat in them made my center tighten. Suddenly the music, a constant stream of classic rock, was so loud that it felt like the only sound between us. "I made you a promise. Do you remember?" Collith asked, his gaze steady on mine.

It took me a few seconds to figure out what he was talking about. This faerie didn't make promises lightly, though, and only one stood out in recent memory. I saw us in my little living room, colorful game pieces between us.

What's your biggest regret?

I can't answer that. I'd have to show you.

"Better late than never," I said with a grin. It occurred to me that I was doing that a lot around him now—smiling. "Are we going somewhere?"

He nodded. "Yes. Back to Court. I'd like to introduce you to someone there."

The prospect of going underground, back to that place, didn't unsettle me as much as it used to. I wasn't sure what that meant or if I was bothered by it. "Are you going to tell me who?" I asked as we walked to the door together.

Collith pushed it open for me. The wind was intense today and it mussed his hair. He looked down at me, oblivious to the strands blowing in his eyes. "The most important one in my life... next to you."

As we started toward the goblins' van, parked in the closest spot to the door, I chewed my lip. I wondered, suddenly, if I was ready to see this part of Collith. To know him better than I already did. We were moving toward something, I could feel it. Instinct told me to slow it down or put a stop to this completely.

Yet I couldn't ignore the curiosity rising up within me, getting heavier with every second, like snow piling up against a door. Open it, and I might find the avalanche would be too much to bear. I knew, though, that it would haunt me if I didn't go.

Collith was still waiting for my answer. "Do I have time to shower?" I asked. We'd reached the van. I stood with my back to the door, gazing up at him.

"Certainly." He tilted his head and appraised me. "Would you like some company?"

The question made my stomach flutter. I hesitated, only for a moment, but then I pictured us there. Tasting each other beneath a hot, pounding stream, free to touch whenever and however we wanted. All that wet, bare skin. "We'd have to be quiet," I managed. I had roommates now, and Damon had been doing projects around the house all week. To forget that he had a son waiting for him in Denver, I suspected. Eventually, though, he would have to face that inevitable truth.

Collith put his hand on my waist and pulled me close, banishing all the thoughts from my head. "I won't make a sound," he promised in a whisper. "My tongue will be otherwise preoccupied."

I shivered.

A single bird mourned the departing sun.

I searched for it in the treetops, then the underbrush, half-expecting to see a pair of yellow eyes staring back at me. But Finn was back at the house, sleeping on the couch. Returning to his human shape had taken a lot out of him; he'd still been unconscious when Collith and I left. I knew he'd probably be furious that I hadn't woken him.

We made our way through the dead forest now. There was no more green in sight, everything having succumbed to the approaching winter. My shoes crunched over leaves that were brown, red, and gold. The trees looked naked and forlorn.

Halfway through our hike, the wind picked up again. It was indifferent to how it made me shiver again, this time for a less pleasant reason. My hair was still wet from the shower... and my head was still light from the sky-cracking orgasm Collith had given me amidst all that steam and hot water. I forgot about the cold as I relived that hot, uninterrupted time in the shower.

We'd spent an hour in there. Then, when we were done with that, the two of us left the bathroom in favor of my room. We fell onto the bed and picked up where we'd left off. Hours went by in those four walls. Never once did we get dressed or stop touching each other.

Only with one other person—a soul that wasn't even real—had I lost myself to like that.

We didn't have sex. For the first time, it wasn't because I hadn't been willing. Collith was the one who stopped us from crossing that line. When I asked him why, he'd just held my hands against his chest, shook his head, and moved to kiss me again. It had been all-too easy for him to make me forget my hurt and embarrassment. Afterward, he'd taken me into the kitchen, where he made us pancakes and bacon. Finn slept through it all.

Now the object of my thoughts looked back at me over his shoulder, the corner of his mouth tilted up. "Stay out of my head, damn it," I called to him.

"Stop broadcasting to me like a car radio with the bass cranked up," he called back. Yet another smile tugged at my mouth. I hurried to catch up with him, since we were almost to the Unseelie Court. I'd spent the journey here trying to spot Nuvian or the other Guardians. I knew they were there, protecting their beloved king, but I had to give it to them—they were good. All I'd spotted in the trees was a lone squirrel.

Minutes later, Collith and I were underground. Like spirits, the Guardians emerged from the shadows. I'd given Lyari the day off—well, ordered her to take it, more like—so the faces surrounding us were unfamiliar, other than Nuvian. If he had disliked me before, he absolutely loathed me now. Since that stunt I pulled at the last tribunal, he had gone from addressing me coldly to acting like I didn't exist.

The path Collith had chosen sloped downward. The air became crueler and crueler, sinking like needles into the tips of my nose and ears. I kept expecting to encounter stairs, but the passageway just steadily declined.

All at once, my heart pounded harder—I'd seen this passageway in Collith's mind once. Even that fleeting glimpse had been filled with emotion. He hated this path. He dreaded where it led. Why would he bring me here? Who could I possibly meet in such a dark place?

My curiosity was still stronger than the rising tide of anxiety. I held Collith's hand tightly as the ground became level again. Yards away, the tunnel came to an end. There was a single door embedded in the wall, its surface painted in blue flowers. Two Guardians stood on either side of it. Were they guarding whoever lived behind that door... or making sure they didn't get out?

I didn't recognize either of the faeries, but Collith's demeanor changed as we drew close—the kingly ice thawed. He murmured their names and shook their hands. He knew these Guardians well, I thought as I watched him. He trusted them. "How is she today?" he asked the one on the right. The dark-skinned faerie reminded me of Tarragon, in how his countenance emanated a serenity I could only imagine.

"Lucid, Your Majesty," he answered, giving my mate a kind smile.

Collith nodded, his expression calm, but a whisper of nervousness drifted down the bond. "Very good. Please don't let anyone disturb us."

The Guardian bowed and looked forward again. Without letting go of my hand, Collith pushed the door open and stepped through. I did the same, knowing it was useless to hide any fear I felt. I followed Collith down another tunnel, noting that none of the Guardians accompanied us. Soon this path, too, ended in a wall. There was no door in sight this time. Just a row of torches on both sides, warm and flickering.

Collith looked from the earth back to me. A combination of apprehension and warmth filled his voice as he finally spoke. "Fortuna, this is my mother, Naevys. Mom, this is my mate, Fortuna."

I stared at him, completely at a loss. His mother? Was this a joke or... or did Collith truly think there was someone in the passageway with us? Another glance told me we were alone, nothing but dirt and rocks for an audience. I was on the verge of asking Collith where he thought his mother was when the wall moved. My first instinct was to run—good things didn't usually come out of the ground like that—but then I saw a bright, blue eye. I went still.

It took me another moment to realize that I was looking at a faerie.

Parts of her body had been completely absorbed into the earth. Roots grew out of her stomach. Tiny ones weaved through her hair, looking more like veins than parts of a tree. This was Collith's mother?

If I ignored the bizarreness of her circumstances, she looked like she could be his sister. Her skin was fair and her hair—what parts of it hadn't already been claimed by dirt—was a dark shade of brown. She and Collith shared the same long, slightly upturned nose.

"Thank you for finally bringing her," the faerie said to Collith, politely ignoring the fact that I was gaping. Her voice was faint, but there was a vein of strength within it, and I could imagine the woman she used to be.

In the next moment, Naevys fixed her gaze on me. Though my mouth was shut now, I knew my expression was probably as horrified as I felt. A faint smile curved the female's pale lips, and if I didn't know any better, I would've said it was amused. "Well met, Fortuna Sworn," she said.

"Hello," I murmured back, feeling sick, dismayed, and confused. No wonder Collith hated coming here; seeing his mother like this probably killed him a little more each time. No wonder he was so insistent on living at Court and coming back every day. In the span of a few seconds, I understood my mysterious mate so much more.

Unaware of my thoughts, Naevys's vibrant eyes studied me. "I've been begging my son for weeks to introduce me to his new bride. His descriptions did not do you justice, my dear. Then again, it's difficult to coax anything out of him. Wouldn't you agree?"

With every second that passed, my mind accepted the terrible magic more. "Thank you," I said to her compliment, somewhat mollified at the revelation that I wasn't the only one Collith kept things from.

After I'd spoken, Collith made a sound. When I frowned at him questioningly, he smiled as if he couldn't hold it back anymore. "Forgive me, Mother. This is just the most subdued I've ever seen Fortuna. It's like seeing a wet cat."

"Thanks a lot," I muttered with a glare.

"You have nothing to fear from me," the faerie in the ground interjected, responding to Collith's comment about my demeanor. Her fingers twitched, as if she were trying to touch me in reassurance. "My request was borne from curiosity, not expectation. I wanted to get a sense of you before I go."

"Mother," Collith growled, all traces of mirth wiped away with her words. *Before I go*, she'd said. "We're not discussing this right now."

"Right, yes, of course. I forgot that you buried your head

right past the sand and into the bedrock of Earth itself. Good thing he's got a hard skull, eh, Fortuna?"

"The hardest," I agreed instantly, not thinking. Now it was Collith's turn to glare. I gave him a sheepish shrug.

Naevys laughed. The sound was surprisingly normal, as if she weren't trapped forever in the dark, slowly getting swallowed by earth and rock. "I think I like this girl, darling," she said.

I liked her, too, and that brought my thoughts back to Collith's state of mind. If I was affected at the prospect of his mother's fate, after knowing her for a minute, I couldn't fathom how he felt. He'd done an excellent job hiding it from me.

"Are you dying?" I asked Naevys bluntly. I knew the question would cause Collith pain, and that wasn't what I wanted—not anymore, at least—but I needed the truth of what my mate was facing every day. What he was going to face later on. As Naevys herself pointed out, he wasn't likely to tell me on his own.

The faerie didn't take offense to this; she just turned her attention back to me. "Dying is not the right word," she answered. "Humans die. Birds die. Beasts die. I am simply... becoming something else. Collith's servants don't even need to feed me anymore; the earth sustains me. With each day that passes, I have more trouble remembering my own name or how to form words. Soon Collith will come down here and there will be nothing waiting for him but an empty shell."

"Mother, please," Collith said hoarsely. In all the time I had known him, he'd never looked more vulnerable. More in pain.

Naevys just smiled tenderly. Once again, her fingers twitched, and I knew she was trying to reach for his cheek. "I will not tell a lie just because you fear the truth."

Their exchange had the echo of things that had already been said many times. Collith didn't reply, and when I looked over at him, his expression made my heart ache. The austere king had been replaced by a lost, devastated little boy. "How much time do you have?" I asked Naevys after a long, thick silence.

"If I had to guess, I would estimate that I'll be gone by spring." Her voice managed to be gentle and matter-of-fact at the same time. *I admire her*, I thought suddenly. I'd have to touch the faerie to know for certain, but there didn't seem to be a drop of fear in Naevys's veins when she spoke of her future… or lack thereof.

"Then I'll be sure to visit you more between now and then," I told her. Even as I said the words, I was half-tempted to stay—I remembered how sharp the knife of loneliness could be. Thinking of all the ways I'd tried to fill that void, I looked around the tunnel. How did she pass the time?

"I would enjoy that. I hope you do," she said before I could ask. With an air of finality, Naevys looked between the two of us. I wondered what she saw. Collith and I stood so close that our arms were nearly touching, but we didn't look at each other or lace hands. "I am glad my son found you, Fortuna. I think you've been good for him. Now go and do whatever it is young people do these days; I need to rest a while."

Collith didn't argue. He stepped forward and kissed her forehead, one of the few parts of her that hadn't yet been affected by the spell. She and I exchanged a nod, then Collith offered his arm and we walked away. Leaving her there didn't feel right, but I didn't know what else to do.

The moment we got through the door, the male faerie closed it behind us. The other hadn't moved from her previous position, not even her eyes, and her devotion reminded me of Lyari. Collith expressed his gratitude to both for keeping his mother safe, then we left them, as well. Nuvian must've been called away while we were with her, since the faeries trailing after us were different than before.

It made sense, I thought, why Collith had Naevys protected around the clock. She was his weakness. Enemies could use her against him, just like they'd used Damon against me. When I fought for the crown, all I had considered was the power. I forgot to consider how it could make me vulnerable, too.

I waited until we were well out of Naevys's earshot to ask the obvious question. "How did that happen to her?"

Collith's jaw worked. He didn't want to talk about this, it was obvious. Who would? Thankfully he stayed true to his resolution to be more open with me. "Irony at its finest," he said at last. "The king knew how much Mom loved tending the earth. Coaxing life from the ground. As punishment for leaving him— along with evading him for so long—he did this. She wouldn't have returned at all if it weren't for me."

"*That's* why you killed the old king." It wasn't a question; Collith's shame spread along the bond like fog. I cleared my throat, feeling helpless. I couldn't figure out my own guilt, much less someone else's. "You can't just pull her out?"

We'd reached the surface. I stepped into the night, inhaling deeply, and turned to watch Collith emerge. "The earth is bespelled," he answered, his voice tight. I knew the anger wasn't directed at me; his mind was still on the old king. "The last time we tried to remove her, we nearly ripped her in half. The bastard had a witch on retainer, and after she did his bidding, he killed her. It can't be undone."

Sorrow formed a knot beneath my heart. There was nothing I could say or suggest, since Collith had probably heard and tried it all. Without another word, Collith started in the direction of home. I walked next to him, silent for a time, and listened to the soothing crunch of leaves beneath our feet. "Why did you show me this today? After all this time?" I asked eventually.

"At the motel, I swore you could ask any question and I would answer truthfully. I didn't want you to think my word is worthless, but I knew my answer was down there, buried with my mother. And she's not always like the lucid faerie you just met, which makes outside visitors... difficult."

I looked over at him, but Collith kept his eyes on the path ahead. "What do you mean?"

"It's why I occasionally leave so abruptly—my mother has episodes. She starts screaming and trying to tear herself free. She seems to have no memory of the past few years, so it's like she's waking up like that for the first time. Usually the sound of my voice brings her back."

As soon as he finished speaking, a memory flashed. It was from the night we'd sat at Damon's bedside, watching over him after the assassination attempt. I could still see the serene firelight flicking over Collith's face.

When we first got to the Unseelie Court, you vanished. Every time I wake up, you're gone. After my coronation, there was no sign of you.

Usually I'm… visiting someone.

He'd been trying to tell me the truth about Naevys. Pain or shame must have made him pull back.

Though I still didn't have any right words, I couldn't let another silence be Collith's response. I'd had no idea he was dealing with all of that, and the burden of wearing a crown was heavy enough. A weaker person would've already broken. "I'm so sorry, Collith," I whispered, putting my fingers through his.

They were words I'd heard countless times throughout my life, every time someone learned about my parents, and they'd lost meaning long ago. Or so I'd thought. Now they encompassed everything I felt and floated to Collith. I could only hope he heard my sincerity.

From the corner of my eye, I saw his mouth soften. He stopped and tugged at my hand until I faced him. "Trust does not come easily to either of us, I think," Collith said. "But, as I told you in that grimy motel room, I'm trying to change that… for you."

The way he was looking at me made my core tighten. Yet another sensation went through my body, this one soft around its edges, but no less powerful than all the others. Without thinking, I reached up and tucked that errant curl back into place.

Collith shocked me by drawing back. Frustration shone in his eyes. It must've been there all along, lurking beneath the surface, because its appearance was so sudden. "Why can't you just admit that you want me, Fortuna? I see it in your eyes. It's in your voice when you're moaning my name. Say the words. Please."

I glared at him again, annoyed and unsettled. Why couldn't he just let me speak when I was ready? Why couldn't he just let this unfold without acknowledging what, exactly, was happening? *Oh, the same way you've let him move at his own pace?* logic pointed out. A childish urge rose in me and I gave in to it.

"What are you talking about?" I asked with a roll of my eyes, pretending with everything I had in me. I turned to walk away.

But this time, Collith didn't relent. He sifted and reappeared, blocking the way. "You want me. Just as badly as I want you."

"I..." Whatever I'd been about to say—probably something flippant or dismissive—faded on my tongue. Those damned vows rose from my memory like one of Savannah's zombies, refusing to stay dead. *I promise to always tell you the truth.* I'd already broken it, so why did it still matter? Had Collith kept every single one of his vows?

For the dozenth time, I thought of the recording on my phone. I really needed to get someone to translate his half of the ceremony.

"Fortuna."

My gaze snapped back to Collith's. He was watching me, waiting for the truth that we both felt every time we were together. When I thought of saying it out loud, panic clawed up my throat. "I can't. I'm sorry. I *can't*," I said, retreating.

"Why not?" he pressed. He matched my every step, and we were forced to halt when I backed into a tree. It was wide enough that he was able to flatten his palms on either side of me.

If I'd had hackles, they would be standing on end right now. I resisted the urge to snarl at him. "Where should I start?" I snapped instead. "How about the way this all started, Collith? You lied and manipulated to force a bond on me. You took my voice away. Oh, how about the fact that you're so blind to your ambitions for this Court that you stood by while I was—"

"Those are all excuses and we both know it. You've forgiven me, and don't try to say you haven't, because I sense it every time we look at each other. And whatever you feel for Oliver, it's separate from what you feel for me, because he doesn't even cross your mind anymore when we're together. So that only leaves one thing."

I hated him for dismissing his sins so easily. I hated that he'd said Oliver's name. Most of all, though, I hated that he was right. Yet, even now, I couldn't admit it. "And what's that, Your Majesty? Since you know *everything*."

"You're scared," Collith said flatly.

At this, I uttered a razor-edged laugh. I ducked beneath his arm and kept going, tossing over my shoulder, "That's the best you've got? I have commitment issues? You know, I'd explain the millions of actual reasons to you, but I'm just fresh out of crayons."

Undeterred, Collith stalked me through the trees. He spoke loud enough that his words reached me in spite of the distance between us. "Over and over again, the people you've loved leave. Your parents, Sorcha, Damon. Why open yourself up to more heartbreak? The best protection is to avoid loving at all, right?"

I swung around to face him again. Collith was still yards back, and I raised my voice instinctively, though he'd have no problem hearing me either way. "Wow, you didn't tell me you had a psychology degree."

"I don't," he countered, drawing closer. "I just have a direct line to your soul."

"Yeah, well, I have one to yours, too," I reminded him. He finally reached me, stopping a mere breath away, and looked every inch like the beautiful, cold hunter he was. "Guess what? I'm not the only one who's terrified. Except the biggest difference between our fears is mine don't ruin other people's lives."

Collith's eyes blazed. I couldn't tell if that hazel fire burned from anger or desire. Maybe both. "You're falling for me, Fortuna. Just as I'm falling for you," he growled.

"You don't even *know* me." I felt like a car alarm, always making the same sounds, annoying even myself. But it was one of the few defenses I had left. Once again, I turned my back on him and continued on.

Collith, of course, just reappeared.

"Oh, really?" He cocked a brow, patronizing me with his amused expression. This time, when I tried to whirl away, Collith caught hold of my arms. His grip was not gentle or hesitant. I was about to use one of Adam's new moves when he went on, "I know that you don't have limits for those you love. I know that you'll put yourself in harm's way to save someone you consider an innocent, like a certain werewolf that now won't leave your side. I know that you gave a pair of shoes to a barefooted slave. I know that—"

"Okay, you've proven your point," I interrupted, feeling a little breathless.

The muscle in his jaw flexed, revealing just how aggravated he truly was. "I don't think I have. Also, there's one more thing I know."

His fingers had loosened somewhat. I didn't think Collith was aware of it. "Yeah? What's that?" I crooned, readying myself to bring him down.

"You let me win that game of Connect Four."

I stiffened. "That's a load of—"

Collith bent his head and kissed me. I felt so much anger in the pressure of his mouth, but it didn't put out the flames between us. If anything, it only fanned them. They climbed higher and higher. Hotter and hotter. But then he tore his mouth away, ignoring my sound of protest, and bent to suck on my neck while his hand traveled lower. I gasped against him, my chest heaving.

"Just fuck me," I whispered, unable to think of anything besides how much I wanted to feel him inside. *"Please."*

"Not until you admit the truth," Collith countered. Never had I wanted and loathed someone more. When I still said nothing, he yanked at my jeans. The button popped open. Something within me snapped, and I shoved at him, the movement hard with frustration rather than refusal. In response, Collith's arm looped around my waist, and in one graceful movement, I found myself being lowered to the ground. Air caressed my bare skin as he pulled down my underwear next. I was about to utter a mindless taunt when his tongue slid along the length of my clit.

The words ceased to exist. I couldn't contain a moan. My entire body quivered with anticipation, but when Collith didn't continue, I raised my head. Our gazes met in a clash of lust and determination. As I watched, he pressed a kiss against the skin just above my pubic bone. His breath teased my center and made it throb. "Did you let me win that game, Fortuna?" Collith murmured.

I stared down at him, knowing defiance burned in my eyes. "No."

With a furious growl, he buried his face between my legs. Within seconds, the things he did with his tongue had me bucking and trembling in equal measures. My legs twined about his head and shoulders. I didn't even have enough frame of mind to be embarrassed or think about where we were. He sucked on my nub without mercy, pulling me toward the edge.

And there, amongst the leaves and the dirt and the beetles, I came with a cry that echoed through the treetops.

CHAPTER TWENTY-SEVEN

*C*hurch bells rang into the still morning.

Leaves crunched underfoot as I made my way back to the house, a half-empty mug of coffee in hand. Another Sunday. It had always been my favorite day of the week. As a child, it was because both of my parents would be home. We all stayed in our pajamas until noon, watching movies and eating Dad's pancakes. Later, when I was on my own, I liked Sundays because of the tips. Maybe it being God's day made people more conscious about how they treated their server. On the Sundays that I wasn't working at the bar, I carried on the tradition Mom and Dad began. Pajamas, TV, and pancakes. It wasn't the same, of course, but somehow their memory was more bittersweet than painful on those days.

Light peeked over the horizon—or what I could see of it through the trees—gripping its edges with luminescent fingers, as though the world was a windowsill. Normally, I would pause or sit to enjoy it. Now, though, I couldn't stop myself from pulling out my phone and hoping there was a text message from Collith. It had been almost a week since we'd last spoken. Or argued, more accurately.

Nothing.

I heaved a sigh, put the phone away, and kept going. After a few seconds, I sensed Finn keeping pace with me, using the trees as cover.

"Creep!" I called with a smile. An instant later, it occurred to me that I didn't know if Finn had a sense of humor. *Shit.*

Just as I feared, Finn seemed to take my comment literally. He emerged from the underbrush, his eyes fixed on the ground. I swallowed a sigh and paused, giving the wolf a chance to catch up. I thought about explaining that I used sarcasm about ninety percent of the time, but I'd already done enough damage with my words. I kept silent and we started walking together. It was an improvement from our last one, considering he'd been walking behind me then.

"You've been changing every night," I said finally. Each word was visible in the frigid air. "Why? Doesn't the transformation hurt?"

Finn's golden eyes continued to rove the woods around us. He was looking for threats, I knew, just like Lyari every time I talked to her. "I prefer the wolf," he answered after a long moment.

"Oh." I didn't want to pressure him to say more, so I swallowed the other questions I'd been wanting to ask.

Finn seemed to sense them, anyway. He frowned, clearly having some kind of inner struggle. "Wearing this form... it's like an animal accustomed to open hills and bright stars finding itself in a cage."

It was the most he'd ever said to me. It was a gesture of trust, his sharing this truth. I thought about giving him one in return, but I didn't want to cheapen his gift by redirecting the conversation to myself. "Well, if there's anything I can do to make the transformation easier, please let me know. I don't suppose Ibuprofen would take the edge off, would it?"

The werewolf smiled at this and I almost tripped over my

own feet. Holy crap, Finn was actually *hot*. "No, it wouldn't. But thank you," he replied, polite even when confronted with my moronic suggestions.

We crossed the yard together in a companionable silence. Finn hurried to open the door for me. I considered telling him he didn't have to do things like that, but I already had plans to force him into the shower. *One thing at a time, Fortuna.*

Lyari stood from the couch when we entered. Damon remained where he was, expressionless, but I got the distinct impression I'd interrupted a conversation between them. He was wearing only pajama pants. It was the first time I'd seen my brother without a shirt since finding him in Jassin's clutches, and I froze at the sight. "Jesus Christ," I breathed.

His skin told a story. A sinister, dark fable. Every scar was a different shape and color. No wonder his mind had shattered—it was a wonder Damon had survived at all.

Tears stung in my eyes. I knew he wouldn't welcome my pity, though, so I muttered something intelligible to the two of them, ducked my head, and hurried down the hallway. Finn dutifully followed.

In the bathroom, I blinked away the pain and turned to face my werewolf. It was a welcome distraction as I took in the streaks of dirt on his neck, the twigs in his hair, and the mud caked beneath his nails. All right. It was time to get tough. We'd been home for a week and Finn had ignored my increasingly desperate urges to use the shower.

"Strip," I ordered.

Finn went from fidgeting with obvious agitation to very, very still. I realized, not for the first time, that I didn't know what he was afraid of. Not really. Maybe he had a genuine fear of water.

Or maybe he'd been a wolf too long and he'd forgotten what was good for him.

"I'm not going to hurt you," I told him gently. "I just want to show you the ropes. This is where we keep the towels. Turning on the shower is easy—turn this left knob, then turn the right one to make it less hot. Those blue bottles are for you. Shampoo, conditioner, and body wash. You use the first two on your hair, then the last on your smelly parts. Oh, I also put some men's razors in the cabinet above the sink. When you're done, your room is at the end of the hall. I'm sorry it took so long to get ready—I put a rush order on the bed but it still was a few days in coming. Then I had to assemble the damn thing, which isn't my strong suit. There's a dresser, too, and I bought some new clothes for you. If I didn't get the size right, I can just go back and exchange them. Let's see... did I miss anything?"

I turned back to Finn, who was staring at me. "Why?" he asked hoarsely. I knew what he meant, even if he didn't say it.

It was so easy to become cynical, to believe this was a world where people didn't help each other. I'd drifted toward that way of thinking too many times to count.

"Because you need to be reminded of your worth," I answered, smiling at him, my hand on the doorknob. "We should never accept treatment less than that, no matter what sadistic faeries or psychotic werewolves would have us believe."

I took a few steps, knowing he'd hear them and assume I was gone. A few seconds ticked by. My heart began to sink... and then there came the squeaking sound of a knob being turned. Water burst from the spout and beat against the plastic tub floor.

Smiling to myself, I slipped away and left Finn to his shower.

I passed the rest of the morning watching a Netflix show with Damon and Lyari.

Well, I turned one on, and neither of them left the room. I caught both looking toward the screen at one time or another. So it felt like we watched it together. If anyone had asked me later, though, I couldn't have told them the name of the show. Something with superheroes, maybe?

Credits started to roll on the screen. We'd watched three or four episodes now. "Remember our Sundays together?" I asked Damon wistfully. "Back when they were alive, I mean."

I expected him to ignore the question or shake his head—he'd been so young when we lived in Denver. But Damon surprised me. "I remember," he answered, keeping his gaze on the TV. He didn't say anything more—he didn't have to, though. It was enough that, in that moment, Mom and Dad were alive again, brought back to life by our sweet memories.

After his shower, Finn never reemerged from his room. The profound silence that came from beneath the door made me think that he'd fallen asleep. It was probably the first real rest he'd gotten since leaving the Unseelie Court, so I didn't bother him, even as afternoon light streamed through the windows.

Just as another episode began to play, my stomach rumbled, reminding me that I hadn't eaten breakfast. It was already past lunchtime. I forced myself to get up from the warm couch.

In the kitchen, the fridge door opened with a reluctant sound. As I bent to examine the shelves, I could see why. No one had gone shopping, so we had nothing except a bottle of ketchup and some old fruit. With a resigned sigh, I reached for the bag of grapes.

After shoving a couple in my mouth—they were old and mushy—I grimaced and grabbed a bottle of water from the bottom drawer. I turned, twisting the cap off. Just as I was about to take a drink, someone knocked on the front door. Probably one of Damon's Tinder dates, coming back for a sock or a wallet. In the past week, he'd had a stranger here every night. I'd laid in my room listening to his headboard thump against the wall we shared.

"You expecting someone?" I asked my brother as I passed. He shook his head. Lyari stayed on the couch but sat rigidly now, one hand on her sword. She watched me with narrowed eyes, ready to leap up if anything went wrong. Finn must've woken from the knocking, because he came down the hall now, also tense and alert.

I swallowed another sigh, then opened the door to reveal Fred and Emma. They both carried totes and wore huge, excited smiles. "What are you guys doing here?" I blurted, automatically stooping to hug Emma. The water bottle crackled in my grip.

"Well, hello to you, too," she said, beaming even more at my warm greeting. "You said we should visit. I brought some fresh corn and my famous butter lettuce salad. I thought we could fire up the grill and have a good, old-fashioned barbecue, just like the old days."

I couldn't think of a reason why they shouldn't come in, and after I moment, I realized there *was* no reason. I'd gotten so used to shutting people out that it had become instinct, to avoid making plans with them. Perturbed by this line of thought, I stepped aside. Emma and Fred immediately shuffled in, both making comments about the loveliness of my house's location and how pleasant the drive had been. "You're being polite, but I appreciate it," I said as we gathered in the kitchen. "I should mention that we don't actually have a grill."

"Oh, that's all right. We'll just use the stove!" Fred said, setting his tote down on the table.

Emma put hers down beside it and unzipped the top. I peeked inside and saw that she'd already done most of the work. My stomach gave an involuntary rumble. She lowered her gaze, but not before I caught a twinkle there. "I brought a snack to tide us over while Fred is cooking," she said. "Fresh from the bread maker. Will you fetch a knife, dear? Damon, come in here, please! I need someone to wash the fruit. Oh, and who are these fine young folks?"

I followed her gaze toward Finn and Lyari. The werewolf

looked fairly normal, as long as he didn't raise those yellow eyes of his, but the faerie definitely drew notice. Despite her modern clothing, she still gave off a sense of... otherworldliness. If she was really going to come with me everywhere, we'd have to work on that. Thank God she'd put her sword away, at least.

I hurried to make the introductions between them—Lyari eyed Emma suspiciously, as though the old woman were hiding the weapons of an assassin beneath her pink shirt—and told the old woman that these were my new roommates. Once that was out of the way, I got started on cutting the bread. Lyari was assigned the job of setting the table for everyone. Fred worked busily over the stove. He asked about music, and Damon opened Spotify on his phone. A song I didn't know floated through the sunlit kitchen.

Finn stood next to me, watching every move I made.

Forty-five minutes later, the food was ready and waiting for us on the table. Steam rose from Fred's fried chicken. They'd also brought chilled wine, which had already been poured for each person. Condensation rolled down the glasses. When everyone just stood there, staring and admiring, Emma urged us to sit. A chorus of creaks drifted through the room as we obeyed. My gaze skimmed over, then backtracked onto Lyari, who stood with her back pressed to a far wall. Emma noticed where I was looking and frowned.

"What are you doing?" she asked the faerie, blinking with obvious bewilderment. "Sit down, you goose. We're about to eat."

"Yeah, join us," I added with a shrug.

"Is that an order, Your Majesty?"

"She's joking," I told Fred and Emma hastily. I twisted back to Lyari and knew I was glaring. "No, but I *do* command you to stop joking around, silly goose."

"Please sit," Emma pleaded. "I don't want to make you

uncomfortable, but I won't be able to enjoy any of this food if you're not."

No one could resist Emma for long. Slowly, Lyari moved to comply. The chair creaked when she sank down, and it felt like a signal. As everyone was getting ready to dig in, there came yet another knock from the front door.

Frowning, I started to rise, but Emma beat me to it. "No, no, start eating. I'll get it," she chirped. She had that determined look on her face, so I didn't argue. We all listened to Emma greet whoever was standing outside, but I didn't hear a response.

Fred bowed his head in a silent prayer. No one joined him, waiting in uncomfortable silence, but I looked at the table for the first time since the couple had arrived. They certainly hadn't come empty-handed—I took in the lovely placemats, silver candlesticks, and flowered centerpiece. I'd made minimal efforts to make my house more welcoming, but Emma Miller had accomplished it in five seconds.

Fred lifted his head a few moments later. He started talking about an upcoming snowstorm and passed the plate of fried chicken to me. Emma's footsteps sounded on the tile as she came back. "Who was it?" I asked without looking up, serving myself one of the biggest legs I could find.

"An idiot," a familiar voice said. "A really, really big idiot."

My head jerked up, and I stared across the room at Collith, feeling everyone else's gazes on me. "Hi," I said uncertainly.

He smiled. He wore a plaid shirt I'd never seen before—it made his eyes look more green than hazel. "Hi."

Emma watched both of us with a knowing glint in her eye. As I noticed this, I saw that she'd put on an apron at some point. A large, red tomato decorated the front, accompanied by the words, *Grab Your Balls, It's Canning Season!* "Fortuna, why haven't you told us about this young man yet?" she asked, raising her dyed brows at me.

I knew my face was on fire. I awkwardly started to rise. "Oh, I'm so sorry, I haven't? Emma, this is... well, this is my..."

"I'm a friend," Collith volunteered, gesturing that I should stay where I was. "Fortuna and I met at the market a few weeks ago. I've had a crush on her ever since."

Emma made a pleased sound and looped her arm through his. "Well, aren't you a cheeky one? Come with me. I have a few questions to ask you."

"Ask away." Collith covered her hand with his as though they were old friends. Damon rose to fetch one of the extra chairs in the living room, and when he came back, he placed it on the other side of me. Everyone sat down. Collith touched my knee beneath the table, our bond pulsing with remorse and longing. I looked back at him and said, without making a sound, *I'm sorry, too.*

He responded with an image of our kiss in the falling snow.

Emma said something then, but I didn't hear it. Collith turned to her, the hum of his voice polite.

As they spoke, I found myself staring at the faces of those around me, convinced that at any moment, they'd all disappear and prove this was a dream. There had never been a meal like this in my house. The table had never been used except for a place to set grocery bags or hold up my sad bowls of cereal.

The meal passed in a warm, dreamy haze. For a time, Lyari was stiff in the chair. Emma had a magic all her own, though, and soon enough the faerie loosened enough to serve herself a pile of salad. I added a piece of chicken to Lyari's plate without looking at her. After that, Fred and Emma focused on drawing my brother out of his silence. They went on to ask Collith things that made him smile and laugh. Even Finn answered a question from Fred, though he still didn't lift his gaze. I sat through it all, secretly wishing it would never end.

It did end, though, as all things do. When it seemed like everyone had finished, I started gathering the used dishes and bringing them to the sink. Emma tried to help, but I waved her away. "No, no, you and Fred cooked. It's only fair that we do the dishes. Right, Damon?"

"Right," he said without hesitation, startling me. He got up from his chair and picked up the dishes I hadn't been able to.

Have you forgiven me? I wanted to ask. But I was too afraid of the answer. As the others continued their conversation, I filled the sink with soapy water and got started.

After a moment, Collith stepped into the space beside me and, without a word, starting drying the dishes I'd just washed. I glanced around for Damon, wondering why he wasn't helping, but he must've slipped away to give us some privacy. *Or just avoid any sort of chore*, I thought dryly.

The silence surrounding Collith and I was louder than any of the words we'd said to each other in the woods. "About our last conversation—" he started.

Someone knocked at the door for the third time. Knowing Emma would get up, I rushed from the kitchen to beat her to it, my hands still wet. I grabbed the doorknob and my fingers slipped right off it. I tried again, muttering to myself, and it happened a second time. When I finally swung the door open, smiling triumphantly, Cora stood on my front step.

I stopped smiling.

Every nerve-ending in my body flared to life, driven by the salty taste of terror. "They're coming," she said flatly, answering the question before I could ask it.

My grip tightened on the edge of the door. For an instant, I was tempted to slam it in her face, as if that alone would stop the pack from coming in. "How did you find us? How long do we have?" I hissed.

Cora hesitated. We both knew that every word was a betrayal to her people. Her alpha. Just coming here to warn me was a risk I hadn't thought she was bold enough to take. "The witch," Cora said after a long pause. "She came to the pack and offered a trade. She would tell Astrid where you lived if she spared Damon from her revenge."

"Fortuna? Is everything all right?"

I turned from Cora, horror gripping my heart with icy fingers. Emma stood behind us, every wrinkle in her face deeper with concern. Judging from the young wolf's grim expression, there would be no time for these humans to run. And the protection spell on this house was probably long faded.

The one thing every species of Fallen had in common was a blood-deep instinct to hide our true selves from humans. However much my parents had trusted these two, our closest neighbors, our babysitters, our friends, Mom and Dad had never exposed our family's biggest secret to them. When I was younger, I'd thought it was to protect us.

Now I knew it had been to protect them.

"I'm so sorry, Emma," I whispered. She frowned. Before she could say anything, I spun back to Cora. Even I could hear the desperation in my voice as I blurted, "Challenge Astrid. You're not like her. I know you're not. This pack could be different. You just have to be brave enough to—"

A howl shattered the air. Cora was already several yards away; with every word I'd spoken, she retreated more and more, instant denial in her eyes. I swung away from her and barreled toward my room. I pulled every weapon there was out of my nightstand. Next I went to the closet and pulled two assault rifles out. Footsteps sounded behind me and I recognized Damon's soft tread.

I stood and thrust the rifle toward him. "Here. Take this. Do you remember how to use it? I know Dad taught you, but that was a long time ago."

He didn't reach for it—my brother had the same aversion to technology as most Fallen. "What's going on?"

I shouldered past him and reentered the living room. "Astrid's pack is coming this way."

Understanding filled Damon's gaze. He glanced toward Fred and Emma, who'd picked up on our terror, unsurprisingly. I gave them weapons, too, then faced the door. "Fortuna?" Emma's voice warbled. "What's happening, sweetheart?"

"Laurelis," I said in a clipped voice. There was no time to explain.

Mist coiled together on the front step. He was putting on a show for an audience that was too confused or terrified to care. "You rang?" Laurie drawled, walking out of the darkness. Belying his tone, though, that sharp gaze of his noted every detail in the room. Fred and Emma huddling in the corner, their wrinkled hands clutching the guns I'd given them. Damon holding a rifle of his own, as well, his face pale and tense. Lyari's drawn sword. Finn—who'd begun returning to his wolf form—watching the door with bared teeth.

I nodded toward Collith and said, loudly enough for him to hear, "Just keeping my end of the bargain."

If I didn't survive this, my mate would ask Laurie what I'd meant. It would force them to actually speak openly with each other. Maybe it would even be enough to end their feud. I liked the thought of having done one good thing for them both, these faeries that had somehow become my friends. And so much more than that.

Collith wasn't looking at me, though. He was staring at the door. No, not the door. Beyond it. "She's here, isn't she?" I asked quietly. He nodded.

My heartbeat was in my skull, somehow. *Boom. Boom. Boom.* Collith said something as I moved slowly to the door—I couldn't hear him over the thunder—and stood on the front steps to wait. I held one of the guns in my hands, but I knew it wouldn't do much good against an entire pack. I stared at the tree line along the edge of my property. Shadows moved among the pines. A stick cracked into the stillness.

Astrid appeared without warning.

One moment she wasn't there, the next she stood a few yards away. Boots planted, arms crossed, head tilted. I could hear that her breathing was short and labored. There was a gray cast to her skin that spoke of more than drug use or bad sleep. I glanced toward her leg, but she was wearing different jeans than the last time we'd seen each other. They completely covered the place I'd shot her. Even so, I'd hazard a guess that the holy water was making certain her wound wasn't healing quickly or correctly.

Her gaze shifted, and I realized that I was no longer alone. Laurie, Lyari, and Collith stood to my right, while Damon, Finn, Fred, Emma fanned out to my left. Looking at all of us, the alpha grinned, revealing two rows of yellowed teeth. "I told you there was no use runnin'. No use tryin' any fancy magic, either, since I had the witch do some mojo on us."

Meaning Laurie's power wouldn't save us this time.

"Oh, is it time for another speech?" I questioned. Out of the corner of my eye, I saw Collith's shoulders move slightly, a slight rise and fall, as though he were heaving the smallest of sighs.

He hadn't guessed my plan, then. Good. I didn't want him to get in the way of it, which was to keep the wolves focus on me. Pissed at me. That way, I would be the one to get every punishment or pain. Thinking this, I propped the gun against the wall and walked down the rest of the stairs, separating myself from the others.

Astrid didn't bother with comebacks or insults—she just walked up and slammed her fist into my face.

Pain exploded through my skull. Already I could feel blood forming a hot river from my nose to my mouth. The taste of metal and rust burst, but this time, this was no fear. It was just real and stark violence. In my peripheral vision I saw Lyari grab at Laurie and Collith, who'd both started forward the moment I hit the ground. She said something too low for me to hear.

I began to push myself up, but instinctively froze when Astrid began to circle me. She was more wolf than person now, and any sharp movements might cause her to attack. Gravel dug into my palms.

"I made you an enemy of the pack," the alpha said, folding her hands behind her back. It was a disturbingly elegant gesture from her. "You may have heard of our enemies before. History has buried their deaths as deeds performed by humans, but so many were us. Always hiding in the shadows, always forced to act as though we belong at the bottom of the food chain. All that has kept our proud members able to endure it was the respect we garnered among the Fallen. We are admired. We are feared. This is because when someone is marked as an enemy, they fucking *pay*."

I snickered. My mouth filled with the taste of rust and pennies. "I don't know who's admiring you, but it definitely isn't Nightmares or fae."

"Don't think I don't know what you're doing," she hissed, leaning down. A glob of spit landed on my cheek. "You think I'm so stupid. I saw it in your eyes. Well, would a stupid wolf know the best way to hurt you is *this*?"

She never took her overly bright eyes off me as two were-wolves appeared, halfway between their forms, holding Damon between them. There was no chance to wonder how they'd gotten to him, because in that moment, I knew what Astrid was going to do. She was going to send Damon's blood spraying all over the ground. She was going to kill him. I opened my mouth, about to offer anything, if only she would only leave him untouched. Even that wasn't quick enough.

Surprise burned through the air, hotter than a lightning strike, when she moved to stand behind Collith instead. Damn it, why had he separated from the others, too? Astrid bent and murmured something in his ear. Then, as I watched, she buried her claws into his shoulder.

Collith couldn't hold back an echoing cry as she dug in. With another vicious grin, Astrid did something with her hand, driving him to his knees. I flinched at the sound of his bones hitting the hard ground.

"Cora, please," I whispered. The young werewolf stood nearby, such a quiet presence that I suspected I was the only one who'd noticed her. At my words, she looked from me to her aunt. And then... she walked away. Disbelief and disappointment raged a war within my chest.

More werewolves had entered the clearing now, creatures that looked plucked out of a child's nightmares. Bits of themselves littered the ground around their feet. One of them had half the face of a wolf and half the face of a human. The effect was grotesque and disconcerting. I swallowed and turned back to Astrid. "Do you want me to beg?" I asked. "Is that it?"

Her upper lip curled into a sneer. "No," she said, "I just want you to suffer."

With that, she buried her free hand into Collith's other shoulder. His head snapped back and a hissing sound erupted between his teeth. An echo of his pain came down the bond, and phantom claws tore into my shoulder. "By the way," she added, loud enough for everyone to hear, "I dipped my pretty claws into some holy water earlier. A present just for you."

I knew, more than I had ever known anything—my name, my fears, the faces of those I loved—that she was about to tear his throat open. And there was absolutely nothing I could do about it.

Too often, people made the mistake of thinking they had more. More days, more hours, more chances. We put things off, said things like *next time* or *soon*, ignored the ticking clocks. It hit me in a star-bright burst. I was falling in love with Collith. Even Astrid had seen it; she'd chosen his death as the way to make me suffer most.

"Wait," an unfamiliar voice said.

As one, every creature in the clearing turned toward it. Several werewolves stepped aside and revealed Cora. She had never looked so small. I hadn't even recognized her voice because it was so wrapped in ribbons of fear and doubt. But she'd come back and it was all that mattered.

Astrid just laughed. "Now you find the courage to challenge me, little wolf? To save a couple of faeries and a Nightmare? You're an embarrassment to your own kind."

Cora's mind must've been blank with terror, because she said nothing.

After removing her clothes, Astrid went through the transformation like it was as natural to her as having a heartbeat. It was also much briefer than Finn's had been. Her flesh tore quickly, almost as though it was paper. When it was done, the wolf left standing there, covered in its own gore and blood, did not tremble from shock or pain. It stared back at us with the cold intelligence of an animal that hunted and howled.

The attention turned to Cora. Slowly, with trembling fingers, she took off her jeans, coat, sweater, and boots. Her throat moved as she swallowed again and again. Her eyes were huge. Once she was completely naked, she just stood there, her pale body quaking. It was as though a child had taken her place. Where was that urgent, brave creature that had helped me escape the oubliette? Where was the wolf that so casually pretended not to see the gun I'd taken with me to visit her pack?

Shit, I thought. *I fucked up. She's going to be killed.*

Though I knew so little about werewolves, it was undeniable that Cora had undergone the transformation few times in her life. Her pain had the echoes of someone in a torture chamber— every crack of bone, every wet ripping sound had her whimpering and screaming in equal measures. She didn't anticipate each new development, as Astrid had, leaning into particular changes and adjusting to meet others. She'd almost made it a dance. A morbid, bloody dance.

389

For the first time, I wished I could instill courage instead of fear.

Cora's transformation took well over an hour. The rigid, white-faced girl was gone. In her place rested a gangly, trembling creature that was more pup than wolf.

I couldn't let this happen. I shifted, about to charge into the space between them and say something that would make Astrid see red. Make her destroy me instead of everyone else. An arm shot up and clamped across my stomach. The pack was so focused on the drama unfolding that no one noticed the silent struggle happening between me and Collith.

"We can't intervene," he murmured against my ear. "This is her battle."

"Fine. Just let go of me."

"Will you stay out of it?"

"*Yes*," I spat.

Collith smiled grimly and kissed my cheek. His grip tightened. "Nice try."

I didn't even have a chance to respond; in the next breath, the fight began. Astrid was not a cat with a mouse, she was a predator through and through. She didn't toy with Cora—the second the younger wolf got to her feet, Astrid was on her. Slashing and biting and snarling. *Killing*.

Collith's hands felt like chains, holding me back with the strength of cold iron. There was already blood in the dirt, and I didn't need to see an injury to know it was Cora's. Several times, she recovered enough to leap back from her aunt, only to be torn into again. Her frightened yips and cries filled the air.

I'd touched Cora, which meant her phobias were within reach, but those wouldn't help now. I remembered that I'd been able to unearth Lyari's worst memory. Granted, this werewolf and I didn't share a bond, but maybe if I dug for it...

It took a disturbing lack of effort to get into Cora's head. Because she was in wolf form, the images were fragmented and more sensory than intellectual. But I still found the truth, laced through her fear like a vein along an arm.

More than anything else, Cora feared her aunt.

There was no one memory that had permanently affected her, but many of them, dozens of brief and sharp moments that left a patterned scar of terror. Astrid had been securing her leadership from the moment Cora was born. She pinched the small girl when no one else was looking, whispered threats when no one else would overhear. Word by word, moment by moment, she'd stripped the girl of her courage, self-worth, and hope.

As a result, Cora looked at her aunt and, instead of a skinny, old female, she saw an omnipotent, all-powerful wolf.

But... what if she feared dying more?

I steeled myself, about to break every rule I'd ever made or my father ever taught me. I closed my eyes to better concentrate. Just as I went rigid, reaching for those flavors and strands that created Cora's fears, a terrible scream rent the air. My eyes flew open, expecting to see the worst—the girl lying dead in the dirt, her pretty blue eyes staring up at the sky.

The scene was like something out of a painting.

Astrid rested on her back, her ears flattened and tail drooping. The lines of her body were sharp with fear. She gazed up with wide, startled eyes at her niece, who stood over her with a fearsome snarl. Cora had one paw, just one, flattened against Astrid's throat. But that was all it would take—one set of claws —to cut her aunt open. There was something between her jaws, too, I noticed. As everyone watched, a piece of skin dropped to the earth with a wet plop. Part of Astrid's shoulder.

Suddenly the alpha's face shifted. In seconds her snout and sharp teeth gave way to a bloody, human mouth. The rest of her remained wolf. I knew what would come out of that newly-formed mouth next before Astrid even opened it. The moment was like something out of a bad horror movie, but that wouldn't stop her from saying it. From meaning it.

"You don't have it in you," the craggy wolf taunted. As though Cora's inability to murder was a mark against her character. As though her value for a life was a sign of weakness. My own hands clenched into fists, wanting to use claws I didn't have on Astrid's neck.

Still, Cora wavered. *This can't end any other way*, I wanted to tell her. If she let Astrid up, she would only die herself. It was a choice I'd faced three times during those wretched faerie trials. Kill or be killed.

Yet the seconds ticked past and Cora didn't move.

That was when I did it.

Just a minute, nearly insignificant nudge. A light exhale of my breath over her thoughts. Suddenly Cora's fear of her aunt was nothing against her fear of leaving her alive. The logic I'd used to reach this point was too twisted, too dark; I experienced a dart of terror. Were the fae making me like this... or just exposing what had been inside me all along?

Either way, the damage was done. Cora blinked and looked at Astrid with less confusion, more dread. In the next moment, so quickly it took my mind a second to comprehend what had happened, she pulled her claws across Astrid's throat. Blood splattered through the dirt.

The older werewolf got out one syllable. Just one. "I..."

And then she died.

Without a single tear among them, the werewolves littering my front yard dropped to their knees. Almost instantly, Cora's gangly body began to tear and crack. The change took even longer this time. Everyone in the clearing observed silently, as if this transformation meant something. Maybe it did, since Cora didn't make a single sound, though I knew she had to be in agony. I pressed my back against Collith's chest, feeling sad and drained. She was just a kid. Like me, like Damon, our world had chosen to disregard this and baptize her in pain and blood.

When it was finally done, Cora found the strength to get up.

She was covered in gore and dirt, but she pulled her clothes back on and moved to stand in the middle of the wolves. She then turned in a slow circle, meeting the gaze of every single one. Each of them dropped their eyes in a clear sign of submission. Cora faced me and held her head up high. "Fortuna Sworn is no longer an enemy of the pack. Let it be known," she declared. Her transformations as a wolf had only begun, but her one as alpha was well under way.

"Let it be known," the pack chorused. Okay, this had taken a weird turn.

The girl made a sharp gesture and replied in a language I'd never heard before. *"Părăsește acest loc acum."*

There was a finality in her tone; she was telling them to leave. The wolves didn't hesitate to obey, and some even tucked tail as they ran. A few paused to retrieve Astrid's body. Cora watched them lift her with an empty expression.

"I'm going to talk to her," I said quietly to Collith, who was still holding onto my shoulders. He gave them a gentle squeeze before letting go, and then he turned away. I watched him walk back to the house, where the others were gathered.

Laurie was saying something to Emma and Fred. The old man had his arm wrapped around Damon's frail shoulders. He nodded at whatever the Seelie King told him, and I remembered that they'd already met Laurie once, back in Denver.

Though Lyari stood near them, her gaze was on me, her sword drawn and shining in the moonlight. Finn hovered a few feet from where I stood, panting with agitation, also watching me. Blood clung to his fur, doubtless from undergoing the transformation back at the house. He'd probably missed most of the action because of it.

I gave him a small, reassuring wave, then turned toward Cora. She was waiting for me, standing in nearly the exact same spot where all this began. I wondered if she had undergone any kind of magical change, as I had after my coronation. I approached the new alpha cautiously. My eyes lingered on her arm, where a patch of skin was missing. The exposed muscles and tendons gleamed. "Do you need a healer to look at that? I know one who might—"

Cora shook her head. She sounded normal enough as she said, "We're not supposed to touch any wounds from a challenge. The scar will have many meanings to my kind... and to me. Listen, the reason I came over here was to thank you."

"For what? Almost getting you killed?"

She lowered her voice. "No, for what you did during the fight. I sensed you in my head. Or smelled you, somehow. Your presence smells like... lilacs, I think. Or some kind of flower, anyway."

There was reverence in the way she talked about my scent. Maybe she wasn't as unaffected by my face as she'd acted all this time. I smiled kindly. "Actually, Cora, you really don't have anything to thank me for. You pulled it off on your own. I was about to interfere, but you killed that old bitch before I could."

"Seriously?" she whispered. For once, she sounded as young as she truly was.

I nodded. "Hey, do you have a cell phone? I want to give you my number. You can text or call if you ever need help or... just to talk, even. Is that okay?"

She fumbled for her phone. It bulged from her front left pocket, but she searched the other three first before remembering its location. Redness spread up her neck as she handed the phone over. I programmed my number and passed it back. "Thank you," I said. "You came back. It reminded me that there are some things more powerful than fear. It's easy to forget, especially for a Nightmare."

The new alpha smiled. Dimples deepened in each of her cheeks. "I'll text you."

With those words, she turned and ran, her feet barely making any sound. The last of the wolves were melting into the trees like shadows into darkness. Not one hesitated or looked back. Then Cora was gone, too.

It was over. It was really over.

Just then, there was a prickle against my skin—someone was watching me. Someone who radiated a chill but had the warmest eyes. Like spring. The revelation I'd had in all the chaos returned in a rush. *Collith. I'm falling in love with Collith.* A faerie. No, not just a faerie, a *king*. Boy, I sure knew how to pick them.

Feeling vulnerable again, I cast my eyes downward as I crossed the yard again, closing the space between us. Collith left the others to meet me halfway. It seemed impossible that he hadn't sensed the truth or couldn't see it now, practically written all over my face. "So what was—" he began.

Finn growled from behind. There was something sinister in the sound, and I turned to see what was wrong. His yellow eyes watched the trees. Wind wailed sorrowfully through the dead branches, but there was no other sound or movement. I frowned down at the werewolf. "Hey, what's—"

A figure lurched out of the woods, drawing everyone's attention. Male, judging from the width of his shoulders. His gait was slow and uneven. A moment later, it was joined by another one. I heard Emma gasp. Finn, whose eyesight was better than mine, let out a snarl. My pulse quickened. Was it the pack? Did Cora change her mind about letting us live?

Before I could voice the worry aloud, a scent wafted past, carried on the cold wind. I recognized it instantly. *Oh, fuck.*

"There's a cemetery one mile from here," I said to Collith under my breath. "Savannah must be nearby."

His hazel eyes stayed on the zombies. I'd told him about Savannah and her newfound necromancy on one of our dates. "I still have some strength left; I can use my fire. Not long enough to kill all of them, though."

"All of them?" I repeated. My gaze scanned the trees farther down, and yes, more were emerging. Coming toward us. I hadn't given Savannah's power enough credit; I'd expected just one or two to rise. In an effort to control my wild heartbeat and frenzied thoughts, I counted them under my breath. Soon I lost count—they were everywhere. Dozens of them.

"Get inside," I breathed. "Now."

No one questioned me; even Fred and Emma broke into a run, despite how confused they must've been. Laurie sifted. The rest of us all burst inside, and once I'd done a headcount, I turned the locks. *Little good that will do*, I thought as I backed away. The zombies arrived less than a minute later. They surrounded my small house on all sides, pushing against the walls and windows. Their growls and moans got louder with each passing moment.

I kept spinning, trying to keep track of the glass, praying it would hold against the pressure. What could we do? How could I protect everyone? As I turned yet again, there was movement behind Emma. At first, I thought it was just one of us, but I did a double-take when an excited moan drifted through the room. *Too close*, I thought. Dread gripped my stomach when I met the red-rimmed gaze of a zombie. It had gotten in somehow—was one of the bedroom windows open?—and was about to attach itself to Emma.

I opened my mouth to cry a warning, but at the last second, Fred shoved his wife out of the way.

And the zombie ripped into him instead.

Emma screamed.

Time unfroze. Now it felt like the Earth was spinning faster, tilting off balance, rebelling against its orbit. I didn't see Fred hit the floor, but that's where he was when I looked for him, his eyes already open and unseeing. The zombie squatted on top of his prone body. With supernatural strength, it had opened the old man's chest and yanked out a handful of his insides. Lyari was shouting, yanking at me, and I saw the bright blue of Collith's flames as he burned our way back outside. Laurie had a sword in his hand and hacked at zombies with a grace and precision that would've captivated me any other day.

Somehow I found myself stumbling on the lawn. I didn't remember running outside. Everyone else—*except for Fred*, a vicious little voice reminded me—had managed to get out, too. Lyari was the last one out the door, and she pulled it shut behind her, cursing when it slammed onto a zombie's finger and made it detach completely.

We'd effectively trapped most of them inside, and the ones we didn't, Collith burned. But as we watched, another window shattered and a hand thrust through the jagged opening. They wouldn't stay contained for long. Already some were wriggling through the windows that had been broken.

"What now?" Damon whispered.

An ache spread through my chest. There was only one way. "Now we burn it."

Emma's faint voice came from behind. "Fred brought some kerosene. For the barbecue, just in case you didn't have any."

I turned toward her, taking in her dazed expression. She was in shock, I thought. The sight of Emma coming undone forced me to think more clearly. "Can we... can we borrow it? Fred's kerosene?" I asked shakily.

The old woman just nodded, staring at the scene before us with dull eyes. I started to pull away from her, intending to go to their vehicle, but Collith and Laurie had already beaten me to it. Streams of kerosene gleamed on the walls of my house. Standing safely apart from us, Collith visibly gathered his strength, the muscles in his back tensing, and then he held out his hands. Those blue and white flames exploded from his skin and latched onto the kerosene.

I watched my house burn, transfixed by both the beauty of it and a sense of loss. I arched my neck back, following the fire.

Ashes and smoke climbed toward the sky. It felt like the entire world was shuddering.

Then, something moved in the distance.

My lungs froze as I assumed it was another zombie. I started breathing again when I saw it was Savannah, creeping through the tall grass, trying to reach the darkness. She'd made the mistake of wearing white, though, and her shirt was like a lighthouse on the sea. As I watched the witch try to slip away, Cora's voice drifted through my head. *She came to the pack and offered a trade. She would tell Astrid where you lived if she spared Damon from her revenge.*

Savannah had betrayed us.

If I let her go now, she'd perform a cloaking spell—we would never find her again. Or Matthew, for that matter, who Damon hadn't even started to know. Without a second thought, I charged after her.

Just as she was about to escape into the cover of the trees, I thrust my hand out. Savannah jerked to a halt, her back arching, and released a shrill scream. I winced but held on, tightening my fist to make the illusion more powerful. In her head, she was surrounded by her dead creations, their teeth and fingers tearing into her, gnawing on her flesh. She watched one of them pull an intestine out of her stomach.

Distantly I realized that the real Savannah had dropped to the ground. She writhed and twitched. To everyone else's eyes, it would look like she wasn't being attacked by anything. Just her own hysteric, broken mind. The wind played with my hair as I stalked toward her, putting so much strength into the illusion that pain began to pound at my temple. Amidst sobs and shrieks, unintelligible words dribbled from Savannah's mouth. She was dying.

Someone stepped in front of me.

I blinked, so startled that I accidentally released my mental hold on the witch. When I saw it was Collith—my rage was so white-hot that it all but muted the bond with him—I scowled. "You just keep getting in my way, don't you?"

"Think of the boy, Fortuna," he said. Though he was pale and drained, his voice was calm. It grated on my senses; the darkness inside me cried out. *Touch the witch. Twist her mind. Make her wish she'd never been born.* "You'll be taking his mother from him. He'll grow up without knowing her, just as you grew up without yours."

Collith was blocking Savannah from sight, but I fixed my gaze on his shoulder, picturing her just beyond him. Clouds shifted over the moon, causing the world to become ghostly and ethereal. "He's in danger as long as she's alive," I said coldly. "She has no control over the necromancy."

Maybe he heard something in my voice or felt it through the bond, because in the next moment, Collith switched tactics. "Fine. Then think of yourself. Your power is already growing too quickly. Choosing mercy is in your best interest. Killing the witch will only make—"

"Fuck your mercy, Collith."

With that, I stepped to the side and lifted my hand. Thinking to end it as quickly as possible, I put every drop of power I had behind the mental strike. But then, at the last possible second, Collith moved in front of Savannah again. It effectively blocked my view of her and my thoughts filled with Collith instead. The power inadvertently focused on him. Gasping, I tried to return my concentration to Savannah.

Too late.

Collith's lips parted as my terrible power claimed his mind. I'd already dropped my hand, but it made no difference. My intention hadn't been to make her suffer, but to kill her. And Collith was already weak from the strength he'd spent on summoning fire.

Everyone stared in stunned, horrified silence. Collith stared back, but there was a hollow look to his eyes that made it obvious he didn't see any of us. A line of blood slid down from his nose. Time seemed to slow as everyone watched Collith collapse face-first onto the grass.

Then, somehow, I was on my knees, screaming his name. His considerable weight was suddenly nothing—I rolled him over and propped his head on my lap without any struggle. Collith's throat worked as he tried to speak. He didn't even have enough frame of mind to use our bond and pull his way out of the illusion. I was grabbing his face, slapping his cheeks, anything to make his lovely hazel eyes focus again. "Collith? Hey, baby, look at me. *Look at me*. Collith?"

I was distantly aware of a presence behind us. A familiar, melodic voice broke the silence. "Fortuna..."

Oh, thank God, I thought. *Laurie*.

I was about to turn toward him, beg him to use whatever power he had to help Collith, when my mate's entire body gave a violent jerk. Then, in the next moment, a long sigh left him. His muscles loosened.

I knew the exact moment he died, because our mating bond snapped like a cord pulled too far, too swift, too hard. It left a hole in the middle of my chest. I gasped from the pain, nearly dropping Collith. Instead, I hunched over him, simultaneously trying to protect him and ride out the agony all at once. Dead. Collith was dead. The thought went around and around in my head.

No. It wasn't possible.

He couldn't be dead. It was just a little magic—a force far less substantial than a car accident or a sword. I could fix this. I could. The stares and the whispers were white noise as I tried to remember the CPR training from my high school years. *Tilt the head back, check breathing, two breaths...*

I lowered Collith all the way to the ground and bent over him. After going through the process twice, I leaned over to check his breathing. Nothing. I breathed into him until my own lungs ached. Sirens sounded in the distance.

Grief clawed up my throat, bursting free into a sob. I forgot about Laurie and bent over Collith. "No, no, don't you dare do this," I pleaded, mindless of our audience. Now, instead of his mouth, I pressed my trembling lips against his forehead. I lingered there, resting against his cool skin. My voice dropped to a whisper. "Please don't leave me alone."

Silence. I gripped Collith's shoulder with bloodless fingers and started to rock. I wanted to shout at the others to do something, fetch Zara, call 9-1-1, but I couldn't look away from him even that long. "Never mind, don't speak," I crooned at him, using my other hand to stroke his cheek. "It's going to be okay. You'll be all right. I'm going to make this better, I promise."

My mind couldn't accept it. Collith was the most powerful faerie I'd ever met. He was King of the Unseelie Court, the most volatile and lethal of Fallen to walk this earth. A simple illusion and one terrible moment couldn't just kill him.

I have weaknesses. I am vulnerable. But all of them are tied... to you.

"I didn't mean to," I whimpered, staring into Collith's eyes, which still stared vacantly up at the sky. *Someone should really close them,* I thought faintly. My body began to quake like a city coming apart. "Someone, help me. Please, please, please..."

My brother knelt beside me and tentatively put his hand my shoulder. "He's gone, Fortuna."

"I didn't mean to," I repeated. Then Laurie was back, his alluring scent all around me. His pale hand reached for Collith. I slapped it away with a hysterical sound that was part-snarl, part-sob. "No, don't touch him. He's my mate, *not yours.*"

"Fortuna, we need to—"

"Don't touch him."

Laurie drew back, his mouth tight, his eyes shuttered. A very distant, very quiet part of me knew that he'd loved Collith, too and it wasn't just my loss. But that didn't matter right now.

Damon just tightened his hold. Eventually, I slumped against him, my fingers digging into his flesh. Exhaustion gripped me. It felt like there were bruises on my bones. A scream crawled up my throat, and it felt like I had no control as I threw back my head and released it into the sky. The sound echoed.

Dozens of birds, startled from their hiding places, flapped away into the twilight.

CHAPTER TWENTY-EIGHT

I lost chunks of time after that.

The little house—the only place I'd truly thought of as my own since leaving the house my parents died in—had been reduced to a pile of charred wood and ashes. Half of the town came, drawn by the sound of sirens and the spot of orange against a gray sky. Savannah disappeared during the chaos.

She was probably terrified I'd finish what I started.

At some point, as I'd knelt there in a shocked daze, Cyrus had moved to stand beside me. "You can stay on my farm, Fortuna," he'd said mildly.

After a moment, or maybe it had been several minutes, I'd just nodded. "Don't call Bea," I added in a whisper. Cyrus didn't answer.

The rest of it was a blur. I remembered the whites of people's eyes and the way their mouths moved so urgently. Darkness consumed everything and the only illumination was red and blue lights. There must've been clouds in the sky, since the moon and stars weren't visible overhead. It just felt like we existed in a world where the sun was just a fairy tale. A children's story.

Emma spoke to the police, silent tears streaking down her face. I knew she was reciting the story I'd heard Laurie give her, since humans wouldn't accept the truth. They couldn't know that people had died here today, or they'd ask more impossible questions. I sat there and watched her fumble over the lies, knowing it was all my fault.

Laurie must have used his abilities to a great extent, because no one asked about the two figures lying prone at my knees or the fact that my house was full of burned corpses.

I didn't remember speaking to the police. I didn't remember Damon helping me up. I didn't remember getting in a car or going to Cyrus's.

What I did remember, however fragmented the memory, was Fred's funeral.

It took place behind Cyrus's house. The ground hadn't frozen yet, which made it possible for Finn and Cyrus to dig a hole. While they did that, the rest of us went inside to get warm. Damon and Emma quickly disappeared into the bathroom. I could hear them speaking in there, see their shadows moving past the crack beneath the door.

Collith's body had somehow ended up on the kitchen table. I sat by his side and stared blankly at that shifting light under the far door. I waited for the inevitable sound of Emma's sobs, but it never came. Instead, within a few minutes, she reemerged. There was evidence of crying, yes, but she'd fixed her hair and put on some lipstick.

"Do you know if your friend owns a Bible?" she asked, approaching the table. "I thought Fred would appreciate if I read some of his favorite verses."

I just shook my head. It faintly occurred to me that I had no idea whether Cyrus was religious or not. I'd never asked and he'd never said.

Emma sighed. "Oh, well, that's all right. We can make do without. Are you ready, sweetheart?"

The question made my brow lower. It made sense, of course, that she would expect me to be at Fred's funeral. I should've wanted to go. Offer my support. But I had nothing left to give, and the thought of leaving Collith's side was impossible to fathom.

Emma must've seen the denial rising in my eyes. "Please," she added, trying to give me a tremulous smile. When I saw that, I got up from the rickety chair. At the same moment, Damon emerged from the bathroom. He, too, had cleaned himself up as best he could without fresh clothes. Wordlessly he offered his arm to Emma. She clasped it, once again trying and failing to smile, and the three of us stepped back into the cold.

It was time to say goodbye to Fred Miller.

Finn and Cyrus had picked a spot beneath a pine tree. As a result, the hole was surrounded by a bed of needles. Fred already rested inside. Someone had wrapped him in a thick quilt, hiding his wounds. Despite how he'd died, the old man's expression was peaceful. I almost envied him.

It was difficult to see Emma's face in the darkness. She gazed down at her husband for several minutes, silent and unmoving. I could only see her breaths, forming clouds in the air, deep and even. "Would either of you be willing to say something?" she asked finally, lifting her head to look at us. "I know he would've loved that."

I couldn't think. Couldn't speak. I just stared back at her.

"I was pretty young when Fortuna and I left Denver," Damon said suddenly. To my faint surprise, his voice was clear and certain. "So I may not have a lot of memories. I can say, though, that I cherish the ones I do have. I remember a tree. A really tall oak tree, right in your front yard, Emma. One day I decided to climb it. I think my mom was distracted, and she'd been telling me 'no' all day, so I ran out there as soon as I got the chance."

Emma still didn't smile, not exactly, but the corners of her mouth deepened as though it wanted to remember how. "Fred told me about this."

My brother nodded. His eyes were bright with unshed tears. "He heard me crying for help. Fred seemed so tall and strong as he climbed up and carried me down. I thought he was a giant."

"He was a giant," Emma said, turning her gaze to her husband's face again. "A giant of a man, with a big heart and a legendary soul. I will never know anyone else like him. God, I was so lucky. He could've had anyone, you know, and he picked me."

Smiling fully now, she went on to tell Fred her favorite memories of him.

Throughout the simple ceremony, I kept forgetting that Collith was dead. It seemed that every few minutes, I reached for him or searched for his face amongst our small gathering.

Afterward, our ragtag band of survivors went inside.

Cyrus's home had a front deck that looked new and smelled like fresh wood shavings. It had wooden rocking chairs and carvings along the railings. Inside, there were high ceilings and cracked rafters. Just like his kitchen at Bea's, everything was immaculate. The surfaces looked freshly dusted and there were vacuum lines on the patterned, red rug in the living room. He had at least three dogs, though I hadn't actually tried to count them. It seemed that a different one came up to me every few minutes and nudged my hand, which hung limply between my legs. I was back in the chair beside my dead mate. I had no idea where the others had gone, but I didn't much care. There was only Collith's closed eyes and white skin.

I promise to keep you from harm to the best of my ability. That was the only vow left I hadn't broken. Now it was shattered into a million irreparable pieces. At the thought, a faint laugh left me. "It's sort of funny, when you think about it," I whispered to him. "If there was a prize for the worst possible way to break a promise, they'd give it to me, don't you think?"

Fingers, light as leaves in the fall, settled on my shoulder. I knew it was Emma without looking; she carried that childhood scent with her.

As though she'd aged a hundred years in the past hour, Emma lowered her frail body into a chair beside me. It was obvious from the wet trails left behind on her cheeks—like footprints in snow—that she'd been crying before entering the room. Again.

"I'm sorry," I whispered. There was a dog laying next to the table, and its long ears perked, as though he was listening closely to my every word.

Emma pursed her lips, probably to hide the way they trembled. "It wasn't your fault, sweetheart. Let's get that straight right now. Bad things happen in this world."

Or bad people, I thought. The werewolves wouldn't have come to the house if I hadn't pissed off Astrid. If I'd just kept my mouth shut that day and found another way to free Finn, instead of going against an entire pack, Fred might still be alive right now. "He deserved a better funeral," was all I said.

She instantly shook her head. "No. He would've liked what we did; it was just like Fred. Quiet. Honest."

I concentrated on my hands, on the movements of my fingers as they tangled and curled within each other. I knew that at some point we had to acknowledge everything that happened. *Might as well get it over with.* "You... you probably have some questions about... about what you saw—"

"There will be plenty of time for that later, sweetheart. I always knew there was something different about your family, of course. It was your mother that gave it away. Everyone on the street talked about how beautiful she was... except every single one of 'em had different descriptions of what she looked like." Emma stopped and sighed. "Well, those boxes aren't going to pack themselves. I better get started."

"Boxes?"

She raised her brows at me. "Yes, boxes. My boxes. I'm selling our house and moving in here as soon as possible. I know it's what Fred would've wanted, too."

Since Collith's death, I'd felt cold. At Emma's words, though, the smallest spot of warmth materialized in my chest. Despite our years apart, she knew me well. I would've let her walk out the door rather than ask for help. "Emma, I can't let you—"

"Would you like to know the real reason Fred and I never moved to Arizona?" she asked suddenly.

I hesitated. "Why?"

"He told you I wasn't ready. That was true. I could never quite let go of the hope that you and Damon would come back someday. *You* are the reason we stayed. No matter how many years passed, Fred and I hoped. You two were like our own, when your family lived next door. A little thing like growing up doesn't change that."

Apparently I did still have the ability to feel, because suddenly my vision blurred, and I was blinking rapidly to keep tears at bay. Emma saved me from having to form a response— she got up, squeezed my shoulder, and went to get her car keys from the room Cyrus had given her.

She left after that, presumably to pack up her entire life so she could move to Granby. I remained in that wooden chair, staring down at the unmoving face resting on a table before me.

The silence was ended only by a knock on the door.

I ignored it. It had nothing to do with Collith. With my grief. But within seconds, the knocking came again. Harder this time. Clearly, whoever it was wouldn't stop until someone answered.

An irrational rage gathered over my head. I stormed across the room and wrenched the door open. A very tall and equally agitated faerie stood on the other side. The smooth planes of his face looked harsh and otherworldly in the yellow light. "How did you find me here?" I asked, the rage departing as quickly as it had arrived. I sounded as empty as I felt.

Nuvian didn't bother with pleasantries. "The Tithe was supposed to begin an hour ago," he said, glaring at me with his blue eyes. "The bloodlines grow restless."

"Well, tell the fucking bloodlines that it'll have to be rescheduled. If that's all…" I started to shut the door.

My mate's Right Hand shoved it open. "There are whispers of treason," he told me grimly, keeping his palm flattened against the wood. Something in his face changed, then, and I knew he was finally noticing the changes in me. I'd seen myself in the mirror last time I was in the bathroom. Anyone in the supernatural world would take a look at my bloodless face or red-rimmed eyes and think, *Vampire*.

I stared back at him. Even now, I felt nothing. "Collith isn't here," was all I said in response.

Nuvian's sharp gaze went past me. I was no mind reader, but I could practically hear him considering whether or not to force his way in. After a few seconds, he evidently decided against it, because he focused on my face again. "With all due respect, Your Majesty, you fought to wear the crown. You spilled blood for it. Why make so many sacrifices only to let it get taken from you?"

"You want to step back. Right now," I said, my patience snapping like a frayed rope. However much I'd just been hating myself for my abilities, I itched to use them on Nuvian again.

He probably saw the truth of this in my eyes, because the formidable faerie wasn't able to completely hide his fear as he obeyed. His hand dropped to the hilt of his sword, and I wondered if it was a conscious gesture. The Guardian's voice was tight as he informed me, "The Tithe is as ancient and sacred as Olorel. While there are some who wouldn't mind keeping the monthly sum, many descendants depend on it. How do you think the Guardians are paid?"

"*Fine*," I snarled. "I'll meet you there."

"I'll be waiting at the entrance," the faerie said just before I slammed the door in his face.

Despite the state of my mating bond, the bond between me and the Unseelie Court was alive and well—waves of dislike traveled from Nuvian and into my mind. I barely noticed; all my attention had gone back to Collith. I didn't want to go. I didn't want to leave him alone, not even for a few hours. Did it really matter if someone else claimed the throne?

It meant something to Collith, that wretched little voice reminded me.

"You should go. I can watch your husband," a voice said from the doorway. I saw the glint of red hair in my peripheral vision. Cyrus.

"How long have you been standing there?" I asked hollowly. I couldn't seem to drudge up the will to care that my friend had probably seen and heard Nuvian, who couldn't pass as a human even if he tried. He'd probably tossed around a royal title or two, as well.

Cyrus settled in the chair that I'd been sitting in for the past several hours. "Since that faerie knocked on the door. I won't let anyone move your husband. You should go," he repeated.

I blinked. How did he know Nuvian was a faerie?

A question for another night. There must've been part of me that still felt alive, still cared, because now that I'd pictured it, the image of some fae usurper sitting in Collith's chair was intolerable. "Thank you," I said to Cyrus, knowing that I owed him so much more than that. If we were going to be seeking shelter underneath his roof, he deserved to know what, exactly, he was protecting.

There would be time for all that later. Not right now. I walked over to the table that Collith was draped across. "I'll be back soon," I whispered in his ear. Without thinking, I brushed a kiss along his cheek. A shudder went through me when I realized how cold he'd become—it was nothing like his usual, pleasant coolness. Agitated, I took my coat off the hook, shrugged it on, and walked out into the night.

Though I'd never gone to Court from Cyrus's house, it wasn't difficult to navigate; I simply found the peak of a mountain that was vaguely shaped like a woman, kneeling on her knees in supplication. I strode through the darkness, faintly enjoying the feel of a breeze on my face. It made me remember how the air often toyed with Collith's hair.

Something moved in the tall grass. Before I could make a move for my knife, a pair of yellow eyes appeared.

"Finn," I sighed. He'd probably been following me from the moment I'd left the house, since I didn't see my protective wolf relaxing his guard anytime soon. Not after tonight. It was on the tip of my tongue to order him to stay, but I couldn't take away his freedom to choose. He'd had enough of that to last him a lifetime. Instead I said simply, "I'm going to the Unseelie Court. I wouldn't blame you if you stayed behind this time."

His only response was to turn around and plunge back into the thicket, clearly heading in the same direction I intended to go. The last I saw of him was the white underside of his tail as it swished back and forth. At least one of us was happy. I wondered how much he understood about what had happened today. Or where I was going now.

We walked through the night for an hour. During the shadowy trek, I avoided letting any thoughts form. I was an automaton only capable of making simple observations. *Oh, look, a tree. A mouse. A creek.* Then, when we reached the mouth of the passageway, I didn't let myself hover outside—there were too many ghosts just waiting for the chance to haunt me. Collith and I had paused outside this door so many times.

Inside the passageway, Finn's demeanor changed somewhat, but not as much as I'd expected. While his tail no longer stood up straight and his wolfy smile was gone, he didn't cower or creep, as he had the last time we were here. His ears were perked and his eyes alert. He was no one's chained pet tonight.

Suddenly the wolf bristled. I followed his bright gaze and wasn't surprised to see Laurie standing in our path, his face expressionless, hands tucked behind his back. "If you're here to offer me advice, don't bother," I said. My voice was as cold as my husband's body.

"Good thing that's not why I'm here, then." His gaze dropped, and slowly, leisurely traveled up the length of my body. "I knew you'd barge onto that stage without the proper costume."

"I don't give a flying fuck about how I look tonight, Laurie. You shouldn't, either, considering how you felt about him."

"Fortunately, one of us has their priorities straight. I've been alive a long time, Firecracker, and death is the only guarantee in this world. If we fall apart every time someone drops, nothing would ever get done." In a confident, deft movement, Laurie took hold of my arm and steered me down a different passageway. Finn snarled, which he promptly ignored. Laurie kicked a door open without pause or effort. In the same moment, Lyari shimmered into view. She must've started to react, because the Seelie King fixed his icy gaze on her, just for an instant. Whatever she saw in those depths was enough to make my fearless guard back down.

We'd interrupted a threesome. At our entrance, they all shot upright in the bed. The female's hair was a mass of snarls and tangles. Their skin gleamed with perspiration. They'd been at it for a while, apparently. The air smelled like sweat and sex.

"Get out," Laurie said in a bored tone. At some point he'd stopped masking his power, and now it permeated the room, as thick and tangible as smoke. The faeries didn't question him. All three moved toward their clothing, which lay scattered across the dirt floor.

Something vicious and vindictive stole over me. "No," I said. "Leave it."

They didn't question me. Stark naked, the three faeries ran from the room. I watched them go and felt nothing. Finn padded to a dark corner and sat down.

Laurie had already gone to pull the rope. Within seconds, a human arrived. Sounding completely unlike the Laurie I'd known up until now, the Seelie King barked instructions at the dull-eyed man. *Maybe he's not as composed as he wants me to believe.* The slave left to find the dress Laurie had brought for me and returned just a few minutes later.

The costume he'd chosen for tonight was black. It had long, dramatic sleeves. The neckline was a single strip of material that gripped my throat like a hand. The front was made of stiff, undecorated material that covered my breasts and sides, leaving everything down to my navel bare. The skirt, too, was long and heavy, but there was a deep slit up its center. Laurie was not a creature of subtlety or modesty. Luckily, neither was I.

As I struggled to secure the intricate straps on the shoes, Laurie once again crossed the room. This time he brought jewelry. The earrings were simple, long, and golden. The bracelets, too, were gold and smooth. They accented the band keeping my crown in place. Laurie gave the pieces to me without comment, then settled on the bed to start on my hair. His summery scent gradually covered the stench those faeries had left behind. Neither of us spoke as he weaved the long strands of my hair into braids. His light, capable touches felt so good. I struggled against the urge to close my eyes and lose myself in them.

Maybe Laurie sensed it, because a moment later, I felt him press a kiss against the back of my neck. The warmth of his lips should've been a shock. Instead, I felt nothing. "Collith isn't even buried yet," I said dully.

The soft warmth retreated. I expected Laurie to make one of

his flippant responses, but he had changed, too. He just put some space between us and continued braiding. "Did he know that you loved him?" Laurie asked.

Any other day, any other version of myself, I would've denied it. Responded with words so scathing that it caused a fissure down the middle of our friendship. Now I just stared straight ahead and felt the hole inside of me widen. "Did he know that *you* loved him?" I asked.

"Touché, Your Majesty. You've learned our ways quickly." There was a faint smile in his voice.

I didn't linger after that. Memories of Collith threatened to break through my wall—I saw a flash of him extending his arm, dressed in all his Court finery—and I hurried out the door. My werewolf was behind me in an instant. Laurie didn't follow, but I hadn't really expected him to.

Guardians closed in around me and Finn. We all walked toward the throne room like expressionless, mechanical dolls. When we reached that enormous doorway, I wasted no time plunging into the crowd. It only took a few seconds for the fae to comprehend that I was among them. Word spread like disease, and between one breath and the next, there was a path leading to those great chairs. Finn walked beside me. Over and over, I heard faeries in the crowd wonder where Collith was. *Where is the king? Did something happen to the king?*

As I lifted my thick skirt and climbed the steps, I couldn't stop myself from looking at Collith's throne. Without him sitting there, I noticed slight details I'd missed before. There was a design carved into the place he would've sat, the shapes forming a snake and a crown. The crest of the previous king, maybe. Brittle roots spread across the armrests, some of them worn or broken. I wondered if Collith's relentless tapping had caused it.

Blinking rapidly, I sat in the chair beside his. Finn clicked past and settled on my other side. As I looked out at the enormous space, the hundreds of fae, a head of bright hair caught my eye. I blinked again and focused on the faerie's face. Laurie looked back at me. He didn't wink or smile, but an odd sort of... steadiness emanated from him. For some reason, that comforted me.

I looked out at the crowd again and said, "There will be no Tithe tonight."

The room broke into pandemonium.

I let them shout and argue for exactly one minute. Counting the seconds in my head helped me control the chaos of thoughts and noise. Nuvian and Lyari hovered closer than usual. While neither of them showed unease on their faces, I could feel it emanating from them, more palpable than a breeze.

At last, I raised my hand. Their curiosity was stronger than their indignation. "There with be no Tithe tonight, because it's my turn to talk. By now, you are all aware that I am not as patient or cautious as my mate. Which is why, from this moment forward, there will be no more slaves in the Unseelie Court."

There was movement behind me—probably the Guardians unsheathing their swords—but I didn't give the Court a chance to react. For the first time, I didn't try to avoid that vibrating, humming bond between me and these creatures. I didn't build a wall. No, this time, I kicked it down and took them all inside me. I welcomed them into the darkness like a witch in a house made of candy, like the Leviathan in its deep pool, like Lucifer to Eve in the center of that beautiful garden. Then, once they were all crowded within my skull, I released the creature living inside me. The creature that I'd denied too long, too often.

Fear.

The change in the crowd was instant. The lights of anger and resentment in their eyes gave way to pain and terror. Screams, cries, and moans filled the room, more lovely than a string quartet.

"You've never had a Nightmare as queen," I hissed, gripping the armrests with my fingers. It already hurt, having so many of them in my head, and I knew I'd pay dearly later. No hint of pain showed in my voice, though. "This is what it means. We do not cower, or cringe, or hesitate. You *will* obey me or know what true fear is."

My gaze settled on Laurie again. His eyes glittered with the amusement I expected... and, to my faint surprise, undisguised desire.

The Tongue stepped closer to the throne, drawing my attention to him. The swell of flesh beneath his chin jiggled and his mottled face had gotten redder. "Your Majesty, perhaps we should—"

"*We* should not do anything. I am wearing the crown. Go back to your dusty books and bloody spells, faerie. I'll send word if you're needed." With that, I stood up. My fingers were damp and aching from such a fierce grip. I felt the skirt dragging behind me as I left the dais. Finn loped ahead, and I remembered how he'd looked when we first met, here in this very room. His prominent ribs and patchy fur had become lean muscles and a shining coat. Seeing that dulled the pain in my soul for a single, incandescent moment. Then it came back with an unceremonious inevitability.

After a few seconds, the faeries started murmuring again, their outrage and hate beating against the newly-rebuilt wall inside me. But there was another sound. With every step I took, it grew louder and louder, until it overpowered even the fae. I searched for the source and saw that it came from the slaves, who were lining the walls and crowding at the far door, all of their gazes on me.

Annika stood among them. She mouthed the chant along with the others. I watched her mouth closely, trying to put meaning to their sound.

They were saying my name, I realized. I walked past Annika,

and what had started with a spark swiftly became a roaring inferno. The din filled my ears—*Fortuna! Fortuna! Fortuna!*—and made me feel alive again.

At the doorway, I paused and looked back. I had never felt more invincible. No chains. No fear. No rules. It was the most freeing sensation, like shedding skin or flying into sky.

"Oh. I forgot to mention this part," I added. Though I didn't raise my voice or direct my words at anyone in particular, I knew every single faerie in the room heard. "Even if one of you manages to kill me, you wouldn't be free of my power. So, really, the only way to ensure your survival is to avoid pissing me off."

No one dared to rebel or reason, but the sounds of their desperation followed me into the passageway.

Laurie was waiting for me there. He stood with his hands in his pockets. Though his stance exuded confidence and control, his eyes said something else. My frown deepened as we stared at each other across a distance that felt like miles rather than yards.

"That wasn't wise," he commented, acting as if the air between us wasn't rank with sorrow.

I smiled bitterly. I rested my hand on Finn's back, knowing that he would lead me safely through the dark. The feel of his fur was at once comforting and a reminder of the potential lurking inside us all, if only we would give it the freedom to become something more.

"Didn't you know, Laurie?" I said, walking away from him, going deeper into the shadows. "The wise part of me just died."

CHAPTER TWENTY-NINE

y feet led me in the opposite direction of the surface.

I'd created a hole in the invisible wall between me and the fae—almost as though I'd removed a single brick—and it was so insubstantial that they didn't sense a thing. But it was enough for me to find the presence I wanted. A consciousness that was ancient and oily.

I soon arrived at a door. This one had no carvings or embellishes. There was only a long, black handle. I glanced over at Finn. "Stay here, please," I ordered quietly. He made a sound resembling a sigh.

"Come in, Your Majesty," a voice called. Foul memories breathed down my neck as I grasped the handle and pushed. The hinges emitted a long, low moan that was like something out of a horror movie. The bedchamber within was equally disconcerting.

The fireplace was mammoth, its light so bright that no one had bothered adding torches in any other part of the room. Big enough, I caught myself thinking, to burn a body in. On the other three walls, instead of paintings or shelves, were chains, shackles, and manacles. The dirt floor was covered in a red Persian rug. For furniture, there was just a wardrobe and a bed. Although calling it a bed seemed inadequate—it wasn't queen or king-sized. This was something else. The twins had clearly put in a special order for the thing, and I didn't want to consider their reasons for needing such an enormous mattress.

Resting right in the middle of it, an unmoving lump beneath the covers, was Arcaena. She looked more like a mummified corpse than a living faerie.

I hadn't seen her since my coronation, and now the memory flashed like a dying light bulb. The top of her head as she hunched over in agony. The thin line of drool hanging from her mouth. The bottom of her bare feet as Guardians dragged her away. It had been weeks since she'd performed the Rites of Thogon, but it seemed even faeries healed slowly when it came to magic.

Ayduin sat on the other side of her in a wingback chair, his eyes unnervingly steady. Maybe it was something with the lighting or the slant to his eyes, but in that instant, I was convinced Jassin had come back from the dead. The same evil permeated the air around him.

Jassin was gone, but as long as there were faeries like this one in the world, more would be taken. More disappearances. More pain.

"She's still too weak to leave this bed. Most days, she can't even speak," Ayduin told me, oblivious to the thoughts rumbling through my head.

"But that doesn't stop her from communicating, does it?" I murmured. I knew from the male's bored expression that I'd guessed right. Faeries were getting predictable now. I stopped at the foot of the bed and regarded him as though he were a mosquito taking up residence on my skin. "You hired the assassin. When that failed, you sought out Sorcha. What's next? Who else is coming?"

He let out a weary sigh and returned his gaze to Arcaena. "Oh, Sorcha. I did have such high hopes for her. You know, I chose that one for her shapeshifting abilities. Your history with the fool was just delicious happenstance."

It was the most I'd ever heard Ayduin say. I realized that, during each encounter with him, Arcaena had dominated most of it. This faerie wasn't like Jassin, not even close—he was just a puppet. A conduit. This wasn't Ayduin talking.

It was his sister.

"You should have left Damon out of it," I told her, my voice heavy with a promise.

All pretense fell away from Ayduin like a cloud of dust. His movements became distinctly more feminine. "Or what?" Arcaena purred, getting to her feet. The chair creaked. She ran the tip of her finger along the bed. "Do you plan to use that quaint ability on me? I was walking this Earth before the first Nightmare spread her legs to continue your miserable little line."

As if to prove how insignificant I was, the faerie turned around to focus on the one in the bed. If she had any intelligence at all, she would've run. It was clear that she lived for the game. Thrived off it.

Too bad I played dirty now.

In a single, practiced movement, I made two cuts on the back of Ayduin's legs. He screamed and crumpled. When his head jerked toward me, Arcaena stared out from his eyes, bright with hatred. "You little *bitch!*" she hissed.

"I'm going to give you what you never gave Shameek," I whispered, strolling up to him. I cupped the back of Ayduin's head, pulling him into me, and stroked his hair. "A quick death. Well... quicker than he experienced, at least."

I stabbed him.

I didn't even think about it. One moment Ayduin was gasping in pain and the next it was blessedly silent. Blood, as blue as Laurie claimed it would be, burst from his mouth. I'd done my research—crushing the ribs into the lungs would render him unable to speak. It wouldn't be an easy death, though. I should have slit his throat, gotten his heart, or smashed his skull, but apparently part of me had wanted to make him suffer. I backed away as he gagged. Slowly, as though the world were a camera and everything had been put into slow motion, he dropped to his knees.

When his face hit the rug, Arcaena screeched like one of the banshees from my mother's stories. I grimaced and wiped the knife off on her twin's shirt. He wouldn't exactly be needing it anymore.

"This is your first and last warning," I said, raising my voice over her keening. "Come after me or my people again, and I will kill you. But that death will be slow and painful."

As I turned away, I knew I had crossed a line, rang a bell that couldn't be unrung. And yet... I still didn't care. About anything. Maybe later I would regret killing a faerie in cold blood. Right now, all I felt was cold triumph.

Just as I reached the threshold again, I paused. My bond with the Court was still tethered to two faeries in this room, but I'd just killed one, so that wasn't possible.

Slowly, I turned toward the darkest corner, seeking out the one who'd stayed so still and so silent that I hadn't even sensed him.

Nym stared at me with his bottomless eyes.

In that moment, I noticed the necklace he wore around his neck. During our last encounter, it had been hidden beneath his shirt. Now the chain rested against his chest, glinting in the firelight. A bloodline crest, forged from silver. The ridges formed a cup and a flame. I recognized it from the book Collith had given to me at the motel.

"You're their son," I said. Nym just kept staring at me, and I wondered if I'd made a new enemy. Even with the bond, I couldn't sense anything from him. I glanced at Ayduin's body—which now rested in a pool of blood—and thought about apologizing. However corrupted he'd been, Nym had still lost someone significant. A father that he'd watched me cut down with his own eyes.

Well, he could join the Dead Parents Club and get over it.

I turned my back on him and walked away. Arcaena's voice touched my mind as I reached the threshold—since she no longer had magic, she used our Court bond. *I'm coming for you, Fortuna Sworn. I will make you scream.*

Her threats were nothing more than a fly buzzing past my ear, and I left her in the dark where she belonged.

It was halfway back to Cyrus's that something crawled out of the hole inside me.

I stopped, actually holding a hand to my chest, willing it to lose its grip and fall back into darkness. It had a good handhold, though, and I felt the beginnings of pain. I knew from past experience that it was only going to get worse. *No. No. Have to keep moving. Outrun it. Shake it off.*

I ran the rest of the way. Leaves crunched behind me—Lyari was following, trying to keep up despite her armor and sword—but I didn't slow for her. When I reached the house, I halted in the driveway and imagined what it would be like going inside. Listening to Emma's muffled sobs. Enduring Damon's silence. Attempting to comfort when it felt like I myself was about to shatter. And I knew that I couldn't bear it. Any of it.

I kept running.

At first, I didn't know where I was going, but Cyrus lived closer to town than I had, and soon enough my feet pounded against the pavement of Main Street. I blew past Bea's, past the grocery store, and into a forlorn parking lot. My lungs burned as I ran to the red door.

The bell jangled overhead, just as it always did. How could so much remain constant when everything had changed? I slipped inside the shop, hoping hard that Adam was alone. A gust of wind came in with me, mussing my hair, but I barely noticed as I scanned the room. No car being worked on. I glanced toward the office. Empty. The radio in the corner blared without an audience. My palms were sweating, and I was trying hard, so hard, not to think about anything.

"Hello?" I called, taking a step. Something crunched under my foot, and I jerked back. Glass glinted. There was more, scattered over the concrete. Where had it come from? Still panting, I moved toward the office anyway. "Adam?"

"Yeah."

His voice came from behind a closed door on the other side of the shop. I turned and crossed the space. Hesitantly, I knocked on the cheap wood. No answer. Normally this would be enough to deter me. Tonight, though, I poked my head in. I squinted in the dimness—the air was so thick with smoke that I could only make out Adam's outline. He was lying on a bed, on top of the covers, fully clothed. His belt buckle gleamed silver in the slant of light I'd let in. "Are you free to train?" I asked, sounding as desperate as I felt.

My eyes finally adjusted to the darkness. The first detail I noticed were the drops of blood. They led directly to where Adam lay on that stained, lumpy mattress.

He was holding something in each hand. In the right, his fingers lightly gripped a cigarette. In the other... I frowned in incomprehension. My other senses were kicking in and I noticed the mechanic's musky smell had been replaced by a coppery scent. I knew instantly what it was, and after a moment, I put together that the crumpled object in his hand was one of those plastic bags hospitals used for blood transfusions.

"There's glass on the floor out there," I said, careful not to meet Adam's gaze now. I wasn't afraid, exactly, but I wasn't a fool. Direct eye contact would awaken the predator in him. In avoiding his eyes, my own fell upon a picture resting on the nightstand.

"Yeah. I'll clean it up later," Adam replied. He didn't offer any explanation and I didn't ask. He fell silent for a few seconds. I could feel him appraising me. The whole of my attention, though, was focused on the grainy image of a girl.

There were two kinds of pictures one framed and kept within sight—memories that brought us joy and memories we couldn't let go of. I didn't need to ask the question to know this girl was dead. It seemed Adam and I had more in common than I thought.

Distantly I heard him ask, "You all right?"

"No," I whispered, surprising myself. "No, I'm not."

"Well, I can't train right now. I might hurt you."

His strained tone brought me back to present. Before I could respond, he drank deeply from the bag. When he lowered it again, his lips glistened from the liquid inside. I fought to keep hold of my mask and sank into the chair next to Adam. The cushion released a long whoosh of air. Oddly enough, this induced the bizarre urge to giggle. I felt it rising up inside of me like a tide. Sensing Adam's eyes on me, I did my best to contain it. "Should I go?" I managed.

"Up to you."

I didn't move. Neither did he. The seconds turned to minutes. We didn't tell each other our dark, tragic stories. We didn't show each other our scars. We didn't even fill the silence with short, pointless words, just to hear someone talk or distract ourselves. I brought my knees to my chest and listened to Adam's music. Let the screams settle through my skin and into my very bones.

For the first time since his heart stopped beating, I was able to think about living in a world without Collith in it. I examined my future in a clinical, detached way. No more murmured conversations in dim bedrooms. No more tender, exploratory touches from his long fingers. No more heady rush when I made him laugh. No more infuriating arguments and exhilarating surrenders.

But... I didn't want to add another picture to my nightstand. I didn't want to lay in a dark room, thinking about what could have been or what had come to pass. I didn't want one more memory to cling to because it was all I had left of a reality I longed for.

"I don't like that look in your eye, Sworn," Adam said suddenly. How long had he been watching me?

It didn't matter, really. I made my face a careful, blank mask again. I stood from the chair, moving slowly so as not to tempt him. "Thanks for letting me hang out a bit. It helped."

"Helped with what?" he called after me. "*Sworn*. It isn't smart to run from me right now!"

I didn't answer, and he didn't come after me, probably because he didn't trust himself. I pushed the door open. The sound felt like a shout in the stillness. I didn't flinch as the cold sank its cruel, bitter claws into me. Clouds glowered overhead, readying to release the burden of their eternal rage. I turned my face toward the open road, where there were no cars in sight. Just the bare branches of slumbering trees and nervous, skittering leaves. Every step I took was firm with resolve.

I knew what I had to do.

CHAPTER THIRTY

A boxelder bug writhed on its back.

I stood in front of the window and watched it die. The bug was a frantic, mindless thing. Its wings were two blurs as it struggled against the inevitable. As I observed the creature's final moments, waiting for dusk, it emitted a high sound that no one else cared to hear but me. Then, all at once, it went silent. Its legs, which had been wriggling, no longer moved.

Night was finally drawing near. Multiple people had come and gone since I got back, attempting to talk to me about burying Collith, getting some sleep, or stepping in the shower. I probably looked like an extra from a horror movie. It didn't matter, though. Nothing mattered but that darkening horizon.

A clock on the wall counted into the stillness. *Tick. Tick. Tick.* It was almost time.

Thinking this, I turned around to face the body on the kitchen table.

It was difficult to think of it as Collith. Everything that had belonged to him, made him the faerie I'd grown to care for, was gone. The intelligent light in his eyes, the subtle tilt of his lips when I'd said something amusing, the restless way his fingers moved. Beneath the numbness that had overtaken me, I knew I wanted him to open those hazel eyes. Lecture me, argue with me, *anything*.

Suddenly exhausted, I sank into one of the chairs. Someone had closed Collith's eyes and arranged his hands so they rested palm-down on either side. In movies or books, the characters always seemed to mention how the dead just appeared to be sleeping. It wasn't true, though. Collith looked very, very dead.

"I've never killed someone before," I whispered. "Not like this, at least. I know I killed during the trials, but that was different. So different, Collith."

His face remained white and still, yet somehow, it felt like he was listening. I ran my finger along his cheekbone with the tip of my finger, and I was helpless to stop the onslaught of memories. Every time we'd touched, held hands, brushed past each other.

"You were my friend," I told Collith ruefully. "I never told you that. Now I'm wishing I had. There's a lot I wish I'd told you, actually. So come back to me, and I'll give you every secret I have, okay?"

Here, I paused, waiting with bated breath, hope pinching my heart. But Collith didn't move. Though he appeared asleep, his face didn't emanate serenity. It was further proof that his had not been a peaceful death. Thanks to me.

The thought caused another wave of nausea. Oh, God, I was going to be sick again. I closed my eyes and swayed from side to side, concentrating on keeping the bile down.

At that moment, the door behind me opened. It was the distraction I needed—as the intruder sat in the chair on Collith's other side, the dizziness subsided. I opened my eyes and met Damon's pained gaze. I waited for him to speak, since he'd clearly come for a reason. Why else would the brother who'd vowed to despise me forever bother to be here?

Thankfully, he didn't say anything about burying Collith.

"When you were..." Damon began. Halfway through the words, his gaze met mine, and whatever he saw there made him falter. After a moment, he tried again. "While you were using your power, your eyes turned red. I've never seen that before."

The revelation had little effect on me. There was probably a lot we didn't know about Nightmares—so much knowledge had been lost over the ages. Within seconds, I'd put the image of my eyes blazing red far, far away. I frowned at Collith, thinking that whoever had arranged his hands had done it wrong. He'd always been a messy sleeper.

"You know, I've been sitting here thinking about every moment leading up to this," I said suddenly. Damon gave a noticeable start. "Collith laying dead on this table, I mean. Because of me. What it comes down to, really, is my tendency to do whatever I want and worry about the consequences later. I also like to blame everyone else for those shitty choices. You would agree with this more than anyone, right?"

I raised my eyebrows at the other Nightmare, waiting for him to nod or confirm it. Instead, he pursed his lips. He didn't look concerned—oh, no, couldn't have that, could we?—but he wasn't able to hide that I'd disturbed him. "We're not supposed to touch any wounds from a challenge. The scar will have many meanings. That's what she said."

Damon couldn't stay silent any longer. "What are you *talking* about, Fortuna?" he burst.

I focused on Collith's still, pale face. I knew that, when faced with the death of a soul mate, most people accepted this reality. After all, stories didn't always end happily. Many battles were lost. Countless loose ends were never tied. Take the siren, for instance, whose story of magic and pain had only ended in her living on inside a white house with a monster.

But I was not most people.

My voice, when I finally answered, was empty and distant. "Choices, dear brother. I'm talking about choices."

He either didn't know how to respond or didn't want to. A few more seconds ticked past, then the chair creaked as Damon stood. This time, I didn't bother looking at him, but I felt his fear radiating through the room. It allured and repulsed me all at once. I wanted to bask in the sensation and vomit from its taste. *I really am a monster,* I thought bleakly. The door closed with a sound of finality. Somehow I knew that no one else would come. Not tonight, at least. I was a lost cause.

Finally, when the clock read 2:30 a.m., I left my position in front of the window.

It was too far to walk, so I got into the van, turned the key quickly, and drove away.

Many of the urban legends had a seed of truth to them. It was easy enough to find a demon—all I needed was a crossroads and the Witching Hour. I'd read somewhere, once, that demons liked to hide in the cracks of old logs, basking in the darkness and rot. But that wasn't true. They hid in plain sight and thrived off pure, unadulterated pain.

By now the road was shrouded in darkness, the moon itself wanting no part of the goings-on below it. At the crossroads I'd chosen, a single streetlight shone down, giving a forlorn flicker now and then.

I pulled onto the side and killed the engine. I wanted to linger there for a moment—cling to the memory of who I was, before doing what I was about to do—but the Witching Hour would wait for no one. I fortified that mental wall, took a shuddering breath, and got out.

My shoes hit the gravel with a familiar crunching sound. I pocketed my keys and scanned the small crossing. A light dusting of snow made the ground glitter. The silence felt empty and vast; every bird and bug had gone.

Then, something moved.

That didn't take long, I tried to say. I'd forgotten how to speak, though, because I was afraid. Truly, deeply, utterly afraid. Were it not for what was at stake, I would've fled then and there.

A human shape emerged from the darkness, but this was no human. As the glow from the streetlight fell upon its face, I saw that it had taken the form of Ian O'Connell. I reminded myself that I was a pit of numbness. Every drop of fear and revulsion tumbled down, down, down.

Rumor had it that demons were ashamed of their true appearance, which had once been beautiful and luminescent. Eons in the dark had made them white and misshapen. They used their telepathic abilities—they'd probably been forced to evolve and develop such powers, to ensure their survival in eternal darkness—to find the faces of those you loathed. Those you dreaded.

The demon paused at the edge of the light. Its eyes gleamed with unconcealed excitement. It began to circle me. I forced myself not to turn; it would make my terror that much more obvious.

Why have you summoned me? the creature asked.

Its voice felt like a fingernail on my brain. Just a tickle, the slightest of touches, but with a single movement it could pierce and bury. I swallowed and kept my eyes on a random tree. It helped to have something to focus on. "I'm here to make a deal," I told it. Somehow there was no tremor in my voice.

What do you want? The demon came to stand in front of me again, every movement fluid. Just like the fae. I scraped together enough nerve to gaze up into its face. There wasn't a trace of sympathy or reluctance in what I saw.

Even now, though, I didn't hesitate. "To bring Collith back."

And here I'd been hoping for something original, the demon sighed, looking genuinely disappointed. *You're no better than a human. They're always mewling about their dead, too. Wasting their deals with us on relighting a tiny soul that will only sputter out again in a few short decades.*

"His is no tiny soul," I said past stiff lips.

The demon just laughed. It was a bizarre sight, how it threw back its head and opened its mouth, yet no sound came out.

Then, switching gears with an abruptness that betrayed its true nature, the demon stopped laughing and bent its head to kiss me. I recoiled, almost tripping over my own feet. I caught myself on the hood of the van. "What are you doing?" I managed, fighting the urge to bolt.

The demon snickered. *How charming. You thought I would want your soul. That's not how it works, sweetheart. No, I take something that you value.*

Its meaning was all-too clear. Bile rose in my throat. What had I guarded so fiercely all these years? What had I held fast to, even when I wasn't sure why? What still meant something to me when so much else had lost meaning?

I wanted my first time to be with someone real.

I knew, then, this thing had already helped itself to my memories. Probably as it had been walking around me in circles. I hadn't even felt it. In those few seconds, it had witnessed every private conversation and intimate moment. It had become part of everything beautiful, painful, hopeful, surprising, and *mine*.

"No," I said, my throat threatening to close before I could get the word out. The idea of giving it yet another part of me was unbearable. "There's another way. Tell me, or I'll walk away."

The demon's eyes glittered with ancient cunning. *I don't think you will.*

"Fuck you."

I'm trying, it countered.

Away, away, had to get away. Spinning, I pointed my key fob at the van. Its headlights flashed. A pointless gesture, since I hadn't locked the doors, but I was on autopilot now. I reached for the door handle.

The demon's voice stopped me. *Shall I tell you what my brothers and sisters are doing to your beloved right now?* it called.

I bowed my head, struggling to breathe. Though I'd never had a panic attack before, I knew I was on the verge of one. No, I didn't want to hear what torments Collith was enduring in another dimension. But I could imagine—I'd heard the stories. From a whispered conversation between my parents, when they thought I'd gone to bed. From a drunken warlock sitting in a booth at Bea's, who bemoaned bringing his wife back from the dead. They'd all spoken of darkness, screams, and pain.

And Collith—my sweet, noble, serious Collith—was lost somewhere in that never-ending nightmare. Because of me.

Slowly, my fingers uncurled from the door handle. I looked down at my shoes, the whiteness of them marred by soot and blood. I frowned, trying to remember the moment I'd put these shoes on, but I couldn't. Strange.

Have you made your choice then? the demon asked, still standing where I'd left it. *The devil's hour waits for no one.*

As I walked toward it, the demon smiled. The light in its eyes was a blend of triumph and excitement. I stopped a few feet away, hoping it couldn't hear the uneven rhythm of my heartbeat. I didn't know what came next. I didn't want to know.

The demon took charge, then, and I didn't fight it. Not once. Not as it took hold of my arms and shoved me back against a tree. Not as it pressed a hard, wet, invasive kiss to my cold mouth. Not as it squeezed my breasts so painfully that I felt its fingernails through my shirt. Not as it shoved its knee between my legs. Not even as it unbuttoned my jeans and yanked them down.

I thought about pretending I was with someone—anyone—else. But I knew it would forever alter my relationship with whoever I chose. I'd never be able to look at them again. So I closed my eyes and pictured the woods. My woods, where I'd spent...

The demon rammed its hard length inside me. I buried my fingers in the tree bark behind me and bit back a scream. *So young and tight*, it breathed. It moved its hips back and forth, forcing itself in and out of my body. I was nowhere near wet, though, and every movement felt like the demon was using a knife.

...all those moonlit nights, wandering over moss and tree roots. Listening to the symphony of frogs and crickets. Feeling power flow through my veins...

The demon grunted and cussed. Called me obscene names. It palms slammed into the tree on either side of my head, bracing itself, plunging harder and harder. The entire time, I kept my head turned, my eyes closed. The demon basked in my revulsion. It grunted just as Ian would have, thrusting even harder. I buried my nails into the bark. Pain laced through me.

...and a rare sense of restfulness. Days, weeks, months passed. I stayed in those night-draped woods, walking farther than I ever had before.

Eventually the demon came with a throaty moan. I was somewhere far, far away, and the sound was faint in my ears. I felt the creature wipe its cock off on the hem of my shirt. *Was it worth the wait?* it taunted. *Is this what you hoped for?*

A memory of Laurie's voice whispered through my mind. *Don't you know what strengthens a Nightmare's power? Unleashed fury. The things bad dreams are made of.*

In that moment, I knew I could easily kill it. My power could obliterate this demon from existence, permanently ending its reign of terror. It would never be able to harm anyone again. That's what I thought about doing. That's what I should've done.

But I wanted Collith back more.

Wasn't that a special memory? the demon crooned, chucking me under the chin. *Thank you for providing some entertainment this evening. It was shaping up to be a bore otherwise.*

It didn't wait for me to respond. In the next moment, whistling cheerfully, it slipped back into the woods. I knew this was the part where I tossed an insult after it. This was the part where I stuck up my middle finger and stomped to the van. But it felt like I'd become as insubstantial as a piece of paper, and the last few minutes had ripped me in half. Second by second. Moment to moment. Now I was barely capable of clinging to the tree and not letting the wind sweep me away.

By the way, the demon's voice added, its voice sliding along my mind like a tongue. *I wonder what your father would say, if he could see you now. Aren't you curious?*

It was a parting gift, apparently, because the demon was long gone when I finally unlatched my fingers from the tree bark. I looked around, absurdly wary of moving. Bare branches stretched across the sky. Shadows had returned to being unmoving, insentient things. As the seconds passed, I considered laying down on the ground, letting sleep take me. No, that wasn't right. Couldn't do that. I had to go back. Collith could already be awake.

This thought was what sent a jolt of memory back into my legs, and I remembered how to walk again. I calmly pushed off the tree, fixed my clothes, and returned to the van. This time, the engine offered no complaints as it awakened, like the old beast knew I had no endurance left. I blasted the heat and cranked up the radio, then left the crossroads behind in a swirl of mist and sound. I didn't let myself glance at the rearview mirror; that place would be forever imprinted on me, anyway.

Halfway home I stopped, opened the door, and vomited onto the road. The sour taste coated on my tongue and teeth. I wiped my chin and kept driving.

No one had noticed my absence—as I drove up the driveway, and the house came into view, the windows were still dark. The night was thick with dreams rather than panic. Maybe some part of me had wanted someone to realize I was gone. To come after me. Silly, really. They couldn't have changed my mind.

Moving gingerly, I dropped down from the driver seat, locked the van up, and trudged back inside.

Collith was right where I'd left him. Eyes closed, white skin, dried blood. All the same as it had been before I'd gone to the crossroads. I didn't let myself consider what I'd do if he didn't wake, if it had all been for nothing. *Change*, I thought. Over and over again. *You need to change.*

I strode past the table, climbed the stairs, and padded down the carpeted hallway. There were doors on either side, behind which Damon, Cyrus, and Emma slept. My room was the last one on the left.

Cyrus took as much care with his home as he did Bea's kitchen; the hinges didn't so much as whimper as I entered. I approached the dresser on feet that didn't feel like mine—I hadn't commanded them to move, to walk forward, but it happened.

With more distant thoughts like these, I rummaged through the drawers. Ever the efficient host, Cyrus had apparently purchased pajamas for whatever guests stayed with him; there was a pair of cotton, plaid pants, complete with a matching, long-sleeved top. I took these out, placed them on the bed, and started peeling off what I was wearing.

When I saw that my underwear was covered in blood, I felt nothing.

Moving methodically, I took them off, too. Everything I'd owned had gone up in flames, so there wasn't another pair to replace them. Next, I put the pajamas on, noting at the same time that Cyrus had also placed a brand-new toothbrush—still in its plastic casing—on top of the bedspread. I brought it to the bathroom and brushed my mouth over and over again, until the vomit taste was completely gone.

Then, with my smarting tongue and aching heart, I slipped

back downstairs, returned to my chair next to Collith, and prepared to wait.

It was a morning of frost and wind.

Though there was no sunlight, it still seemed wrong that morning should arrive at all. Not when so much had come to an end.

I was still in the wooden chair, my hands resting limply in my lap. I didn't move, not even to get water or use the bathroom, because moving meant remembering. Every shift or action caused a twinge of pain between my legs. And I was being very, very careful not to think about the origins of that ache. I was an empty seashell. I was a dry canyon. I was a white room.

Cyrus came into the kitchen just as a weak ray of light touched Collith's face. I hadn't taken my eyes off him from the moment I'd sat down. *Any moment now. He's going to wake up any moment.* "Would you like some eggs and coffee?" I heard Cyrus ask.

In the hours that I'd been sitting there, it felt like I'd forgotten how to act human. It took several moments to remember how to form words. "Yes to coffee, no to eggs. Thank you," I rasped.

Even the thought of coffee made my stomach roil, but I needed something to keep me conscious. Needed to act as normal as possible for the sake of everyone around me. I could feel all of us breaking, no, we were standing on the edge of a sharp drop. Someone had to step back. Pull everyone to safety.

There was a clicking sound as Cyrus turned a burner on. Seconds later, another presence entered the room. "I'm going to pick up some things from town," Damon muttered. Any other day, I would have considered it a victory that he bothered to tell me his plans. "Emma needs more tissues and I've got to buy clothes. Do either of you... what's going on?"

He must've seen something in my face. "Do you really care?" I asked tonelessly. The response was more automatic than anything. I still didn't look away from Collith. *Please come back. Don't let it all be for nothing,* I thought, sending my words down the space where our bond once existed.

Nothing happened.

Collith remained white and still.

I felt something inside me wither as I accepted two terrible truths—the first was that the demon wearing Ian's face had lied to me. The second was that Collith was truly dead. There was no coming back from what I'd done. What I'd lost. Soon I would have to get up from this chair, and I had no idea how to be alive anymore. It felt unimaginable, working at Bea's, being a sister, training with Adam, attending the Tithes. Fortuna Sworn no longer existed.

"Fortuna? Did something else happen?" Damon pressed. His voice was closer this time. *Wow, he must really be worried,* I thought bleakly. The old Fortuna would've cared. She would've marveled at the fact that he was starting to forgive her.

Just as I started to respond, Collith's eyes opened.

END OF BOOK TWO

FORTUNA'S STORY
CONTINUES IN...

DEADLY
DREAMS

AVAILABLE NOW!

ACKNOWLEDGMENTS

With this book, my world expanded in a way I never could've imagined when I began writing it. I met an incredible group of Bookstagrammers and authors, who've already been such a big part of my writing process that here I am, mentioning them in the acknowledgments.

The first of which must be authorpreneur extraordinaire Jessi Elliott. I've said before that I can never properly thank you for how integral you were in the creation of this book, but hopefully this is a start. *Thank you*, from the bottom of my heart, for all the hard work and wisdom you lent to this project. Without you, it wouldn't be what it is now.

Then there are the Bookstagrammers who posted about the books, sent me encouragement during the drafting process, and have ultimately been every author's dream turned reality. @Bibliophilic_Ferret, @PaperbackBones, @Books_Over_Everything, @Redrchl.Reads, @SophiesReadingCorner, @MugsnLeaf, @SuspenseThrill, @HeirofBooksandRoses, @Morrigans_Books, @B.B.LynnReads, @TheDarklingOne, @WiinterTide, @Lookin_aBook, @Moonlight_Rendezvous, @The_Bookish_Astronaut, @FearYourEx, @JenacidebyBibliophile, @B00kDragon, and

@STFUSara to name a few. I am so, so lucky to be part of this community.

I also want to express my undying gratitude to the amazing women of Storygram Tours, Bridget and Kristen. You've created something fun, beautiful, and rewarding. Thank you for spreading the word and sharing the love for my first indie series!

ABOUT THE AUTHOR

K.J. Sutton lives in Minnesota with her two rescue dogs. She has received multiple awards for her work, and she graduated with a master's degree in Creative Writing from Hamline University.

When she's writing, K.J. always has a cup of Vanilla Chai in her hand and despises wearing anything besides pajamas. She adores interacting with fellow writers and readers. Until then, she's hard at work on her next book. K.J. Sutton also writes young adult novels as Kelsey Sutton.

Be friends with her on Instagram, Facebook, and Twitter. And don't forget to subscribe to her newsletter so you never miss an update!